Also by Maggie Craig

The River Flows On

When The Lights Come On Again

Maggie Craig

HEADLINE

First published in 1999
by HEADLINE BOOK PUBLISHING

First published in paperback in 1999
by HEADLINE BOOK PUBLISHING

10 9 8 7 6 5 4 3 2 1

ISBN 0 7472 5865 1

Printed and bound in Great Britain by
Clays Ltd, St Ives plc

HEADLINE BOOK PUBLISHING
A division of the Hodder Headline Group
338 Euston Road, London NW1 3BH
www.headline.co.uk
www.hodderheadline.com

Dedicated, with the utmost respect, to the people who
experienced the dramatic events which form the
background of this story:
those who died,
those who did their bit,
and those who lived to tell the tale.

and to my aunts and uncles,
remembering always amongst that group
of indomitable people
Elizabeth Dewar Craig McCulloch.

Author's Note

The characters in this story spring from the imagination of the author. Their activities during the Clydebank Blitz are also fictional, but they were inspired by the real-life gallantry of a nurse and a group of medical students who risked their own lives to go to the aid of the injured. Their true story is recounted in I.M.M. McPhail's *The Clydebank Blitz*.

Acknowledgements

I should like to thank Grace Howie, Joen McFarlane and Jean Morrison for telling me of their experiences as wartime nurses. Among many other things they spoke of being on duty at Rottenrow Maternity Hospital in Glasgow during the Clydebank Blitz, training and working as VADs and living and working in the Western Infirmary as student nurses. Thanks for the yellow liver, Jean!

Andrew Ross Caddell Hamilton told me what it was like to be walking up Kilbowie Road as the bombs were dropping. Maisie Nicoll was also in the thick of things. She gave me many lovely anecdotes, several of which have found their way into this book. All five gave me a great deal of useful information and not a little inspiration.

I should also like to express my thanks to all my writing friends for much help, support and encouragement, particularly my adverbial, medical and spiritual advisers. They know who they are.

PART I

1938

Chapter 1

The disappointment was so bitter she could almost taste it.

It knocked her off balance, made her ignore the warning signs she was usually so good at reading: her mother's white face and anxiously clasped hands, her brother's silence. Eddie normally had plenty to say for himself.

The expression on her father's face should have been warning enough. William MacMillan was frowning, his dark eyebrows drawn together, his mouth a grim and rigid line. That alone should have stopped her in her tracks. Only it didn't.

'You opened my letter?'

Liz was so angry she could hardly get the words out. All of her careful control, won at such cost over the years of her childhood, shattered in that moment.

'How dare you open a letter addressed to me!'

She thought her father was going to explode. Nevertheless, she took a quick little breath and refused to lower her eyes under the glower he was directing at her over the remains of her birthday tea. Her mother and Eddie, occupying the other two sides of the square table, had gone very still.

Holding her father's angry gaze took an enormous effort. In her lap, out of his sight, Liz curled her fingers round the overhang of the white damask tablecloth and gripped hard. She wasn't going to back down this time – however hard it was. This was too important.

'How dare I?' he demanded. Making a fist of his right hand he brought it down on the table with a thump. The force of the blow rattled the cups and saucers and shook the plate which

3

held what was left of the cake her mother had baked for her birthday.

'Because I'm your father, my girl, and while you're under my roof, I've got a right to know what you're doing!'

'Well, I might not be under your roof for much longer!' Liz flung at him. 'If the Preliminary Training School accepts me I'll have to stay in the nurses' home!'

There was a silence. It was broken only by the noise of a blackbird chirping in the back garden and the distant hum of the traffic up on Dumbarton Road. Her father locked eyes with her once more.

'If you think you're going for that interview, you've got another think coming, my girl.'

Then he really let rip. Her place was at home with her family. He hadn't paid good money for her to train as a shorthand-typist when she left school for her to throw it all up. And for what? To work as a skivvy in uniform, cleaning up other folk's messes and getting paid a pittance for it?

He went on and on. How were they to put her brother through university without her contribution to the family finances? His bursary only stretched so far. Eddie shifted uncomfortably in his chair and studied his feet at that one.

'And who do you think is going to help your mother in the house if you're not here?' her father thundered. 'I'm not having you swanning off to some nurses' home – having a high old time with girls who're no better than they should be—'

Liz couldn't take any more. She rose from the table so quickly that her chair fell back on to the floor, hitting the linoleum with a loud whack. Her mother, Sadie, leaped up from her own seat and righted it. Her father stayed where he was, glaring up at their daughter. His eyes were cold, but his nostrils flared with the effort of mastering his anger. He wasn't used to having any member of his family question his decisions.

'Where do you think you're going, young lady?'

'Up the road to my grandfather's,' Liz flung back. 'I suppose that's allowed!' She had never openly defied him before, but

4

the depth of her disappointment was giving her a courage she hadn't known she possessed – even if it was making her heart beat faster and the blood pound in her ears. Was there a medical term for that? If William MacMillan had his way, Liz was never going to find out.

She took a step away from the table. Her mother, who'd been hovering nervously behind her, moved away to stand by her own chair. Miserably aware of the distress this confrontation was causing her, Liz knew nevertheless that right now she had to get out of the house before she said something she would really regret.

'I'm going up to Radnor Street,' she said, consciously lowering her voice. She'd not get anywhere by shouting and stamping her feet. Not that tantrums of that sort had ever been tolerated in the MacMillan household anyway.

Taking a deep breath, she forced herself to calm down. She was eighteen years old now. A young lady. She should act like one.

'Grandad's expecting me,' she said.

'It's that old bugger who's put half these daft ideas into your head!' her father shouted. He flung an angry glance at his son, sitting opposite him at the table. 'And in your brother's head too!'

Sadie swallowed. She was clearly forcing herself to speak.

'William, it's no' right that you should speak about your father like that . . .'

Her husband turned his implacable gaze on her. Sadie's voice trailed off, her eyes dropped and she sank into her chair. Liz, seeing how her mother seemed almost to grow physically smaller under the onslaught of her husband's disapproval, felt the old familiar anger boil up inside her. It was rare for her mother to contradict her husband, and she only ever did it in defence of others, never of herself.

'I'm going,' said Liz, her voice rough-edged. 'I'll see you all later.'

She ran from the room, grabbing her coat from the dark oak

5

hatstand in the hall with one hand and opening the front door with the other. Once she was out, she was safe. He would never dream of making a scene in the street. Perish the thought that the neighbours, many of them his fellow managers in the shipyard, should know that there were any problems in the MacMillan family. Although – unless they were stone deaf – the Crawfords who lived next door would have heard at least some of the argument.

Her brother caught up with her on Dumbarton Road, grabbing her by the elbow as she went to step off the pavement.

'Liz, slow down. You'll get a stitch. Or run over by a tram.'

He was trying to make her laugh, but she was in no mood for that. She whirled round to face him, her eyes big and filled with hurt.

'Thanks for standing up for me back there, Eddie.'

He dropped her arm and let his breath out on a sigh of exasperation.

'Liz, you know I agree with him on this one. You *will* be a skivvy if you become a nurse. Another working-class lassie being exploited. Doing the dirty work for the bosses and the bourgeoisie.'

'Oh, Eddie! Don't talk *at* me! I'm not one of your political meetings!' Quick tears of anger and frustration sprang into Liz's eyes.

'Och, Lizzie, I'm sorry. Don't cry.'

He laid a hand lightly on her shoulder. Then he lifted it and ran it through the unruly waves of his hair, dark brown like her own. Since he had gone up to Glasgow University two years before, he had adopted a bohemian appearance to go with his enthusiasm for radical ideas and radical politics.

He had let his dark hair grow over his collar and he wore soft and unstarched shirts, usually without a tie. Recently he had taken to sporting a floppy black scarf, loosely knotted at the neck. Their grandfather muttered darkly about the days when 'men were men and pansies were flowers'. That made

Liz laugh. In his own quiet way, Eddie was a very masculine man.

Indeed, striding along hatless, with his tousled hair blowing in the breeze, wearing the loose black coat he had bought during his first term at the Uni, Liz thought he cut rather a romantic figure. That opinion was obviously shared by one of Eddie's old friends from school. Spying him across Kilbowie Road last week the lad had shouted, 'Hey, Lord Byron, are you gonnae write us a wee poem?' Eddie, characteristically, had grinned and waved back, not a bit put out.

His father approved neither of his politics nor of his appearance, but he had been persuaded to tolerate both for one simple reason. Eddie was doing extremely well at university – a star pupil in both of his chosen subjects of history and politics.

'Ma gave me a bit of your birthday cake to take up to Grandad.' He raised one hand to indicate the brown paper bag he held. 'Come on, let's get over the road.' He took Liz's elbow with his free hand, guiding her across.

'Look at it this way,' he said, when, with the ease born of long practice, they had snaked their way between a slow-moving tram, a horse-drawn lorry and two private cars and reached the safety of the other pavement. 'In a few years' time you'll probably get married and settle down.' He shot her a sideways grin as they walked along. 'If Father and I consider there's anybody good enough to deserve you.'

Liz lifted her shoulders in a gesture of irritation. When were men ever going to take women seriously? Thinking about her brother's attachment to radical ideas, something else occurred to her. She stopped dead on the corner of Kilbowie Road, forcing him to come to a halt too. The light of battle shone in her eyes as she turned to face him.

'Edward MacMillan, you're a right hypocrite! I thought you didn't believe in marriage – that you were all for this Free Love that you talk about.'

'Not when it applies to my wee sister, I'm not,' he growled. With shameless inconsistency, he compounded the offence.

7

'Any fellow who tries anything on with you will have to answer to me.'

Exasperated with him, Liz tried a different tack. 'You want to change things, Eddie, don't you? Try to improve life for everybody?'

Quiet for once, he waited for her to formulate her thoughts. She was taking her time about it, not finding it easy to put her most deeply felt and cherished hopes into words.

'I want to change things too,' she said slowly. 'Only not in the same way as you do.' She laid a hand on his arm and looked up into his face. 'You're going to do it through getting involved in politics and becoming a teacher, and that's great. I don't begrudge you your chance. I really don't. I'm going to be so proud of you when you graduate from the Uni. I'll be there cheering you on.'

'Don't think I don't appreciate it,' he said, his voice gruff with emotion. 'I do.' He tweaked her nose and grinned. 'Not that I would tell you that, wee sister.' His smile faded. Liz was looking at him with a very serious look on her face. 'But?' he suggested.

'There's so much that's wrong with the world, isn't there?'

Eddie nodded, knowing exactly what she meant. They had discussed it often enough. Their own family's position might be a lot more solid since their father's promotion to manager, but anyone who had grown up in Clydebank knew what was wrong with the world: the constant threat – and reality – of unemployment; damp, overcrowded houses; the illnesses bred of poverty, ignorance and bad working and living conditions.

'I want my chance too,' Liz said passionately. 'To change things. To do some good in the world.'

Eddie sighed heavily. 'Oh, Liz . . . why would you want to be shut up in a nurses' home being bossed about by some dragon of a matron when you could be doing a job that would give you some fun – and a better wage – for a few years?'

'Like at Murray's?' asked Liz.

'Like at Murray's,' he repeated, with the confident air of a

8

man who had just won an argument by reasoned debate and discussion.

He hadn't caught the dryness in her voice, but then why should he have? She'd never told him about the problems she had with Eric Mitchell – hadn't dared to, for fear of him getting himself into trouble by rushing helter-skelter to his little sister's rescue.

Given what he had just said about anyone trying anything on with her, she was more convinced than ever that her decision to keep that particular worry to herself had been the right one. If she told Eddie, he'd go straight up to the shipping office in the Broomielaw in Glasgow where she worked and punch Eric Mitchell in the mouth – and what a stushie that would cause. He could get suspended from the University if he pulled a stunt like that. She'd been on the point of telling him several times, desperately wanting to share the burden, but she couldn't risk it.

She lifted her head and saw Tam Simpson, one of their grandfather's neighbours. A small man, he was bustling down Kilbowie Road towards them, heading for the pub on the corner outside which she and Eddie were standing.

'The old man's waiting for youse two!' he said cheerfully, touching his bunnet – his flat cap – to Liz. 'I'm just away for a wee refreshment!'

Once he had disappeared into the pub, Eddie cocked his head to one side.

'Can we stay up the road until the pub pours him out on to the pavement, do you think?' he murmured. 'Then we could listen to that charming old Clydebank ritual of Mrs Simpson's welcome home to her husband.'

Liz grimaced at the irony in Eddie's voice. You didn't have to be near a pub to know when it was closing time in Clydebank. Not if you lived within shouting distance of the Simpsons. They had a flat in the same tenement in Radnor Street as Liz and Eddie's grandfather. Liz and Eddie themselves had been born and brought up in the same building until their father's

9

promotion had brought about a move to the neat little row of terraced houses close to the River Clyde where they now lived.

A few minutes after the pubs called time, Nan Simpson would throw up the sash window of her top-floor flat. Then, when her errant husband hove into view, she would start berating him. The volume and severity of the insults, as well as the coarseness of the swear words, increased the closer he got to home.

After he had negotiated the difficult task of locating the entrance close – as folk said, that must be a bit like trying to thread a needle in the dark – Tam always took a zigzag course up to his own flat, stoating up the stairs, bouncing first off one wall and then the other. Eddie likened his precarious ascent to a tennis ball flying back and forth over a net.

'Aye, I know. It's funny, isn't it?' Liz took her brother's arm as they started walking again. 'Funny peculiar, I mean. Not funny ha-ha. D'you mind how it used to perplex Granny?'

Eddie nodded.

'I can see her shaking her head now.' He raised the pitch of his voice, putting on a Highland accent in affectionate mimicry. '"A decent respectable God-fearing body the rest of the week, but at closing time on a Saturday night she's got a mouth on her like a sailor."'

'She's got provocation, mind,' said Liz. 'Six children to bring up and a husband who'd spend all of his wages on drink if she didn't get to them first. People laugh at folk like Tam Simpson, but it's not funny at all.'

'No,' agreed Eddie. 'It's not. On the other hand,' he went on, 'at least he doesn't bounce his wife's head off the wall when he gets home. There's plenty as do.'

'And she's supposed to be grateful for that?' asked Liz, her voice rising in indignation.

'No,' said Eddie consideringly. 'That's not what I meant. I think it's . . .' He paused, searching for the right word. 'I think it's *despicable* for a man to behave that way. In either of those ways.'

They walked in silence for a few moments, passing the entrance to Singer railway station. It was named for the sewing-machine factory which occupied a vast area to their left. The complex of buildings was dominated by an imposing clock tower, a landmark in Clydebank and for miles around.

Eddie was obviously still thinking about Tam Simpson.

'I don't know though, Liz. Maybe you can understand why people reach for the bottle. I suppose it blots out all their problems – for a wee while, at least. Men like Tam Simpson have to worry all the time about when they're next going to be laid off, how they're going to feed their wives and children when that happens.'

'Don't you see, Eddie,' said Liz eagerly, 'that's one of the reasons I want to go in for nursing – it's all tied up together. It has to do with what you want to fight for – jobs and decent houses and good wages and better health and all those sorts of things.'

She turned to him in her enthusiasm. The quick movement blew a strand of brown hair across her face, and she tucked it impatiently behind one ear. 'But it's about education too – health education for a start. I mean, people needn't have such big families. There is such a thing as birth control – but there need to be doctors and nurses who can tell folk about it.'

Edward MacMillan, revolutionary and free thinker, blushed to the roots of his hair. Liz guessed he wasn't too happy about discussing the controversial subject of birth control with his kid sister, but he did his manful best to control his embarrassment. They were children of the twentieth century, after all.

'That's what's wrong with all your Free Love theories,' Liz added. 'It's the woman who ends up paying the price.'

Eddie's only response to that statement was a noncommittal grunt. Liz had a shrewd suspicion – given added weight by that betraying blush – that her brother's theories on Free Love were just that – theories. He might dress unconventionally, but in other ways he could be surprisingly shy – especially when it came to the opposite sex. Not unlike his sister, she thought

11

wryly. Although what she'd had to put up with from Eric Mitchell over the past two years might possibly have something to do with that . . .

They turned the corner into Radnor Street.

'Ah!' said Eddie. 'Here we are at last!' There was just a little too much relief in his voice.

Peter MacMillan swung open the heavy door to his ground-floor flat. His craggy face lit up when he saw Liz and Eddie standing in the close.

'Come in, come in,' he said, 'I'll lead the way.'

Out of sight of their grandfather, Eddie winked at Liz. Peter always spoke about leading the way, as though he were conducting you into some palatial dwelling, full of rooms and corridors in which you might very well get lost without him to guide you safely through.

His two-room apartment was actually tiny. A minuscule lobby led to a small bedroom-cum-parlour looking out over the back court, and to an even smaller kitchen at the front. This was the room where he spent most of his time and to which he was conveying Liz and Eddie now. It was smaller than the corresponding rooms on the floors above because the space for the entrance close to the tenement had been taken out of it. Yet Granny had given birth to six children here, four boys and two girls.

Both of the girls had died young – of scarlet fever, which had nearly taken Liz herself as a child. With no effective treatment for infectious illnesses, there weren't many families who escaped that sort of loss. Liz and Eddie's wee brother George had died of it.

Her father's eldest brother had fallen in the Great War. Of the three boys who had survived, only William was still in Clydebank. Bruce was in the Merchant Navy and dropped in and out of their lives erratically, turning up on the doorstep every two or three years with an armful of exotic presents. Bob had emigrated to Canada when he was eighteen, married and settled down in Ontario. Unlike Bruce, he was a faithful correspondent, his long letters about his life and family out there eagerly awaited by his parents. It wasn't the same as having him round the corner, though, as Granny used to sigh.

The relationship between Peter MacMillan and his youngest son was a fraught one. Since Granny's death it had become nonexistent. There had been a furious argument the morning of the funeral, although Liz and Eddie had heard only the aftermath of that: slammed doors and angry footsteps.

After the church service, William MacMillan had helped his father, Eddie and friends of the family lower his mother into the earth. Then, walking out of the cemetery, he had announced that he would not be attending the purvey, or funeral tea. In a carrying voice, he had said that as far as he was concerned, both of his parents were now dead.

Liz had never forgotten the look which had passed between her father and grandfather that day – shuttered bitterness on one face, hurt on the other. Now William MacMillan was quite capable of passing his own father in the street without a word. She'd seen him do it.

She had no idea what the argument had been about. She had summoned up the courage to ask her grandfather once, but he had shaken his head, such a sad look on his face that she hadn't ever had the heart to pose the question again.

Whatever it was, she knew that it caused both her grandfather and her gentle mother a great deal of distress. But that wasn't something, she thought bitterly, likely to keep her father awake at night.

Having conducted his young guests safely into his inner sanctum, Peter MacMillan gave them the usual command.

'Sit yourselves down. I'll make the tea.'

Liz chose a chair as far as possible from the black range which filled most of one wall. Being so small, the kitchen could get as hot as a blast furnace. Eddie made a face at her at being forced to sit close to the heat.

13

'My birthday treat,' she murmured to him. 'Take your coat off and stop moaning.'

They both looked up brightly as their grandfather approached. Not for all the tea in China would they have hurt his feelings by complaining about the heat, which he himself didn't seem to notice. He had a package in his hand.

'Well, hen,' he said to Liz, holding it out to her. 'Happy birthday, and many more of them.'

The parcel was small, but solid. He had wrapped it in the newspaper – the *Glasgow Herald* – which he read avidly from cover to cover each morning. With the interested eyes of the menfolk on her, Liz unwrapped her gift. Then she burst into tears. He had given her a pocket nurses' dictionary.

Chapter 2

Two cups of tea and Eddie's explanations later, Liz's grandfather was looking at her with deep sympathy in his piercing blue eyes.

'Och, lass, I'm so sorry. You've been that patient, too.'

'I have, haven't I?' she gulped. 'I've done everything he wanted me to do. First that commercial course and then the job at Murray's, and I thought maybe that if I did all that he would relent when it came to the bit – when I was old enough to apply to the Infirmary – but he hasn't!' Her voice rose on a sob. 'And now I can't see any way that I'm ever going to get to be a nurse!'

'You could always do it when you're twenty-one,' said Eddie uncomfortably.

'Och, Eddie, that's ages away!' wailed Liz.

A father's word was law where his children were concerned. Liz might consider herself quite grown up at eighteen, but the law wouldn't recognise her as an adult for another three years.

'Wheesht,' said Peter. 'Dry your tears and lift up your head – isn't that what your granny used to say?'

Applying her sodden hankie to her eyes, Liz nodded. 'It's such a disappointment, Grandad. That's all.'

He leaned forward and patted her on the knee, the room small enough to allow him to make the gesture without leaving his chair.

'I know, hen, I know.'

The only sound in the room was the ticking of the old clock on the high mantelpiece over the range. Liz looked up at its familiar face. She couldn't remember a time when she hadn't known those solid black Roman numerals.

Dry your tears and lift up your head. How many times had she sat in this room and heard Granny say that? She and Grandad had always been ready to listen, always ready to offer consolation when she or Eddie had come storming down the stairs after another dressing-down from their father. Liz blew her nose.

The two men were looking very sombre. It wasn't fair to burden them with this. They'd both done what they could to comfort her.

'Well, Grandad,' she said, 'what do you think of the international situation?'

Eddie visibly relaxed, leaning back in his chair and exhaling a long breath. The question was a joke between the three of them. Whenever the conversation flagged, some one would come out with it.

Peter MacMillan smiled, but he answered her seriously, lifting his pipe and tobacco pouch from a small shelf beside his chair as he did so.

'Well, lass, to be perfectly honest, I think the international situation is looking pretty grim.'

'You don't think Hitler's going to stop at Austria?' asked Eddie.

His grandfather, filling his pipe, gave him a searching look from under his bushy eyebrows. 'Damn the fear of it, I should say. I think he'll not be satisfied until the whole of Europe is under his blasted swastika.'

Liz shivered. Germany's annexation of Austria the month before had led to an influx of Viennese Jews into Britain. The stories they were telling about what was happening to their people in Germany were hard to believe . . . but chilling all the same. All of a sudden the little man with the toothbrush moustache who was running Germany didn't seem such a figure of fun.

Now Herr Hitler was making threatening gestures towards

Czechoslovakia, insisting that a part of that country called the Sudetenland belonged to Germany – and that his Nazi stormtroopers would take it by force if they had to. The question was: were Britain and France going to let him?

'The man's a megalomaniac,' said Peter MacMillan. 'He wants to rule the world.' Turning his pipe around, he used the stem of it to emphasise what he was saying, pointing it at Eddie. 'You mark my words. It'll be our turn soon enough.'

'We're an island,' said Eddie. He shifted in his chair. 'We don't have to get involved in a bosses' war.'

'No?' said Peter, his voice sharp. 'So what happened to "all men are brothers"? Eh?' He leaned forward, giving his grandson another of those penetrating looks. 'What's the difference between a Scottish family in Clydebank and a Jewish family in Austria or Germany? Or, for that matter, a Spanish family? Answer me that, young man.'

Putting his pipe to his lips, he sat back with an air of expansive confidence, knowing only too well that his grandson wouldn't be able to give him an answer.

'But Grandad,' protested Liz, 'you don't have to be a communist to be a pacifist.'

'Christ, hen,' said Peter MacMillan with sudden passion, 'only a madman wants another war. I know that better than anybody.' He paused, and Liz knew that he must be thinking of his firstborn, who had died at Passchendaele. 'But that's exactly what we are dealing with here – a madman.'

The emotion in his voice was enough to silence even Eddie, and for a few moments they sat saying nothing, contemplating the awful prospect and terrible reality of a world stalked by the spectre of fascism.

It had been bad enough when Mussolini had ordered the invasion of Abyssinia two years before, pitting all the power of modern warfare against primitive tribesmen who had tried to turn back tanks with bows and arrows, but that, God forgive them all, had seemed a long way away. Film footage from the civil war currently raging in Spain was much closer to home.

Almost exactly a year ago the Basque town of Guernica had been bombed from the air. It had been their market day and thousands of unarmed men, women and children had been killed. The horror of that aerial attack had sent shock waves around the world.

Aviators had been heroes – symbols of the modern age, of man's triumph over the forces of nature, of the progress of humankind. Now they were angels of death, raining destruction down from the clouds, slaughtering innocent men, women and children in their own homes. And the airmen who were honing their terrible skills most efficiently in Spain were the men of the German Luftwaffe: the men who would be attacking Britain if it came to war.

There was supposed to be a non-intervention agreement about the Spanish civil war. Germany and Italy were blithely ignoring it. The suspicion was growing that what folk were learning to call the Axis Powers were using Spain as some dreadful sort of training ground, a rehearsal for a larger theatre of war.

There was widespread revulsion at the prospect of Britain once more involving herself in a European war. The dreadful years between 1914 and 1918 had blighted the lives of one generation and made an indelible mark on the next.

Aware of the strength and depth of pacifist opinion, Prime Minister Neville Chamberlain was trying desperately to stop Britain being dragged into war, adopting a policy which had come to be known as appeasement. Let the Nazis have something of what they want, ran this philosophy, and we'll be able to pacify them, keep the ravening beast at bay, the hounds of war firmly on the leash.

The trouble was, anyone who had a conscience was becoming more and more uncomfortable with the reality of appeasement. Liz knew that Eddie was one of them. He was not in principle opposed to fighting for what you believed in.

A year ago Liz had needed all of her powers of persuasion to stop him from throwing up his studies and going off to join the International Brigade fighting in defence of the beleaguered democratic government of Spain against the fascist rebels led by General Franco. In the end she'd told him it would break their mother's heart if he went off to war – and that had been the argument which had finally convinced him to stay at home.

Now, with the international crisis growing more serious every day, she knew he was having a great deal of trouble reconciling his political convictions with his innate sense of honour and decency, although he wasn't going to let go of those convictions without a fight. The two men were talking about the Soviet Union now, a country which Eddie idolised.

'Eddie, Eddie,' her grandfather was saying, shaking his head in despair, 'I'll grant you that the October Revolution was one of the great events in human history, but it's been corrupted. Look at the show trials in Moscow last year. What were they, if not the revolution eating its children?'

'No, no,' cried Eddie, 'don't you see? They have to constantly keep purifying the revolution – and if that has to be done by blood,' he declaimed, tossing his tousled locks, 'then so be it.'

Liz snorted. 'This from the man who has to ask his mother to take a spider out of the bath? And then asks her to be sure not to kill the poor wee thing?'

Eddie scowled at her.

'The end justifies the means,' he said. 'That's what we have to remember.'

'Edward, my child,' said Peter MacMillan, 'if you don't mind me saying so, what you've just said is – excuse me, Lizzie – a load of shite.'

They were off once more, amiably trading insults and casting aspersions on each other's intelligence, shrewdness and political judgement. Liz wouldn't interrupt again. They were both enjoying themselves far too much.

She looked at the old clock on the mantelpiece. If she listened carefully she could make out its reassuring tick-tock underneath the men's raised voices.

Dry your tears and lift up your head. She could hear her grandmother's voice saying it. She lifted her chin. *I'll do my best, Granny.*

Liz stretched her legs out, then hurriedly drew them back up again as her feet hit the cold patch of sheet at the bottom of the bed. As she did so, the memory of yesterday evening's confrontation with her father came flooding back. She curled herself up into a tight little ball of misery. So much for her resolution to count her blessings.

She had thought that turning eighteen would solve all of her problems. She'd been fourteen when she had first composed a letter to the Western Infirmary up in Glasgow about nursing training. When she had received a polite and businesslike reply telling her that she couldn't be considered until she was eighteen it had seemed such a long way away.

All through school and after – when she had done a course at commercial college to learn how to type and do shorthand, activities which didn't interest her in the slightest; when she had gone to work at Murray's – eighteen had been the magic number. It had twinkled on the horizon, out of reach but edging slowly closer, full of hope and promise, offering her the opportunity to fulfil a dream which had matured over the years into the desire to do something useful with her life: to help others, to make a difference.

She could remember every detail of the time she had spent at Blawarthill Hospital when she'd had scarlet fever as a child. Being carried down the stairs at Radnor Street wrapped up in a red blanket, her mother and Granny waiting anxiously on the pavement by the horse-drawn ambulance which was to take her away.

Sadie, a young mother who'd already lost one child to the dreadful disease, had been pale and silent, her face stricken with grief and fear. Granny, a comforting arm laid along her daughter-in-law's thin shoulders, had smiled at Liz and told her to be a good girl and get better soon. Her father had been standing on the pavement a step or two away from his mother and his wife.

Liz, just eight years old, had known only that her brother George had gone off in a closed carriage like the one to which she was being carried – and had never come back. One afternoon, without any sort of an explanation, she and Eddie had been taken to his funeral. Liz watched the small white coffin being lowered into the ground, turned to her mother and asked, 'Is that heaven down there? Where they're putting Georgie?' No one had given her an answer.

About to be put into the ambulance, her father opening the door for the nurse who was carrying her, Liz made the terrifying connection between what was happening to her and what had happened to her little brother. Turning to her father, she reached out for him.

'Daddy, Daddy! Don't let them put me down the big hole!'

But William MacMillan, his face shuttered, had taken a step back from his daughter's outstretched arms. Without a word of farewell to his daughter or comfort to his wife he turned on his heel and walked back into the close. The next thing Liz knew she was in the darkness of the ambulance, weeping as though her heart would break.

And then, small and scared and lonely, Liz's paroxysms of grief had subsided to an exhausted sobbing, and a nurse at Blawarthill had laid a cool hand on her hot brow and told her that everything would be all right. The woman had sat with her and talked to her, offering much-needed comfort and reassurance to a very frightened little girl.

Her mother had been allowed to visit once a week, and even then they had only been permitted to look at each other through a window. They hadn't been able to talk to each other. Her father hadn't visited at all.

But she had survived, gradually regaining her health and strength, and eventually being allowed to go home. She had never forgotten the kindness of that nurse, and of the others who'd looked after her during her six weeks away from home.

21

As she grew older, Liz came to realise that nursing was what she wanted to do with her life too.

Now, at long last, she had got there – only for the dream to be cruelly snatched out of her reach. By her own father. She'd always believed he would have preferred it if Georgie had been the one to survive, not her. He was proud of Eddie, but he didn't seem to think daughters were much use for anything.

Liz groaned, and pulled her knees up more tightly. She tried not to revisit the bad memories too often. Sometimes they seemed to crawl to the surface of their own accord. The door of her room creaked. Cocooned in her sheets and heavy blankets, she looked up and saw her mother peering round it.

'Come on, Lizzie,' said Sadie MacMillan in an anxious whisper. 'You know your father likes us all to have breakfast together.'

Always what her father wanted. Liz bit back an angry retort.

'Aye, Ma. I'll be two ticks.' She gestured towards her underwear, lying folded in a neat pile on the upright chair which stood against the wall. 'Hand me those, would you? I'll need to warm them up.' She must be a better actress than she'd thought. Her mother's face cleared a little. That was good.

Clutching her underclothes to her, Liz suppressed a shriek as the smooth artificial silk of her petticoat made contact with her own warm skin. It had never been this cold in the old house in Radnor Street, where she had slept in the box bed in the warmth of the kitchen, listening to Eddie snoring on the hurly bed on the other side of the curtains.

There, she'd had to perfect the art of putting her clothes on in bed for modesty's sake. Here, she did it to prevent her skin breaking out into goosebumps as big as Ben Lomond.

She knew her mother missed the old place, but to her father moving into Queen Victoria Row had been a great mark of achievement. Eddie, with his firebrand communist politics, was less happy about it. Their father was now one of the 'bastards in bowlers', the choice of hat as much a mark of status as anything else.

22

His new position set them apart from a lot of the people they'd been friendly with before. As far as some of them were concerned, William MacMillan had now gone over to the enemy. That made life difficult for his wife. She was a shy woman, but she had known people up the road – had appreciated having her parents-in-law just down the stairs. Brought up in an orphanage after the early death of her own parents, she had been close to her in-laws, who had taken her to their hearts in a big way when their son had first brought her home.

Now it was much more difficult and time-consuming for Sadie to visit Peter MacMillan. Because of the dispute between him and his son he wasn't able to visit her at all.

Performing the various contortions needed to get into her bra and knickers, Liz sighed. Her mother's life wasn't easy. For her sake she'd better go through there and play the dutiful daughter.

Her father did not drink to excess. Nor was he a physically violent man. Liz couldn't remember that he'd ever given her and Eddie so much as a smack when they'd been little. But then he'd never hugged them either.

To the best of Liz's knowledge he'd never lifted a hand to her mother. He didn't need to. He dominated her quite successfully by sheer force of personality, bullying and undermining her at every turn, belittling her whenever she had the rare temerity to contradict him.

To Liz's way of thinking that made him little better than the Tam Simpsons of this world – or the men who came home from the pub on a Friday and Saturday night and, in Eddie's memorable if gruesome phrase, bounced their wives' heads off the wall.

Liz slipped into her place at the kitchen table and scowled at the handsomely framed print which hung on the wall opposite her. It was one of her father's most prized possessions: Prince William of Orange crossing the Boyne in 1690 to defeat the Catholic army of King James.

23

It's all your fault, she silently told the bewigged monarch, resplendent on his white charger. One of the arguments her father had advanced against her going in for nursing was that she might end up having to care for Roman Catholics. Honestly, he was quite ridiculous!

'Good morning, Elizabeth.' He hadn't lifted his head from his newspaper, and he had used her full name. She was still in the doghouse, then.

'Good morning, Father,' she replied. Had she ever really called him Daddy? And her father, despite his allegiance to the monarch his fellow Orangemen familiarly addressed as King Billy, got his own name in full. It was always William. There was a formality about him – a coldness – which prevented anyone from shortening it.

Liz felt a fresh wave of despair sweep over her. Was there no way she could persuade him to let her do what she wanted? Maybe, just maybe, if she was polite and obedient and kept her nose clean . . .

Her father lifted his head at last, looked at her coolly and dashed that faint hope to smithereens.

'You'll reply to that letter as soon as you come home tonight, Elizabeth, telling the Infirmary you will not be attending for interview – that you no longer wish to be considered for a probationer's position. Then you will give your reply to me and I shall post it.'

The full bitterness of her disappointment threatened to engulf her completely. She did want to be considered for a probationer's position. It was all she had ever wanted.

'Do you hear me, Elizabeth?'

She heard him all right. There was to be no shouting this morning, but the message was as clear as though it had been delivered by foghorn. She was to do as she was told. What he wanted her to do.

'Do you hear me?' he said again. 'I'll have no dumb insolence from you, miss, I'm warning you.' He hadn't raised his voice, but her mother jumped all the same. Only for her sake then, thought Liz, only for her sake. Her voice dull, her eyes downcast, she answered him. She had to force down the lump in her throat to get the words out.

'I hear you, Father,' she said.

Chapter 3

Rising to her feet after extracting a file from the bottom drawer of the filing cabinet, Liz kicked it deftly shut with her foot, turned – and let out a small shriek of alarm. Eric Mitchell, chief clerk of Murray Marine Agents, was standing right behind her.

'Oh, Mr Mitchell, what a fright you gave me!'

Eric Mitchell laughed. He didn't, however, stand aside to let her past.

'Excuse me, please,' said Liz, looking pointedly over his shoulder towards her own small desk in the middle of the room the two of them shared with Miss Gilchrist, Mr Murray's secretary. Realising that they were practically nose to nose – Eric Mitchell wasn't much taller than her – she also took a step backwards. At least, she tried to, but there wasn't really anywhere to go.

The solid green filing cabinets which ran nearly the entire length of the back wall of the office left only a narrow space in the corner formed by the other wall. Somehow Liz managed to sidle into the gap. Only after she'd done it did she realise what a mistake she'd made.

Instead of moving away, he took a step towards her. He had her cornered – and they were alone in the sunny room. Her mouth dry, Liz had to moisten her lips before she could speak. The man standing far too close to her smiled when he saw the nervous gesture. The gleam in his pale eyes made her skin crawl.

'Excuse me, please, Mr Mitchell,' she said again. She hoped her voice wasn't rising nervously. She had learned to be careful in the office, cautious about how and when she moved about

26

the place, but she wasn't thinking straight today.

She'd been day-dreaming for weeks of how she was going to hand in her notice and leave Murray's. She'd gone so far as to imagine herself telling Eric Mitchell exactly what she thought of him. Some hopes.

'I have to get on with my work.' She clutched the buff folder she'd taken from the filing cabinet closer to her chest. He smiled his creepy smile again and put a hand up on the wall beside Liz's head.

'Mr Mitchell? Haven't I told you before to call me Eric?' He glanced towards the door which separated their office from the boss's room. 'Not when Mr Murray or Miss Gilchrist are about, naturally. But when we're on our own.'

Her eyes followed his. The door into the inner office was half-glazed, but with frosted glass. In any case, they were standing at the wrong angle for anybody in the boss's room to be able to see them. Miss Gilchrist was in there, taking dictation from Mr Murray. If only they would hurry up and finish . . .

Liz felt like a trapped animal, her back pressed against the wall, her left shoulder feeling the cold metal of the filing cabinet through the thin crêpe de Chine of her short-sleeved blouse, Eric Mitchell's arm blocking any escape on the other side.

'Isn't it better to be businesslike at work?' she asked desperately.

'Och, little Lizzie,' he said, shaking his head at her in mock despair. 'So conscientious.'

She hated it when he called her that. She hated almost everything about Eric Mitchell: the way he looked her up and down, the way he stood behind her while she was typing, the way his hand – accidentally on purpose – managed to brush against her leg as she passed his desk. She shuddered.

'Cold, little Lizzie? Perhaps I could do something about that. Mmm?' He moved closer, looming over her, one sandy eyebrow raised in interrogation. She could smell the cigarette smoke which clung always to his clothes, practically count the hairs in his moustache. Oh, Mammy, Daddy, what was she going to do if he tried to touch her? Or even, horror of horrors, kiss her . . .

She looked at him, her heart thumping wildly. She wished she could tell him to get lost, give him a real good mouthful. She'd never actually used the words, but she knew them well enough. Living beneath Nan Simpson for several years had seen to that.

There were several reasons why Liz couldn't swear at Eric Mitchell. Nor could she remind him that he had a wife and child, that he shouldn't be pestering her in this way, that he was fifteen years older than her, that she herself wasn't very far away from being a gawky schoolgirl, that it just wasn't fair.

He was a member of the same Orange Lodge as William MacMillan and had 'put in a good word for the lassie' when Murray's had been looking for a junior member of staff to assist Mr Murray's personal secretary. And she couldn't afford to antagonise him.

As her father had reminded her the other night, Eddie had to be seen through college. He had won a bursary to go to the Uni, but it didn't pay for everything. Her pay really was needed at home.

The door of the inner office opened and Miss Gilchrist came out. Eric Mitchell moved rapidly away from Liz and she scurried back to her desk, laid the file to one side of the solid Underwood typewriter and sat down. She was all fingers and thumbs as she searched through the papers to find the address she needed for the next letter she had to type.

Liz thought grimly that maybe she could understand why Nan Simpson swore at her husband. Even saying the words to yourself helped relieve your feelings.

Damn you, Eric Mitchell, and damn being only eighteen and damn having no say in anything and damn having to work here—

Her index finger slid on to the wrong typewriter key. Did she have to work here? She'd been at Murray's for two years, surely long enough to repay the favour done when Eric Mitchell had recommended her for the position. Maybe she could find a better job, one that paid a bit more. Her father wouldn't be able to object to that. And waiting the three long years until she was twenty-one would be a lot pleasanter if she didn't have to put up with unwanted attentions day in, day out.

Over the next week Liz made enquiries about three shorthand-typist's jobs she saw advertised. She went to the relevant offices either during her midday break or at the end of the afternoon so that neither Miss Gilchrist nor Eric Mitchell would know she was planning a move.

At the first office, a lady quite as formidable as Miss Gilchrist looked her up and down and told her that they were looking for an experienced stenographer. Liz was far too young.

They were friendlier at the second place, but the pay was lousy, even less than she was getting at Murray's. At the third they seemed interested in her, and cheerfully asked when she could attend for interview. They reminded her to be sure to bring a reference from her current employer when she came.

'Oh,' said Liz, her face falling. 'Maybe I'd better think about it a bit more. I'll let you know if I'm interested. Thanks all the same.'

Only ever having been in one job since leaving school, she had forgotten those two important facts. She would need time off to attend an interview, and she would need to get a reference.

Asking for time off meant explanations. She imagined that looking for a new job wasn't going to go down too well as an excuse. Miss Gilchrist might even contact her father to ask if he approved of his daughter making a move. Liz wouldn't put it past her.

Murray's might also refuse to give her a reference. No other firm was going to take her on without one, or perhaps even with one. Liz had few illusions about her abilities as a shorthand-typist. Any reference she received wasn't going to be a glowing one. She'd get herself into extremely hot water, with no guarantee of a new job at the end of it.

Trudging up the stairs of the railway station on Friday

evening, Liz walked out on to the pavement. There was a man standing in front of her, barring her way. She glanced up.

'Grandad! What on earth are you doing here?'

The station was only a few hundred yards from her home. By tacit agreement, she and Eddie never met Peter MacMillan except at his house.

So far, their father continued to tolerate the visits. It was one of the few things about which Sadie had dug her heels in. It had been an enormous effort for her to stand up to her husband, but she had won. Eddie and Liz were not to be prevented from seeing their grandfather.

Valuing each other's friendship and company as they did, none of the three of them wanted to put that in jeopardy. Appearing so close to his son's house might just be sufficient annoyance to make William ban the visits – which meant that her grandfather had to have a very good reason indeed for coming to meet Liz off the train.

'Read that,' he said, thrusting a crumpled *Glasgow Herald* into her hand. 'Page twelve. Under "Women's Topics". You get some real good articles on that page, you know.' He gave her an outrageous wink. Curious, Liz scanned the article. He had folded the newspaper open for her at the right spot.

The piece was about the Red Cross. With international tension rising, the reporter wrote, recruitment to the Voluntary Aid Detachment of the organisation was being stepped up. Public-spirited citizens prepared to volunteer would receive training in the various skills required. The Red Cross was particularly keen to hear from men or women who could drive and from women prepared to train as nursing auxiliaries. It would be remembered, of course, that VAD nurses had given sterling service during the Great War.

Liz looked up. She said the words out loud, her voice high and breathless.

'Nursing auxiliaries?'

Peter MacMillan gestured excitedly towards the newspaper. 'Read on,' he said. 'You haven't got to the best bit yet.'

Impatient, he snatched it from her hands and read the article out loud to her.

'While VAD nursing assistants may be sought on a full-time basis if the crisis continues to worsen, the organisation will also be happy to hear from girls and women who would be able to make their contribution on a weekend or evening basis, thus combining this valuable work with their domestic duties or existing employment responsibilities. The Red Cross will shortly be establishing an intensive programme of first-aid classes to which both sexes will be warmly welcomed. Initially, all those interested in becoming nursing auxiliaries should enrol for these classes.

'There,' he said triumphantly, folding the newspaper and tucking it under his arm. 'What do you think of that?'

'I think it's the answer to a prayer,' breathed Liz, hardly daring to believe her eyes and ears. Peter beamed at her and they began to walk together along the pavement, chattering excitedly.

'It would be great experience,' she said, 'until I'm old enough to apply to the Infirmary again.'

Peter nodded enthusiastically. 'Aye. They'd surely snap you up if you already had three years' experience with the Red Cross.' He handed her the roughly folded newspaper. 'Take it home with you, lass. There's something about a recruitment session one night next week up in Glasgow—' He broke off. They were getting close to Queen Victoria Row.

'I'd better not come any further with you, hen.' His gaze went over her head. 'I'd like fine to have popped in to see Sadie . . .'

His voice trailed off and he sighed. 'But it wouldn't do to be caught committing the unforgivable sin of talking to my own granddaughter in the street,' he said wryly. He sketched her a very passable bow. 'And now, like the great Houdini, I disappear.'

Liz grinned at his departing back. He was a hoot, he really was. Whatever would she do without him?

* * *

Once her father was safely out at an Orange Lodge meeting that evening, Liz spread the newspaper over the kitchen table and read the article out loud to her mother and Eddie. Her voice grew warm with excitement as she read it for a second time and the details began to sink in. This was a real possibility.

With growing excitement she read of plans to pay full-time VAD nurses a wage if the international situation continued to deteriorate. During the Great War they'd all been volunteers. If that worked out, she might manage to get away from Murray's sooner rather than later. Her first step was obviously to enrol for the first-aid classes.

The recruitment evening for those was to take place in a church hall in Glasgow on the following Tuesday – thankfully another evening when her father was out regularly. If the classes were also on a Tuesday she was in clover.

Lifting her head from the paper, Liz saw her mother regarding her with a worried frown. No prizes for guessing why. Suppressing her irritation at how her father managed to dominate his wife even when he wasn't there, she set about reassuring Sadie.

'He can't object to me doing a class, Ma. Surely. I do other night classes, after all, and he's never said anything about them.'

'I don't know, Lizzie,' said her mother nervously. 'He might think you were trying to get round him, do what he forbade you to do.'

'Forbade me?'

The MacMillan family seemed to be living not only in a street named after the old Queen, but also during her reign. Liz turned eagerly to Eddie. He would back her up.

'You can't be serious, Liz.' The words were clipped, his voice harsh.

'Why not?' she asked, genuinely puzzled by his reaction. He'd always been her champion and he knew better than anybody how devastated she'd been by their father's ban on her going for the interview at the Infirmary.

'Don't you see, Eddie?' she asked. 'This would let me start nursing almost straightaway – well, it's not quite nursing, but I'd be learning about first aid and there's the possibility of becoming a part-time auxiliary—'

He interrupted her. 'Don't *you* see what this is all about, Liz? It's all part of getting ready for war – and the more we do that, the more likely it is that we will go to war. We'll be sucked into it.'

He rose to his feet, pushing his chair back with a loud scrape. The strength of his feelings clearly required movement. He strode about the kitchen as he made his points, gesturing wildly at the newspaper lying open on the table in front of Liz.

'That,' he began. '*All of that*. Everything that you read in the capitalist press. It's designed to create the war mentality—'

'Eddie,' said Liz, beginning to get angry herself, 'we're talking about the Red Cross. You know? The organisation that helps alleviate the sufferings of war? Do you know what VAD nurses did during the Great War? They worked at the front, in field hospitals, tending the wounded.'

Eddie snorted.

'The vastly overprivileged daughters of the bourgeoisie and the upper classes playing at being Nursie?'

Liz lifted her chin, infuriated by that sneering response. Sitting beside her at the table, Sadie had gone very still. She hated arguments, especially on the rare occasions when they broke out between her children, but Liz was too angry now to consider her mother's feelings.

'Don't talk rubbish, Eddie,' she snapped. 'If there's going to be a war, there's going to be a war. Nothing you or I do is going to make a blind bit of difference. And if it's coming anyway, wouldn't it be better to get ready for it?'

He stopped pacing, came forward and gripped the back of his empty chair. 'Liz, for God's sake! I never thought you were that stupid!'

Bristling, Liz sat up straight, more than ready to retaliate. Eddie, however, was in full flow. Taking one hand off the back

33

of the chair he pointed once more at the newspaper.

'That article's appealing to naïve, idealistic girls like you who can't see that it's all designed to put the whole country – and the economy – on a war footing. People say we're pulling ourselves out of the Depression. D'you know how we're doing that?' he demanded.

He answered his own question. 'By gearing up for war, that's how. Factories and businesses – and hospitals. If you join the Red Cross you'll be part of the capitalist war machine too!'

That one took the biscuit.

'That, Edward MacMillan, is the biggest load of—'

Seeing her mother's shocked face, Liz stopped herself just in time. She flung Eddie's words back at him. 'So I'm naïve, am I? Idealistic too? Well, pardon me for breathing. I didn't realise either of those were hanging offences!'

'Och, Liz, you don't understand!' He gripped the back of the chair with both hands and looked down at her despairingly.

Her eyes flashing green fire, Liz lifted her face to him. 'And you do, I suppose!'

Abruptly, Eddie folded his arms across his chest, his demeanour all at once much calmer. Frighteningly calm.

'I've studied history,' he said. 'Politics too. I know how things happen. History repeats itself. All the time.'

Liz felt a tightness in her chest. The constriction rose into her throat and her head swam briefly. Shaking it to clear away the feeling, she met Eddie's eyes. Then looked away again. Continuing this argument wasn't going to get them anywhere – apart from upsetting Ma.

'I think we'll have to agree to disagree, Eddie.'

'You think so?' he asked stiffly. However, when Liz made an almost imperceptible movement of her eyes towards their mother, she saw by the answering flicker that he had caught the unspoken message.

'Aye,' he said, unfolding his arms, pulling out his chair and sitting down at the table. 'You're right. There's obviously not much point in continuing the discussion.' He put a smile on his face and turned to Sadie.

'Shall we have another cup of tea, Ma?'

Chapter 4

In the middle of the following Tuesday afternoon, Miss Gilchrist sent Liz out on an errand. The office boy was off somewhere else, and there was an urgent letter to be delivered to Murray's solicitor, who had offices further along the river towards Glasgow city centre.

Liz was glad of the break: to get away from Eric Mitchell's leers, because the office was hot and sticky and because she had a decision to make. Tonight was the enrolment evening for the first-aid classes.

She had robustly defended the Red Cross to Eddie, but she had thought a lot about the points he had made. Could he possibly be right? Were they rushing pell-mell towards war, carried along by the sheer momentum of the thing?

There was a kind of terrible drama about it all which was almost exciting, and her chances of becoming a full-time auxiliary nurse were all tied up with the possibility of war. Did that make her a warmonger?

Walking along towards Jamaica Street Bridge, enjoying the breeze coming off the Clyde, Liz lifted her chin in defiance of that accusation. No, it damn well didn't. Of course she didn't want there to be a war, and she really couldn't believe that her joining the Red Cross was going to influence things one way or the other. That was a stupid argument – and she would tell Eddie so . . . just as soon as they were speaking to each other again.

Stopping to cross the road, she glanced at the newspaper vendor who had his pitch at the junction where the Broomielaw gave way to Clyde Street. There was a poster on his stand. *Another Spanish city suffers aerial bombardment. Pictures.*

Liz wondered who went to the aid of the injured and the survivors there: the Spanish Red Cross, she supposed.

She delivered the letter and stood for a moment on the stone steps of the lawyer's office. The imposing entrance doorway was flanked by two huge stone figures, their limbs clothed in the garb of Ancient Greece. Their mighty heads bowed, they each supported a globe on their broad shoulders. That reminded Liz of her grandfather's strongly voiced belief that Adolf Hitler wanted to rule the world.

She gazed out across the busy street to the river and the houses beyond it. There was a dirty big grey cloud hanging over the Gorbals. Good. A downpour was exactly what this oppressively hot day needed. She made her way down on to the pavement.

How would she feel if the bombs were raining down on Clydebank? What would she do if it was her own home town which was suffering?

Her shorthand and typing skills wouldn't be much use. *Let me through, I'm a stenographer. I can take dictation at eighty words per minute and sometimes I can even manage to read it back again afterwards.* No, she didn't think so.

Eddie was going to accuse her of being part of the capitalist war machine once a day and three times on Sundays. Liz tossed her head, her generous mouth curving in reluctant amusement. A man walking past in the opposite direction threw her an admiring glance and tipped his hat. She didn't notice him. Me and Adolf, she was thinking. Both of us out to rule the world.

She couldn't believe it. After all it had taken her to get here, the effort, the soul-searching, the sheer trouble it might be going to cause at home, and between her and Eddie, the woman sitting in front of her was telling her that she was too young to join the Red Cross.

'But I'm eighteen,' she said, quite consciously squaring her shoulders and drawing herself up to her full five foot six. Sometimes Liz found her few extra inches a problem. She was taller than most women she knew – and a good few of the men.

Tonight she was glad of her height – anything which would help impress the imposing-looking woman sitting behind a table in a draughty church hall at the top of Buchanan Street in Glasgow.

Pen poised over a list, she looked up at Liz, her eyes narrowing. She was middle-aged, beautifully dressed and formidably elegant, her smooth blonde hair swept back into a French roll.

Liz felt her cheeks grow pink under the careful appraisal. She was being sized up. She hoped she was making a good impression, but somehow she doubted it.

Coming out of work at the end of the afternoon, she had made it along Clyde Street, through Dixon Street and up into St Enoch Square before the fat raindrops bursting as they hit the pavements had marshalled themselves into the torrential summer rainstorm which had been threatening all afternoon.

She had thought about seeking the shelter of the huge Victorian railway station which occupied one whole side of the square, then decided against it. She'd be better off making a run for it. She'd no idea how long it might take to enrol and she didn't want to risk getting in after her father came home at the end of his evening out.

So she had crossed Argyle Street and made a mad dash up Buchanan Street, the skirts of her raincoat getting soaked, passing traffic more than once splashing water over her feet and ankles. A horse-drawn coal lorry passed her. She spared a thought for the beast, a solid Clydesdale getting ready for the extra pull as the road began the climb towards the eastern end of Sauchiehall Street. Wisps of steam were rising off the animal's warm back as the raindrops struck him.

Liz herself was feeling unpleasantly warm on the inside, the rubberised material of her mackintosh sealing the heat of her exertions firmly in. The summer shirt-waister dress she wore beneath the raincoat was clinging to her. Since the morning had been hot and sunny, she hadn't worn a hat today either. That meant that her dark brown hair had done what it always did in the wet – gone into a mass of unruly curls and waves. She could feel them, curling round her hot and sweaty temples. She must look like something the cat had dragged in.

'I'm eighteen,' she repeated, leaning forward and gripping the edge of the desk in her determination to put her case.

The elegant lady smiled – and instantly seemed much less fierce.

'I'm afraid that's my point, my dear. You see, the Red Cross doesn't have a junior branch – not as yet, anyway – and there might be things our helpers would be called upon to do . . . well . . . that we feel youngsters like yourself shouldn't see.'

She was very refined, her cultured accent only just recognisable as belonging to the west of Scotland.

'It's very good indeed of you to come along to offer your services in the current crisis. Perhaps you'd like to leave your name and address and we can get in touch with you at a later date. If necessary.'

The smile was apologetic. It was also dismissive. Any minute now she was going to raise her beautifully modulated voice in a shout. *Next!* Liz lifted her head and looked about her. Surely she couldn't be the only younger person interested in enrolling?

There was half a dozen registration tables set up around the hall. They didn't have many customers as yet, potential volunteers presumably waiting for the rain to go off. The men and women waiting to receive them all looked ancient to Liz's young eyes.

A small knot of people stood a few yards away. Looking at the clothes and listening to the accents, she mentally categorised them as Bright Young Things. She was unlikely to get much help there. Anyway, they all looked a bit older than her, in their early twenties perhaps. She caught the eye of a tall young man who glanced over with an expression of polite interest on his face. He smiled at her.

Hearing a discreet cough at her elbow, Liz turned. A pretty

39

fair-haired girl stood there. Judging by the damp patches on the heavy woollen coat she wore, she too had only recently come in off the street. She took the few steps necessary to bring her to stand beside Liz. She was almost the same height as her, and about the same age.

'I-I'd like to enrol too,' she said. 'I was w-wondering if you m-might be running classes in Clydebank?'

Liz turned to her enthusiastically.

'I'm from Clydebank as well.'

The girl, clearly nervous, gave her a little nod of acknowledgement. Both she and Liz turned to look anxiously at the woman behind the desk, who surveyed them for a moment or two before letting out a long, exasperated sigh.

'My dear girls . . . you're both very young—'

Liz's patience snapped. 'Would we be too young to be bombed? If the war does come?'

Her impassioned outburst fell into an uneasy silence. Every head in the echoing hall seemed to turn towards her, the other conversations going on grinding to an abrupt halt. The pale, shocked faces indicated that everyone present knew exactly what Liz was talking about. She obviously wasn't the only person to have been struck by the newsreel pictures from Spain.

Support came from an unexpected quarter.

'The young lady has a point.'

It was the tall man who had smiled at her. He moved to stand behind the woman sitting at the desk, and Liz wondered if he was her son. While his accent wasn't quite so refined as hers, he was very well-spoken, and their colouring was the same, his lanky frame topped with a thatch of hair the colour of a corn field. Assuming hers owes nothing to the peroxide bottle, thought Liz irreverently.

Young lady, indeed! He could only be a few years older than she was. What did her age matter, anyway? She was old enough to be out at work earning a living – which was probably more than this well-off chap had ever done. On the other hand, he did seem to be trying to help.

Liz felt a spurt of amusement. To think that she, a daughter of Red Clydeside, was considering using one of the Idle Rich as an ally in her plans to join the Red Cross! Eddie would be doubly horrified.

Mind you, what was that phrase he had used when he and Grandad had been arguing about the show trials in Russia? The end justifies the means? If this posh young gentleman could help her get enrolled, that was fine by her.

She gave her unexpected knight in shining armour a broad smile and received one as warm and friendly in response. He had nice eyes. They were a warm hazel, a striking contrast with his fair hair.

'After all,' he said, 'if the worst does come to the worst, Clydebank's going to be one of the places that—' He broke off, looked embarrassed, and started again. 'The Red Cross could do with a lot of volunteers in Clydebank . . .' His voice trailed away.

Liz knew exactly what he had been about to say. *Clydebank's going to be one of the places that'll get it.* If war did come, the town on the banks of the Clyde, full of shipyards and factories, was going to be a prime target for enemy bombs. And all those yards and factories sat cheek by jowl with the packed three- and four-storey tenements which housed the people who worked in them.

Unexpectedly, somebody laughed. It was one of the Bright Young Things, a pencil-slim young woman with hair the same colour and length as Liz's. Hers, however, was beautifully coiffed, curling smoothly under at the ends.

'I thought you were all conchies down there,' she observed, her voice an amused drawl. 'Just waiting for the Germans to parachute down and help you start the revolution. Send all us lot to *Madame la Guillotine*. Isn't that right, darling?'

Coming forward, she slipped her arm through that of the fair-haired young man. Her last comment had been addressed to him, and now she turned and looked up at him with an expectant smile.

Eddie would have said that the Bright Young Thing's reading of modern politics was somewhat defective. She didn't seem to know the difference between fascism and communism. All Liz knew was that the comments had made her blood boil. How dare she?

It was true there was little appetite for war in Clydebank, its inhabitants still pinning their hopes on the League of Nations being able to find a peaceful solution to the continuing crisis. Damning her home town as being full of potential fifth columnists was, however, too much for Elizabeth MacMillan to take. Tossing her unruly head, she prepared to do battle.

'Surely no sane person actually wants there to be a war?' she asked haughtily.

'And,' she finished up, having made her points in her usual forceful and forthright manner, 'personally I'm of the opinion that conscientious objectors deserve our respect. They stand up for their beliefs.' She swallowed. Eddie might be going to be one of them.

Squashing that thought, Liz smiled sweetly at her adversary. 'We've got some in Clydebank,' she said. 'You've probably even got them in Bearsden,' she added, 'or wherever it is that *you* live.'

'Well, really!' came an older female voice, the precursor to a chorus of disapproving murmurs. Liz couldn't make out all the words, but she could guess what was really being said. *The lower orders just don't know their place any more.*

Serves them bloody well right, she thought. It is 1938, after all, not the dark ages. Then her momentary satisfaction at answering back evaporated. *That's you cooked your goose, MacMillan. They're never going to let you join now. Not after that performance. When are you ever going to learn to hold your tongue, you stupid bisom?*

She'd forgotten about the girl standing beside her, who now began to speak. She seemed to be battling against shyness, traces of a nervous stammer in her voice. All the same, she managed to sound both persuasive and conciliatory.

Somehow smoothing over the awkwardness of the last exchange, she brought the discussion back to the point at issue. Wouldn't it be useful to have people of all ages who knew what to do in an emergency? Especially somewhere like Clydebank – as the young gentleman had said, she added, flashing Liz's champion a shy smile.

They could perhaps be enrolled for classes on a probationary basis. How about a trial period of three months? The crisis might even be over by then. Whether it was or not, the powers-that-be could then make a decision about keeping them on.

Liz could see that the woman was wavering, impressed by both the argument and the gentle maturity with which it had been put, not to mention the skilful pouring of oil on troubled waters.

'Well, if you're both sure . . . if you're happy to be enrolled on that basis . . . there is going to be a class starting up in Clydebank. Let me take your details.'

Liz turned to her new friend and smiled.

Chapter 5

'Are you a communist? You were that fierce in there.'

Both girls were standing in the lobby of the church hall, making preparations to brave the downpour. The force of the deluge had diminished, but a steady rain was continuing to fall on Buchanan Street.

Liz laughed at the question, and the way in which it had been put – a mixture of disapproval and reluctant admiration. Her voice was tinged with scorn as she answered.

'Why is it that everyone thinks you're a communist just because you speak your mind and don't let people like that walk all over you? No,' she said irritably, pulling on her gloves and getting ready to put up her umbrella, 'I'm not a communist.' Preparations complete, she turned to the girl. 'My brother Eddie is, though. He says it's the way of the future.'

Her companion's blue eyes grew wide.

'But they do the devil's work!'

Liz snorted.

'That's just propaganda. Don't tell me you believe everything you read in the capitalist press?'

The girl's face fell. I'm taking it out on the wrong person, thought Liz. She held out her hand.

'I might have been fierce, but it was you who managed to get us enrolled. Thank you. I'm Elizabeth MacMillan – Liz.'

The other girl shook Liz's hand with a firmness which belied her ethereal appearance.

'Helen,' she said, with a shy dip of the head. 'Helen Gallagher.'

44

'Oh!'

Cursing herself for the reaction she hadn't managed to suppress, Liz felt the firm clasp on her hand relax. Helen took a step back, lifted her chin and gave Liz a wry smile.

It was her surname that had done it, marking her out immediately as coming from an Irish – and therefore Roman Catholic – family. It went along with the universal question: what school did you go to? Clydebank High provoked one response; Our Holy Redeemer's quite another.

'Well,' said Helen Gallagher after a tiny pause, 'perhaps I'll see you when the class starts.'

She turned and headed for the doorway and the rainy street beyond. The street lamps had been lit early. One was casting a pale glow over the slick wet pavement, the illumination it gave fighting a losing battle with the spring twilight.

Liz, following her out, noticed for the second time that the other girl wasn't wearing a mac, but a heavy winter coat – a rather shabby one at that. That told its own story. She didn't seem to have an umbrella either, so Liz swung her own up to cover the two of them.

'I'll get you home,' she said. 'Do you take the tram or the train?'

'Train to Singer's,' said Helen shortly. She was obviously reluctant to accept the shelter of Liz's umbrella, maintaining a slight distance between the two of them.

'I can go that way too!' exclaimed Liz. 'Where do you live?'

'The Holy City,' said the girl, naming the group of tenement houses in Clydebank which had acquired their nickname because their flat roofs were said to resemble those of the houses in Jerusalem.

'The Holy City!' repeated Liz. 'I was brought up in Radnor Street! Just up the road a wee bit! What a coincidence!'

She wasn't getting much response. She also seemed to be speaking in exclamation marks.

'Look,' she said urgently, putting a hand on Helen's damp sleeve, 'I've really got nothing against Catholics.'

Helen's voice was as dry as the evening was wet.

'That's big of you.'

Liz grinned. She had deserved that. She must sound as patronising as the Red Cross woman had sounded to her.

'Yes, it is, isn't it? What about you, though? Do you have anything against Protestants?'

Helen gave her fair head a decisive shake.

'I don't have anything against anyone.'

She was holding herself less stiffly, her posture more relaxed.

'Come in a wee bit under the brolly,' urged Liz. 'Your hair's getting wet. Can we start again?' she asked, when Helen had done as she had asked. 'Chum each other home?'

Helen tilted her head to one side. She was really pretty, eyes the colour of the summer sky, a straight little nose and a Cupid's bow of a mouth. Despite the rain, her short blonde hair continued to sit in perfect waves. I ought to hate her, thought Liz ruefully.

'Why not?' said Helen.

Walking closely together, the two girls began to negotiate the puddles on the broad pavement.

'Are you working?' Liz asked.

'Aye. I'm an assistant at Woolie's in Sauchiehall Street. How about you?'

On the point of answering, Liz was interrupted by a deep-voiced shout from behind them.

'Ladies!'

'Can he mean us?' murmured Helen. Liz laughed and turned, somehow not at all surprised to see the tall young man hurrying towards them. He was smartly dressed in a belted trench coat, but, like Helen, he didn't have an umbrella.

'Ladies,' he said again when he reached them, taking off his hat in greeting. 'Could I offer you a lift home to Clydebank? It's such a filthy night. Fine weather for ducks, what?'

Liz looked at him. He looked back at her, his face open, the expression on it friendly.

'And are you heading for Clydebank?' she demanded.

'More or less,' he said. Then the look on his face turned sheepish. 'Well, Milngavie, actually, but it's only a mile or two out of my way.'

'It's quite a bit out of your way!' She was back to speaking in exclamation marks.

'Shouldn't you put your hat back on?' suggested Helen. 'You'll get drookit.'

He turned his hazel eyes and his pleasant smile on to her.

'Drookit? That's a good word.'

'And this is a daft place to be holding a conversation,' said Liz firmly. 'We're all going to be drookit if we don't get out of this rain soon. Thanks for the offer, but no thanks.'

'Och, go on,' he said, suddenly sounding a lot more Glaswegian. 'I'm quite trustworthy, I assure you.' He gave a quick nod of his increasingly damp head, indicating the door of the church hall behind him. 'I could get my mother to supply you with a written character reference, if you like.'

Helen chuckled. Liz wished she hadn't. It would only encourage him.

'I'd be happy to give you a lift to your homes in my little bus.' He half turned, gesturing. 'She's parked just round the corner.'

He stood waiting for their answer, seemingly not at all perturbed by the rain running down his face and dripping off his eyelashes. They were darker than his hair, thought Liz, or maybe they looked darker because they were wet.

'She?'

His smile grew broader. 'I call her Morag,' he confided.

In the name of the wee man, she thought, this one's a real numpty, a complete eejit.

'Thank you,' she said again. Polite but firm. 'I'm afraid my friend and I shall have to decline. After all,' she said grandly, getting ready to walk away from him, 'we don't know you from Adam.'

He laughed out loud. Amusement had put a twinkle in the hazel eyes.

47

'Oh, that's very good.' And then, as the two girls stared uncomprehendingly at him, 'Adam,' he said. 'That's my name, you see.' He looked first at Helen, then back at Liz. 'Adam Buchanan.'

They were standing in Buchanan Street. Helen asked the obvious question.

'Named after the street?'

Young Mr Buchanan looked embarrassed. 'I believe it *was* named after one of my ancestors.'

That did it for Liz. She'd had quite enough of consorting with the Idle Rich for one evening. She opened her mouth to once more turn down the offer of the lift. Helen Gallagher got there before her.

'It's very kind of you,' she said decisively, 'but we couldn't possibly take you so far out of your way. Goodnight, Mr Buchanan. Come on, Elizabeth.'

Liz felt her arm being taken in a firm grip. Helen set the pace, marching them both firmly in the direction of Queen Street railway station. It occurred to Liz that her new friend was turning out to have some surprising characteristics.

When they were safely under the shelter of the great glass and steel roof of the railway station and she could lower the umbrella, she said as much. Helen shrugged.

'Folk like that,' she said, 'I'm never exactly sure what to say to them. I'm no' very good at social chit-chat. Isn't that what they call it?'

She turned her pretty mouth down in mock dismay. The gesture brought her face alive, revealing a mischievous intelligence behind the chocolate-box prettiness of her features.

'Mind you,' she went on consideringly, 'he was quite nice. Gorgeous eyes. Did you no' think so?'

Liz shrugged. She had noticed the eyes. Not that she was going to admit it.

'I suppose so. Not my type, though. Far too posh.'

Helen laughed. 'Are you sure you're not a communist?' Then the amusement left her face and her features took on a wistful look.

48

'I'd like fine to have had a hurl in a car, though. I've never been in one. Have you?'

'No,' Liz admitted, 'but maybe we'd prefer one that wasn't called Morag!'

Laughing as she scanned the departure board, Helen grabbed Liz's arm.

'Platform five. A Helensburgh train. We'll have to run for it!'

The man at the barrier waved them through and they ran up the platform, flinging themselves into a compartment with only seconds to spare. The door was slammed behind them, the whistle blew and with a great puff of steam from the locomotive the train pulled away from the platform.

'Let's give the train a name,' gasped Liz as they sank together on to the cushions.

'Adam?' suggested Helen.

'Then we could call that one Eve,' said Liz, pointing to a train snaking its way in to another platform.

Those two remarks brought on a fit of the giggles which lasted until they were nearly through the tunnel which linked Queen Street to Charing Cross, the next station down the line. Recovering slowly, Liz rose to close the window against the blackness of the tunnel and the smoke and steam drifting back from the engine.

Her task completed, she took a seat opposite Helen and found the girl regarding her with a very odd look on her face.

'What?'

'I was just thinking,' began Helen, 'that here you are trapped in a railway carriage with a Fenian. Does that not worry you?'

Liz winced. Fenian was one of several insulting names Protestants gave to Catholics. She had heard her father come out with most of them: Fenian, pape, left-footer. She'd probably used some of them herself, she thought guiltily . . . when she was a wee lassie and hadn't known any better.

As the liberal-minded young lady she was now, she'd never have dreamed of coming out with any of them in front of an actual Catholic. She knew exactly why Helen Gallagher had done so. The girl was issuing a challenge, testing Liz to see whether or not the two of them could be friends.

This was exactly what she needed, of course – a Catholic friend. Her father would love that. But she liked this girl. She really liked her. She saw her old schoolmates occasionally, but they'd all moved on. Everyone was busy working and doing different things. There was no one she was particularly close to.

It had been a long time since she'd had a really good laugh like the one she and Helen Gallagher had just shared. With everything that had happened over the past days and weeks she could do with a friend – and right now she couldn't have cared less whether she was a Roman Catholic, a Jew or a Mohammedan.

'I told you,' said Liz, looking Helen straight in the eye, 'I've got nothing against Catholics.' The train, which had stopped at Charing Cross, lumbered back into the tunnel. Nobody had got into their carriage. Helen was still surveying her with that appraising gaze. For someone so pretty, she could look real stern when she chose to.

'Mind you,' Liz went on, not entirely happy at being put on the spot like this, 'my brother Eddie does say that religion is the opium of the masses.'

'Your brother Eddie says a lot more than his prayers, doesn't he?' observed Helen, her tone deceptively mild.

'He doesn't say his prayers at all. He's an atheist.'

About to add more, Liz caught herself on. Her defence of her big brother had been automatic. She loved Eddie dearly – nothing could shake that, not even their current estrangement. Although if she were being strictly honest, she might have to admit that he'd taken to preaching lately – an odd thing for an atheist to do.

He'd always loved arguing the toss about politics. However, since he'd joined the Communist Party last year, he'd shown a wee bit of a tendency to ram his beliefs down everyone else's throat – as with Liz over the Red Cross business. All the same, he was her brother.

'Och, Eddie's all right,' she said. 'You'd like him. Honestly.'

Helen looked doubtful, but tactfully changed the subject.

'So where do you work?'

'I'm a junior stenographer. I work for a shipping company down at the Broomielaw.'

'That sounds like a good job.'

Liz shrugged her shoulders.

'Don't you like it there?'

Liz looked out of the carriage window. They were clanking up to the surface now, passing Queen's Dock and Yorkhill Quay on their way to Partick Station. She turned back to Helen, who was looking at her with an expression of keen interest on her face.

'I hate it,' she said.

'That's a terrible thing to have to put up with,' said Helen twenty minutes later as the two girls climbed the stairs from the platform at Singer station up to street level. Her voice was full of sympathy and righteous indignation. 'Is there not anybody you can report him to?'

Liz sighed. 'I tried telling Miss Gilchrist – she's the boss's secretary – when it first happened, but all she did was read me this lecture about girls having to be careful not to lead men on – as though I'd done anything of the sort!'

Her voice rose as she recalled the outrage she had felt at the time. The suggestion that she had encouraged Eric Mitchell in some way had been humiliating and hurtful.

She certainly didn't flirt with him. She was too shy to flirt with anybody. She knew she was quite shapely, but she couldn't help that. That was the way she was made, and she went out of her way not to wear clothes which emphasised her figure. Did she somehow sit or stand in the wrong way? Was that what Miss Gilchrist had meant?

'Aye,' said Helen. 'They always try to blame the lassie, don't

51

they? Could you not change your job?'

Liz let out a heavy sigh. 'Not really. Eric Mitchell's in the same Orange Lodge as my father.' Helen's eyebrows went up at that, but she said nothing, and Liz went on. 'He put in a good word for me to get the position – besides, it's not that easy to find another job.'

She told Helen why, listing her unsuccessful attempts and the difficulties about getting a reference. 'I don't think I'm a very good shorthand-typist, anyway.'

'Because your heart's not in it?' suggested Helen, for Liz had also confided her burning desire to become a nurse. Handing her ticket to the collector, Liz followed the other girl out of the station.

'Well,' said Helen, as they emerged on to Kilbowie Road, 'I'll say goodnight, then. I go up the way.' She gestured with her hand in the direction of the Holy City. Built where Kilbowie Road gave way to Kilbowie Hill proper, the tenement terraces overlooked the sewing-machine factory and the rest of Clydebank. 'It's been nice talking to you,' she said.

Liz blurted out a question. 'D'you fancy going to the dancing together one night?'

Helen Gallagher looked suddenly awkward, her graceful poise and self-possession evaporating. Her nervous stammer had come back. 'I d-don't know. I'm n-not sure if my d-daddy w-would let me . . .'

'What's the matter? Is he scared you might get a lumber from a Proddy?' asked Liz. Getting a lumber was the local slang for completing an evening successfully by getting a boy to walk you home who hopefully would then ask you out on a proper date on a subsequent evening.

She smiled broadly at Helen. If a Catholic could happily use an insulting name for herself, then Liz was happy to match her with 'Proddy' – though somehow it didn't sound nearly so bad as 'Fenian'.

'I don't suppose you'd fancy going to the flicks instead?'

'That would be great,' said Liz cheerfully. 'Do you know

what's on at the end of the week?'

They made a date, wished each other goodnight, and went their separate ways. Walking down the road towards Queen Victoria Row – thank goodness the rain had finally stopped – Liz felt happier than she had in a long while.

She and Helen Gallagher had clicked. It was wonderful to have found someone she could talk to about Eric Mitchell. Confiding in her mother had always been out of the question. Like her brother, Liz tried not to burden Sadie with her problems. Their mother worried too much as it was.

As Liz crossed Dumbarton Road and walked past John Brown's, an uncomfortable thought surfaced. If her father found out that her new friend was a Roman Catholic, she'd be for the high jump. She'd just have to make sure that he didn't . . .

Chapter 6

'Well, that was all very interesting.'

The girl sitting next to Liz didn't look so sure. She was Janet Brown, who'd been in Eddie's class at school. They'd just had their first lecture on the effects of poison gas and how to deal with an attack of it.

'I don't know,' said Janet slowly. She gave a little shudder of distaste before walking over with Liz to the long trestle tables at the back of the hall where they got their tea and biscuits midway through the evening.

'All that stuff about how the gas gets into your body. It's a bit frightening.' She handed Liz a cup of tea, her face troubled. 'D'you no' think so, Liz?'

The lecturer had gone into some detail about the effects of poison gas: how it attacked the eyes, the ears, the throat, the skin. Everybody knew of the horrors of its use in the Great War. Nobody who'd seen films or photographs of soldiers blinded by mustard gas could ever forget them.

Liz squared her shoulders. She and Helen were only a few weeks into their probationary period with the Red Cross. They couldn't afford to give the impression that they were too young to cope with all the grisly details. Besides, Janet was looking really worried. Agreeing with her wasn't going to make her feel any better.

'Och, yes,' she said, 'it does give you a bit of a thought, but look at it this way, Janet. At least we're being trained how to deal with it. We'll be able to help ourselves – and other folk. And didn't the speaker say that the government's planning to issue protective masks to everybody?'

'Oh, aye,' said Janet. The lines on her forehead smoothed out. 'That's true. I suppose you're right, Liz.'

The lecturer had shown them drawings of the masks, emphasising how important it was that the straps which held them in place should be fastened very tightly to keep out the gas. How effective they were really going to be was another matter, one on which Eddie had already offered his opinion.

He and Liz had agreed to make up their quarrel. He had approached her first, pointing out how upset their mother was about their disagreement. For exactly the same reason, Liz had been on the point of saying something to him. So they had shaken hands on it and agreed to disagree amicably.

The government was using psychology, he declared, promising the distribution of gas masks to keep folk busy and make them think there was some way they could protect themselves if the threatened war did come. When it came to offering protection from mustard gas, Eddie maintained, the psychology became kidology. No gas masks issued to civilians were going to be any good at keeping that out.

In any case, he'd gone on cheerfully, it wasn't going to be much use sitting there wearing your wee gas mask if a dirty great German bomb fell on your head . . . but maybe Liz wouldn't repeat that particular comment to Janet.

She laid a comforting hand on the other girl's arm.

'Maybe it won't come to that. We're not at war yet, are we? Perhaps the statesmen can sort it all out.'

She wished she could believe that herself.

'But are you really not going to get married, Liz? Not ever?'

Liz flicked back a wayward strand of brown hair before she answered Helen's question. They were sitting opposite each other in the small tearoom near Singer's station to which they had got into the habit of repairing after their class.

She had dealt with the problem of her father's disapproval by simply not telling him what she was doing on a Tuesday evening. She was getting away with it because William MacMillan was so regular in his habits.

Coming home from his own night out, he pushed open his front gate at exactly twenty-five past ten. You could set your watch by him. Sadie MacMillan did, timing her husband's supper of tea and cheese on toast for exactly half past, giving him five minutes to get in, hang up his coat and wash his hands.

Their father's precision had always given Liz and Eddie a private chuckle, but now she was grateful for it. The Red Cross class finished at half past nine, which gave her time to have a cup of tea and a chat with Helen and still be safely home a quarter of an hour before her father.

'Och, maybe when I'm really ancient,' Liz conceded, with all the insouciance of a young woman not long past her eighteenth birthday. 'When I'm about thirty-five or something.'

She lifted her cup and took a sip of tea. 'But only if Robert Donat or Cary Grant are available. Or maybe James Stewart,' she added, placing the cup back in its saucer and giving every appearance of considering the matter seriously. 'I quite like him.'

'Well, Robert Donat will be ancient himself by then,' Helen pointed out. 'And I think Cary and James are probably spoken for.' She gestured towards the door of the tearoom. 'Added to which, the chances of you bumping into any of them out there on Kilbowie Road are no' all that high.'

'No bother,' said Liz confidently. 'I'll be a sister at the Western Infirmary by then – maybe even the matron. Cary Grant'll be visiting Glasgow to open some big new picture house and he'll fall ill with an exotic ailment—'

'Which only you can cure?' suggested Helen.

'Aye,' said Liz, nodding her head enthusiastically. 'Or maybe he'll be injured heroically saving some child in the crowd from going under the wheels of a tram—'

'And you'll patch him up and nurse him back to health, and he'll be so smitten that he'll whisk you back off to a life of luxury in Hollywood. By which time, of course, you'll have done your best work and found a cure for various dreadful diseases which have afflicted mankind for centuries and people will be calling you the Florence Nightingale of Clydebank.'

Picking up the last tiny morsel of her Tunnock's caramel wafer, Helen popped it into her mouth. Then she wet her index finger and dabbed it over the wrapper to get any last crumbs. She had a tendency to eat treats slowly and with great delicacy because, Liz assumed, she didn't get very many of them.

As she'd suspected when she first met Helen, the Gallagher family were as poor as church mice. Her father Brendan and her three grown-up brothers were casual labourers, taking work as and when they could get it. Along with her younger brother Dominic and her mother Marie, the whole family lived crammed into a two-apartment house in the Holy City tenements.

Having finished her biscuit at last, Helen spoke again. 'They'll probably put up a statue to you on the pavement in front of the town hall.'

'That's it,' said Liz. 'Do you doubt it?'

'Not a bit,' said Helen stoutly. Then, lifting her hand from the biscuit wrapper and holding it palm downwards, above the table, she rocked it from side to side in a balancing gesture. 'Well . . . there's maybe a few details that sound a wee bit iffy . . .'

They grinned at each other. A few short weeks after their first meeting they had become firm friends, close enough to trade the occasional amiable insult – and a great many confidences.

They had learned the hard way to be careful about two subjects: religion and politics. Helen's church was very important to her. She had little interest in politics, and disapproved of extremes in either direction. However, she did have a strong sense of justice and, like Liz, she hated unfairness with a passion.

They talked about silly things too. That was what Liz liked most about her friendship with Helen. They could be having a

57

great serious discussion one minute and the next they'd be on the latest fashions. Liz had always enjoyed talking with her grandfather and Eddie, but neither of them was much good on what length skirts were going to be next season.

Taking a final sip of tea, Helen pushed her cup and saucer away and fixed Liz with her cornflower-blue eyes. The picture of innocence. Liz pursed her lips and returned the look with a wary one of her own. Miss Gallagher was up to something.

'Seen Mrs Buchanan's wee boy recently?'

'Who?'

'Come off it, MacMillan,' said Helen robustly. 'And while you're at it, pull the other one. It's got bells on. You liked him. You know you did.'

'He was all right,' conceded Liz, 'but we don't exactly move in the same circles. Do we?'

'I don't know about that. We see quite a lot of his mother.'

For although their Red Cross class was led by a local lady, Mrs Galbraith, she was helped out from time to time by local doctors, visiting lecturers and other members of the organisation, including Amelia Buchanan.

'He liked you,' Helen pointed out. 'Otherwise he wouldn't have come running out into the rain that night to offer you a lift. Would he now?'

'How do you know he wasn't coming after you?'

'A woman knows these things,' said Helen, putting on what both girls referred to as her mysterious voice. It was copied from a fortune-teller they had visited a couple of weekends previously. The woman, sporting a Russian name and corresponding accent – neither of them could decide whether or not either characteristic was genuine – had predicted that they were both shortly going to meet a tall, dark, handsome stranger with whom they would fall deeply in love.

'A tall, dark, handsome stranger,' Liz had scoffed once they were safely back out on the street. 'You'd think she could have been a bit more original.'

'At least we're getting one each, Liz,' Helen had pointed

out. 'We won't have to fight over just one of them!'

'Besides,' she went on now in her normal tones, still talking about Adam Buchanan, 'he was perfectly nice and polite to me, but he looked at you in a different way.' She raised her fair eyebrows. '*Quite* a different way.'

'Might I point out, Miss Gallagher, that the fortune-teller spoke of a tall, *dark*, handsome man?'

Helen batted her eyelashes at her. 'And you said that was a load of baloney.'

Liz snorted and determinedly changed the subject.

It hadn't taken Liz long to find out the real reason why Helen wouldn't come to the dancing. Having worn out her last evening dress some time ago, she had nothing suitable to wear. Working behind the make-up and perfume counter in Woolworth's, it was a hard enough job ensuring she had some decent outfits for work. She rang the changes with two skirts and four pretty, but businesslike blouses.

When her supervisor suggested that one of the skirts was becoming a bit threadbare, it hadn't been easy to find the money for the material to make another, so a new dance dress had gone way down the list. And of course, as the only girl in a family of boys, Helen had no sister to borrow from.

Liz had a solution to that particular problem. It was hanging at the back of her wardrobe. Bought at Copland & Lye's January sale six months previously, the dress had been a real bargain and she'd thought it exquisite. It had an orange satin underslip and draped brown georgette overdress. A boat neckline was set off by a graceful floaty collar in the same material. Little cap sleeves completed it and the hem danced attractively on the knee. As she and Helen had agreed, skirts were getting shorter again.

Once Liz got the dress home, trying it on in the privacy of her bedroom, she saw that it did absolutely nothing for her. Her own colouring was too dark. The beautiful rich brown of the dress needed a blonde.

Soon after she met Helen, she realised that the dress would look great on her. Her golden hair would set it off to perfection. The two girls, both fairly tall, were also much of a muchness in size. Helen was perhaps a little less full in the bust, but the dress could be easily adjusted for that.

So far, however, Helen had refused even to try the dress on. Looking unusually haughty, she had informed Liz that she most certainly was not prepared to accept it as a gift. Until she had the money to buy it from her, the dress would have to stay where it was.

Passing the town hall on her way home, Liz glanced up at the clock. Twenty past ten. Helen was so stubborn, but she'd look fantastic in the georgette dress. There must be some way she could make her take—

Twenty past ten? Hell's bells, she must have been dawdling down the road. Her father would be home in five minutes' time!

Chapter 7

Breaking into a run, Liz rounded the corner – and stopped dead. Her father was a hundred yards in front of her. Oh, Mammy, Daddy! What was she going to do?

Then it came to her – the muddy lane which ran behind the houses on Queen Victoria Row. She could dash along there and get in the back door just before her father reached the front one. She'd need the luck of the Irish to do it, especially as she would have to give him another half-minute. If she ran down behind him now, he might hear her.

She counted out the thirty seconds, her eyes on the back of his head. *Don't turn round, don't turn round.* Then she ran like the wind, sticking close to the hedges of the gardens which bordered the road. Her heart was thumping. She hadn't moved this fast since she'd been at school.

With a sob of exertion and relief she wheeled into the lane – and caught her skirt on a nail sticking out of a fence. Damn, damn, damn. Pulling herself free, Liz pushed open the garden gate, sped up the path, flung open the back door and threw herself into the kitchen.

The occupants of it greeted her sudden arrival with upturned faces and looks of astonishment: her mother, Eddie and Mrs Crawford from next door. They were even more amazed when Liz flung her jacket off and ran out to the lobby to put it on the coat stand. Were those her father's steps she could hear coming up the front path?

Rushing back into the kitchen, Liz switched on the big wireless set which sat on its own solidly built wooden shelf to the left of the kitchen door. There was a dance music programme on. The band was playing 'The Lambeth Walk'.

Eddie was sitting at the table. Liz seized his hand and pulled him to his feet.

'Dance with me,' she said breathlessly. She threw a glance at her mother. 'Don't tell him I've been at my Red Cross class, Ma. Please!'

Mrs Crawford looked puzzled. 'Why should her father object to her doing that? I don't understand.'

Liz and a bemused Eddie started dancing. The music was very loud. In her haste, she'd turned the dial too far. Then it suddenly stopped.

'What's the matter with the wireless?' asked Eddie, whirling round to check. 'Oh!'

His father was standing in the doorway, his hand on the knob of the substantial machine.

'What do you lot think you're playing at? I could hear that cheap music from halfway down the street!'

He wasn't to know that everyone present knew that wasn't true. From the front door maybe . . . but not from halfway down the street.

'Mrs Crawford. I didn't see you there.' His voice had changed, become much less cold. Liz hated him for being able to do it. He would give his family the rough side of his tongue, not because he had lost his temper and couldn't help himself. That, though unpleasant, she could have understood. No, they were all in for it because he had found them acting in a way he didn't consider proper. In some obscure way it threatened the control he seemed to need to exercise over his house and his family.

Mrs Crawford was on her feet, aware as everyone was of the sudden chill in the air.

'Good evening, Mr MacMillan. You'll be wanting your supper. I'd better be getting home. I'll be seeing you, Sadie.'

Liz saw her father's eyebrows rise at the use of her mother's first name. The gesture infuriated her. She wasn't going to allow

62

him to spoil her mother's new friendship. She just wasn't.

Taking a mental deep breath, she rushed in. Where angels fear to tread, she thought.

'Why don't you see Mrs Crawford to the door, Ma? I'll get on with the supper.'

With grim pleasure she saw that her father was torn between the desire to assert his authority and the desire to defer to Mrs Crawford as the wife of one of the senior managers. Deference won. That didn't mean the storm wasn't about to break – only that it had been delayed.

Sadie crept back into the room and lifted her apron off its hook. Her hands were clumsy as she tied the strings around her waist.

'Here, Ma,' said Eddie gently, 'I'll get that for you.'

He completed the task and sat down. Liz began slicing the bread. The icy silence was too much for Sadie to bear.

'They were just having a wee dance, William. You and I used to enjoy that, don't you remember?'

Liz and Eddie exchanged a look. Couldn't their father hear the plea in their mother's voice?

'That's where we met,' Sadie told her children as she unwrapped the cheese. 'Your father was a lovely dancer. Real good-looking, too. All the other girls were jealous when he asked me up.'

For the merest second, Liz saw something flicker in her father's eyes. It was gone so quickly she wondered if she had imagined it.

His lack of response was making Sadie more and more nervous. She dropped the teaspoons on the floor and had to run them under the tap. When she put the cups and saucers out, they rattled noisily. Her husband sat waiting to be served, breathing heavily and tutting whenever she did something wrong. It made Liz so angry . . . but if she or Eddie stood up for their mother, it only made matters worse.

Her own escapade tonight hadn't helped. Liz laid the milk jug and sugar bowl on the table. Her father glanced up at her.

'You look like a hoyden, Elizabeth. When did you last brush your hair? And you've torn your skirt.' He pointed to the threads which had been pulled by the nail as she had hurtled round into the lane. 'That's sheer carelessness.'

What was she supposed to say to that? *Yes, Father, I probably do look like a hoyden. Thanks for the compliment. Nice of you to take an interest in my appearance.*

'Well?' he demanded.

'Sorry, Father,' she mumbled as she slipped into her seat. She hoped that would do. She should have known better. The tirade began with 'Sorry's all very well, my girl.' It went on through the cost of clothes and the necessity for a young lady like herself – especially now that she was the daughter of a shipyard manager – to look neat and smart at all times. *Ye gods!*

The tongue-lashing ended as it usually did, with a shaking of the head over Liz's ingratitude – to him for providing her with a roof over her head and to her mother for all the cooking and cleaning she did for her children. That was the only time he ever said anything remotely complimentary about his wife – when he was using her as a stick to beat Liz over the head with.

Liz had learned a long time ago not to answer back. Not out loud, at any rate. She suspected her father knew that very well. There was something in her character which infuriated him. He called it a rebellious streak. She called it survival – a refusal to be bullied.

Last week she had read an article in the *Evening Citizen* about how so many girls didn't fancy nursing because of the discipline of nurses' homes. It couldn't be worse than this. She'd happily submit herself to it.

The possibility was there. The Voluntary Aid Detachment nursing auxiliaries were to be split into mobile and non-mobile. If you were mobile, you might be sent anywhere. Away from here.

She shot a swift glance across the table at her mother. Listening to her husband lambasting their daughter, Sadie was white-faced and drawn.

Liz experienced a huge flood of guilt. She was putting her mother in a difficult enough position as it was. There was no way she could apply to become a mobile VAD. It was completely out of the question. She couldn't leave Sadie to cope with him on her own, or to deal with the ructions which would inevitably follow her departure.

Funny to think that her parents had once loved to dance with each other. Almost unimaginable. Not because they were old. They weren't. Sadie wasn't forty yet, and her husband had reached that milestone only a few months before. The MacMillans had married young.

The wedding photograph hung on the wall in the front room. Liz had always found it difficult to relate the smiling young couple to the people her parents had now become. They had loved each other once, she supposed.

Her father was still going on at her. All this for a few pulled threads and some music that was a bit too loud. How was he going to react when she announced that she was going to become a volunteer auxiliary nurse in her spare time? Liz's stomach lurched.

Chapter 8

'The thing is,' said the extremely large young man with the extremely large dog, 'we go everywhere together.' He stretched down and patted the huge grey beast which lay at his feet. 'My faithful companion on the hill. He and I have brought home a good few rabbits for the pot. Haven't we, Finn, my lad?' He scratched the dog's ear, laughing at the soft growl of pleasure the caress provoked.

'What kind of dog is he?'

'An Irish wolfhound,' said Finn's master. 'Do you have a dog, Liz?' He gave the animal a final pat and looked up at her. 'You don't mind if I call you Liz, do you?'

She didn't mind at all. She just wished she could return the compliment, but she was still having some difficulty in sorting out Helen's brothers. She'd worked out that the older ones were called Danny, Joe and Conor, but she couldn't have said which one of them she was talking to at the moment. Pity she couldn't have had a quiet word with the dog.

While the whole of Helen's family seemed disposed to like Liz, Finn's master had taken a real shine to her. She was pretty sure she knew why. A gate-leg table, pushed back against one wall to make room for all the people in the room, held a generous array of home baking. Alerted for some reason, Liz had turned round a little while ago and seen the big dog, his head on a level with the table, quietly slipping first one and then a second piece of gingerbread into his wide mouth.

Having swallowed the goodies and licked his lips once or twice, the dog had moved over to join his master, a look of complete innocence on his wise grey face. Liz had smiled in admiration and kept her own mouth firmly shut. Observing both the snaffling of the cakes and the visitor's reaction to it, his master had spoken out of the side of his mouth to her.

'He's smart enough not to take too many, you see, Liz. He knows how to get away with it.'

Liz tried not to frown. Just which brother was she talking to at the moment? He was using her name frequently, but she was scared to respond in kind in case she got it wrong.

Dominic, the youngest member of the family, was easy enough to identify, but the older brothers were more difficult. They were all tall, broad-shouldered young men, big and burly like their father, Brendan. Like him, they were all red-haired too.

Helen had obviously inherited her golden hair from her mother, Marie, a small woman whose husband and children towered over her. Her personality, however, more than made up for her lack of stature. There was absolutely no doubt about who ruled the roost in the Gallagher household.

The Gallaghers could not only all talk the hind legs off a donkey – they had clearly all kissed the Blarney Stone at an early age – they were musical as well. Not long after Liz had arrived this afternoon, Brendan Gallagher had brought out a penny whistle and started playing it. His children had then produced from various places in the cramped flat an assortment of musical instruments – an accordion, a fiddle, a bodhrán drum – and an impromptu ceilidh had started up.

Everybody sang along with all the songs, but they also had their own particular party pieces. Helen sang a haunting song called 'She Moved Through the Fair'. It should really have been sung by a man, lost in admiration of his sweetheart, but she did it so beautifully that that didn't matter.

> *She stepped away from me*
> *And she moved through the fair,*
> *And fondly I watched her,*
> *Move here and move there . . .*

Clapping along to the music of a livelier song, Liz caught Helen's eye.

'Don't the neighbours mind the noise?'

Brendan Gallagher, leaning back in a rocking chair by the range, gave Liz a lazy smile and a wink.

'We invite them along,' he said in his warm Donegal brogue. 'Then we soften 'em up with some of Marie's home baking. Don't we, me lovely girl?'

He laughed and gave his wife a playful smack on the bottom; at which point she laughed and told him that he was a daft Irish fool. Liz tried to imagine her own parents acting in the same way. Her normally vivid imagination failed her on that one, however.

Crammed into their two rooms as they were, the Gallaghers played host to a bewildering number of visiting neighbours and friends. Several had come and gone since Liz's own arrival an hour or so before; friends of both the parents and the children, girlfriends of the older boys. Names and banter and jokes were tossed about the room faster than Liz could keep up. That was part of her problem with the boys' names.

Her eyes came back to the big grey dog. She was fascinated by the size of him.

'We hide him from the factor, of course, Liz,' said Finn's master. 'I'm not sure if you're allowed to keep animals here at all – certainly not giants like him.'

'So how do you exercise him?' asked Liz, glancing up to see Helen approaching her with a cup of tea. Her friend winked.

'The two of them tend to go out after dark. We never ask Conor where the rabbits come from. Some of them taste remarkably like chicken, too, as a few people round these parts could tell you. Particularly a few farmers up Duntocher way, I should imagine. And Finn can't tell us anything. Can you, darling boy?'

She slipped off one shoe, balanced herself with the back of her hand on Liz's chair and rubbed the dog's chest gently with her stocking-soled foot. Finn rolled over on to his shaggy grey back, the better to receive the petting, a look of sublime pleasure in his big dark eyes.

Conor. Right. Conor was the one with the big dog.

'Does going out at night not make you too tired for your work the next day, Conor?' It was a relief to be able to use his name at last.

'Och, I'm not working at the moment,' said Conor, leaning back and putting one ankle up on the opposite knee. He gave Liz a wry look. 'Sometimes having a name like Gallagher isn't very helpful in that direction.'

'I'm sorry,' she said, uncomfortably aware of the truth of what he was saying and remembering also her own initial reaction to Helen's surname.

'Och, Finn and I do all right,' Conor said easily, 'and I've no great wish to be a wage slave anyway. You see, Liz, the thing is' – he uncrossed his legs and leaned forward in his chair, the better to impress the point upon her – 'I'm an anarchist anyway – and an atheist,' he added for good measure.

'Oh,' said Liz gravely, sipping her tea and keeping one wary eye on Finn. If the wolfhound decided to stand up he might well knock the cup and saucer out of her hand without meaning to. She smiled at Conor. 'You must meet my brother. He's a communist and an atheist.'

'Sure, it would be a pleasure and a privilege, Liz.'

What a family. The boys and Helen sounded as Clydebank as herself, but there was something different about the way they used words. In the case of the parents, it was all served up in that rich Irish accent. Helen's father was from Donegal, her mother from Cork. They argued all the time, so Helen had told her, about where they were going back to in Ireland once their children were grown up.

She'd observed for herself that Helen's parents argued with each other about almost everything, but unlike her own mother, Mrs Gallagher gave back as good as she got. And there was affection underlying the fighting – it was all part of the general

69

family banter. Liz couldn't figure it out at all, but she knew that she liked it.

She glanced round, taking in the telltale stains of dampness where the walls of the room met the ceiling. That's what you got for building flat-roofed houses on a wet Scottish hillside. It was a perennial problem in the Holy City houses.

Despite the damp, the room was immaculately kept, dotted with earthenware pots of flowering bulbs which Helen had told Liz she had grown, germinating them under her parents' bed over the winter. The walls of the room were covered with religious pictures. There was the Pope, whom they referred to as the Holy Father, and the Virgin Mary in a blue cloak. There was a wee statuette of her on the high mantelpiece over the range too. Liz's father would have been horrified by what he would have called idolatry. Then again, she thought, taking a sip of tea, wasn't his print of King Billy crossing the Boyne his own version of a religious idol?

Liz liked the picture the Gallaghers had of Jesus. He looked so kind, His eyes beautifully gentle. He had a lantern in His hand and He was knocking at a solid old door in a deep and dark forest.

'The door to our hearts,' Helen's mother told Liz, seeing her studying it. 'All we have to do is let Him in.' Then she crossed herself.

They were obviously a very devout family but they seemed to have no objections to Helen having a Protestant friend or, judging from what Conor had said, to one of their sons being an atheist. Remarkable, thought Liz, lifting her teacup to her lips.

The next thing she knew, Helen's mother had appeared out of nowhere, fetching Conor a wallop on the back of his coppery head. Finn growled, opened one eye, saw who was attacking his master – and stayed where he was on the floor. The big animal had obviously decided that discretion was the better part of valour. Liz didn't blame him one little bit.

'An atheist, is it?' cried Marie. 'And your brother going in

70

for the priesthood? I ought to wash your mouth out with soap, Conor Gallagher!'

'Ma,' protested her large son, putting his hand to the back of his head and doing a fair imitation of a man who'd been mortally wounded. 'Please!'

Liz took another sip of tea, the better to hide her amusement. Conor's hair was very thick. His mother's hand was very small. However, he was obliging enough to pretend to be suffering.

'Ears like a hare,' he observed ruefully to Liz. 'Much better, in fact. I don't know how she does it, but she always manages to hear the things you don't want her to. If what Finn and I go after had hearing like that, we'd never catch a bloody thing.'

That earned him another smack.

'Mind your language,' said his mother. 'There's ladies present – in case you hadn't noticed. As to how I manage to hear you – our Lord Himself helps me,' she went on primly. 'That's how. Otherwise how would I keep you lot in order?'

She turned with a smile to Liz. 'Will you have another piece of gingerbread, Miss MacMillan?'

'Thank you,' said Liz. Then, a little shyly: 'And please call me Liz, Mrs Gallagher.'

'So are your parents not like that, Liz?' asked Helen when she saw Liz downstairs and out on to the street.

'That,' said Liz, 'might very well be the understatement of the century. By the way, have you got another brother?'

Helen looked blank. 'No. Why do you ask?'

'Well, your ma said something about one of them going in for the priesthood. I thought maybe he was away studying somewhere.'

'Oh,' said Helen, realisation dawning. 'She thinks Dom's going to become a priest.'

'And he doesn't?'

'Not unless he can travel about his parish in a spaceship,' laughed Helen. 'He's daft about Flash Gordon at the moment.'

71

'Well,' said Liz comfortably, 'I'm quite fond of old Flash myself.'

Helen smiled. 'It's either that or steam locomotives. You know this one called the *Mallard* that's just broken some speed record? Last week, in fact?'

Liz was forced to admit that she didn't.

'Don't worry about it,' said Helen easily. 'I only know because Dominic's so interested in it.' She ticked the relevant points off on her slim fingers. 'She was designed by a man called Nigel Gresley – chief engineer for the London and North Eastern Railway, and one of Dom's heroes – she achieved a speed of a hundred and twenty-six miles per hour and she's built to a streamlined design.'

'I don't even know what that means,' cried Liz in mock despair.

'Neither do I, really,' admitted Helen. 'Although Dom does try to explain it to me. Quite frequently.'

Liz grinned.

'Well, brothers are like that. Speaking of which, are you coming to the exhibition with Eddie and me next Saturday?'

The Empire Exhibition had opened in Bellahouston Park on the south side of Glasgow in May. Everyone was talking about it. A showcase for the commercial, industrial and cultural achievements of the countries which made up the British Empire, it was also designed to be a splash of colour in a Scotland beginning to pull itself out of the Depression, a symbol of confidence in the future.

It had proved to be a grand way to inaugurate the reign of the new monarch. It had been widely feared that George VI, taking over the throne two years before in the unfortunate circumstances following the abdication of his brother, wasn't up to the job. For one thing, he was known to be extremely shy. There were reports of a paralysing stammer.

However, with his Queen at his side, the King had come to Glasgow to perform the opening ceremony of the exhibition. He had made a fine speech, marred by not one hint of a stammer.

It was Helen who had first raised the subject with Liz, telling her that Woolie's had a whole counter full of exhibition souvenirs, but the summer was wearing on and they still hadn't been. Liz thought she knew why. Helen's next question confirmed her suspicions.

'Do you know how much it costs to get in?'

'A shilling,' said Liz, wondering if she dared offer to pay for both of them. Probably not. To her relief, the little frown furrowing Helen's forehead disappeared.

'Oh, that's not too bad. I can manage that. But would you want to go to one of the restaurants while we're there? I hear they're gey expensive.'

'No,' said Liz decisively, having already anticipated the question and rehearsed her answer to it. She would actually have loved to have tried one of the various eating places at the exhibition. They'd all been written up in the newspapers. The Atlantic Restaurant sounded wonderful, but far too expensive. Her grandfather had laughingly shown her a cartoon entitled 'The man who asked for a pie and chips at the Atlantic Restaurant', the joke being that it was far too grand an establishment to serve that kind of fare. Liz wouldn't have minded splashing out at one of the others, though.

The Treetops Restaurant sounded intriguing, with real trees growing up through the floor, but Liz knew how short of money Helen was. Any of the restaurants would be too expensive for her.

'Apparently there's lots of refreshment tents where the prices are very reasonable,' she told her cheerfully, 'and some of the pavilions have free samples of their country's produce: fruit juice and cheese and that kind of thing. We thought we'd do that if we got hungry.'

Surely Helen wouldn't see anything of charity in that? Apparently she didn't. 'That sounds like a great idea,' she said.

'I thought I might wear my houndstooth check costume to the exhibition,' said Liz innocently.

'The oatmealy one with the nipped-in waist and the peplum?'

73

'Yes. With my cream blouse with the big cutwork collar that sits outside the jacket. What do you think?'

Helen nodded consideringly. 'Yes, that'll add the right touch of femininity. And your brown hat with the wee red brim?'

'You think that's the best one?'

'Definitely.'

'What about you, Helen?'

'Well, I havenae got that much choice, have I? I'll just wear my best blouse and my old coat and hat.' Her eyes narrowed suddenly. She had just realised what Liz was up to. 'No thank you.'

'I didn't say a word,' protested Liz.

'No, but you were about to,' said Helen sternly. 'And don't offer me the georgette dress again either. I've told you already. I'll maybe buy it off you, but I'm not taking it for nothing – and I don't have enough spare cash at the moment. What did it cost you again?'

Swiftly deducting ten shillings, Liz quoted her a price.

'And the rest,' said Helen laconically. 'You really shouldnae tell lies, Elizabeth MacMillan. You're no good at it.'

Liz looked at her with affectionate exasperation. 'Oh, Helen! You know I don't really want any money for it at all. It's just hanging in my wardrobe attracting the moths. You're so stubborn!'

'Well,' said Helen, her expression softening into an equally affectionate smile, 'if that isn't the pot calling the kettle black, I don't know what is.' She turned to go back into the close. 'Safe home, now. Oh,' she added, suddenly remembering. 'Ma told me to say you're welcome here any time. You don't need to wait for an invite.'

'That's *very* kind of her. I love visiting your family.' Liz hesitated. 'I'd really like to have you round to my house—'

'Don't worry about it,' said Helen immediately. 'I know your daddy wouldn't exactly be keen on the idea. And you know my lot love having visitors. Don't worry about it,' she said again.

Liz couldn't help worrying about it. The Gallaghers had given her such a warm welcome. It would have been fine to have had Helen over for the evening. They could have gone into Liz's room and gossiped and tried on clothes and generally set the world to rights.

But it was out of the question. She'd told her mother about her new friend, but she had carefully forgotten to mention her last name. She hadn't spoken about Helen at all in front of her father.

She'd told Eddie, of course, giving him Helen's full name and watching with grim amusement as the prejudices with which both of them had been brought up warred with his new-found love for all mankind – black, white, Jewish, Mohammedan – even Irish Catholic. His egalitarian principles had won the day.

Naturally, when the visit to the Empire Exhibition had first been discussed, Eddie had lectured Liz on the morally indefensible nature of the British Empire. Visiting the exhibition did not in any way imply that he, Edward MacMillan, approved of the iniquitous system by which Great Britain kept half the countries of the world in subjugation.

Liz told him gravely that she understood this perfectly, and Eddie, equally as grave, told her that he would be delighted to escort her and Miss Gallagher to the Empire Exhibition next Saturday.

Chapter 9

Bustling about making a pot of tea for her returning daughter, Sadie MacMillan listened with interest as Liz told her what had happened at the class that evening. Eddie, sitting at the kitchen table reading a history textbook, was keeping ostentatiously out of the conversation.

'And we're going to have this thing soon – they call it an exercise – where we'll get to practise everything we've learned – dressing wounds and bandaging and all that.'

The words came tumbling out in her enthusiasm.

'It'll be on a Saturday in August and we've to ask all our friends and families if they'll be volunteer casualties for us. They wouldn't have to stay for the whole day – even half an hour would be helpful, Mrs Galbraith says, because that would make it like a real emergency, where you don't know what's going to be coming at you next.'

Liz paused at last to draw breath. 'Would you maybe consider being one of our volunteers, Ma? You could ask Mrs Crawford to come with you.'

She looked expectantly up at Sadie, who was setting a cup and saucer in front of her. Liz was doing everything she could to encourage the friendship with the next-door neighbour, although sometimes she feared she was fighting a losing battle against her mother's shyness and reserve.

Sadie was frowning, not wanting to disappoint her daughter. 'I'm not sure, Lizzie . . .'

'Oh, go on, Ma. Helen's family are going to come. Well, her brothers, anyway.'

That would raise another problem. If the Gallagher boys came to the exercise she couldn't expect them to change their surname to something more neutral just for her. Her mother would find out and she would have to ask her to keep that secret as well. Liz knew that was an unfair burden to lay on her. The alternative was a confrontation with her father . . . although that was going to have to come sooner or later anyway.

Liz smiled up at her mother. She would cross that bridge when she came to it. It would do Sadie good to get out of the house. That was the important thing.

'Go on, Ma,' she said again. 'You'd enjoy it.'

Eddie coughed and turned another page of his book. He definitely wouldn't be one of the volunteer casualties. No doubt he would consider that as participating in the capitalist war machine.

'Well,' said Sadie, although she still looked very doubtful, 'if it would help you and your friends, Lizzie . . .'

'It really would, Ma.'

Eddie didn't quite tut-tut, but he wasn't far off it. Liz was beginning to find his silent disapproval profoundly irritating. She was distracted from it by a sudden brainwave.

'You could think about joining the Red Cross, Ma. Coming along to the class.'

'Och,' said Sadie dismissively, slipping the tea cosy over the pot and setting it on its stand, 'you wouldn't want an old wifie like me there.'

'Ma,' said Liz in exasperation, 'you're hardly an old wifie – and anyway, there's all ages at this thing. I told you, Helen and I had a real hard job persuading them to take us on – they thought we were too young. They want older people too.'

Sadie's face lit up.

'I'd like fine to do something like that – something interesting, and useful, too.' She shook her head. 'But no, I'm too old for it.'

'Ma, Mrs Simpson was there tonight. She's going to join the class.'

That stopped Sadie in her tracks. Even Eddie looked up from his overstudious scrutiny of his book.

'Nan Simpson? You've got to be joking.'

Liz shook her head. 'No, it's the God's honest truth.'

Sadie laughed. 'Fancy her having the brass neck to show her face at something like that after the way she curses at Tam.' Her face was alive with amusement.

The three of them turned at the sound of the front door opening. Even before William MacMillan entered the kitchen, the animation which had shone in his wife's face only thirty seconds before had faded.

It was like a light going out, as if the leerie had been along on his morning round to extinguish the gas mantles. My God, thought Liz, watching it happen, now she really does look like an old wifie. And yet, less than a minute ago . . .

'Will you have a wee cup of tea, William?' Sadie asked anxiously, but then she always sounded anxious when she spoke to her husband.

'Aye. I will that.'

Liz blinked. His acceptance had sounded almost friendly. He too normally had a special tone of voice when he spoke to his wife: one of exaggerated exasperation. Tonight, however, there was an air of suppressed excitement about him.

'Well, Lizzie? What would you say if I told you that I've just been entrusted with some very good news?'

'I'd want to know what it was, Father,' she said politely. That seemed to be the answer that was called for.

'Well,' he said again, 'if your mother will stop fussing and pour us all a cup of tea, I'll tell you.'

'Aye, William. Right away, William.'

Liz suppressed the bubble of irritation at the deference in her mother's voice. Couldn't she stand up to him? Just once? If Liz herself were married to a man like her father, she'd pour the blasted tea all over his head – leaves and all. That would set his gas at a peep.

'Something amusing you, Lizzie?'

'No, Father,' she said hurriedly.

'So, what have you been doing this evening?'

'Oh . . . nothing much.' Nervously, she waited for him to quiz her further, but he didn't, turning to look across the table at Eddie.

'How about my son and heir? I hope you haven't been misspending your youth tonight?'

Liz blinked. It wasn't like her father to be jokey in any way, shape or form. Whatever his news was, it had to be very good indeed.

'I've been studying, Father.' Eddie put a paper marker in the book, closed it and reached behind him to place it on the sideboard. 'For an essay I've to write on the causes of the Great War.'

Sadie, her preparations complete, smoothed the back of her skirt and sat down. Lifting the pot, she began pouring the tea. Her husband gave a long sigh.

'How many times do I have to tell you? I like my milk in first!'

'I'm sorry, William,' she said, half rising from the chair she'd only just sat down in. 'I forgot. I'll get a fresh cup—'

'Sit down, woman!'

Sadie subsided into her chair.

'What is your news, Father?' Liz asked quickly. Anything to deflect the irritation from her mother. He might be in an unusually good mood, but he was still snapping at her. Liz supposed it had become a habit he couldn't break: one he didn't want to break. He was, however, unable to keep his news to himself any longer.

'I have this evening been to a meeting called by yard management for senior foremen and managers,' he said, unable to keep the pride out of his voice that he now belonged to this august group. 'Then, together with the management representatives, we all repaired to a public house for a small refreshment.'

Across the table, Eddie gave Liz an unobtrusive wink.

William MacMillan had a tendency to use pompous language, which his children, with the cruelty of youth, had an equal tendency to laugh at.

Liz gave Eddie the ghost of a smile back, along with the silent signal which meant, *We'll have a laugh about this later*.

'The order books are full,' William MacMillan announced, finally getting his big news out. 'There's work assured for the next five years. At least.'

'That *is* good news,' said Liz, and meant it. Anyone who had grown up anywhere along the Clyde knew the importance of a full order book.

She had been eleven when work had stopped on the 534. Now the ship which had borne that job number for so many years was the *Queen Mary*, the greatest passenger liner ever to sail the Atlantic. Since then another *Queen* had been ordered. She was nearing completion, her launch due to take place any day now.

People seemed to have forgotten the hard times, the two years during which this new ship's predecessor had lain rusting on the stocks at John Brown's, when Cunard had run out of money to build her and the whole workforce had been laid off. Liz would never forget those years, though. Never.

It had been shortly before Christmas 1931. She and Eddie, sliding along the icy patches on the pavements which all the feet before them had polished to thrilling – if hazardous – perfection, had come bounding into the close at Radnor Street. They were as high as kites as they ran up the stairs because it was nearly time for school to break up for the holidays. Then, bursting into the house, they had seen their parents' faces.

Both William and Sadie MacMillan had been white to the lips, staring silently at each other from their chairs on either side of the range, her mother tearful and her father . . .

How *had* her father looked that day? Buttoned up, tight . . . humiliated. At that age Liz hadn't known what the word meant, but she had understood the feeling it described, had seen with

80

painful clarity that William MacMillan was crushed by the knowledge that he wasn't going to be able to support his family, that he was dreading the inevitability of having to go on the parish and accept the meagre dole money which would be offered.

Liz knew the importance of a full order book, all right. So did her mother.

'Oh, aye, William,' Sadie was saying warmly. 'That's great news.'

He actually smiled at them both, and for a moment there was unusual unanimity in the MacMillan household. Then Eddie spoiled it all.

'And do any of you know *why* the order books are full?'

His tone of voice was ostensibly calm, but as she turned to look at him, Liz realised that he wasn't calm at all. He was furiously angry and upset.

'The books are full because the Clyde's getting ready to go to war. Along with every other shipbuilding river in the country. That's why. The mobilisation has started. The river's running to war.'

Startlingly pale, his voice shaking with emotion, he waved an unsteady hand towards the history book lying on the sideboard.

'Wasn't the last time bad enough? Haven't we learned anything? No. We're rushing headlong towards it: to bombs and fires and destruction. It'll be even worse this time. Everyone will be involved: killed and maimed while they're sitting at their own firesides. Like in Spain.'

His voice quivered with passion.

'Can none of you see that? Are you all blind as well as stupid?'

'Oh, Grandad,' said Liz, reporting it all to Peter MacMillan the next evening. 'It was terrible. They kept shouting at each other and then Eddie stomped out of the house and didn't come back till after midnight, and Father waited up for him and then they

81

shouted at each other some more and Ma was crying all the time – oh, it was dreadful!'

Peter MacMillan patted her shoulder, then sat down opposite her in front of the range.

'There, there, lass. They're both too much like each other, that's the trouble. Both hotheads.'

'My father?' she asked doubtfully. 'A hothead?'

'Your father has strong feelings,' said her grandfather. 'About a lot of things.'

'He keeps them well hidden then,' said Liz. She raised her arms, clasping them together on the nape of her neck, lifting her heavy hair. 'I wish he wasn't so against Catholics, either.'

Peter gave her a shrewd look. 'You're not walking out with a Catholic lad, are you, Lizzie?'

'No, it's not that. I'm not walking out with anybody.'

She told him about Helen, and their developing friendship. 'If he knew I'd got friendly with a Catholic lassie—' Liz stopped, a wave of anxiety flooding over her.

'He'd try to stop you seeing her?'

'And the rest,' she said drily. 'I'd never hear the end of it. So I haven't told him, and I feel like I'm denying her.' She gave her grandfather a half-smile. 'And I cannae invite her home because he'd have to know what her surname is and then he'd know that she's a Catholic – and I feel bad about that too. Her family have been real hospitable to me.'

'You can invite your friends here any time, Lizzie,' said Peter stoutly. 'You know that, hen. Don't you?'

'Aye, Grandad,' Liz said, her voice soft. 'I know that. And I appreciate it. I really do.'

Peter shook his white head. 'I don't know how your Granny and I managed to produce a child with ideas like your father has. As the Bard said, "we're all Jock Tamson's bairns",' he declaimed, quoting one of Robert Burns' most famous lines. 'How we raised a bigot I'll never know.'

'You did your best, Grandad,' said Liz, edging herself gingerly back into her chair. It might be the end of July, but the range was lit, her grandfather using the excuse of the wet summer. She'd lay a bet the *Queen Mary*'s engine room wasn't any hotter than this. 'Calling him William Wallace MacMillan was a good start.'

Her grandfather's face lit up. 'Aye, that was your Granny's idea – to call him after the national hero. We visited the Wallace monument at Stirling when we were courting, you know. She was scared, but I managed to persuade her to climb to the top.'

He turned his face towards the open fire in the middle of the range.

'She always rose to a challenge. Even if it scared her.' He paused, gazing into the flames. His blue eyes, normally piercing and intense, went soft and dreamy. 'Especially if it scared her.'

Before Liz could think of something comforting to say, his head snapped up again. 'You're like her, lass.' Liz felt a warm glow which had nothing to do with the heat from the fire. 'Now, of course,' Peter went on, 'your father forgets about the Wallace, likes to think he's called after King Billy. As if Jenny and I would have done any such thing!'

Liz allowed herself an inner smile at the indignation evident in his voice.

'Shall I make the tea?' she suggested, sitting up in her chair.

'Damn the fear of it. You sit there and make yourself comfortable and I'll see to it. You've had a long day, pet.'

Resisting the temptation to help him, Liz did as she was bid. It was a novelty to be waited on, after all. In her own home, the division of labour was strictly traditional – which basically meant that she and her mother did all the housework.

Her grandfather, on the other hand, had always done his best to be helpful around the house. Right now he was cutting some of Sadie's fruit loaf which Liz had brought with her. The slices were a bit thick, but he put them out neatly on a plate with a wee paper doily underneath them. Keeping up Granny's standards. That brought a lump to Liz's throat.

'So, hen,' Peter said once they were both settled opposite each other, 'what else have you been up to lately? The Red

Cross exercise is still going ahead?'

'Yes, Grandad,' she said. 'It's all arranged.' He'd already promised to be one of the volunteer casualties. 'And Helen and Eddie and I are going to the Empire Exhibition this weekend.' She took a small bite of fruit loaf and chewed it thoughtfully. 'At least I think we are. If Eddie's still speaking to me, that is.'

Chapter 10

Considering the upsets of the week, Saturday started well enough. However, the day wasn't very old before Liz was seriously wondering if it was too much to hope for that a great big hole might open up in the middle of Bellahouston Park into which she could conveniently slide. Her dismay had nothing to do with the exhibition itself. That was as exciting as everybody had said it was. No, her problem was with Helen and Eddie.

It had looked promising at first. Apart from the expected acerbic comments about the British Empire, Eddie was on his best behaviour. He had even laughed out loud at something: the giant model of a merino sheep on top of the Wool Pavilion.

There was a minor hiccup when Helen mentioned the forthcoming Red Cross exercise, asking innocently if he was going to be one of the volunteer casualties.

'No, I don't think so,' he said, enunciating each word of his answer so carefully and with such a sarcastic edge to his voice that Liz could cheerfully have thumped him one.

On the plus side, judging by the look on his face, he obviously thought that his sister's friend was a very pretty girl. Sensing the embarrassment that might cause him and knowing how shy he could be with the opposite sex, Liz wasn't therefore too bothered when conversation on the tram going to Bellahouston was polite but stilted. They needed time to get used to each other, that was all.

Casting around for subjects of conversation, they started on the journey itself. Being 'Bankies, they had been born and brought up on the north bank of the Clyde. Travelling to the south side of Glasgow was a big adventure. The two halves of the city seldom visited each other.

The tram itself was one of the new ones, its design very much in the modern style, built to commemorate the crowning of the new King and known therefore as Coronation Class.

'It's a streamlined design, of course,' Eddie explained to both girls, 'for style and speed.' His tone was a little too patient – as though he were explaining some terribly complicated machinery to small children who couldn't possibly be expected to grasp anything overly technical.

'A bit like Flash Gordon's spaceship then,' said Helen contemplatively. 'Or the *Mallard*. Apparently the streamlining of the locomotive was an important contributory factor towards the breaking of the speed record.' Helen turned to Liz. 'A hundred and twenty-six miles per hour, you remember, Liz? That Nigel Gresley, he really knows his onions.'

'Ah . . . yes . . .' said Eddie. He looked startled.

Liz exchanged a look with Helen, noted the mischievous glint in her baby-blue eyes and knew she was amused that Eddie was quite obviously struggling to come to terms with the fact that she possessed some brains. Modern men. Huh! They were as bad as the Victorians. But if Helen were disposed to laugh at Eddie, that was surely better than finding him irritating – which was what Liz had feared might happen.

Once they got to Bellahouston, however, things began to go badly wrong. Firstly, and disastrously, Eddie the revolutionary was seized by a sudden fit of gentlemanly behaviour. He tried to insist on paying both his sister and her friend into the exhibition.

He did it with a bit too much of a flourish. Liz suspected that embarrassment was a factor in that, but the offer went down very badly with Helen, who bristled immediately.

'I can pay myself in, thanks, Mr MacMillan,' she said frostily, opening her purse and extracting a shilling with that stiff pride which only those who've ever been truly poor can understand.

Groaning inwardly at that rigidly formal *Mr MacMillan*, Liz then watched helplessly as the situation went from bad to worse. Spotting a volunteer first-aider sporting a Red Cross armband, Eddie proceeded to make a sarcastic comment about both girls' involvement with the organisation.

Helen, the sparks really flying now, answered back. That sent Eddie off into his son-of-the-revolution routine, pontificating about the capitalist war machine. Liz did her damnedest, but there didn't seem to be any way of stopping him. Even the admiration which the exhibits evoked brought only a temporary respite. Such a pity, she thought, when it was all so interesting.

Stylish buildings – startlingly modern – had been specially built to provide pavilions to display the industry, produce, culture and achievements of the huge variety of countries which made up the British Empire.

They had come in by the Paisley Road West entrance, close to the two Scottish pavilions. Those were painted a rich blue on the outside, to match the colours in St Andrew's flag, but also to contrast with the pastel hues of many of the other buildings. That information was volunteered by one of the policemen on duty, who also told them that the colourful paths which linked the different pavilions were made of red asphalt mixed with chips of white granite from Skye and pink granite from Banffshire.

On the other side of the main path from Scottish Avenue was the Palace of Art and, some distance behind that, An Clachan, the Highland Village. Liz had read about the latter in the newspapers. It had traditional white-walled cottages from Skye and black houses from the Outer Isles, and even a burn with a wee bridge over it which flowed into a tiny sea loch. As a city girl, Liz thought the country scene in miniature was perfectly lovely.

And then you looked up and saw a skyscraper behind the Highland cottages. The Tower of Empire dominated the whole site and had quickly become the symbol of the exhibition.

According to people who knew about such things, lots of buildings in Glasgow were going to look like that in the future.

Glaswegians had nicknamed the structure Tait's Tower after the architect who had been in overall charge of the design of the exhibition. They told each other proudly that the illustrious Mr Tait was a Paisley buddy, from the town a few miles along the road from Bellahouston, and that he was already famous as the architect of Sydney Harbour Bridge.

As well as being tall, Tommy Tait's tower was spectacularly futuristic in style. It reminded Liz of something out of a Flash Gordon film, and she said so to Helen.

'Aye, Dominic would love it. He'll need to come with us the next time. The Stratosphere Girl would be right up his street, too.'

That was a female acrobat who performed at the top of a two-hundred-foot-high pole. Liz could hardly bring herself to look at her. It made her feel really dizzy.

Helen seemed to be enjoying the exhibition, if not the company. Eddie had lapsed into a sullen silence. Honestly, he was much use as a . . . Liz thought of the most useless thing she could think of. A stookie, that was it: a handy word which meant either sheaves of corn set up to dry in a field, a plaster cast on a broken arm or leg, or a stupid and silent person – one who made no contribution to the conversation.

Liz's mouth set in a grim line. She tried giving her brother a dirty look, narrowing her eyes at him so that he would get the message. He paid not a blind bit of notice. Stookie was exactly the right word.

Trying desperately to fill the conversational gap and having bought the exhibition guidebook, Liz began reading out snippets of information to her two companions as they walked around the site.

'The tower's three hundred feet high apparently, and constructed on the highest point of the park.' She looked up and gave Eddie a smile. '*We'll* need to bring Grandad the next time. He told me that he and Granny once climbed the Wallace monument at Stirling.' She bent her head back to the guidebook. 'They reckon that you can see for eighty miles from the top of it.'

'If it's not raining,' grumbled Eddie. The summer was proving to be depressingly wet.

'Och, but that doesn't matter once you're inside the exhibition,' insisted Helen. 'Everything's so colourful and interesting – even today, when it's a wee bit overcast.'

Liz would have said that it was more than a wee bit overcast – *gey dreich* would have been her assessment of today's weather. Trust Helen to look on the bright side. Unlike Eddie, who was watching her friend without a smile on his handsome face.

At the South African pavilion they tasted passion fruit juice, unlike anything they'd ever drunk before. The Empire Tea Pavilion offered them more familiar refreshment, but even there they found something unusual to admire: enchantingly polite Indian women, graceful in their flowing saris. The colours and materials from which they were made fascinated Helen. Eddie, still silent, stood looking at her as she crouched down to admire them, the women delighted by the interest she was taking in their national dress.

A second visit to the Highland Village provided some distraction, but strolling along a path which led away from it they soon found themselves outside the Roman Catholic Pavilion. It was a beautifully decorated building, but unfortunately it set Eddie off again, and on one of his favourite hobbyhorses too: the one about religion being the opium of the masses.

'And the Roman Catholic Church is the worst of the lot,' he said. To Liz's growing dismay and anger, he went on to attack her friend's faith. According to Eddie, Catholic priests had a complete stranglehold over their flock, who were apparently totally incapable of thinking for themselves.

In a state of horrified fascination, Liz saw Helen take a deep breath. A huge one. She rushed so vociferously to the support of her Church that she sounded like the mother superior of a strict and particularly humourless order of nuns. Then, by some tortuous logic, they got on to the war in Spain . . .

When Helen described General Franco as a Christian gentleman rescuing priests and nuns from the excesses of the left-wing government, an increasingly desperate Liz began racking her brains for something which would distract them both. Eddie was about to blow a gasket. Any moment now.

Somewhere not very far away she heard the strains of bagpipes tuning up. The wave of relief was so powerful it threatened to make her go weak at the knees.

'Oh, listen! Can you hear a pipe band? I think it's coming from this direction!'

Cutting in between Helen and Eddie, she took them both by the arm and more or less frog-marched them in the direction of the music.

The next ten minutes passed pleasantly, if ear-splittingly enough, but when the pipers stopped playing and the drummers stopped drumming, Eddie looked across Liz to Helen, his dark brows angry over stormy grey eyes.

'What you were saying just now,' he began, 'about Spain . . .'

In the name of the wee man . . . what had she done to deserve this? Liz looked around her. They were standing in a large open area with a bandstand in the middle, not far from the main entrance on to Mosspark Boulevard. There had to be something here. Didn't there?

Then she saw it. The building could only be the Australian Pavilion, judging by the animal which stood on top of it. Incredibly, a man was holding it by a lead.

'Oh, look!' she cried. 'What's that? It surely can't be a kangaroo!'

Good grief, she sounded like one of the Bright Young Things she despised so much. But any sacrifice was worth it if it achieved the desired result. It did. Eddie shaded his eyes, the better to see, and Helen laughed in delight, clapping her hands like a child.

'Och, the poor wee thing,' she said with quick sympathy.

'Poor big thing, surely,' murmured Eddie. Helen either didn't hear him or chose not to.

'I wonder if it misses the sunshine,' she said as they moved closer to the Australian Pavilion. 'We've had so much rain.'

'It doesnae seem to mind,' said one of the exhibition attendants, who had overheard her. He gestured towards the kangaroo. 'Princess Margaret Rose liked him too. She was here last week. Clapped her hands when she saw him, just like you did.'

He beamed at Helen's pretty face. Liz, in the meantime, was sending up a silent prayer. *Don't let Eddie start on the royal family and the monarchy.* Oh Lord, he was opening his mouth to do exactly that. He never thought to lower his voice, either. Helen would stomp off in high dudgeon and they'd probably get lynched into the bargain.

'Oh, look,' she said again, spotting a poster on a wall. She'd no idea what it was about, but it had to be about something, didn't it? She was getting really desperate now. Hell's bells, this was hard work.

'It's an advert for all the concerts they're having during the course of the exhibition. Is there a concert hall, then?'

'Oh, aye,' said the attendant proudly. 'There's an entrance to it off Bellahouston Drive – no' far from the junction with Paisley Road West.'

'What a pity,' said Liz, scanning the poster, 'we've missed Gracie Fields. She was here two weeks ago.'

Well, she had shut Eddie up, but both he and Helen were now staring at her like stookies. When they weren't scowling at each other, that was. Hadn't they ever heard of the art of conversation?

'You haven't necessarily missed Gracie Fields,' said the attendant. 'She's made quite a few private visits to the exhibition. Stood in front of the Atlantic Restaurant last week – you know, the bit that's shaped like the prow of a ship? – and sang "Sally". It was magic, it really was.'

The man shook his head, lost in admiration of Gracie. Then

he added, on an afterthought, 'Paul Robeson's coming back to do a second concert in September, if you like him.'

'Paul Robeson? Oh, aye,' said Helen with enthusiasm. 'I've heard him on the records at work. What a voice! See when he sings "Ol'Man River"? It makes the hairs stand up on the back of my neck.'

'You like Paul Robeson?'

It was Eddie the stookie who had spoken, apparently shocked into speech. Hallelujah, thought Liz, praise the Lord, a point of contact at last. Never mind if part of Eddie's admiration for the black singer who'd made his home in Britain for the past few years had something to do with the entertainer's well-known communist sympathies. It was a start. If she could just keep the conversation on his songs . . .

'I wanted to hear him last time,' Eddie told the girls, as the attendant gave them a friendly nod before moving away, 'but the tickets sold out real quick. Do you know,' he said admiringly, 'he gave all his fee for the last concert to the Spanish Civil War Relief Fund.'

Bloody hell, thought Liz, here we go again. She really must stop swearing, even though it was only to herself. On the other hand, this pair would try the patience of a saint.

Then, for the second time in as many months, salvation came to Liz from the same quarter.

'Well, hello there!'

She spun round. Standing there, smiling all over his face, his hat politely swept off, was Adam Buchanan.

Chapter 11

'Miss MacMillan, how very nice to see you again!' He turned politely to Helen. 'And Miss . . .'

'Gallagher,' supplied Helen. 'How are you, Mr Buchanan? It's so nice to see you again too. Isn't it Liz?' she asked sweetly, turning to her friend with an expectant air.

Liz just managed not to do a double-take. Helen's bad temper had vanished like snow off a wall. What was she up to? For his part, Adam Buchanan was now looking at Eddie, waiting for an introduction. Liz did the honours.

Adam and Eddie shook hands. It was a little wary. Liz had noticed that men were often like that when they met for the first time. Sometimes it made her think of two wild animals circling around each other.

'How very nice to see you,' Adam Buchanan said again to Liz, smiling warmly. 'Are you enjoying the exhibition?'

'It's great,' she replied. Looking up at him – gosh, he was tall – she returned his smile and saw the hazel eyes crinkle at the corners in response. There was a pause which threatened to go on for too long. Now that the social niceties were out of the way, no one seemed very sure what to say next.

'I say,' he said suddenly. 'I'm meeting some friends at the Atlantic Restaurant. Why don't you join us for lunch?' He turned to Helen and Eddie. 'The three of you, of course.'

Eddie, still doing the sizing-up business, answered for all of them.

'Sorry, *old chap*, the Atlantic Restaurant's a bit out of our league. Not for the likes of us, you might say. In fact, you and your friends probably would say that.'

Liz blinked. Had she heard him properly? It was Adam Buchanan, however, who seemed to be covered in embarrassment.

'Oh, yes, of course—' He broke off, realising he was appearing to agree with what Eddie had said. 'Oh, I say, I'm terribly sorry. I really didn't mean anything by that. I mean . . . I do apologise,' he finished lamely.

Helen stepped into the breach.

'It's very kind of you to offer, Mr Buchanan, but we've already made alternative arrangements. And,' she added, smiling up at him, but with an edge to her voice which was unmistakably meant for someone else, '*you* have no need to apologise for anything. I hope you enjoy your lunch.'

Once Adam had taken his embarrassed leave of them, Helen spoke, her voice steely.

'I'd like to go back to the Roman Catholic Pavilion, Liz. Will you meet me at the Tower in about half an hour?'

Liz nodded. Expecting Helen to turn on her heel and go immediately, she was surprised when she spoke again.

'I have to get my daily dose of opium, you see. And be told what to think, of course.' Eddie coughed, and shifted his weight from one foot to the other.

Helen looked him straight in the eye. 'I don't see that there was any call for you to be so rude to him. He's a very nice man, and he was only trying to be friendly. See you later, Liz.'

She stalked off without giving Eddie the chance to reply. Liz wasn't sure he would have managed to. He spent the next minute or two in silence, watching Helen's retreating figure grow smaller and smaller until she finally turned a corner in the path and went out of sight.

Liz coughed, measuring her words carefully before she spoke. She was very angry, but she wasn't going to fall out with Eddie in public.

'Do you want to go back home now? I'll easily wait for Helen by myself.'

His voice was expressionless. 'I said I'd escort you both, didn't I? I'm hardly going to go off without you. Credit me with some manners. You don't have to speak with a marble in your mouth to know how to act like a gentleman.'

Oh, dear. She'd wanted so much for Helen and him to like each other.

'Cheer up, Helen. It might never happen.'

Helen grimaced at Janet Brown's teasing comment, following it with a rueful smile to indicate that she appreciated the impulse which had provoked it.

'We seem to take it in turns to cheer each other up, don't we?' observed Liz as the three girls sat waiting at the tea table for the second half of the evening's programme to commence. The first part had been a rather sombre affair, going into more detail about the consequences of a chemical attack. Helen and Liz had been discussing the gas mask question again, as Liz explained to Janet.

'Helen was wondering if they're going to make any specifically designed for dogs. Or cats too, I suppose,' she mused, thinking about it.

Janet laughed. 'For dogs and cats? Do you want one for your budgie too, Helen? How about special miniature masks for goldfish?' she added, warming to her theme.

'No,' said Helen, shaking her head, 'I'm perfectly serious, Janet. My brother dotes on his dog. If he couldn't protect Finn, he'd take to the hills with him. I'm sure of it.'

Liz saw Janet's laughter fade as she registered Helen's real concern. Her own observation had been an accurate one. As anxiety continued to rise, they did all seem to take turns at being strong and bolstering each other up when the seriousness of the situation facing the country suddenly hit one of them really hard.

Liz was pretty sure it hadn't yet occurred to Helen that her brothers might be called up to the army if war broke out with Germany. Conor and Finn would have to be separated then.

He'd hardly be allowed to take the big dog with him.

'How's Eddie doing these days, Liz?' asked Janet. 'Still wanting to storm the barricades?'

Helen dropped her head, murmuring something about the buckle on one of her shoes having come undone. About to answer Janet, Liz noticed something which distracted her completely from her gloomy thoughts.

Her own chair was pushed back from the table. She could see Helen's feet without moving her head. The buckles on both of her shoes were fastened perfectly neatly. Liz could also see the side of Helen's face. Miss Gallagher was blushing.

Because Edward MacMillan's name had been mentioned? That couldn't possibly be the case. Could it? Yet why else would Helen have invented that story about her buckle, if not to hide her embarrassment?

Well, well, well, thought Liz. That was interesting. Very interesting indeed.

Mrs Galbraith called them to order for the second half of the evening, reminding them about the practice exercise.

'So please get all your family and friends to volunteer to come along as casualties for you to practise your new skills on!'

Next week, she told them in the same bright tone of voice, they would be learning how to deal with bomb, blast and shrapnel injury – just in case, as she put it, the worst came to the worst.

'And now,' she said with obvious relief, 'it's a great privilege for me to introduce Mrs Buchanan, who's going to tell us about the Voluntary Aid Detachment of the Red Cross. We know her well, of course. She's been a good friend to our Clydebank group – so let me ask you to give her a warm welcome. Mrs Buchanan?'

Adam Buchanan's mother was a good speaker. She knew what she wanted to say, had her information well organised and was surprisingly witty. It wasn't so much what she said, as the way that she said it. Several of her comments provoked laughs and chuckles.

She related the history of the Voluntary Aid Detachment, and told them how the Red Cross, particularly in the current crisis, would be looking for volunteers of both sexes and all ages – at this point she directed a big beaming smile towards Liz and Helen – and for all branches of their work.

'Drivers, cooks and, of course,' she went on, 'nursing auxiliaries.'

Helen gave Liz a discreet elbow in the ribs.

'Now,' Mrs Buchanan was saying, 'I can speak about this with some authority, as I was myself a VAD nursing assistant during the Great War. Gentlemen, close your ears for a moment, I've got something that's just for the ladies . . .'

Liz had to admire the technique. All the men present looked instantly as alert as the women.

'Well now. You might find this hard to believe, but I was once a slim and attractive young thing—'

'You still are, hen,' came a rough but gallant voice from the back of the room. Amelia Buchanan acknowledged the compliment with a graceful inclination of her head. In the midst of the general merriment, her eyes – hazel like her son's – sparkled. With some surprise, Liz realised that she must be enjoying the banter. Funny, that. She would never have thought that a refined lady like Mrs Buchanan would have got on so well with a crowd of rough and ready 'Bankies.

She seemed to thrive on it, responding to her audience, relaxing and telling ever more outrageous stories about her experiences as a field nurse on the Western Front. Digging deep into a capacious handbag, she brought out a bundle of hatpins and passed them around.

'Uniform buttons,' she explained. 'Gifts from grateful patients. We VADs used to get them made up into hatpins, as you see here, or sometimes brooches.'

She gave the assembled company a sheepish look. That reminded Liz of her son too.

97

'Until the powers-that-be found out about it and clamped down on the practice. The British Army was running out of tunic buttons. Never mind the ammunition. The colonel couldn't have his men looking sloppy on parade.'

There was general laughter.

'Not just the British Army either – you'll see some French and Belgian ones in my collection.'

'Hang on a wee minute,' came the same rough male voice which had made the earlier compliment. 'This one I've got here looks German.'

She gave him a charmingly rueful smile.

'Well, he was very handsome, we had shot him down, and he did speak impeccable English.'

By the time Mrs Buchanan sat down at the end of her talk, the room was reverberating to great gales of laughter.

'Oh, that was good,' said Janet Brown, wiping tears of mirth from her eyes. 'Did you not think so, Liz?'

Liz pursed her lips in disapproval.

'I think she should have treated it a bit more seriously. The Great War's hardly a subject for jokes and funny stories.'

'Has it not occurred to you,' chipped in Helen, sitting on her other side, 'that she saw we were all looking a bit worried and decided to cheer us up?'

Liz swung round in the hard wooden chair to face her friend.

'You know what your biggest fault is, Helen Gallagher?'

'No, but I'm sure you're going to tell me!'

Helen, an impish grin on her face, waited patiently for Liz to speak.

'Your biggest fault, Miss Gallagher,' she told her with mock severity, 'is that you always see the best in people. Just when I want to get a good dislike of someone going, you manage to find their redeeming features. It's very aggravating.'

Helen grinned. 'Well, Miss MacMillan, all I can say is that I'm sure it's very good for your soul.'

'You mean Proddies have got souls?' asked Liz in tones of

astonishment. 'Well, fancy that. Who'd have thought it?'

'Miss MacMillan? Miss Gallagher?' Liz spun around. Amelia Buchanan was standing there, a sheaf of papers in her hand.

'I enjoyed your talk, Mrs Buchanan,' said Helen shyly.

'One does one's best,' she murmured, looking pleased, but with a decided twinkle in her eye. This woman knows how to laugh at herself, thought Liz, surprising herself with the observation.

'So have I convinced any of you young ladies that you should apply to join the Voluntary Aid Detachment?'

'Not me, I'm afraid,' said Helen, 'but Liz wants to join. Janet too.'

'Good, excellent. You'll need these then.' She handed both girls some sheets of paper. 'Application form and further information.'

Liz took them with a murmur of thanks, thrilled at the knowledge that she was getting closer and closer to her goal.

'And I could really become a VAD, but still keep working – do it in the evenings and at weekends?'

Mrs Buchanan, now wearing gold half-moon glasses, smiled at Liz over them.

'Yes. You would then be a non-mobile VAD, based at one of the hospitals, where you would probably be asked to do a certain number of hours per week. Oh,' she said absently, 'there's one form I've forgotten to give you.'

Excited, Liz held out her hand for the further sheet. Extracting it from the bundle of papers she held and handing it to Liz, Amelia Buchanan enumerated each one.

'Information sheet, application form – and consent form.'

Liz's blood ran cold. 'Consent form?'

'In view of your age, my dear, we must get your father's permission. You too, Miss Brown,' she said, handing Janet a copy of the form. 'Well then,' she said brightly, 'I'll look forward to receiving your completed forms as soon as possible.'

She swept off. Neither Helen nor Janet said anything for a

while. Then Helen spoke, her voice full of sympathy.

'Oh, Liz,' she said. 'Oh, Liz.'

Chapter 12

He had touched her. His hands were on her body. He had crept up behind her while she was standing sorting out some papers on her desk and she didn't hear him until it was too late – when he slid his arms around her from behind, pushing her lacy jumper up over her petticoat.

Liz jumped and tried to turn around, but he was holding her too tightly, one arm and hand clamped round her waist. His other hand slid upwards, tightening over her breast.

She tried to say, *How dare you?* but her mouth had gone dry. She couldn't get the words out. She struggled, and felt his mouth at her ear.

'Stop pretending you don't want it,' said Eric Mitchell. 'You little temptress.' The softness of his voice terrified her. She struggled some more. That only made matters worse. His hands squeezed harder, pulling her into his body. He laughed at her futile attempts to resist the contact.

'Can you feel me, little Lizzie?' he whispered. 'Is that nice?'

She moved her head from side to side in frantic denial, feeling the strands of her hair passing over his face.

'Let me go.' She was so panicky she could hardly get the words out. The blood was whooshing through her ears and her skin was hot and clammy. She felt as if she was going to be sick. The pressure of his body repelled her. Oh, dear God, how was she going to get out of this? A prayer to St Jude? Helen had taught her about that.

'If ever something seems really desperate and you can't see

any way out of it, then send up a wee prayer to St Jude. It always works.'

She had laughed all over her pretty face when an anxious Liz had asked if a prayer to a Catholic saint would work for a Proddy. Liz didn't hesitate now. Anything was worth a try.

The patron saint of lost causes was clearly not at all prejudiced against Protestants. Liz's body grew limp with relief as she heard footsteps in the corridor outside the door to the outer office. With a muttered obscenity, Eric Mitchell released her, moving swiftly back to his own desk.

Liz pulled her jumper down just in time. The door opened. She had been expecting to see the sharp features and cheery grin of the office boy. Instead, a young woman was coming into the office – closely followed by Adam Buchanan. What on earth was he doing here?

His open face lit up with pleasure when he saw her, and he came forward with his hand outstretched.

'Why, Miss MacMillan, what a surprise to see you again! Although a very pleasant one,' he added gallantly. 'My mama must be right. She always says that Glasgow's a village. How delightful it is that we keep bumping into each other!'

'Delightful,' agreed Liz. Reeling from the shock of what Eric Mitchell had done, it was a miracle she could get any kind of coherent answer out – even one consisting of only one word.

Adam Buchanan introduced his dark-haired companion.

'Miss Elizabeth MacMillan – the Honourable Miss Cordelia MacIntyre.'

The girl turned a laughing face up to him. 'Cordelia MacIntyre will do fine, Adam. These courtesy titles are a bit ridiculous in this modern age.' She looked at Liz, her discreetly made-up mouth grimacing in rueful distaste. 'Don't you think so, Miss MacMillan?'

'I'm sure I couldn't say,' said Liz, dropping the girl's hand as soon as she reasonably could. She'd remembered where she knew her from. She was the young lady who'd made the disparaging comments about Clydebank the night of the Red Cross enrolment.

Eric Mitchell had never done anything as bad as this. Her skin crawled at the memory of his hands on her body, the way he had pulled her against him, the feel of him . . . What in the name of God was she going to do about it?

She wasn't in any fit state to be standing here making small talk with Adam Buchanan and his fashion-plate companion. The Honourable Miss MacIntyre was pencil slim, but shapely with it, her dark hair, long when Liz had first met her, now fashionably waved and cropped close to her head like an elegant cap.

'Oh, come on, Miss MacMillan,' said Adam Buchanan, a mischievous twinkle in his eyes. 'I'm sure you've got an opinion on the matter. You don't strike me as a young lady who's backward about coming forwards.'

Cordelia MacIntyre laughed and looked expectantly at Liz, eager to play the game. Something snapped in Liz. She could have sworn she heard it: like the crack of a dry and brittle twig breaking as she put her foot on it.

Eric Mitchell, her disappointment about the Voluntary Aid Detachment, the country careering towards war. Yet you still got people like this pair – have another cocktail, go to another party, bury your head in the sand and it'll go away. They found life so *frightfully amusing*.

'All right then,' said Liz. She folded her arms across her chest. 'All titles – and the whole rotten class system – are the ruination of this country. We're in the modern age. People say that man will even travel to the moon this century.'

The people who said that were largely Dominic Gallagher, but Liz was sure he knew what he was talking about. She lifted her chin.

'Every day it looks more and more likely that there's going to be another war – in which we'll all be expected to participate and do our bit. Yet we're hidebound by an utterly stupid class system which exercises a complete stranglehold on society –

where privilege and birth count for more than intelligence and common sense.'

It was an impressive speech. She should probably have stopped there. She didn't, her cool grey-green gaze sweeping contemptuously over the two of them.

'Do you have any idea of the sort of poverty some people are forced to live in? Do you realise what a waste of potential that is?'

Cordelia MacIntyre looked very earnest.

'I do so agree with you, Miss MacMillan.' She turned to her companion. 'She's absolutely right, you know, Adam. We need a better system.'

That was all Liz needed – an upper-class young lady with a conscience.

'Would you excuse me, please?' she said coldly. 'Mr Murray pays me to work, not stand around talking.'

That went beyond rudeness. She knew it did. If Miss Gilchrist had heard her, she'd have been for it. Eric Mitchell, a hateful smile on his lips, was standing aside from the conversation. He knew exactly why she was so rattled.

Helen would have read her a lecture on manners – and she'd have been right. Liz knew she was taking out her feelings of helpless anger and rage towards Eric Mitchell on the wrong people, but she couldn't seem to stop. She wasn't going to be very proud of herself when she thought about this later. Adam Buchanan, however, simply laughed.

'Oh, come on, Miss MacMillan. My Uncle Alasdair's not a slave driver.'

Uncle Alasdair? So she'd really put her foot in it. Added to which, Adam Buchanan was perfectly right. Mr Murray was by no means a slave driver. He could be strict sometimes, but he was always fair.

The door to the inner office opened and Miss Gilchrist came out. She positively simpered when she saw Adam Buchanan and Cordelia MacIntyre.

'Miss MacIntyre! Mr Buchanan! How delightful to see you!

Why, it must be fully two years since we last had the pleasure. I hope Miss MacMillan's been making you welcome. Elizabeth, why have you not made some tea for our visitors?'

As she turned to Liz, her expression changed and hardened. Now Liz was for it. She wondered if she could have cared less.

Adam Buchanan and Cordelia MacIntyre both started speaking at once. They laughed and Adam made a funny little bow to Cordelia, indicating that she should speak first. He had lovely manners. Unlike myself, thought Liz.

'Miss MacMillan has been making us very welcome, Miss Gilchrist – and we didn't want any tea. We've been drinking the stuff all day. Swimming in it, in fact. Isn't that right, Adam? It's all this going around with the begging bowl.'

She smiled at Miss Gilchrist and then turned, including everyone in the warmth of the gesture. So she wasn't a clype. She had chosen not to mention Liz's rudeness and belligerent attitude. That was one tiny little point in her favour. It didn't mean Liz was going to smile back. She had no idea what the girl meant by the begging bowl – a little light charity work, probably.

The two visitors were shown into Mr Murray's – Uncle Alasdair's – office. Ten minutes later Cordelia MacIntyre came out alone. Miss Gilchrist leapt to her feet. Cordelia, fastening white kid gloves which buttoned at the wrist, looked round the office and gave another of those all-encompassing smiles.

'Well, I must be off. I only really came along to say hallo to Uncle Alasdair. I hear you're doing well at the Red Cross classes, Miss MacMillan.'

Liz, back behind her Underwood, looked up at her stupidly. How did she know that? Adam Buchanan via his mother, she supposed.

'Yes,' she managed at last. 'My friend and I are enjoying them.'

'They're good, aren't they?' agreed Cordelia, nodding her head enthusiastically. 'I'm doing one in the West End. It's so nice to feel that one is doing something useful. Especially for a social butterfly and generally useless person such as myself.' She laughed gaily. 'Maybe it'll be enough to keep me from the guillotine come the revolution, eh?'

'I wouldn't count on it,' said Liz, the words shooting out of her mouth before she could stop them. The Honourable Miss MacIntyre seemed, however, disposed to find them amusing and took her leave of them all with a friendly wave.

The door had barely closed behind her before Miss Gilchrist gave Liz the look and the command.

'Elizabeth. In front of my desk, now. If you please.'

And whether she pleased or not. The ticking-off which followed – on rudeness to visitors in the office 'who also happen to be close relatives of Mr Murray's, young lady!' – was administered with a smirking Eric Mitchell listening to every word.

It didn't help that the lecture was delivered by a seated Miss Gilchrist with Liz standing in front of her, arms behind her back like a naughty schoolgirl. Or that having finished berating her, her supervisor stood up, scooped a pile of folders from the filing tray and dumped them in Liz's arms.

'You'll file these before you leave tonight.'

'But Miss Gilchrist, I'll be late home!' wailed Liz, glancing up at the office clock. *Not to mention the row I'll get from Father – especially when he finds out why I had to stay behind.*

Adam Buchanan, coming out of the inner office at that moment, must have heard the comment. His uncle, following him out, didn't notice what was going on, but then why should he have? He hadn't witnessed the conversation which had provoked the reprimand. Adam Buchanan, however, by the faint raise of his eyebrows, showed that he had a fair idea of what was going on.

Alasdair Murray took his leave of his nephew, clapping him affectionately on the shoulder. Then he called Miss Gilchrist into his office. Liz knew they were planning to work late themselves. He was in the middle of dictating a long report to his personal secretary. They'd spent the morning pulling out

106

information from lots of different files, hence the large amount which now needed to be put back into the cabinets.

His visitor came over and stood in front of Liz.

'Miss MacMillan, I'm heading for Clydebank this evening. Can I offer you a lift home, by any chance?'

'I have to work late,' she said, indicating the files. The huge bundle was threatening to slide all over her desk.

'I'll stay if you like, Lizzie,' said Eric Mitchell. 'Help you put them away.'

'No need for that, Mr Mitchell,' said Adam Buchanan smoothly, not taking his eyes off Liz's face. Had it betrayed the panic she had felt when Eric Mitchell had made his suggestion? 'I'll give Miss MacMillan a hand and afterwards I'll give her a lift home so she won't be too late.'

Once Eric Mitchell had left, Adam Buchanan pushed some of the files out of the way and half sat on Liz's desk, perched on the corner.

'If you'll excuse me, Mr Buchanan,' Liz said firmly, 'I'd better get on. There's really no need for you to stay and help me with the files. I can manage.' Now that her tormentor had gone, she could afford to be brave.

Her rejected helper clapped a hand to his chest. 'Miss MacMillan, you wound me, you really do!'

Liz curled her lip. 'I doubt it, Mr Buchanan.'

'My friends call me Adam,' he said.

'How very nice for them.'

'Oh, well,' he said, 'bring on the tumbrels and the knitting needles. Do you have a basket to catch my head?' he enquired politely. 'We wouldn't want the blood to splatter all over your clothes.'

'Ha, ha,' said Liz. 'Very funny.' But she did feel a twinge of amusement, and she couldn't help letting it show.

One long leg swinging, he grinned at her, then made a sudden request.

'Come and have tea with me after we've done the files.'

'What?'

'Tea,' he repeated. 'A popular reviving drink. The cup that cheers but does not inebriate. Enjoyed by all classes of society – even revolutionaries and Red Clydesiders.'

'Ha, ha,' said Liz again. 'Very droll. Unfortunately I shall have to decline. It would make me even later home.'

He looked around him and spotted the phone on Miss Gilchrist's desk. 'Couldn't you telephone your folks? Tell them you're going to be a little late?' He clapped his hand to his chest again, a comical expression on his pleasant face. 'But that you're in safe hands?'

'Only with extreme difficulty. We're not on the phone.'

She said it with a smile. The relief now that Eric Mitchell was no longer in the room was enormous. And Adam Buchanan was funny and nice. She was beginning to warm to him.

'Ah,' he said, pushing himself up off the desk. 'Well, then, we'd better get going. Working together we'll get through these files like a hot knife through butter. Co-operate in this time of crisis. Put our noses to the wheel and our shoulders to the grindstone and all that – or should it be the other way about?'

'Uh-huh,' said Liz, wondering why listening to her boss's nephew talking nonsense was making her feel so much better. It was kind of him to help her. Really kind.

Twenty minutes later they had put all the files away and, somewhat to her own surprise, Liz was allowing him to lead her to his car.

'Morag?' she asked when they reached the Austin 7 parked just round the corner from Murray's. The rain had come on again. It didn't seem to want to stop this summer.

'Morag,' Adam murmured. 'She'll be flattered that you remembered.' He put a gentlemanly hand under her elbow to help her into the car. It was the lightest of touches, but Liz jumped back as though she'd been stung, his innocent good manners evoking all too vividly her terrifying experience of earlier in the afternoon.

'Sorry!' Swiftly, he removed his hand. 'I didn't mean to startle you.'

'I'm all right,' said Liz, but it was quite clear that she wasn't. Her breath was coming too fast, for one thing. The hazel eyes narrowed thoughtfully.

Once he had started up the car and they were driving along the street, raindrops drumming against the windscreen, he seemed inclined to continue the bantering conversation they'd been conducting earlier.

'Isn't it fine to be out of the rain? Passing the *hoi polloi* all getting *drookit*?' He gave a teasing emphasis to the last word. 'I only hope it doesn't compromise your revolutionary principles.'

Suddenly it was all too much. Today had been just hellish.

'Hey,' he said, glancing across at her. 'What's the matter?'

'Everything,' she blurted out. 'Everything.'

Without a word, he carefully steered Morag into the side of the road, pulled on the handbrake and turned to face Liz.

'Cup of tea?' he suggested, surveying her critically.

Liz blew her nose. 'I thought you were swimming in the stuff.'

'Coffee, then. I know exactly the place.'

Chapter 13

He took her to a café in Byres Road, not far from the Western Infirmary. Putting his hand on the bold diagonal chrome bars of the glass door, he pushed it open, ushering Liz in front of him.

Behind the counter, framed by tall sweetie jars on shelves behind him and dispensers of pink and white paper straws on the glass counter in front of him, stood a man in late middle age. A little heavy around the cheeks and greying at the temples, he was nonetheless still handsome, an impression confirmed when he smiled broadly at Liz, teeth startlingly white against olive skin.

The café owner obviously knew her escort, greeting him by name.

'Adam! Come in, come in – and close the door. The young lady will get cold.'

He was Italian, of course. Café owners always were. The cadences of his native Tuscany were clearly to be heard in a voice which also bore the unmistakable imprint of a long residence in the west of Scotland.

'Hello, Mr Rossi. Is Mario about?'

'Not yet, but he'll be back soon, I think. Now, what can I get for you and the *signorina*? Coffee?'

'Please.'

Liz slid into one of the booths which Adam indicated. They were set down one wall of the café, opposite the counter. A small oval marble-topped table was bolted to the floor in each one. The wooden bench seats on either side of the table were painted a glossy black and each alcove was big enough to seat

110

four – maybe six if you were prepared to get really friendly with your fellow coffee drinkers.

Gazing out at the street, Liz saw that the rain was into its stride now: a typical west coast summer rainstorm, the water falling in elongated drops like darning needles which bounced back up off the pavement as soon as they struck it.

Inside it was all cosy and warm. Liz unbuttoned her mac. The man brought their coffee.

'It's fair stoating, eh?' he said, pointing to the rain outside. Adam shared a smile with her, and she could see that, like herself, he was secretly amused by Mr Rossi's use of the vernacular. She applied herself to the coffee, white and frothy in a glass cup and saucer.

Everything was glass in here – or chrome – even the sugar dispenser. You tipped it up over your cup and it measured out exactly a teaspoonful of pure white sugar. Liz didn't drink coffee very often. At home and at work they always had tea, and the coffee she had tasted before hadn't been nearly as nice as this. Despite her attack of the miseries, she felt herself begin to relax as she sipped the hot, sweet liquid.

Looking around, she caught a glimpse of herself in one of the mirrors which lined the walls. Her hair had done what it always did in the rain: gone into an unruly mass of waves and curls. So what? She wasn't trying to get a lumber with Adam Buchanan. He wasn't her type. She most definitely wasn't his. She didn't have an *Honourable* in front of her name, for one thing.

'That's better,' he said, watching her smile. 'Now, tell your Uncle Adam all about it.'

Liz stalled for time, glancing once more at their surroundings. 'Nice place.'

'Yes,' he agreed, his voice deep and measured. 'We come here all the time. It's handy for the Infirmary.'

Liz stared at him uncomprehendingly.

'I'm a medical student,' he said. 'So's Mario. Mr Rossi's son. We're in the same year.'

111

She ignored the information about the unknown Mario.

'You're a medical student?'

She hadn't succeeded in keeping the surprise out of her voice. An unholy gleam of amusement crept into young Mr Buchanan's eyes.

'Ah-hah! I see. You had me down as one of the Idle Rich, I suppose. A well-off wastrel. Thought I spent all my time going to cocktail parties. Or huntin', shootin' and fishin'. That sort of thing.'

'Yes. N-no,' she stammered. That was exactly what she had thought.

'You Red Clydesiders,' he sighed in mock dismay. 'You'd have us all strung up from the nearest lamp-post, wouldn't you?'

'I'm sorry,' she said. Her voice trembled. She was making a mess of everything today.

He leaned forward across the narrow table, peering anxiously into her face.

'Hey! I think it's probably me who should be sorry. Have I upset you in some way?'

'No,' said Liz. She turned her head to look out at the street. She wasn't seeing it. In her mind she was back at the Broomielaw with Eric Mitchell. Suppressing a shudder, she forced herself back to the present, meeting Adam's eyes across the table. 'No, you haven't upset me. It's something else.'

'Want to talk about it?' he asked.

Unconsciously catching her bottom lip with her teeth, Liz looked doubtfully at him. Confide in him? A man, a posh man, a medical student? Who even if he had just shot up in her estimation because of his chosen profession was so far outside her social circle he might as well be in the stratosphere that Dominic Gallagher kept going on about? At this precise moment, she couldn't think of anyone better.

She didn't tell him about Eric Mitchell of course, but she told him about wanting to become a VAD and about her father's opposition to her becoming a nurse.

112

'What exactly are your papa's objections? Could you persuade him to change his mind if you tried to pinpoint them and argued your way logically around them?'

'I wish I could,' said Liz wistfully. She rested her elbows on the table and gazed at him. 'Logic doesn't really seem to come into it.'

Adam looked thoughtful. 'Is he a bit authoritarian?'

'You could say that.'

He squared his shoulders and spoke slowly, thinking it out as he went along. 'Well . . . in that case . . . if he's not susceptible to a reasoned argument – what you have to do is manipulate him into being unable to refuse his permission.'

'Och, I don't know,' said Liz, sinking her cheek on to her fist. When it came down to it, her father's objections were completely illogical and unexplainable. That made them all the more difficult to fight. 'My brother doesn't want me to do it either.'

'Why ever not?'

Liz told him. She got a very scornful look in return.

'It's your life,' Adam said, 'not your brother's. I'd tell him to take a running jump if I were you.'

'Maybe he's got a point,' she said gloomily. 'Mrs Buchanan gave us this talk about it – what a lovely time she'd had being a nurse in the Great War – "how all the officers would fall in love with us".'

Unthinkingly, she had mimicked Amelia Buchanan's polite tones for the last phrase. 'Honestly, that woman's so *frightfully posh—*'

She stopped dead, realising just too late who she was talking to: Mrs Buchanan's wee boy, as Helen called him.

Flushing scarlet, Liz sat up straight and forced herself to look him in the eye. 'I've just opened my mouth and put my big foot right in it, haven't I? That's always been one of my greatest talents.'

Adam laughed out loud. 'That's what Cordelia says about herself too.'

'I'm sorry,' said Liz. 'I'm really sorry. I do apologise.'

'I should think so too,' he murmured. 'Insulting a chap's mother like that. Not quite the thing, you know, dear gel.'

He was putting it on. He had to be. Quite that posh he wasn't. But she had been terribly rude. She apologised again. He waved a languid hand.

'Think nothing of it. I have to admit that my mother in full flow is quite a prospect. It's a bit like a natural phenomenon – a river bursting its banks or those pictures of streams of molten lava in Iceland that you see on the newsreels. Personally, I think that if the Germans knew we had her on our side, they'd sue for peace straightaway. The people of Czechoslovakia could sleep safe in their beds at night.'

He was doing it again – talking nonsense until she had recovered. Helen was right. Adam Buchanan was a very nice man – even if he did talk posh.

'Can I call you Elizabeth?' he asked suddenly.

'I only get Elizabeth from my father – usually when I've done something wrong,' she responded with a shy smile. 'You said that your friends call you Adam. Mine call me Liz.'

He extended his hand across the narrow café table.

'Hello, Liz.'

'Hello, Adam.'

His grip was firm, and this time the touch of his warm hand didn't make her feel at all uncomfortable.

'So, Elizabeth called Liz, have you always wanted to be a nurse?'

'Since I was wee,' she confided. 'I used to bandage my dolls and pretend to take their temperature – my brother too when he'd let me. I would tuck them up in bed and pretend to nurse them. And I took the pillowcase off my bed and fastened it around my head with pins so that I looked the part.' She made a face, laughing at herself. 'Daft, eh?'

'Not daft at all,' he assured her.

He was real easy to talk to. Liz found herself telling him things she hadn't even told Helen, like about the time she had

114

spent at Blawarthill as a child, how lost and alone she had felt until the nurse there had been kind to her.

'That must have been tough.'

'No doubt it was very character-building.'

'I'm sure,' he said politely. 'Probably what made you want to be a nurse, as you say. Would you like another coffee?'

She shook her head. 'No thanks. I'd better be getting home. My mother'll be up on the ceiling if I'm not back soon.'

'I'll take you,' he said immediately. He lifted a hand to forestall the protest Liz had started to make. 'It's no trouble. No trouble at all.' He leaned forward conspiratorially. 'In fact, my dear girl, it's essential to my cunning plan.' He sat back in his seat, tapping the side of his nose in a significant manner and putting on a look which reminded her of Helen's mysterious voice and face.

'Which is?'

'To ask your mama if it would be convenient for my mama to call on her and your father to persuade him that it's his patriotic duty to let you join the Voluntary Aid Detachment.'

'What?' Liz's face broke into a joyful smile. 'Would she really do that?'

'Of course she would. She's a good sport.'

'But why should she go to all that bother for me?'

Adam smiled. 'Because you'd make a great nurse and you'd be an asset to the Red Cross – which needs as many volunteers as it can get at the moment. And to which my mother is devoted.'

'Because she was a VAD in the Great War?'

'That,' he said, 'and also because it was what kept her going after my father died. There was some bad timing there,' he said ruefully. 'I'd just started at the Uni, you see, and I was all caught up in that.'

'You don't have any brothers and sisters?'

'No. After she had me she had a post-partum haemorrhage and as a result she had to have a hysterectomy.'

Liz tried to show nothing more than polite interest. She knew what a hysterectomy was, of course, but she'd never actually

115

heard the word said out loud. Even in all-female company it tended to be spoken in a whisper. The young man sitting opposite her seemed belatedly to realise that.

'Oh, I say, I do beg your pardon. I don't suppose this is really a very suitable subject for mixed company – certainly not for a well-brought-up young lady like yourself.'

Liz, who'd decided to take it as a compliment that he thought he could discuss such subjects with her, made a face.

'And do you know how fed up well-brought-up young ladies get with that sort of censorship? Especially when the topic of conversation is our own bodies, and our own health.'

He grinned. 'Yes. Cordelia tells me quite frequently.'

That was the second time in this conversation that he had mentioned the Honourable Miss MacIntyre.

'You were saying,' Liz prompted, 'about when your father died?'

'Yes – well, we lost a lot of money in the Crash, and basically he worked himself to death during the last few years of his life trying to leave Mother and me with something. We moved to a smaller in Milngavie – it's a very nice house, but we used to have a much bigger one. Out Strathblane way. Bit of land, a couple of ponies, that sort of thing, you know.'

She didn't, but she sensed he wasn't trying to show off in any way. She supposed he couldn't help talking posh either.

'Cordelia and her family were our nearest neighbours. They've still got their place out there.'

Childhood sweethearts, then. That must be it.

'Would you know me again?'

'Sorry, was I staring at you?' asked Liz. 'I was wondering if it's going to work. Your mother trying to persuade my father, that is.'

'O ye of little faith. Of course it will. Her powers of persuasion are legendary in Milngavie and Bearsden.'

'But will they work in Clydebank?'

'Of course they will. Liz?' he asked, smiling diffidently at his still novel use of her first name. 'Is becoming a VAD the only thing that's worrying you?'

'How do you mean?'

Adam Buchanan fixed her with a very level look. He might be extremely adept at talking nonsense, but there was a keen intelligence at work behind the quiet good looks.

'There isn't anything wrong at Murray's, is there? I mean, are you having a problem with anything – or anybody – there? I could always speak to my uncle about it if you were.'

He looked so sympathetic, sitting there across the table from her. She was sorely tempted to tell him the whole story. She thought better of it. As Helen had said, they always tended to lay the blame at the lassie's feet. She didn't want Adam Buchanan to think badly of her.

'No,' she said slowly. 'No, it's just the nursing thing.' Out of sight underneath the table she crossed her fingers so the lie wouldn't count.

'You're sure?' He seemed disinclined to let the subject go, one arm along the back of the bench, his fair brows knitted in concentration.

Anxious to change the subject, she allowed her mind to leap ahead on to something else which genuinely troubled her.

'The only thing is . . . my chances of becoming a nurse are all tied up with there being a war.' She lifted her eyes to Adam Buchanan. 'Do you think there's going to be a war?'

'Do you know,' he said in a quiet voice, 'I'm awfully afraid that there is.'

And for a moment, in a douce Glasgow café, two young people sat silent, gazing into the abyss which had opened up at the feet of their generation. The experience of the war to end all wars was something that had belonged to their parents, not to them, a prospect they had never dreamed they would have to face. Yet every day the dreadful possibility seemed to be edging closer.

As Liz and Adam sat there in sombre contemplation, the door of the café opened. There was a sudden influx of cold, damp air, the noise of traffic from the road outside – and a young man who stood there with a student's briefcase over his dark head, laughingly protecting himself from the downpour. By the way he was being greeted – and by the strong physical resemblance – he had to be the son of the café owner. He was also, Elizabeth MacMillan decided, the most handsome man she had ever seen in her life.

Chapter 14

'And?' demanded Helen, busily engaged in bandaging the arm of a volunteer casualty.

'And what?'

'In the name of the wee man!' Helen dropped the end of the roll of bandages she was holding and put her hands on her hips. 'And what happened then? You can't stop there.'

'No, ye cannae,' said the volunteer, who happened to be Helen's young brother Dominic. The other three lads were there too, Finn as well. As a joke, Liz had bandaged one of his paws, unaware that Mrs Galbraith was standing behind her, tapping her foot and doing her best to look disapproving.

Liz shouldn't have done it, of course, but she was in the oddest of moods today. Her whole future hung in the balance this weekend, dependent on the outcome of Mrs Buchanan's visit to her parents the following day. Yet she was curiously light-hearted, ready to laugh at anything and everything.

She was probably hysterical. She had looked it up in her nurses' dictionary before she came out this morning. *Hysteria: Nervous disorder characterised by violent mood-swings. More common in women than men. A firm hand and sharp words, rather than sympathy, usually produce good results.* Yep, that sounded about right. She should ask Helen to slap her face.

Her mother hadn't made it to the exercise, nor had Mrs Crawford. Good-hearted soul that she was, she had volunteered to help a panic-stricken Sadie get organised to receive Amelia Buchanan for tea on Sunday afternoon. Liz arriving home – late – by car had been the first surprise. Seeing the lace curtains twitching in several of the neighbouring houses, Liz had thought ruefully that her method of arriving home on this particular Friday evening was going to be the talk of Queen Victoria Row for some time to come.

Her escort being a well-spoken young gentleman unknown to her parents had been another shock, but when he casually mentioned that he was the nephew of Liz's boss, the stern look on her father's face disappeared as though someone had wiped it off with a cloth.

He offered young Mr Buchanan a small refreshment. A wee dram of his best malt, perhaps? That was when Liz knew that Adam had really made an impression. Her father's best malt, kept tucked away in the sideboard in the front room, was his only malt. Apart from at Hogmanay, William MacMillan never drank at home. Like most Scottish families, however – even some of the teetotal ones – there was always a bottle of whisky in the house for special guests.

Adam had gracefully declined. Turning to Sadie, he had asked if his mother might have the pleasure of calling on her and her husband on Sunday afternoon. Sadie had more or less gone into a tail-spin, or, as Liz had put it to Helen, 'I thought she was going to have kittens.'

She and Mrs Crawford were spending most of today doing home baking and getting ready for tomorrow's visit. That solved one problem. Her mother wasn't going to find out Helen's second name. Not yet anyway. That was just as well. Liz was in enough trouble as it was.

Adam had barely driven away in Morag when her father had barked out an order.

'The front room, Elizabeth. Now. You've got some explaining to do, young lady.'

It had all come out. William MacMillan had listened to most of it in ominous silence. He had one question for his wife. Had she known that their daughter was attending Red Cross classes? On the point of rushing in to deny that on her mother's behalf, Liz had been astonished when Sadie had answered for herself,

120

admitting that she'd known all along about Liz's Tuesday night activities.

The expression on her father's face had been almost comical. He'd been so taken aback, especially when Sadie, screwing up her courage, had gone on to say that most people would think it was commendable that Lizzie wanted to do something to help other people.

Commendable. It wasn't one of her mother's words. Liz suspected she was repeating something Mrs Crawford had said. The unexpected rebellion on his wife's part had rather taken the wind out of William MacMillan's sails. He'd actually said something about waiting to see what Mrs Buchanan had to say. Liz couldn't quite believe that her father hadn't come down on her like a ton of bricks, locking her in her room on a diet of bread and water, perhaps. Hence the hysteria, she supposed. She might just be able to allow herself to hope.

In the meantime, two members of the Gallagher family were growing impatient. Helen was looking curious and Dominic put it into words.

'Come on, Liz. I want to hear the end of the story too.' Despite having grown up in an overwhelmingly male household, the youngest member of the Gallagher family had none of the usual embarrassment of the adolescent male in female company. Over the months since Liz had met Helen, he had quite simply adopted her as an extra big sister.

'You be quiet, Master Gallagher,' said Liz, pursuing her lips. She picked up the bandage roll and went to work on him. 'You're supposed to be unconscious, or suffering from a poison gas attack or something. Any more cheek and I'll bandage you up like Boris Karloff in *The Mummy*.'

'Do what you like,' said Dominic cheerfully. 'Only for Pete's sake tell us the rest of the story. Helen's going to explode of curiosity otherwise.'

Liz, feigning exasperation, let out a long and theatrical sigh.

'Well, if you absolutely insist . . .'

121

'We do, we do,' chorused brother and sister in unison. Liz laughed. She loved all this banter.

'Well . . . his name's Mario Rossi, his father owns the café near the Western and he's a medical student and a friend of Adam Buchanan. What else do you want to know?'

Helen winked at her brother.

'Well, was that fortune-teller we went to right? Is he tall, dark and handsome?'

'Yes,' admitted Liz reluctantly. 'Although not as tall as Adam.'

'Adam, is it? My, my, we are a fast worker.'

Liz gave a sigh of exasperation. 'Adam Buchanan is very nice – a really friendly chap. He's being so helpful to me over this VAD thing.'

Her friend pounced on the implicit admission.

'Ah-hah! So the other one was something more than nice. Tell us, does he have liquid brown eyes?'

'He does, as a matter of fact.' Extremely beautiful eyes, she thought, and a fantastic smile. It sort of flashed, dazzlingly white against his darker skin. And he had beautiful hands, too, his fingers slim but strong. Funny how she'd managed to notice all that although she'd spent only a few minutes in his company: not very long at all, actually.

Shortly after Mario Rossi's arrival at the café, Adam Buchanan had murmured something apologetic about time getting on. If Liz was worried about being home late, perhaps they should think of making a move?

Dominic, helpfully angling his elbow so that Liz could bandage around it, fluttered his eyes and tried for the soulful look.

'And did he look at you with longing in his beautiful brown eyes?'

'No, he did not,' said Liz crossly, pausing in her bandaging. 'He was friendly and jolly like Adam and he hopes that if I do become a VAD we'll meet up from time to time at the Infirmary. I'll probably volunteer to work there at the weekends if I get

122

into the Detachment. That's all. I think we could just be good friends.'

'Ah-hah!' said Helen. 'But that's what Mrs Simpson said about King Edward. And look what happened to them.'

'I shall treat that statement with the contempt it deserves,' said Liz grandly. 'Now, let's get on with bandaging this extremely obstreperous casualty. He seems to have sustained some nerve damage from a poison gas attack. Anyway,' she went on, applying herself anew to the task, 'nothing can come of it. His family's Italian, so he's bound to be a Cath—'

She had stopped herself in time. No she hadn't. Both Dominic and Helen were looking at her with pursed lips and pained expressions.

'Stop hiding your horns and tail, Dom,' said Helen in her driest tones. 'We'll need to bandage them too.'

'Och, Helen!' Liz frowned at her friend, annoyed that she might have offended her, especially after the bad feeling there had been between her and Eddie at the Empire Exhibition over the religious question. 'You know I don't think like that. But you also know what my father's like. That's all I meant. He'd kill me if I took a Catholic boy home.'

Janet Brown sauntered across the hall to them, throwing a laughing comment back over her shoulder.

'Lizzie MacMillan!' she boomed. 'That grandfather of yours is an old devil!'

'Why, what's he done?' Liz peered over Janet's shoulder. Her grandfather was on the opposite side of the hall, looking rather dashing with a bandage around his head. He waved to her and she waved back. Helen gave him a wave too. Peter MacMillan was fond of young people and shared none of his son's sectarian beliefs, and the two friends sometimes met at his house – especially when they wanted to get away from the noisy Gallagher household to have an intimate tête-à-tête.

'Asked me if I was winching,' laughed Janet. 'Said he could fill the gap if I was between boyfriends! I told him I was spoken for,' she said smugly, stretching out her arm so that she could

123

admire her engagement ring. She'd recently plighted her troth with a boy who was nearing the end of his apprenticeship in the sewing-machine factory.

'Mind you,' she said, dragging her eyes away from the tiny stone. 'At least he comes along and gives you his support, Liz. Unlike your brother. Off starting the revolution somewhere, is he?'

'Aye,' said Liz, 'something like that.' She had tentatively asked Eddie if he would reconsider his refusal to come along to the exercise and he had told her with a toss of his dark head that he would have nothing to do with the march towards war. Honestly, she was getting tired of his attitude.

Turning back to Dominic, her mouth open to ask Helen to hand her the scissors, she observed something very interesting. Helen Gallagher was blushing. That was the second time a mention of Eddie's name had provoked that particular reaction.

What had she just said? That her father would kill her if she took a Catholic boy home? Reverse the genders and the same would hold true for Eddie and Helen. Liz wondered if that was something else she needed to worry about. She also wondered if Helen's apparent feelings towards Eddie were reciprocated.

Somebody was tapping a tumbler with a piece of cutlery.

'If I could have your attention, please, ladies and gentlemen?' It was Mrs Galbraith, up on the stage at the end of the hall. As the hubbub subsided, she began explaining how the next part of the morning's programme was to be arranged.

'So that we can all get the maximum benefit from the exercise, I'd like the helpers to complete what they're doing and then form themselves into groups of six and we'll go round the casualties.'

She paused and smiled. 'To whom we all say a big thank you. After I've given you the say-so, please make your way to the canteen – through the door at the other end of the hall – where the ladies of the new Women's Voluntary Service have kindly agreed to serve soup, tea, coffee and home baking.'

An appreciative murmur ran through the assembled company. For most of them it was their first contact with the WVS. Newly formed, it was another response to the growing crisis in Europe and the imminent possibility of war.

The first-aiders toured the room. Bandages and splints were examined, mistakes pointed out and sometimes rectified by demonstration.

'Bear in mind, of course,' said Mrs Galbraith, who was leading Helen and Liz's group, 'that in the real thing the injured would very likely be confused, perhaps suffering temporary memory loss because of the shock. That also would be part of our job – to coax them out of it.'

'You can coax me any time,' said the next patient, a shameless twinkle in his piercing blue eyes.

'Behave yourself, Grandad,' murmured Liz.

Mrs Galbraith was ready for him. 'Please also bear in mind that real casualties wouldn't be half so cheeky as this lot.'

'Don't put money on it, lass,' said Peter MacMillan. She moved on to the next patient, once more doing her best to look stern, but clearly delighted that Peter MacMillan had addressed her as 'lass'.

The next casualties were a man and a woman lying next to each other on camp beds. Her leg had been put in a splint and he, like Peter MacMillan, had a bandage around his forehead. The bandage looked startlingly white against his thick dark hair. The two of them were chatting quietly to each other, oblivious to the approach of the stretcher party.

Many of the volunteer casualties were talking among themselves. What was different about this couple was the concentration they were giving to each other.

As Liz watched, the man lifted one hand and stroked a strand of the woman's chestnut-coloured hair behind her ear. The smile she gave him in response was very tender. They're in love, thought Liz. It was just like something you would see at the pictures. And they had to be nearly thirty years old . . .

Mrs Galbraith coughed. The pair on the camp beds turned

125

their faces up to the group, expressions of intelligent interest and readiness to be helpful on their faces.

Mrs Galbraith went through the imagined injuries and the way they had been dealt with, then smiled at the couple.

'Right then, once you've had the bandages removed, please do have something to eat. And thank you once again very much for coming, Mr and Mrs . . . ?'

'Baxter,' said the woman, smiling in response. 'And you're very welcome.' She looked at her husband. 'Aren't they, Robbie?'

'Oh, good grief,' said Liz. 'Whose brilliant idea was it to spread this over a whole day? We're going to be dead on our feet by the end of it and it's not even dinner-time yet.'

It had been decided that the volunteers should take their lunch breaks in two batches before returning for an afternoon session. Liz and Helen weren't due to be off duty until one o'clock, and it was only twelve now.

'What?'

Liz turned to Helen. She had made the oddest noise – something like a mouse's squeak. She was staring across the hall, watching the young man who had just appeared.

'Look what the cat dragged in.'

It was Eddie. He was making straight for them, a ferocious scowl on his pale and handsome face.

'Well?' he demanded as he reached the two girls. 'Where do you want me then?'

The question seemed to be addressed to Helen, so Liz let her answer it.

'Want you?' she asked, looking Eddie up and down. 'What would I want you for?' She was giving him back look for look, her arms, apparently casually, behind her back. It was a pity for her that Liz could see that she was clenching her fists.

'A volunteer casualty, of course,' growled Eddie. 'I thought you needed all the practice you could get.' He shrugged out of his jacket and looked around for somewhere to put it. Helen hadn't moved. Eddie looked at her from under his dark brows and sighed heavily.

'I can't stay long, I've got studying to do this afternoon. You can have me till one o'clock.'

Helen shifted position at last, lifting her eyebrows, a roll of bandages and a pair of scissors.

'We *are* honoured.'

Before he had time to retaliate she gave him his orders. 'Put your jacket over the back of that chair over there and sit down on this one.'

Eddie glowered at her.

'I never knew Hitler had Irish blood in him. You and he are obviously related. Adolf one of the traditional family names, is it?'

'Maybe I should bandage your mouth,' said Helen levelly as she approached him. 'It could do with a rest.'

Liz stifled a laugh. Not very successfully. As one, they both turned and glared at her. She went off to find Janet Brown. Somehow she felt it would be a good idea to leave Helen and Eddie to it.

One hour later, Helen Gallagher still had a rosy glow on her face, although Eddie was long gone. He had submitted to her ministrations, allowed her to deal with an imaginary broken arm, been examined and unbandaged and left, stiffly declining Mrs Galbraith's friendly offer of a cup of tea. Liz and Janet were studiously quiet at the meal break, speaking only when strictly necessary. Eventually, Helen couldn't stand it any longer, laying down her knife and fork.

'Well?' she demanded.

'Well what?' replied Liz, in a cloyingly sweet tone of voice. 'I've got absolutely nothing to say, Miss Gallagher. Nothing at all. Not a dickie bird.' She turned to Janet. 'Have you got anything to say, Janet?'

'No, Liz. I've got nothing to say either.'

Janet and Liz exchanged deliberately arch smiles. Helen's

expression was thunderous. Then it changed, her eyes sliding past them both to the door of the hall. It was her turn to have some fun.

'Oh, I think you might have something to say, Miss MacMillan,' she said, her voice as sweetie-sweetie as Liz's had been. 'That cat's having a busy day today. Look what it's dragged in now.'

'She's like the old Queen, that woman,' muttered Janet Brown as Amelia Buchanan swept into the hall. 'She knows how to make an entrance.'

Liz, however, was not so much struck by Mrs Buchanan's resemblance to Queen Mary as by the fact that what one could only call her entourage consisted of several white-coated medical students. It wasn't a great surprise to see that Adam Buchanan was one of them. The appearance of Mario Rossi at his shoulder was a different matter entirely.

Chapter 15

'Would you look at that?' hissed Janet. 'Is he God's gift to womankind, or what?'

'Close your mouth, Elizabeth dear,' said Helen. 'You'll catch flies. Oh look, he's coming over. Your description of him was excellent, by the way. I'd have known him anywhere.'

It was Liz's turn to make an inarticulate sound. Mario Rossi was indeed heading straight for her, closely followed by Adam Buchanan and the other medical students. Introductions were made and then Mrs Buchanan appeared, smiling at Liz, Helen and Janet.

'Whilst I understand the attraction, young gentlemen, there *are* other helpers in the hall – and many simulated injuries worthy of your attention. Miss MacMillan – I'm really looking forward to meeting your parents tomorrow. I do hope you'll be there too.'

She was aware of him for the rest of the afternoon: the dark good looks, the laughing eyes, the flashing smile, the way he was making everybody laugh. So what? He was a Roman Catholic. He was out of bounds.

Not to mention the fact that a man as good-looking as he was would never be interested in someone like her anyway. Liz had her good days, but she knew she wasn't a stunner like Helen.

However, when he spotted her leaving at the end of the exercise, Mario Rossi cut off a conversation with one of his medical student colleagues, and came running across the room to request, with surprisingly old-fashioned courtesy, if he might have the honour of walking her home.

Flabbergasted that he had asked, Liz opened her mouth to turn him down and heard herself saying yes instead.

It was about quarter to four, and the event was tailing off. Three of the Gallagher boys had already left. Only Conor had stayed, waiting to walk his sister home. Finn was at his side as usual, an intelligent look on his craggy face, ready for whatever his master required of him.

'That's a magnificent animal,' said Mario warmly.

Finn's proud owner preened visibly.

'Do you know something about dogs?' he asked, looking down at Mario, who was bent over – not very far, Finn being such a large dog – patting the shaggy grey head.

'Oh, aye,' said Mario, offering Finn the back of his hand to sniff. 'Back in the village where my family comes from – in Tuscany – we have a breed of hunting dogs not unlike this . . .'

The two young men were off, happily talking dogs until Helen coughed. 'Mr Rossi was about to walk Liz home, Conor.'

'Oh – I'll not hold you back then,' said Conor. 'You're Italian, then?'

'Aye,' said Mario, giving him a smile. 'Although my mother was Irish.'

Conor grinned hugely, his wide mouth filling the whole of his good-natured face. 'You'll have to come and visit us sometime. Our ma would love you. A good Catholic boy' – Conor paused, a question in his voice, and Mario nodded – 'and half-Irish into the bargain.'

Helen coughed again. Her brother obediently took his cue.

'Right then, I'll not hold you back. Liz's father will probably come out waving a string of garlic at you, mind,' he said to Mario. 'Don't go all the way with her.'

Then the big red-haired lad blushed scarlet, suddenly realising what else his words could mean. He stammered an apology which succeeded only in making Liz as embarrassed as he was. She was aware of all the faces around them: Helen,

Conor, Adam Buchanan. He was looking unusually serious. Somehow Mario Rossi managed to extract them from it. Soon they were out in the fresh air, heading down the road.

He made no reference at all to poor Conor's disastrous comment, chatting easily about other topics until Liz began to relax. In time the blush faded from her face and she began to feel able to give more than monosyllabic replies. She even managed to look at him from time to time. That was no hardship. He was real handsome.

Having met her the day before, she supposed he was walking her home out of some extravagant sense of courtesy. She'd heard that continentals could be like that. His father had certainly been a charmer.

He couldn't possibly fancy her – not someone like him. All the same, she was aware of a little thrill of excitement at having him walking by her side.

That didn't prevent her stopping some distance before they got to the corner of Dumbarton Road where she always turned off to go home. Mario Rossi stopped too, looking at her with polite curiosity.

'Is this where you live?'

'No,' she said. 'Our house is along a wee bit.' She waved vaguely in the direction of Queen Victoria Row. 'I'll be all right from here.'

'You don't want your parents to see me?'

'It's not that—' she began. She realised it was exactly that. 'I'm sorry,' she finished lamely. 'My father's very against Roman Catholics.' She dropped her eyes, not wanting to see the reproach in his.

'What about you?' came his voice from above her dipped head. 'Are you very against Catholics?'

She shook her head, embarrassed.

'My best friend's a Catholic. Helen. You met her back there at the exercise.'

'So does that mean you'd contemplate going out with a Catholic? To the pictures, maybe?'

She darted a nervous look up at him. Was he actually asking her out? She was flattered. Very flattered. Unfortunately she could think of two extremely good reasons for saying no.

Firstly, she had enough problems at the moment with her father. If Adam's mother did manage to persuade him tomorrow – please God, let her do that – she'd have to be careful not to give him any chance to change his mind. From now on, she couldn't afford to put a foot wrong.

Secondly, if her suspicions about Helen and Eddie's interest in each other were true, there was going to be enough trouble in the MacMillan family as it was. One mixed-religion romance was more than enough to be going on with.

And he had asked her to the pictures: to the cinema, with its soft, dark intimacy, a place where people held hands and kissed. After what Eric Mitchell had done to her yesterday – and before – she just wasn't ready for that yet. But it was her father's bigotry which made her turn him down.

'I'm sorry. I can't.'

'So you *are* prejudiced against Catholics?'

'No,' she denied, shaking her head, hating the note of wry resignation she could hear in his voice. 'No, I'm not, but it would cause me too many problems at home.'

He would go away now, wouldn't he? Only he didn't. He stood there gazing at her out of those soulful brown eyes. You could drown in those depths, thought Liz, carried away on an uncharacteristic flight of fancy.

She wondered how Mario Rossi would go about kissing a girl. Would he cup her face between those long-fingered hands before he bent his head to hers?

'W-well,' she stammered. 'I-I expect we'll see each other at the hospital when I start my VAD training. If Adam's mother manages to persuade my father, that is.'

Mario smiled a slow, lazy smile.

'Oh, she'll manage. She's a formidable lady, Mrs Buchanan.'

That smile did things to Liz. She hoped the effects weren't visible on the outside. She was horribly afraid that they were.

Mario, however, relaxed the intensity of his gaze and spoke briskly.

'Some of us are organising a trip to the Paul Robeson concert at the Empire Exhibition,' he told her. 'We thought it might be fun to go as a group and we're planning to hire a bus. That'll be cheaper the more participants we get, and we're going to drop people off as close to home as possible on the way back. Why don't you come with us? Bring your brother and your friend Helen, if you want,' he said easily.

Liz looked at him, undecided.

'Safety in numbers,' he suggested.

'Could Helen's brothers come?' she asked. 'They're all dead keen on music. And maybe my grandfather too?'

The dazzling smile flashed. 'Would you like me to get a ticket for the big dog as well?'

Aided and abetted by her son, Mrs Buchanan's arrival in Queen Victoria Row the next afternoon was a bit like a visit from royalty. Acting as her chauffeur, Adam handed her out of the car as though she really were Queen Mary. The effect on William and Sadie – and the rest of the street, watching from behind the lace curtains as usual – was not at all marred by the huge wink he gave Liz behind everyone else's back.

Liz's father was completely overawed. Amelia Buchanan's task was easy. Liz wondered how much Adam had told her. Perhaps it was her own desire to gain as many recruits as possible for her beloved Red Cross which did the trick.

In less time than Liz could have believed, Mrs Buchanan had done the impossible: the form giving parental permission for his daughter to join the Voluntary Aid Detachment as a nursing auxiliary was signed. Liz was bubbling over with excitement.

With unerring instinct, Amelia had appealed to William MacMillan's snobbery.

'We do get a very superior class of girl in the VADs, Mr MacMillan, I can assure you of that. A very *nice* type of young woman. And Elizabeth would be making her contribution without having to leave home.'

She launched into a great exposition of the plan of action *should the worst come to the worst* – that phrase again. There were plans, she told them, to evacuate children from industrial areas, and the manning – or more probably *womaning*, as she put it with a winning smile – of first aid posts.

'And of course, VADs could prove very useful in freeing trained and experienced nurses for field hospitals and the like. We all hope it won't come to that, of course, but we do have to be ready for every eventuality.'

By the time she began drinking the first of two cups of tea, taking time out to compliment Sadie on her 'absolutely delicious fruit loaf, Mrs MacMillan, you must let me have the recipe', Liz's father was nodding sagely, agreeing with all the points which his charming guest was making.

By the time she had finished with him, he was ready to take on Hitler in single combat.

Both Liz and her parents saw the Buchanans to the door when they left. Going on ahead down the short garden path, Adam held the gate open for Liz to go through in front of him. He glanced back at his mother, still on the doorstep saying her farewells to William and Sadie.

'It's the British disease,' he observed. 'An inability to say cheerio and just go. You see it all the time.'

Liz beamed at him, and on a wild impulse stretched up and kissed him on the cheek. If it hadn't been for his kindness none of this would have happened. His arm came round her for a second, his hand resting lightly on her back. It was dropped almost as quickly as it had been raised, and he took a step back, looking down at Liz with a quizzical air.

'Unhand me, woman. What was that for?'

'To say thank you,' she said happily. 'For what you've done for me.'

'Any time, Liz. Any time at all.' He moved towards the kerb where Morag was parked. 'I hear you're coming to the Paul Robeson concert with us.'

She nodded.

'Did Mario ask you?'

'Yes,' she answered, thinking that it was a strange question. He must have known it was Mario who had asked her.

He looked over her head. She liked his height. It made her feel dainty, not a sensation often experienced by a girl of five foot six who lived in Clydebank and worked in Glasgow.

'They're still at it. How long can it take to say goodbye, I wonder?'

Before she could answer, he posed another question – one which made her immediately uncomfortable.

'Liz, you are sure there's nothing troubling you at Murray's, aren't you? I'd be more than happy to speak to my uncle, as I told you on Friday. Only if you want me to, of course.'

'There's nothing,' she said quickly.

'The thing is,' he said, 'sometimes it can help to face up to something – or someone – that's bothering you. Simply show them you're not prepared to put up with it any more. Not rudely, of course.' He smiled. 'Not in a way that might get you into more trouble. But firm and definite, all the same.'

Suddenly she realised what he was getting at. Having witnessed her ticking-off from Miss Gilchrist, he thought that was her problem – that his uncle's secretary was bullying her.

'It takes quite a bit of guts to do it, but I reckon that's not a problem for a girl like you.' His voice changed, became louder and less intimate. 'Ah, Mother, here you are at last! Liz and I were thinking we might have time to read *War and Peace* while we were waiting for you.'

'Impudent young pup!' said Amelia Buchanan, flicking an elegant hand at her son. 'The cheek I have to endure from him, Miss MacMillan. You've no idea.'

Adam had been wrong about the source of her troubles at Murray's, but his words stayed with her for the rest of Sunday all the same. It had been an eventful weekend, allowing her to

135

put what had happened on Friday afternoon to the back of her mind.

It all came rushing back as Liz got ready for bed on Sunday evening. Despite all the good things which had happened, she realised with a sinking heart that she still had to face him the following morning – and a lot more mornings to come.

Could Adam possibly be right? Was it a matter of standing up to Eric Mitchell, telling him that she wasn't prepared to put up with his behaviour any more? Lying in bed before she went to sleep, Liz thought of that horrible hand on her breast, at the way he'd forced her to feel his body. The remembered sensations made her shudder.

It had been bad enough before, when he had brushed his hand against her leg or put an unwelcome arm around her shoulders. Friday had been much, much worse. It had to stop.

Chapter 16

In the cold light of Monday morning, Liz's determination to square up to Eric Mitchell seemed an awful lot shakier. If she was going to do it, she'd have to get him on his own. That meant actively seeking him out, watching his movements as carefully as she'd ever done, only this time not because she was trying to avoid being alone with him. This time she would have to steel herself to do the opposite.

That was scary. Her going looking for him might make him think she wanted what he had done to her on Friday afternoon. But if she let it go again, he'd think he could keep on molesting her.

It took Liz two days to summon up the courage to confront him, and in the end it wasn't for her own sake that she spoke, but for someone else's: the new girl who was getting a start that week to be trained up as a junior shorthand-typist. She was a shy little thing, but bright with it. By lunchtime on her first day, Liz had learned that she lived in the Gorbals, the eldest child of a large family.

She confided to Liz that she and her parents were tickled pink that she had landed the job at Murray's. Not only was her small wage going to make a big difference at home, everyone was delighted that she was in a job where she was going to have the chance to go on to better things.

Keeping a close eye on Eric Mitchell's movements on Monday afternoon, Liz saw him go across to the young girl and lay a hand on her shoulder. He was doing the kindly bit, telling her how the outgoing mail should be dealt with. Liz could see that the new recruit was trying desperately not to shrink away from him.

Liz wondered if the female of the species was born knowing the difference between a genuinely friendly touch – like the way Adam Buchanan had put his arm around her on Sunday afternoon – and the other sort. If not, it was certainly a skill you learned early on in life.

Eric Mitchell's pestering over the last two years had affected her own response even to a friendly touch, not to mention the kind which went – willingly – a bit beyond friendship. An image of Mario Rossi flitted across her mind's eye.

Liz took a deep breath. She couldn't let the new girl suffer as she had. Adam Buchanan thought she had guts. Maybe this was the time to prove it.

It was late on Wednesday afternoon before she managed to get Mitchell on his own. Everyone else was out of the office on various duties and errands.

Getting up from her desk took an enormous effort of will, as did crossing the room towards him. He glanced up as she approached, and Liz could see that he was surprised. First point to her. She stood in front of his desk and spoke without preamble.

'What happened on Friday afternoon – there won't be any repeat of it. And you'll leave the new lassie alone as well. She's not to be bothered.'

He pushed his chair away from the desk, tilting it so that only the two back legs were on the floor.

'Really, Lizzie? Might I ask how you propose to stop me?'

How she hated him! He sprawled back in his chair, and his cold eyes roamed over her body, lingering quite deliberately on the swell of her breasts.

'I'll speak to Mr Murray.'

I mustn't sound angry, she thought, resisting the impulse to fold her arms protectively over her bosom. She had to appear cool and relaxed, even a little amused.

'After all,' she said, trying to emulate Adam's elegant drawl, 'his sister did have tea with my parents last weekend.'

That surprised him. She could see it in his horrible pasty face. Liz pressed her advantage.

'And I've got friendly with his nephew too. We're on first-name terms now. You heard him on Friday – we keep bumping into each other all over the place.'

'He giving you one, is he?'

She managed not to shudder in distaste. *Don't react to it, that's what he wants you to do. Keep cool and keep the heid.*

'I rather think that he and the Honourable Miss MacIntyre are walking out together. Not that it's anyone's business but their own.'

Eric Mitchell tilted his head back. 'Ah, but you know what toffs are like, Lizzie. They've got the morals of alley cats.'

'You're one to talk.'

He slammed forward on the chair, startling her. As the two front legs hit the floor he got up and came to stand in front of her. Right in front of her.

'Perhaps he fancies the both of you,' he said softly. His face was only inches from her own. 'At the same time, even. Pretty perverted, the upper classes. Or maybe he wants to watch the two of you together first.'

Innocent as she was, it took a minute or two for the penny to drop on that one. When it did, she took an involuntary step back from him.

'You're disgusting!'

He smiled his horrible smile. 'I've got some very interesting literature at home I could let you see. More in the way of photographs, actually. Hidden from the little woman, naturally. My wife doesn't like that sort of thing, but you might, Lizzie. I'd be more than happy to show them to you.'

His cold, hateful eyes reminded her of those of a dead fish on a marble slab. 'I certainly wouldn't blame young Mr Buchanan if he couldn't control himself around you. Any man might have the same problem.' His eyes dropped to her mouth. 'Little prick-tease,' he murmured.

That was it, *that was it*.

'Your mind's really in the gutter, isn't it?'

Trembling with fury, she took another step back, putting some space between them. To hell with not getting angry with him.

'I won't listen to any more of this. I'm not prepared for you to speak to me in that way. Ever again. Or the new lassie either.'

'Going to run to Mr Murray, are you? Or his relatives that you're so palsy-walsy with all of a sudden? That's very clever, little Lizzie, ingratiating yourself with the boss and his family. Going to become a part-time nurse, I hear. Should be right up your street. Angels of mercy? Tarts, more like.'

If it hadn't been so pathetic it would have been laughable. He had no idea – no idea about anything.

'Yes,' she said simply. 'If you try anything else either with me or with the new girl, I'll go to Mr Murray. Without asking Miss Gilchrist first. And if that fails, I've got a friend who has three extremely large brothers. All good men in a fight, I understand.'

That was pure invention, the idea popping into her head from nowhere. She wouldn't dream of inciting someone to commit violence. Fear of possible fisticuffs had, after all, been the reason why she hadn't told her own brother about Mitchell long before now.

'You accommodating all three of them too?'

He was still sneering, but she had rattled him. She could see it in his face. She felt a sudden odd little spurt of energy.

She wasn't sure if Adam was right about her having guts, but she did know she was experiencing a new-found confidence, a sense that she could do anything she set her mind to. She was going to become a VAD, and she was going to stop Eric Mitchell in his tracks. Right now.

It was the threat of physical violence which had tipped the scales in her favour. In which case she might as well be hung for a sheep as a lamb.

'How long do you think you'd last here if I let it be known

how you've molested me over the past two years? Or if you came in to work with a black eye after having been in a brawl? I daresay I could arrange for that sort of thing to happen quite frequently.'

Bloody hell, where had that come from? She sounded like some sort of gangster's moll out of a third-rate American film. Lizzie MacMillan, tough-talking broad. Just as long as he didn't notice how nervous she still was, even at this stage in the game.

It was a wee touch melodramatic. *Interfere with me again and I'll summon my henchmen.* Oh, come on. Could he really be that stupid? She looked into his eyes and realised that he could. It was hard not to let the elation show on her face.

The door of the inner office opened. Miss Gilchrist peered at them both.

'Is there a problem?'

Liz turned towards her, her head high, graceful as a queen.

'No, Miss Gilchrist, there's not a problem. Mr Mitchell and I have just succeeded in resolving one. Haven't we, Mr Mitchell?'

'So not only have I sorted Eric Mitchell out – he really backed down when I threatened him with your lot – I'm also going to get to become a VAD. Isn't it wonderful?'

'Wonderful,' agreed Helen. 'I'm so pleased for you, Liz.' She had been aghast when Liz had given her the details of her conversation with the chief clerk.

'The slimy creep! Imagine him having the sheer brass neck' – she paused, searching for the right word – 'the . . . the effrontery to say disgusting things like that to a respectable girl like you. I'm proud of you for standing up to him, Liz. I really am. The boys would be perfectly willing to teach him a lesson.' Helen's pretty mouth settled into a determined line. 'I know they would. You'd only have to ask. They all like you, you know.'

'I wouldn't ask them,' said Liz. 'Not really.' She stretched out an impulsive hand to touch Helen's arm. 'But it's great to know that I've got such good friends.'

141

'Likewise, I'm sure,' said Helen, mimicking the Cockney charlady who'd been one of the characters in a film they'd recently seen. Her indignation vanishing, she put her elbows on the table and rested her chin on her clasped hands.

I wouldn't be at all surprised if Eddie does fancy her, thought Liz. Not only is she pretty, she's so sweet-natured too – honest and fierce and loyal and funny.

'So,' Helen asked, 'when do you start your training, will you and Janet do it together and – much more importantly – what's the uniform like?'

Liz laughed. 'Quite flattering, actually. Apart from the length of the dress.'

'Several inches too long?'

'How did you guess?'

'Well, they couldn't run the risk of any of the nice young doctors catching a glimpse of your knees. Or the patients. It might drive them wild with desire.'

Liz laughed again. 'But it is a very nice shade of blue. The coat and hat are darker, navy blue really. Very smart and neat, both of them.'

'And you'll wear a nurse's apron over the dress? And a cap?' asked Helen.

Liz nodded. 'Aye. The apron has a big red cross on the bib and the cap has a smaller one. And we wear an armband as well, to tell the world that we're VADs and belong to the Red Cross. And both Janet and I should start our training sometime in the new year. Probably the end of January, Mrs Buchanan says. It seems like ages away.'

'It'll pass soon enough,' said Helen. 'Will you need to ask off work for it?'

Liz shook her head. 'No. It'll be done over several weekends at one of the hospitals. That's why there's a delay. They can only take so many of us at a time. I hope we both get sent to the Western.'

'Won't that be automatic? Seeing as how you're from Clydebank?'

Liz shook her head. 'Apparently not. It might be the Victoria, or the Royal.'

'I suppose they're good hospitals too, Liz.'

'I'm sure they're great hospitals,' she said warmly. 'But I'd feel more at home at the Western.'

While Clydebank was well served by several highly respected small local hospitals, it was to the Western you always went for serious emergencies and more major ailments. Like the other big teaching hospitals, it was dependent for its income on freely given donations. The people who lived in the areas served by them raised money for those by holding regular dances and sales of work.

Donations also came from businesses, trade guilds, professional associations and charitable institutions, hence Cordelia MacIntyre's reference to the begging bowl the day she and Adam had come to Murray's. As Liz had subsequently discovered, Alasdair Murray was a regular contributor to hospital funds. Miss MacIntyre herself was one of the Infirmary's volunteer fund-raisers.

'Well, I'll keep my fingers crossed,' said Helen. 'Do you know what the training will be like?'

'Lectures and some practical stuff and then I'm inclined to think we're going to be thrown in at the deep end.'

'On the wards?' Helen asked. 'With real, living, breathing patients?'

Liz grinned at her affectionate sarcasm, opening her eyes wide in mock alarm.

'Apparently. I only hope the patients are still living and breathing after they've had me looking after them for a while.'

'Och, you! You'll be good at it. I know you will.'

'I hope so. I certainly intend to do my best – even if I am in with a crowd of bourgeois young ladies playing at nursing!'

Helen shook her head. 'Elizabeth MacMillan, sometimes you sound just like your brother.'

'Oh?' asked Liz innocently. 'And is that such a bad thing?'

There was a pause. Then Helen resolutely changed the

subject. Liz let it drop. It wasn't fair to tease her about it. Helen and Eddie might well be attracted to each other, but encouraging the relationship wasn't doing them any favours. Liz couldn't imagine that either set of parents would be exactly over the moon if a romance did develop.

September arrived, and with it the end of the brief dry spell they had enjoyed during August. The rain which had characterised the whole of the summer of 1938 was back with a vengeance. The wet weather made one of the year's hit songs – 'September in the Rain' – all too appropriate.

Everybody was singing it – while they slipped and slid on the real leaves of brown which came tumbling down and turned into a sludgy mass on the wet pavements quicker than they could be swept up. The party going to the Paul Robeson concert sang it on the hired bus on the way over to Bellahouston. Adam Buchanan and Mario Rossi, carried away by an attack of high spirits, sat next to each other and belted it out crooner-style, stroking imaginary moustaches and giving all the girls ludicrous come-hither looks. Peter MacMillan, in his element among the young people, laughed uproariously at them.

As they filed into the concert hall, Liz noticed the lengths to which Eddie and Helen went in order to avoid sitting next to each other. She also noticed the way the two of them looked at each other when they thought they were unobserved. Oh, dear. Ought she to help them out after all?

Without quite knowing how she had managed it, Liz herself ended up between Adam and Mario. She felt more than a little awkward about that, especially as Cordelia MacIntyre was sitting next to Mario rather than Adam.

When the great singer took to the stage, she forgot it all in the sheer pleasure of listening to his magnificent voice. He sang all the numbers for which he was best known: 'Ol' Man River', 'Swing Low, Sweet Chariot', 'Curly-Headed Baby'. He further delighted his audience by singing a couple of Scottish songs, even managing one in Gaelic. Entranced, impressed and complimented, his listeners almost clapped their hands off at the end of that one.

One song was new to Liz: the ballad of 'Joe Hill'. Listening attentively to the words, she decided that it was terrific. It told the story of an American trade union leader who'd been framed for murder because he was causing the bosses too much trouble.

Although he'd been executed for the crime he did not commit, the message of the song was that they hadn't been able to kill his fighting spirit: *Where working men defend their rights, that's where you'll find Joe Hill . . .*

Glancing along the row of seats when the song was finished, joining in the rapturous applause, she caught Eddie's eye.

'Wasn't that great?' she mouthed over the noise of hundreds of hands clapping. Her brother gave her the thumbs-up. He'd loved the defiant song too.

At the interval, Adam asked Liz if she would like an ice-cream. Leaning forward, he looked along the row and extended the invitation to Cordelia and Mario as well.

'I'll come and help you carry them, shall I?' asked Liz, hurriedly rising to her feet. Most people had already shuffled out and were heading for the foyer. Except Mario Rossi. Leaning back comfortably in his seat, he clearly had no intention of moving during the interval.

'No need for that,' said Cordelia with a smile. 'I'll go. You stay here and chat to Mario.'

She meant to be friendly, Liz supposed. The only trouble was that the last thing in the world she wanted to do was stay here and chat to Mario Rossi. And he knew it. She could see the amusement in his eyes, along with something else she couldn't quite interpret. Whatever it was, it was making her very uncomfortable. Liz tried desperately to think of something to say, but her mind seemed to have gone a complete blank.

'Are you enjoying the concert?'

'It's marvellous,' she said, momentarily forgetting her awkwardness in her enthusiasm. 'He has a wonderful voice.

Thank you very much for asking me.'

'I asked you something else, too,' he said quietly. 'Any chance that you've changed your mind about saying no?'

Liz dropped her eyes. 'I'm sorry. I can't.'

'Pity,' he said. His voice was light, but when Liz darted a glance up at him she saw that all trace of amusement had vanished from his eyes. They looked almost bleak. Without taking them off her face, he gestured with his head towards the stage.

'He does have a wonderful voice, doesn't he?'

She nodded. There was no doubt about that.

'One of the greatest singers in the world today, in fact,' Mario went on. 'Wouldn't you say?'

Liz nodded again.

'Yet they had difficulty finding a hotel prepared to take him.' He paused briefly. 'Because he's a negro.'

'That's terrible,' cried Liz, genuinely shocked. 'What does it matter what colour he is?'

She had walked right into it. The smile which curved Mario's mouth was a bitter one, and it didn't reach his eyes.

'Prejudice *is* a terrible thing, isn't it?' He held her gaze for a few unforgiving seconds, then glanced over his shoulder.

'Ah. Here come Cordelia and Adam with our ice-creams.'

The following Sunday afternoon, Liz popped her head round the door of Eddie's bedroom. She found him bent over the table under the window where he did his studying.

'Am I disturbing you?'

'No,' he said, turning and greeting her with a smile. 'Come in. I'm needing a break. I thought you'd gone up to the Holy City.'

'I'm about to go now,' she answered, perching on the end of his bed. 'I wondered if you might like to come with me. Have a break from your swotting.'

'Och, well, Liz, I'm not sure. I've got an essay to finish for Tuesday . . .' His voice trailed off, and he blushed.

Liz stood up.

'Oh well, then. It's just that one of Helen's brothers is really interested in politics. Conor,' she went on briskly. 'He was at the concert and the Red Cross exercise. The one with the big dog?'

Eddie nodded. Liz moved towards the door of the bedroom.

'He's an anarchist, he says. What with you being a communist, I thought you might enjoy a discussion with each other.'

Why was she encouraging this? The answer came winging back to her. Because she had seen the way they looked at each other, because she loved them both, because they were so obviously made for each other. What did it matter what religion they were? Mario Rossi would never know how much she agreed with him.

'But if you haven't got the time, Eddie . . .'

Liz smiled regretfully. She ought to be in pictures. And she had given him a legitimate excuse to visit the Gallaghers. It took him five seconds to close his books and follow her.

Edward MacMillan and Conor Gallagher went at it hammer and tongs for a good forty minutes, putting the world to rights according to their own respective political philosophies. They covered it all: the current crisis and what had caused it, appeasement, the rise of the Nazis in Germany, the civil war in Spain, the inadequacies of the current British government, the Irish Question.

On some points they were in agreement, on others they argued from diametrically opposed points of view. Inevitably, the discussion came back to the crisis in Czechoslovakia.

'But people say that the Sudeten Germans have been persecuted by the Czechs,' said Conor. 'That they want to be part of Germany.'

'If Hitler takes the Sudetenland, he'll take the rest of Czechoslovakia,' insisted Eddie. 'And he'll not stop there.'

Brendan Gallagher, tolerant by nature, eventually called time on the two young men. 'Enough! Let's have some music.'

Eddie joined in enthusiastically with the songs, especially when it came to the Irish republican ones. Any louder, thought Liz, and we'll all get arrested for treasonable behaviour.

Then the Gallagher lads, who had clubbed together to buy a Paul Robeson songbook at the concert, performed some of the songs they'd heard. Joe had the deepest voice, so he sang 'Ol' Man River'. Then Danny, Conor and Dominic gave the assembled company 'Swing Low, Sweet Chariot'. After they had finished, Helen stood up to sing.

At first she sang her party piece, the hauntingly beautiful 'She Moved Through the Fair'. She really had a lovely voice, sweet but strong, surprisingly low-pitched and mellow.

> *She said this to me,*
> *And then she did say,*
> *It will not be long, love,*
> *Till our wedding day.*

Conor nudged Liz's elbow. With a discreet lift of his head he indicated that she should look at Eddie, who was sitting on the opposite side of the room from them. Leaning forward, his chin propped on his fist, he was giving Helen his complete attention, his serious grey eyes fixed intently on her.

'We heard this song at the Paul Robeson concert, too,' Helen told her parents. She didn't look at Eddie, but as soon as Liz heard the first line, she knew that Helen was singing it for him.

> *I dreamed I saw Joe Hill last night,*
> *Alive as you or I,*
> *But Joe, said I, you're ten years dead,*
> *Said Joe, I didn't die . . .*

If Eddie had looked entranced before, he looked completely moonstruck now. Any doubts Liz had had vanished at that

148

moment. Helen's growing feelings for her brother were fully reciprocated.

Chapter 17

A few days later, Liz walked up to Radnor Street. She had arranged to meet Helen there. She took the brown georgette dress with her. Having made sure she arrived before her friend, she asked Peter MacMillan for a coat hanger, took the dress out of the Copland & Lye bag and hung it on the back of the door.

Coming through that same door ten minutes later, Miss Gallagher guessed immediately that something was up. She'd often told Liz that she was no good at either telling lies or keeping a secret. It always showed on her face. Peter MacMillan was smiling broadly, happy to be party to the plot. That helped give the game away too.

Looking around for it, whatever it was, Helen spotted the dress.

'Oh no, Liz. I've told you. When I've got the money to pay you for it. Not before.'

'Phooey! I don't want a penny piece for it, and you know that fine well, Helen Gallagher.'

Helen started shaking her fair head, but Liz waltzed over to the door, lifted the dress down and held it against her, pushing her over to stand in front of the small mirror which hung on the wall opposite the range.

'Look,' she said, 'you can only see your top half, but even at that you can see how much it suits you. Don't you think so, Grandad?'

'I do.' He smiled fondly at the two girls. 'It's the right shade for your colouring, lass,' he said to Helen.

'I never knew you were a fashion expert, Mr MacMillan. Did she put you up to this?' she asked, glancing at Liz in the mirror.

'Who's she? The cat's mother?' Liz replied sweetly. 'Grandad's got eyes like the rest of us. He can see that the dress is all wrong for me and all right for you. Isn't that right, Grandad?' she asked, spinning herself and Helen round to face him.

'Absolutely, pet.' He smiled at Helen. 'Hen, you're a wee smasher whatever you wear, but you'll be a right bobby-dazzler in yon frock.'

Liz could sense Helen's resolve weakening. Time to wheel out the big guns. She spun them both round once more to the mirror.

'You could go to the dancing if you had it.'

'Mmm,' murmured Helen, as noncommittal as possible.

'My brother Eddie's a good dancer, you know.'

Helen gave their combined reflections one of her stern looks.

'Oh, really? How terribly fascinating. Although I can't imagine why you think that piece of information should interest me.'

Liz could be arch too. 'Can't you? You know, for an intelligent woman you can be very stupid sometimes.'

The wireless was on when Liz got home. She could hear the strains of dance music as she walked up the front path. Lifting the brass door knocker, shaped like a lion's head, she gave it three sharp raps.

She should really have a key, but her father had decreed that she had to wait until she was twenty-one. Eddie had been given his own key when he had started at the Uni at the age of seventeen. He was a boy, of course. That made all the difference as far as her father was concerned.

She heard her mother's footsteps approaching from the other side of the door. Sadie MacMillan swung it open, her face alive with animation.

'Och, Lizzie,' she cried, seizing her daughter by the arm to pull her into the lobby, 'come away ben to the kitchen. We're having a right laugh!'

In the kitchen Liz found Eddie steering Mrs Crawford round the linoleum floor, the square table pushed back against the sink and the window which overlooked the back garden. She was laughing and protesting, but obviously enjoying herself.

'Here's your sister,' she called out. 'You'd be better dancing with her than with an old woman like me.'

'Not at all, Mrs C,' said Eddie gallantly. He put on a terrible French accent. 'It eez you for who my 'art she beat faster – not my leetle seester – lovely though she eez.'

He threw a grin at Liz. She returned it. It was good to see him playing the fool.

Mrs Crawford snorted with mirth, pushed Eddie away and collapsed on to one of the kitchen chairs, laughing and putting her hand to her bosom. It was heaving with exertion and amusement, straining the buttons of her flowery print blouse.

'I'd better sit down before I fall down!' She laughed up at Sadie MacMillan. Then she looked at Liz.

'Well, Lizzie, did you not get a lumber tonight?'

Liz took off her hat and coat, laughing. She liked Annie Crawford. She might be the wife of one of the senior managers but she was really down to earth.

'Hardly, Mrs Crawford, I was up at my grandfather's this evening – although we were dancing, right enough. A friend of mine who lives nearby came round and we were teaching ourselves how to do the Lambeth Walk.'

Liz smiled at the memory. After she'd persuaded Helen to accept the dress, the two of them had ended up in a fit of the giggles when they had tried to work out how to do the steps of the year's dance craze from diagrams on the back of some sheet music.

Peter MacMillan had joined in with the impromptu dance class, causing even more hilarity, exacerbated by the difficulties of trying to do a dance which involved lots of walking steps in such a small kitchen.

Excusing herself for a moment, Liz went out to the lobby to hang up her coat and hat. Eddie followed her out.

'Did you have a nice evening, Liz?'

'Yes thanks.'

'How's Grandad?'

'He's fine.'

'Good . . . I'm glad to hear it . . .'

She wasn't cruel enough to keep him dangling any longer. 'Don't you really want to know how Helen is, Eddie?'

His mouth twisted wryly.

'Is it that obvious?'

'Every time you look at each other,' Liz said softly. 'Did the two of you think I was blind?'

He continued to look ruefully at her. Then realisation dawned.

'You just asked if the two of us—' He broke off, obviously arrested by the thought.

Liz nodded encouragingly. He'd get there in a minute. He got there in three seconds.

'You really think she likes me?'

'I know she does.'

Watching the happiness spread over his face, Liz thought about how she had wrestled with herself over encouraging this romance. Oh God, the two of them had a rough and rocky road ahead of them, but she knew one thing. It was going to happen whether she helped it along or not. Eddie's grey eyes were sparkling like silver.

'What does she say about me?'

'That's for me to know and for you to find out. But I've made her take my georgette dress so she can go to the dancing. She'll maybe be needing a partner. Do you think?'

Eddie's smile was cautious. Liz poked him in the chest.

'Ask her out, you great numpty.'

He grinned at the affectionate insult, but then his smile faded.

Standing in the lobby looking at his sister, he sighed and ran a hand through his dark locks.

'She and I – well, we haven't exactly got off to a very good start, have we? Every time we meet the sparks seem to fly.'

'And does that not tell you something, Eddie? Ask her out,' she said again.

'I'm scared she'll say no, Liz,' he confessed.

'She'll not say no.'

Eddie's grin spread from ear to ear. Liz put a hand on his arm.

'Promise me one thing. When you go out with her, try to restrain yourself from banging on about religion being the opium of the masses, and don't talk to her like you're addressing a political meeting.'

He had the grace to look sheepish.

'I'll do my best. How about if I ask her to go dancing at the weekend? You could come too, Liz.'

She guessed that the invitation had been issued on a surge of affection for her. That gave her a nice warm feeling. It didn't mean she was going to accept.

'No thanks,' she said briskly. 'I'll paddle my own canoe if you two start going out together. I have absolutely no desire to play gooseberry, brother dear.'

'Well,' he said enthusiastically, 'why don't you and I have a wee dance now?' Grabbing her hand, he waltzed her back into the kitchen. 'Pretend I'm about to ask you up on to the floor,' he murmured. 'Ma's been having a good laugh this evening. Let's keep it going a bit longer.'

Throwing herself into the role, Liz stood leaning against the kitchen wall, arms folded, adopting an air of boredom. Eddie swaggered up to her. The two older women, seated now at the kitchen table, leaned forward in anticipation.

'Hi, gorgeous,' said Eddie. 'Where have you been all my life?'

Liz looked him up and down without speaking, the picture of contemptuous young west-of-Scotland womanhood.

'D'ye come here often?' asked the eager young man.

'Only in the mating season,' replied Liz, lifting her hand and pretending to examine her nails.

Mrs Crawford laughed.

'Are ye dancing?' Eddie said.

Liz gave him the traditional reply.

'Are ye asking?'

'I'm asking.'

'Then I'm dancing.'

They kept up the patter as he birled her around the floor. 'Could I see you home after this wee soirée?' He gave it the local pronunciation – *swarry*.

'Aye,' said Liz, exaggerating her accent. 'Why no'?'

'Where d'ye live, doll?' he asked.

Sadie chuckled.

'Helensburgh,' said Liz, naming the resort town on the Firth of Clyde, thirty miles away down the river.

Her swain let go of her abruptly.

'Helensburgh! It's no' a lumber you need, hen.' Eddie paused for effect before delivering the punch-line. 'It's a pen-pal.'

Mrs Crawford gave a great hoot of laughter. The upright chair in which she sat creaked in protest as she leaned back.

'Oh dear,' she said, wiping her eyes. 'That pair should be on stage at the Glasgow Empire, Sadie. I haven't laughed so much in ages!'

'Will you have another wee cup of tea, Annie?' Sadie was beaming, basking in the praise of her beloved children.

Liz and Eddie exchanged a private smile. Then Eddie, one ear cocked to the wireless, grabbed his sister's hand again.

'It's the tango. Come on, Liz!'

They danced cheek to cheek, exaggerating the movements and turns. Eddie, playing the Latin lover to perfection, swung Liz back over his arm at the appropriate moments. Brother and sister gave each other smouldering glances all the while, until they couldn't keep it up any longer and could hardly dance for laughing.

155

The next day it was announced on the wireless that the Prime Minister had flown to Germany for crisis talks with Herr Hitler about the Czechoslovakian situation.

Neville Chamberlain made three separate visits to Germany during the last fortnight of September 1938, during which period it felt like the whole country was holding its breath. At the same time, feverish activity was going on. Defensive trenches were dug in Britain's towns and cities, plans for evacuating children from the industrial areas were scrutinised and the promised gas masks finally appeared.

Some folk took one look and said they just couldn't. They would feel as if they were choking and the smell of the rubber would make them feel sick.

Liz could see what they meant. The masks had a sinister appearance which gave everyone the heebie-jeebies. Their very existence was depressing, making the threat which had hung over the country all summer that much more real. How awful that one civilised European country was actually contemplating releasing such a terrible weapon upon another.

Children were to have their own versions of the respirators, known as Mickey Mouse masks. It was recommended that mothers play a short game with their children each day to get them used to putting on the claustrophobic devices. There was some concern over how babies were to be protected, and there were no respirators for cats or dogs.

The atmosphere was curious: a mixture of ill-concealed nervousness, gallows humour and a feeling of something like relief that the threatened showdown with Germany might be happening at last.

Clydebank appreciated the seriousness of the situation – if it hadn't done so before – when it was deemed impossible for the King to come north to launch the new liner waiting to go into the river at John Brown's. Fortunately it was considered that his wife might be spared, although the launch was a low-key affair. The Queen gave the new ship her own – and Liz's – name.

'They'll not be able to bomb us,' some folk said, trying to reassure themselves and others. 'We're too far away. Their planes would never be able to carry enough fuel. And how would they find the Clyde among all the other rivers and lochs on the west coast? I feel sorry for the Londoners, though. Germany's only a hop, skip and a jump away from them. And London's that big ye cannae miss it.'

Hundreds of thousands of Britons decided in the last fortnight of September 1938 that it was high time they made their wills. Tam Simpson was one of them. His wife went her dinger about that.

'A will! He thinks he should write his will!'

'You don't think it's a good idea, Mrs Simpson?' asked Helen.

'He's got nothing to leave, pet. Apart from a few empty whisky bottles, that is.' Nan curled her lip. 'That's what I said to him. And do you know what he said to me? Do you know what Thomas Simpson had the black effrontery to say to me?'

Helen shook her head. The conversation was ostensibly between her and Tam's aggrieved wife, but everybody was listening in. Behind Nan's head, Liz and Janet were making apologetic faces at Helen, thankful that the older woman had caught her and not them. The tirade had been going on for some time.

'What did he say, Mrs Simpson?' asked Helen politely.

'He said he wants to leave me and the weans comfortable if he gets bombed. So, says I to him, we've never been comfortable afore. Why should it bother you now? Especially if you're deid? If you get bombed, says I, we'll probably a' get bombed tae. None o' us'll be very bloody comfortable then. Sure we'll no', hen?'

She paused for breath, looking to Helen for confirmation.

'Probably not,' she obliged.

Mrs Simpson drew herself up, the picture of embattled womanhood. 'My man seems to think Adolf Hitler himself is making a wee special bomb with *Tam Simpson* written on it –

one that'll get him and leave the rest of us alone.' She gave a magnificent sniff. 'Chance would be a fine thing.'

Despite Tam Simpson's worries, Adolf Hitler was rather tied up with his own concerns. He was determined to have the Sudetenland. Only Britain, France and Russia, who'd all promised to help Czechoslovakia in the event of a German attack, stood in his way. German public opinion didn't seem to.

At a huge rally in Nuremberg at the beginning of September he had spoken of atrocities perpetrated against the German-speaking inhabitants of Sudetenland by the Czechs.

Most honest people weren't sure whether to believe the stories or not, but Neville Chamberlain and his civil servants were getting very fed up with the long-drawn-out negotiations and the stubbornness of the people they referred to as *those Czechos.*

After his second meeting with Hitler, at which he agreed to most of the German leader's demands, the Prime Minister spoke to the nation via the wireless:

'How horrible, fantastic, incredible it is that we should be digging trenches and trying on gas masks because of a quarrel in a faraway country between people of whom we know nothing.'

Listening to that, Eddie grew pale. When the broadcast was over, he made a grim prediction.

'It looks as if we're about to sell Czechoslovakia down the river. Not a very honourable course of action.'

He was right. Two days later, on 29 September, Chamberlain, Hitler, Mussolini and Daladier, the French prime minister, met at Munich. Czechoslovakia, the country whose fate was being decided, and the only democratic state left in Central Europe, was not represented. The great powers simply made a decision. The Sudetenland would be incorporated into Hitler's Germany within the space of the next two weeks. The crisis was over.

Neville Chamberlain flew home flourishing a piece of paper

which held an agreement that Britain and Germany would never again go to war with each other. It was, he told the people of Britain, nothing less than peace in our time. The tension of the long wet summer exploded into acclaim for Chamberlain. He was even nominated for the Nobel Peace Prize.

Not everyone rejoiced. Many thought as Eddie did. Winston Churchill was one of them, describing the outcome of the Munich Conference as the blackest page in British history.

But the war everyone had feared so much had been avoided. There was to be peace, and because people longed so much for that, many of them chose to ignore their misgivings. They didn't ask searching questions and they turned a blind eye to the shaky foundations on which the peace sat, and the cost at which it had been achieved.

It had been too close to call, and the relief was enormous. The last night of the Empire Exhibition in October 1938 gave thousands the chance to celebrate this most narrow of escapes.

Chapter 18

Liz felt wonderful. Judging by the noise and laughter, so did everyone around her. Not even the fact that it was raining cats and dogs could dampen the mood. And the wet weather had some advantages. Trying to do the Lambeth Walk whilst simultaneously holding your umbrella over your head meant that it didn't really matter whether you knew the steps or not.

You couldn't dance properly in this size of crowd anyway. That didn't matter either. Noisy and high-spirited, but well behaved at the same time, people were intent on enjoying themselves and marking the end of the exhibition which had meant so much to them.

They were grateful for the pleasure which the event at Bellahouston had brought into their lives: the pavilions, the displays and exhibits, the fountains and cascades, Tait's Tower and the Highland Village, the music, the knowledge that half the countries of the world had come to this small corner of Glasgow.

It had been a bright splash of colour during one of the wettest summers on record. It had helped them forget the crisis in Europe and the worries and struggles of their own lives.

Liz felt all that. Something else too. She was counting off the weeks. She and Janet had just had it confirmed that they'd be doing their training at the Western. She could hardly wait.

There were two small flies in the ointment. One was Mario Rossi. He was here, but with a girl. He'd given Liz a wee smile accompanied by a curious little downturn of the mouth. Liz had thought it a very continental gesture. Did it signify regret?

If she were being strictly honest, she might have to admit she felt some of that herself. Not to mention a sharp little pang of jealousy when she had seen him with the other girl. And she was just a wee bit put out that despite his bitter observation the night of the Paul Robeson concert, it hadn't seemed to take him very long to get over his disappointment.

Well, what did she expect? She had turned him down, after all. Twice.

The other minor irritation was the Honourable Miss MacIntyre. Liz couldn't get on with her at all. Unfortunately, the girl seemed to like her. She had sought her out earlier in the evening to ask which hospital Liz had been allocated to for her VAD training and when she was due to start.

Cordelia had been delighted. She was heading for the same place at the same time. Liz had been sorely tempted to say, 'Oh, goody,' or perhaps, 'Really? How frightfully spiffing!' She managed to restrain herself.

Never mind. She was going to do her VAD training; she seemed, touch wood, to have more or less solved the Eric Mitchell problem; there wasn't going to be a war – not this week anyway; and she was with friends. What more could she want? She resolutely ignored the wee voice in her head which whispered, *Mario Rossi*.

There was some romance in the air. Helen and Eddie had eyes only for each other, although things were still at an early stage. Liz had a shrewd suspicion they hadn't even kissed properly yet. She thought that was nice, kind of romantic, like the way they were shyly holding hands tonight.

Adam Buchanan had complained vociferously about them making what he called sheep's eyes at each other and declared that it was positively revolting. Liz wondered what Cordelia thought when he made comments like that. Eddie himself had laughed. After the disaster of his and Adam's first meeting, they seemed to be getting on well enough tonight.

Not long after they arrived at Bellahouston in the early evening they had a spirited but amiable discussion about the exhibition and the Empire itself. Adam asserted that the British had done a lot of good in many of their colonies – introducing democracy and the rule of law and encouraging trade and commerce. The Empire Exhibition was surely a manifestation of that. Eddie, of course, disagreed with him.

They were standing around eating ice-cream in one of the refreshment tents, the rain drumming on the canvas above their heads. Eddie licked his cone contemplatively.

'As a spectacle,' he agreed with Adam, 'it's been magnificent, second to none, but its very existence is an affront to the countries we've subjugated and exploited. We should dismantle the British Empire and give the native peoples their countries back. With an apology,' he added for good measure.

A hand was laid on his shoulder. It was Helen.

'But have you enjoyed the exhibition, Eddie?' she asked slyly.

'Oh, aye,' he said, his eyes creasing at the corners as he turned to smile at her. 'It's been magic. I've had a great time. I loved the kangaroo, and the big model of the sheep on the Wool Pavilion. The Palace of Engineering, too.' He gave himself a shake. 'Oh, and lots and lots of other things. I wish it could stay open forever.'

He looked puzzled when everyone burst out laughing at him – which only made them laugh all the more. Cordelia took pity on him, turning to Adam with a question.

'What did you like best?'

Young Mr Buchanan pretended to give the matter some serious consideration, but Liz could see the joke coming.

'Well,' he began expansively, 'I might suggest the sheer variety of the exhibits, or the innovative architecture of the pavilions.' He paused and looked very thoughtful. 'However, on careful reflection I think I'd have to plump for the demonstrations by the Women's League of Health and Beauty. All those long legs and short skirts!'

Cordelia hit him.

* * *

162

The crowd grew larger and the weather wetter as the evening wore on. Spirits remained high, even though the final display of the exhibition gave some people pause for thought.

As the visitors watched, three aircraft staged a mock attack on Bellahouston Park. They were caught in searchlights manned by the City of Glasgow Squadron of the RAF and, of course, successfully driven off. That produced much ribald and irreverent comment.

As the countdown to the end of the event came closer, the singing grew louder, everyone swaying happily together. Eddie was right, Liz thought. It had been magic. Funny to think it was soon going to be over, in the past: something you would tell your children and grandchildren about.

She turned to say something to Helen and found that the swaying and shifting crowd had separated her from her friends. She couldn't see any of them. In the midst of a vast sea of humanity, Liz all at once felt very small and alone.

Then the lights went down. There was a great sigh of anticipation and the huge crowd fell silent.

At that very moment and to her immense relief, Liz turned and found herself shoulder to shoulder with Adam Buchanan. She could just make out his features in the gloom.

'All right?' he asked, whispering the words into her ear. 'I saw you here all on your lonesome. I've been trying to get through to you for the past ten minutes. All right?' he asked again. 'I thought you looked a bit sad.'

'I am sad,' she admitted. 'Sorry to see it end.'

'I know,' he said, his deep voice soft in the darkness. It was absurdly comforting that he understood how she felt. 'Would it help if I put my arm around you?'

He meant to be kind. She knew that, but she shook her head and in case he couldn't see her properly declined verbally as well.

'No, I'm all right, thanks. Anyway, Cordelia might object to that. Where is she, anyway?'

'Oh, she's somewhere about,' he said vaguely. 'Why would

she—Look!' A warm and heavy hand was laid on her shoulder and he turned her round to face the tower up on the hill.

Obediently, Liz looked in the direction he had indicated. With the rest of the park in darkness, the floodlit Tait's Tower stood out like a beacon. It must, she thought, be visible miles away, from all round the city.

It only remained for two songs to be sung: the National Anthem and 'Auld Lang Syne'. Then they saw the Union Jack on the tower being slowly lowered, and the lights on the tall structure dim.

As the lights died away completely, a disembodied voice spoke, thrilling in the velvety blackness of the wet October night.

'*Let the spirit of the Exhibition live on!*'

A huge cheer went up.

'Are you crying?' came a voice close to her ear.

'Y-yes!'

'Och, Liz, you wee daftie!' Laughing, Adam gave her shoulders a squeeze.

'I don't know,' she said, pulling out from under his arm as the lights which illuminated the paths came back on and conversations started up again. 'I've got such a funny feeling. More than just because the exhibition's closing.' She shook her head, trying to banish the uncomfortable thoughts.

'It's trepidation,' he said. 'Fear of what the future might hold.'

She blinked. That hadn't sounded like Adam's voice. Then he looked at her and smiled.

'You're drookit.'

'We're all drookit,' she said ruefully. A raindrop ran down her nose. She stuck out her tongue and caught it, and he laughed.

It was nearly two o'clock in the morning before Liz and Eddie got home. Sadie was waiting up for them. She'd kept the fire in for their return and insisted they changed into their night clothes and dressing gowns straightaway and sat by it for a

164

wee while to warm themselves up. She'd put a piggy – a hot-water bottle – in both their beds, too.

She brought them cocoa and fussed over their wet things and they told her about their evening, speaking in quiet voices so as not to waken their father.

Lying in bed later, Liz allowed the memory of the sights and sounds of the evening to wash over her. *Trepidation. Fear of what the future might hold.* But the future was going to hold peace, wasn't it? Peace in our time.

You're drookit. Liz smiled. She liked Adam. He was sweet. Pity about Mario Rossi, though . . . Yawning, she stretched her legs out. The bed was lovely and warm. She pulled the covers up over herself. Within minutes she was sound asleep.

PART II

1939-1940

Chapter 19

Liz hung up her uniform hat and coat in the small cloakroom at the Infirmary allotted to the VADs, and brought out the square of white cloth which had been carefully ironed and starched for her by Sadie the day before. Doing her best to look nonchalant, she put it over her smoothly tied-back hair, transforming the material into a cap by tying it carefully in butterfly wings at the nape of her neck.

Lifting her head again, she checked in the mirror over the washbasin. Perfect. The wee red cross was right in the middle.

'Oh, gosh,' came a voice, 'you've done that really well. I seem to be making a bit of a dog's breakfast of it.'

Liz turned slowly. Cordelia MacIntyre was giving her a rueful grin in greeting, her cap still a square of white cloth dangling from her fingers – a rather crumpled one at that. She must have made a couple of unsuccessful attempts to put it on.

'Would you mind giving me a hand, Miss MacMillan? I seem to be all fingers and thumbs today. Nervous, I suppose.'

Liz found that hard to believe, but she took the scrap of cloth from her, giving it a brisk shake to try to remove the creases.

'Bend your head forward a wee bit,' she instructed, swinging the cloth up and over Cordelia's short and beautifully styled hair. 'Now turn around and I'll tie it at the back.'

She wondered if she sounded as reluctant as she felt. Was she being churlish to resent being asked for help? To feel that she was being treated like some sort of a lady's maid?

If Cordelia noticed anything, she certainly didn't show it,

169

expressing her gratitude at some length. 'Oh, I say, that's great,' she said, turning her head first one way and then the other to see how she looked. Her eyes went to Liz's reflection. 'How clever of you. You must just have the knack.'

Liz had been practising how to tie her cap for the past week in front of the mirror on her wardrobe door. She wasn't going to tell Cordelia MacIntyre that. She, still busy admiring her butterfly wings, suddenly looked wryly amused.

'We almost look like real nurses, don't we?'

Liz was forced to smile at that one. She'd been thinking exactly the same.

'I'm sure they'll probably knock that idea out of us, Miss MacIntyre,' she replied, gesturing towards the cloakroom door to indicate the hospital beyond.

Cordelia hesitated and then plunged in.

'Would you mind if I called you Liz? And would you call me Cordelia?'

'It seems to be the done thing to use surnames,' Liz said. That was true. It was also true that she didn't want to be the Honourable Miss MacIntyre's friend. They had absolutely nothing in common, after all.

Cordelia grimaced. 'I know . . . but perhaps when we're on our own? It would be friendlier. Don't you think?'

'Maybe. We'd better go now. We'll be late.'

'I'm coming,' said Cordelia with a quick smile. 'Just let me take a deep breath.'

Holding the door open for the other girl to follow her out, Liz was struck by a thought. Could Miss MacIntyre really be feeling as nervous as herself? She shrugged that off as swiftly as it had come to mind. That was a daft idea. People like her were born confident.

Sister MacLean, the nursing tutor from the Preliminary Training School who'd been put in charge of the VADs, initiated their training by imparting a piece of philosophy. Medicine, she told them gravely, is a science. Nursing is an art.

She also gave them two maxims. One: never go up the ward

170

empty-handed. There was always something which needed to be transferred from one place to another. Two: come hell or high water, the patients must always come first.

As Liz had predicted, she wasted no time in letting them know her opinion of their lowly status. Fixing them with a steely glare as they sat eagerly in the lecture theatre, she delivered her verdict.

'You may have lovely red crosses on your brows and on your breasts,' she told them in her lilting Hebridean accent, 'but that doesn't make any of you nurses. Not in my book.'

'Well,' said Cordelia while they ate their luncheon in the nurses' dining room, 'it's nice to know that you're the lowest of the low.' She glanced around her. 'They seem to have thrown a cordon sanitaire around us, don't they?'

Liz could recognise that the words were French. She didn't know their exact translation, but she understood what Cordelia meant. The other nurses – the proper ones – were making it quite clear that the VADs were not part of their group.

'I say,' said Cordelia, 'why don't we go across to Mr Rossi's café tomorrow instead?'

'Where's that?' asked Janet Brown. Cordelia explained. Janet and the other girls at the table enthused about the idea. It would, Liz supposed, look a bit odd if she didn't go with them.

Aldo Rossi greeted the six young women who walked into his café the following lunchtime with considerable charm. Cordelia he obviously knew well, and he remembered Liz from her previous visit. Taking her hand between the two of his, he shook it enthusiastically.

'I will call Mario,' he said when the girls were seated. Bestowing a warm smile on them all, he headed for a door at the back, behind the counter. As he swung it open, Liz saw a flight of stairs. Presumably he and his son lived in a flat above the café.

'Oh, don't disturb him, Mr Rossi,' said Cordelia, half rising again. 'We can help set the tables and all that. Can't we?' She

171

looked around her for confirmation.

'Yes,' said Liz hurriedly, also rising to her feet. It was too late. Mr Rossi was already shouting something up the stairs.

'Sounds so poetic, doesn't it?' murmured Cordelia to Liz.

It did, as did the stream of Italian which floated back down to them. Liz wondered if he was up there with the girl she'd seen him with at the Empire Exhibition. They might be sitting on a sofa, perhaps, his arm draped about her shoulders, or . . .

A succession of pictures flashed through Liz's mind. None of them had any business at all being there. Then Mario appeared in the doorway. Alone. And yawning hugely.

He was a bit rumpled. A dark waistcoat swung open over a blue and white striped collarless shirt, unbuttoned at the neck and the cuffs. His dark hair was tousled. Another set of pictures entered Liz's mind. They had no business being there either.

'*Scusi,* Papa,' Mario began. His long fingers went to his wrist, doing up his cuff buttons. Spotting that his father had customers, he switched seamlessly into English. 'I should have been down to help you earlier, but I fell asleep.'

'They work you too hard in that place,' grumbled his father. Bustling about with napkins and cutlery, he paused long enough to make a very Italian gesture with his head which took in the hospital, the University and everything else down the road from his café.

Mario had just registered who the customers were. He came forward, his hand outstretched.

'Cordelia! How nice to see you! And Miss Brown, and Miss MacMillan too, of course.' He shook hands enthusiastically with all three of them, leaving Liz till last. There was a mischievous gleam in his brown eyes as he lifted her hand – and kept hold of it rather longer than was strictly necessary. 'Won't you introduce me to the rest of your friends?'

'Uh . . .' said Liz.

It was Cordelia who did the honours, faultlessly managing to remember the other three girls' names.

'You're a medical student?' one of them asked.

'Yes. Perhaps we'll meet on the wards sometime. I certainly hope so.' He flashed her a smile. Like father, like son, obviously, thought Liz.

Finishing a plate of delicious tomato soup some time later, she looked up. Aldo Rossi was in the kitchen doing the cooking, and Mario was attending to the serving of the meal. There didn't seem to be a Mrs Rossi. Then she recalled that Mario had spoken of his mother in the past tense when he'd been talking to Conor Gallagher at the Red Cross exercise. Under cover of the general hubbub, she asked Cordelia.

'Poor Mr Rossi's been widowed twice,' she told her quietly. 'That's Mario's mother up there, next to the bust of Mussolini.' She indicated a high shelf to the side of the door to the upstairs flat. It was too far away to see properly. All Liz could make out was that it was a formal portrait of a woman. As she studied it, a hand came over her shoulder. It was Mario, lifting her empty soup plate.

'Oh! Thank you!' Embarrassing somehow, to have him serving her. He had heard Cordelia's reference to his father's bust of Il Duce.

'Embarrassing, isn't it? Especially for a socialist like myself. Although,' he said reflectively, stacking three soup plates together and transferring the spoons to the top one, 'I suppose I was a little fascist once. When I went to school in Italy I could sing all the songs with the best of them.'

'Why were you at school in Italy?' asked Janet with unabashed curiosity.

'Because my mother died when I was ten,' he said matter-of-factly, smoothly and efficiently swapping soup plates for main courses. 'My father couldn't cope with building up the business and bringing my brother and me up as well. My mother's family were willing to take me in, but not Carlo.'

'Why ever not?' asked Janet, looking shocked.

'Carlo is Mario's half-brother,' Cordelia explained. 'The son of Mr Rossi's first wife.' Glancing swiftly around to check that Aldo was still safely out of earshot in the kitchen, she went on:

'All her other children died, didn't they, Mario?'

He nodded. 'One in the influenza epidemic back in '19, one of diphtheria and one of scarlet fever.'

'Is that why you decided to become a doctor?' asked another of the girls.

'Probably,' he said a little absently. His eyes were ranging over the two tables between which the girls had divided themselves. 'Although I'm planning on becoming a surgeon rather than a physician. Hang on, you haven't got salt.' He went behind the counter and was back in a couple of strides. 'Right, there you are.'

Six sympathetic female faces were looking expectantly up at him.

'Have I forgotten something else?' he asked, looking faintly puzzled.

'Only the rest of your life story,' said Cordelia. 'D'you mind?'

'Not at all, but don't let your food get cold. *Buon appetito,* ladies.'

'*Grazie,*' said Cordelia in response, picking up her knife and fork.

'*Prego, signorina.*' Mario gave Cordelia a funny little bow and leaned back against the counter, watching them all eat. A large white apron tied around his waist, the sleeves of his striped shirt now rolled up, he looked as though he was enjoying the sight.

'Well, then Carlo's mother died, and a few years later my father met my mother. Her family disapproved of a good Irish girl marrying a struggling Italian immigrant. So we were sent to my grandparents in Italy when my mother died, because Carlo and I refused to be separated.'

Cordelia shook her head. 'How could your other grandparents have been so hard?' She thought about it for a minute. 'Prejudice, I suppose. It's a terrible thing.'

'It certainly is,' said Mario lightly.

'How long did you spend in Italy?' asked Janet. Liz thought

174

she was being extremely nosy. They all were, firing questions at him like this, although he didn't seem to mind. And Liz had to admit, if only to herself, that she wasn't at all averse to listening to his answers.

'Four years. I came back to Glasgow when I was fourteen.'

'That must have been a bit of a shock to the system.'

Mario shrugged. 'Oh, they stopped calling me a dirty wee Tally after I had worked out what my fists were for.'

The other girls laughed, but Liz had caught the hint of dryness in his tone.

'And once I remembered how to speak English again I was able to give back as good as I got verbally as well.' He laughed. 'And tell them jokes, too. Always an excellent form of defence – and a lot less painful on the knuckles.'

'You're completely bilingual?'

He struck a pose. 'Trilingual, if you don't mind.'

'Italian, English and . . .' Janet stopped, her brow wrinkling in perplexity.

'Glaswegian,' supplied Liz. Her reward was an appreciative little smile.

'What about your brother?' asked another of the VADs.

'He stayed out there, married a local girl.' Mario straightened up from the casual slouch in which he'd been standing and walked round behind the counter, bending down to look for something underneath it.

'They've just had a baby,' he said, his voice muffled. 'I've got a photo here somewhere that Carlo sent me in his last letter.' He found what he was looking for and came back out to the girls. Extracting the photograph from an envelope, he handed it first of all to Cordelia, who studied it and passed it round. 'That's Mariella,' he said proudly. 'Isn't she the most beautiful wee thing you ever saw?'

Any more of this and they're all going to swoon, thought Liz, watching Janet and the others going all dewy-eyed over the picture of the baby and this evidence of Mario's paternal streak.

'You and your father must miss them,' said Cordelia sympathetically.

'Yes, but they're going to come over once the baby's old enough, eventually take over the café from Papa. Now, ladies,' he said briskly. 'Anyone for dessert?'

'Wow!' said Janet as the girls walked back across the road. 'Is he spoken for, Miss MacIntyre? Do you know?'

'You're spoken for yourself, Janet,' said Liz mildly.

'I know, but I don't like to think of a man like that going to waste,' said Janet with a sly little sideways glance at Liz. Cordelia laughed.

'No, he's not spoken for.'

'What about the girl he was with at the Empire Exhibition?' asked Liz.

'Didn't last long,' said Cordelia. 'I don't think it was very serious.'

'Doesn't it simply turn your insides to melted butter when he says something in Italian?' said one of the other girls.

'Oh, yes,' agreed Janet in a dreamy voice. 'And see when he came downstairs all sleepy . . .'

There was much more in the same vein, but Liz had stopped listening. She didn't disagree with anything that had been said. Mario Rossi was a very attractive man.

It wasn't thoughts of the man which were filling her head at the moment, though. She was thinking about the little boy who'd lost his mother and whose grieving father had been forced to send him off to grandparents he'd probably never met before.

At least he'd had his brother with him then. It sounded as if they were close. When he'd come back to Glasgow as a fourteen-year-old, he'd had to go through it all on his own. *They stopped calling me a dirty wee Tally after I had worked out what my fists were for.*

And then he had stopped his tormentors by making them laugh. A lot less painful on the knuckles, he'd said. She was surprised how much it upset her to think of those beautiful hands – those surgeon's hands – being scarred and bruised.

'What?'

'Pay attention, Liz! Miss MacIntyre just asked you a question.'

'Oh. Sorry. What were you saying?'

Janet and Cordelia gave each other a smile.

Chapter 20

'Look lively, MacMillan! You haven't got all day! And when you've finished the floor, the patients' lavatories need cleaning.'

On her knees in the corridor which ran between the male and female surgical wards, a galvanised bucket of soapy water in front of her and an increasingly grimy floor cloth in her hand, Liz raised her head. Sister MacLean's sensibly shod feet were already marching off in the direction of Male Surgical.

Gone to torture some poor soul in there, no doubt. The deceptively soft-spoken nursing sister ruled the hospital community with a rod of iron. Even the medics and junior doctors were terrified of her: not to mention the VADs under her tutelage.

Many of them had already gone off to postings in the military and naval hospitals which had been established throughout the country, gearing up to receive the casualties expected when hostilities finally broke out between Britain and Germany.

That could only be a matter of time. The euphoria which had greeted the settlement at Munich hadn't lasted long – a matter of weeks. The news of Kristallnacht – the Night of Broken Glass – had seen to that.

One Wednesday evening in early November 1938, synagogues and Jewish shops and businesses in every town and city in Germany had been systematically attacked by what Eddie called the bully-boys of the Nazi party. They had beaten up many Jewish people as well. Hundreds of them had died from the terrible injuries they had received.

It was a chilling indication of the evil growing at the very heart of Europe, the brutal character of the regime which had taken over Germany, poisoning and distorting every aspect of that country's life.

Then, in March, the German Army had invaded the rest of Czechoslovakia. When Britain and France did nothing in response there was a feeling that the country had been betrayed a second time. When it became obvious that Poland was the next place on Hitler's shopping list, the two great European democracies took a stand. If Poland were attacked, they would come to her aid. The British government quickly introduced a limited conscription of its young men.

As one of the VADs wryly put it, it was a bit like knowing that someone was about to slam a door. You knew it was coming and you knew you were going to jump when it did, but boy, did it stretch the nerves waiting for the bang!

Janet Brown's fiancé, having completed his apprenticeship at the sewing-machine factory, was called up almost immediately. In the same age group as him, Eddie was granted an extension to allow him to finish his degree.

With her boyfriend away, Janet decided she would go off and do her bit too, volunteering to become a mobile VAD. Liz tried not to feel envious. Her father had refused point-blank to give his permission for her to do the same.

With the other volunteers at the Infirmary, including Cordelia MacIntyre, who had chosen to stay at home, Liz found herself becoming a member of the newly formed Civil Nursing Reserve. Everyone expected air attacks to follow almost immediately after the outbreak of war. Fearing high levels of civilian casualties, the non-military hospitals were also preparing for the worst.

Till that day came, Liz was convinced that Sister MacLean was going out of her way to make sure that the volunteers never got anywhere near real nursing duties. Scrub the floors, clean the toilets, make the tea, do the washing, fetch and carry for the proper nurses.

'We're skivvies,' declaimed one of the girls with a dramatic flourish one day – safely out of earshot of Sister MacLean, of course. 'Nothing but high-class skivvies.'

'Speak for yourself,' said another cheerfully. 'Some of us are low-class skivvies. Eh, MacMillan?'

Liz gritted her teeth and stuck it out. There was no way she was going to complain about her lot at home and let her father or Eddie say *I told you so*. Only Helen knew how much time she was spending cleaning floors and toilets.

But as the weeks and months went by, little chinks of light began to appear. One day she was allowed to feel a few pulses and take a few temperatures. On another a staff nurse supervised her as she administered eye drops. The patient, an elderly man in one of the medical wards, joked with her as she did it.

'It'll be worth it if it means I can see a pretty little thing like you a bit better, Nurse!'

Despite what Sister MacLean said, being addressed as *Nurse* gave Liz a real thrill. She was, quite happily, a 'floater', working in whichever part of the Infirmary she was most needed: sometimes on the wards, sometimes in Accident and Emergency or Outpatients.

She'd been asked to make a commitment to do fourteen hours a week. She spread that over the weekend, plus two short sessions on weekday evenings.

It was hard going at first. She was putting in a full week's work at Murray's as well. However, she was young and fit and doing something she enjoyed – and it had an unlooked-for bonus. The volunteers had been asked to be as flexible as possible. Could they be ready to stay on longer if the hospital was under pressure? Could they come in on a different day if there was an emergency?

Liz found herself enjoying a freedom she'd never known before. It simply wasn't always possible to say what time she'd get away from the hospital. That was something her father had to accept. The war might not have started yet, but Liz felt as though she'd already won a battle.

* * *

Still on her knees on the floor of the corridor, Liz thought with grim determination that if she had to be a skivvy, she'd be the best one around. And after this, she had the toilets to clean. Oh, goody.

'Say one for me while you're down there, MacMillan,' came an amused drawl.

It was Adam Buchanan. Like Mario and the other senior medical students, he was beginning to spend more time on the wards, gaining practical experience.

'What is it about this place that makes everyone in it think they're a comedian?'

'Who stole your scone?' he asked mildly.

'Ming the Merciless,' Liz said sourly.

Adam's hazel eyes widened in delight. He and Liz shared a love of Flash Gordon films.

'Ming the Merciless? Sister MacLean, you mean? The Florence Nightingale of the Inner Hebrides?'

'The very same,' said Liz, finishing her task and throwing the dirty cloth into the bucket with considerable relish. 'I volunteered to nurse, not to scrub floors,' she complained automatically. 'Thanks,' she said, as he extended a hand to help her up from her knees. Jings, they were sore. She gave them a rub with her free hand, Adam still being in possession of the other.

'And you a Red Clydesider, too,' he said lightly.

'My hand?'

'What about it?'

'Can I have it back?' she asked.

'Oh! Sorry!' He loosened his grip. Liz lifted her released hand and wiped her damp and sweaty forehead with the back of it.

'What's me being a Red Clydesider got to do with it?' she demanded.

'I thought you lefties were all about working together for the common good,' he said teasingly. 'Don't tell me you're too grand to scrub floors?'

'Certainly not, but I'd like to learn some nursing too.'

'Another complaint to Ming the Merciless then? Or perhaps the heid bummer?' asked Adam, his mouth quirking with amusement.

Such was Liz's irreverent name for the Infirmary's medical superintendent, a gentleman of immense dignity. Adam had loved another of her descriptions of the hospital hierarchy. She had described the superintendent and matron as God and the Archangel Gabriel. Agreeing with her, Adam had added that it would have been a brave man who would have said which was which.

'Haven't either of you young people got any work to do?'

It was Sister MacLean, returning from her errand to Male Surgical.

'We'd better get on with it, Flash,' muttered Adam under his breath as Sister swept past them. He put on a middle-European accent. 'I shall prepare zomezing in my laboratory to help us fight ze Martian forces. My God, zey have infiltrated ze hospital! Vun of them is advancing rapidly along ze corridor even as ve speak!'

The maligned Sister MacLean, who never wasted a moment of any day, was already at the stairwell which marked the mid-point between the male and female wards.

Liz laughed and sketched Adam a salute.

'Very well, Dr Zharkov. Let us rendezvous later.'

She meant at Aldo Rossi's café. Conveniently near the hospital and the University, it was a favourite meeting place for students. Liz had discovered that Eddie knew it well. She teased him when he started appearing there on Saturday afternoons.

'How kind of you to come and escort me home after my shift, brother dear.'

In fact, it had proved to be an ideal place for him and Helen to meet after she finished her work on a Saturday, well away from the danger of either set of parents bumping into them. The café was particularly popular with medical students and nurses: patients too, sometimes. A week ago Liz and another girl, searching for a female post-operative patient, had found her in there. It wasn't the first time such an incident had occurred.

Less than a fortnight after having her appendix out, the woman had quietly put her dressing gown over her nightie, walked down the stairs from the surgical ward, along the corridor and out of the door, shuffling up the road in her slippers. The girls caught her red-handed, happily tucking into a cheese beano and declaring defiantly that she'd had enough baked cod – 'that doesnae taste o' anything at all' – to last her a lifetime.

Mr Rossi maintained that he would have escorted the lady back down the road in due course, but only after she had finished her meal. Liz put her hands on her hips.

'Mr Rossi, really! She's supposed to be on a special diet.'

He shrugged. 'But Elisabetta, can I help it if the poor woman was starving to death? How come you not feed your patients in that place?' He struck his forehead with the heel of his hand. 'How come a *bella ragazza* like you is so cruel to poor sick people?'

She tried to look severe, but she was as susceptible to the charm as anyone else. It was completely indiscriminate. Any woman from nine to ninety was a *bella ragazza* – a beautiful girl. Any woman with a pulse, Cordelia MacIntyre said.

Liz took the continental courtesy and accepted it for what it was – a novelty, at any rate. As a rule, the male population of Clydebank didn't go around paying extravagant compliments to their female counterparts. Most of them, thought Liz wryly, wouldn't know a compliment if it came up and hit them in the face.

How she felt about Aldo Rossi's son was a different matter entirely. As she got to know him better she could see there was a lot more to him than good looks and a winning smile. And she liked him. She liked him a lot.

She admired the way he chose to see humour in almost every situation. She was touched by how protective he was towards

183

his father. That was nice to watch. *He* was nice to watch, moving efficiently about the café, cheerfully serving meals and snacks and coffees.

He was unfailingly charming to Liz. Whether that charm was as indiscriminate as his father's was another question. No new girlfriend had appeared. Liz didn't flatter herself that he was waiting for her to change her mind, but she wondered, all the same. Sometimes there was an odd little look or a sideways smile or an enquiring tilt of the head. Was she imagining what the question might be?

She had to keep reminding herself that he was as out of bounds as he'd ever been. She wondered how long she could go on believing that.

'The thing is,' Adam was saying, 'people go down the road there expecting to be cured of whatever ails them.' He waved an elegant hand in the direction of the Infirmary. 'But when it comes down to it, what an awful lot of people actually need is a prescription for fresh air, good food and better housing.'

Liz listened attentively. Sometimes the café was better than a lecture theatre. She had learned a lot from these sorts of conversations. Very occasionally, it got embarrassing, like when she and Cordelia had come in to find a discussion going on about the mechanics of menstruation. It had taken the boys a good five minutes to realise they were there. There had been a lot of coughing and shifting of position and red faces when they did.

'What we need is an improvement in living conditions all round,' said Jim Barclay, another of the medical students.

'And better-equipped hospitals,' chipped in Mario. Finance was a perennial problem. The voluntary hospital system, dependent on donations, wasn't an ideal one. Discussion often centred on the pressing need to create some sort of national health care provision – for rich and poor alike.

'But Adam,' Cordelia broke in, 'you say that the doctor's bag of tricks isn't very large, but what about this new wonder

184

drug that we hear about? Surely that will make a huge difference in the treatment of infection?'

'Penicillin will save lives,' said Jim Barclay solemnly. 'No question about it.'

'When we finally get it,' said Adam in disgust. 'The problem is that Professor Fleming hasn't been given the research resources he should have had. It's damnable. He made the breakthrough discovery in nineteen-twenty-eight. Nineteen-twenty-eight,' he repeated, 'and we're still waiting.'

'At least we've seen the development of sulphonamides in the last year,' put in Jim. 'They're proving effective against some infections.'

'That's true,' conceded Adam thoughtfully.

'Sulphonamides?' asked Cordelia.

'I think they're also called M and Bs,' Liz told her. 'They come in tablet form. Who developed them?' she asked.

'Various people,' said Jim Barclay. 'I believe it was a German chemist who did a lot of the pioneering work.'

'You mean not everything coming out of Germany is bad?' It was Cordelia who had spoken. Liz looked at her in surprise. Her voice had been more than dry: almost bitter. She saw a look pass between the Honourable Miss MacIntyre and Adam and wondered briefly what that was all about.

Twenty minutes later, on her feet and ready to depart, Liz was watching her friends with an indulgent eye. It was like Adam had said. People couldn't seem to simply say goodbye and go. As soon as they thought about taking their leave of each other, they suddenly seemed to find several fascinating new topics of conversation.

Standing waiting for the log jam at the door to clear, she glanced up at the photograph of Mrs Rossi.

'She was my mother,' came a voice.

Embarrassed, Liz turned and smiled shyly at him. He stretched up for the picture and handed it down to her. 'There. Now you can see her properly.'

Touched that he had taken the trouble, Liz studied the

photograph. 'She was fair-haired?'

'Yes. I get my colouring from my father. Most of my looks, in fact. I don't think I look at all like her.'

'Oh, I don't know,' said Liz, examining the face in the photograph and then glancing up at him. 'There's something about the mouth that you've got too.'

'D'you really think so?' He came to stand behind her, looking down at the picture.

'Definitely,' she said. 'Is this how you remember her?'

'Yes, except that she looks a bit serious. I remember her as being funny, always laughing and telling Carlo and me stories. She never made a difference between him and me. And she didn't have her troubles to seek, as they say, but she always chose to see the funny side of life.'

'Like her son,' said Liz softly, tilting her head back and looking at him over her shoulder. She seemed to be staring straight at his mouth. She hadn't realised how close together they were standing.

His voice was as soft as her own. 'And here was me thinking you didn't appreciate any of my good qualities.'

Their eyes met and locked.

'Liz . . .'

She thrust the picture into his hands.

'I've got to go,' she said breathlessly, and headed for the door.

The University and the Infirmary couldn't have been more convenient for each other. There was an internal gate between the grounds of the two institutions and a path which led from the Uni up on Gilmorehill down to the hospital.

The gate was a handy short cut for the medical students. Some of the senior professors, doctors and nursing staff thought it was a bit too handy, especially for the nurses' home, situated with the Preliminary Training School on the University Avenue side of the Infirmary.

However much their elders disapproved, remembering

perhaps the hot blood of their own youth, human nature was human nature. Liz smiled as she listened to the story of an escapade which had occurred earlier in the week. After an illicit late-night date with her boyfriend, one of the probationers had got back into the nurses' home by climbing through a window which she'd asked her friends to leave open for her.

So far, so good. However, the window was in a small scullery at the back of the building, above a deep sink used for soaking clothes. The friends of the pupil nurse had thought it a brilliant idea to fill it full of cold water . . .

'I'd have killed them,' said Cordelia solemnly.

'She very nearly did,' said Naomi Richardson, the student nurse who was relating the story to a mixed group of probationers and volunteer nurses sitting around a table in the nurses' dining room. As individuals got to know each other, the barriers between the two factions were gradually breaking down. 'They tried to convince her they were only trying to cool her down after her date, but she's still gunning for them apparently!'

'Well, I suppose they might have had a point,' said one of the volunteers. 'I imagine a girl would need some cooling off after a date with certain people. Like Mario Rossi, for example. Don't you think so, MacMillan?'

Somebody giggled. The rest of them were grinning at her like idiots.

'I'm afraid I'm not in any position to comment,' said Liz loftily. 'Shouldn't we be getting back to the sewing room?'

'Tell it to the marines, MacMillan,' said Naomi drily.

Four of the volunteers had been dispatched to the sewing room that morning to make up what seemed to Liz like several hundred yards of blackout material into curtains and screens. The Infirmary had a lot of windows.

A depressing task in itself, the stiffness of the cloth they were sewing made it a tiresome one too. Having spent all morning doing it, it was only half an hour after lunch when everyone began complaining that their fingers were aching again – just as Sister MacLean arrived to see how they were getting on.

The permanent seamstresses weren't in on a Saturday, and the four sewing machines in the room were sitting idle. The volunteers had been told at the start of their stint that they weren't to touch them. That didn't make any sense to Liz.

'Why can't we do this on the sewing machines? Isn't it a waste of effort doing it by hand?'

'It keeps you well out of our way, MacMillan,' came the lilting, if unforgiving, reply, 'so that we can get on with the business of looking after the patients. Added to which, I don't want any complaints on Monday morning from the sewing room staff that they've had amateurs playing with their machines. You might break something.'

There was silence for a minute or two after Sister MacLean left. Then, with a groan, one of the girls threw her needle and thread down in disgust.

'My fingers are like pin cushions! Hey, MacMillan, see when you storm the barricades, can I come with you?'

There were murmurs of assent. Cordelia MacIntyre's voice rang out.

'You can count me in too. This is one of the most ridiculous things I've ever had to do in my entire life. Especially with four perfectly serviceable sewing machines sitting there.'

Liz gave her a polite smile. She was still thinking about the teasing comments the other girls had made about Mario and her, and she remembered what Eddie had said when she had first told him she knew how he felt about Helen. *Is it that obvious?*

Chapter 21

Eddie was devastated, so upset that their grandfather didn't have the heart to say *I told you so*. It was the beginning of the last week in August and the signing of the Nazi-Soviet Pact had just been announced. Hitler and Stalin, arch enemies ideologically and in every other way, had agreed not to go to war with each other.

'How could they?' he kept saying. 'How could they?' Sitting beside him in Peter MacMillan's flat, Helen reached for his hand. He tried to give her a smile in response, but it was a pathetic effort.

'Aye, lad,' said Peter sympathetically. 'Betrayal always cuts deep.'

Helen looked anxiously up at Liz and Peter. 'What will it mean?' she asked. 'For this country, I mean?'

'It means we can't rely on the Russians for help,' said Peter. 'When it comes to the crunch – and that can only be weeks away – Britain and France will have to stand alone.' He gazed sadly at the three young people. 'I'd hoped your generation wouldn't have to go through this,' he muttered, 'but it hasnae turned out that way.'

He'd joined the ARP in the spring, persuaded by a friend that he wasn't too old to do his bit. As the man had said: 'The young lads will all be marched off, Peter. They'll need old fogies like us on the home front.'

Peter MacMillan had thought of his firstborn, dead in the mud and blood and suffering of Passchendaele. He had thought of his beloved Eddie and of the Canadian grandsons he had never met . . . and then he had tried not to let his thoughts travel any further.

'New medical journal?' Liz asked, not recognising the colourful cover of the magazine Adam was reading. She'd come on duty to find him in the kitchen of the ward to which she'd been allocated today, putting his feet up and having a break.

It had been a hell of a week. With everyone saying the war was now only days away, plans for the evacuation of hospital patients who were well enough to be moved had swung hurriedly into action. It had taken some organising. Everybody had mucked in to help, including the medical students. Those with cars, like Adam, had helped with the transportation of the patients. Others had acted as ambulance escorts for the more serious cases. Then there had been all the blackout screens and curtains to be put up.

Slouched in an upright chair, his long legs stretched out on another, Adam had been intently reading when she had come in. Standing up to greet her, he laughed.

'Not a new medical journal. A new comic. Well, I think it's been out for about a year. Mario loaned it to me. It's called *The Beano* and it's the funniest thing I've ever read in my entire life.'

'I'll take your word for it,' she replied, getting ready to help serve the lunches for the few patients who remained in the hospital. 'I suppose you need some respite from all those great medical tomes you have to read.'

He and Mario had a long road ahead of them. Gaining their medical degree from the University wasn't the end of the story by any means. Until they had done a year as hospital residents, living and working on the premises, they wouldn't be considered fully qualified.

Even if they decided to become general practitioners, they had to complete several more years of hospital work. If they did their first residency in medicine, they might try to get an appointment as a junior house officer on the surgical side, or vice versa.

Mario had told everyone that his aim was to work his way up through the surgical specialities, first to a registrar's post, then a senior registrar's. He made no secret of his ambition to reach the top of the tree: consultant surgeon.

'Can you imagine having those hands working on you?' Naomi Richardson had breathed.

'You'd be anaesthetised, you dope,' had come the robust reply.

That daft exchange had stayed in Liz's head longer than it should have. She was thinking about it now, while she was putting out the lunches.

'MacMillan?'

'Mmm?' she responded, not bothering to turn round.

'You wouldn't fancy the flicks tonight, would you? I could offer you a Flash Gordon film: *Mars Attacks the Earth*. Take our minds off that other forthcoming attraction: *Germany Attacks Poor Wee Us.*'

'Sorry, Adam,' she said, away in a world of her own. She hadn't even noticed the joke. That private world seemed to have only one other inhabitant: Mario Rossi. 'I'm a bit tired. It's been a busy week. Maybe another time? Tell the others I'm sorry, won't you?'

She turned and gave him an absent-minded smile in apology, but he was already reading the comic again.

'Nae bother,' he muttered politely.

Liz smiled fondly at his bowed head. They all pronounced it the Glasgow way. *Nae bother.* It had become their catchphrase.

Liz glanced at the clock behind Miss Gilchrist's head. An hour to go. She wondered why the minutes seemed to slow down at the end of the day – because you were desperate to get out of the place, she supposed. Her time at the Infirmary always went past quickly. Time flies when you're having fun.

Oh, jings, she was talking nonsense to herself. She must be tired, and the busy week wasn't over yet.

On Friday the evacuation of thousands of children to places of safety was scheduled to begin. Mr Murray had agreed to give Liz the day off so she could help. She'd been allocated to a train taking some children down the Ayrshire coast.

A wasp flew in through the open windows of the office. Predictably, Miss Gilchrist leaped up from her chair and started having hysterics. Apart from Liz, everyone else decided to join in.

In the name of the wee man! Jumping up and down and waving your arms like some sort of demented windmill was a sure-fire way of getting stung. If you kept still the beastie usually moved on. It did, buzzing out the way it had buzzed in, and the occupants of the room settled down once again to their work.

'Oh, don't close the windows, Miss Gilchrist. It's real hot in here.'

That was the office boy, uncomfortable in his stiff collar and tie. Liz had overheard a snatch of conversation during her lunch break.

'How can they be going to declare war when the weather's so lovely and warm?'

Eric Mitchell was studying a list of ship movements on the Clyde. 'I see the *Athenia* leaves Princes' Dock at midday on Friday. Rats deserting the sinking ship,' he sneered. The Donaldson Line passenger ship did a regular North Atlantic run. The demand for tickets for this particular crossing had been high.

Miss Gilchrist looked up from her work. 'Oh, I don't think you should say that, Mr Mitchell. Many of them will be Canadians and Americans trying to get home before it all starts. You can hardly blame them.'

I'd go if it was me, Liz thought. No question about it. She yawned. Catching a disapproving glance from Miss Gilchrist, she hastily covered her mouth with her hand. She'd better have a few early nights this week. She'd need all her energy for

192

Friday. A train full of wee horrors, no doubt.

The appeal for helpers had been targeted at women and girls, but someone had suggested that a few men would come in handy in case the wee boys got raucous. Jim Barclay and Adam had volunteered. They'd both be on Liz's train. Cordelia too, she expected. She and Adam usually went together.

Liz wasn't so sure now that they were romantically involved with each other. They were very discreet about it if they were. They called each other 'darling' and 'sweetie', but people like them always did. They never held hands and she had never seen them kiss except for a peck on the cheek: a friendly salute when they met or parted.

Helen still maintained that Adam fancied Liz. Liz couldn't see it. He'd never said anything to make her think that. They were friends, that was all, sharing the same quirky sense of humour and sense of fun.

She yawned again.

'Late night with your boyfriend, Miss MacMillan? You really ought to get more sleep, you know.'

She gave him a level look. As far as Miss Gilchrist was concerned, the comment had probably sounded harmless enough. Only Liz and Eric Mitchell understood what lay beneath the words.

Since she had stood up to him, there had been no more incidents. She was pretty sure he'd left the other girl alone too, but he managed to get in the occasional barbed comment and he still sometimes looked at her in a way that made her skin crawl. Liz supposed she could put up with that.

'A man?' queried Miss Gilchrist of the office boy. 'Asking to speak to Miss MacMillan? On a private matter?' She made it sound like a hanging offence.

'Aye, Miss Gilchrist,' said the office boy. 'I mean yes,' he hurriedly corrected. 'Shall I show him in?'

'Do so,' said Miss Gilchrist with a regal inclination of her head. Adam's mother wasn't the only woman who could do a

Queen Mary impersonation. Liz looked up with interest to see who her visitor was.

The lazy autumn afternoon was suddenly vibrantly alive. Mario Rossi had walked into the room.

Chapter 22

Miss Gilchrist rose to her feet and went forward to greet Mario. Greet wasn't perhaps the correct word. That implied a friendly, or at least civil, welcome. The senior secretary looked more like a Pole or a Czechoslovak discovering a German at the border. *Back, you dog! Get off my territory!*

She raised a hand as though to ward him off. Perhaps she thought she could simply push this unwanted intruder out of the office. Liz wouldn't have put it past her to try, but stopping Mario's confident progress into the room made her think of King Canute attempting to hold back the waves.

At least Miss Gilchrist was doing something. By the look on her face she was about to give young Mr Rossi a suitable dressing-down. Liz doubted that she herself could have strung three sensible words together at the moment. What was he doing here? And how on earth had he known where to find her during the working day?

'I feel I should point out, young man, that personal callers are not—'

She got no further. Mario seized her hand, shook it firmly and introduced himself.

'Good afternoon – or should it be good evening at this time of day?' The quizzical air was quite charming. 'I'm never quite sure. I'm Mario Rossi. And you must be . . .'

'Lucy Gilchrist.' Despite the Queen Mary act, she was finding it difficult not to sound taken aback. Liz didn't blame her. Having the Rossi smile trained on you could rock any female's composure. Miss Gilchrist was a woman like any other.

Well, maybe not exactly like any other . . . but it was obvious that even she was finding the Italian charm difficult to resist.

'Of course,' he murmured. 'Miss MacMillan's told me so much about you – how you've helped her in her work, how much she looks up to you.'

'She has?' Miss Gilchrist swivelled round to Liz, who hastily adopted an expression of admiration. At least she hoped it conveyed admiration. It would be a pity if it made her look like a half-wit instead.

'Miss MacMillan and I work together at the Infirmary, you see,' Mario was explaining to Miss Gilchrist. 'I'm a medical student. There are some things which need to be sorted out regarding the evacuation of the children on Friday. Administrative matters. I'm sure you understand.'

Miss Gilchrist asked him something. Liz didn't quite catch it, but she heard the reply.

'Yes, it is good to feel that one can do something to help the country during these difficult times.'

What a ham. As far as she knew, he wasn't involved with the evacuation arrangements at all. The flattery was outrageous too, but Miss Gilchrist – could she possibly be called a sweet, pretty name like Lucy? – was drinking it in as eagerly as Mario was dishing it out.

Liz caught Eric Mitchell's eye. She wished she hadn't.

Ten minutes later, Liz was walking along Clyde Street with Mario. Miss Gilchrist had taken her breath away by allowing her to leave work early. In fact, she'd insisted upon it, 'If it's to do with the arrangements for the poor little children who have to leave their homes.'

Miss Gilchrist the humanitarian? That was a good one. Could the beaming approval of a handsome young man have anything to do with her change of heart? *You're getting cynical, MacMillan.*

'You ought to be on the stage.' She shot Mario a sideways glance, and he returned it, a gleam in his dark eyes.

196

'And there's one leaving at sundown?'

'I didn't know you were involved in the evacuation. There's nothing to discuss anyway. It's all organised. And I've never mentioned Miss Gilchrist to you. You don't know her from a hole in the road.'

The observation, or the way she had put it, earned her one of his flashing smiles, the ones which were beginning to do strange things to her insides. Who was she trying to kid? They'd always done strange things to her insides. Since the day she'd first set eyes on him.

'Nope,' he said cheerfully, 'but I thought you were about to get into trouble for having a personal caller – of the male variety too,' he added mischievously. 'Are you heading for the subway?'

'Yes, it's one of my nights for the hospital.'

'That's what I thought.'

She sent him another curious glance. 'I've been going there for some time now. I think I know the way.'

He smiled, but said nothing, putting out a protective arm to stop her stepping off the pavement. She hadn't noticed that there was a tram coming along the road.

'Now it's safe,' he said after it had clanked past. They crossed over to the other side of the street.

'How did you know where I worked?'

'Oh, I managed to get the address out of Adam. Eventually. And I am involved in the evacuation,' he added. 'I'm not coming with you, but I'm helping organise things at the station on Friday morning.'

They made their way through into St Enoch Square. Outside the subway station Liz stopped, turning to face Mario.

'Why did you come to my office?'

He returned her steady gaze. He wasn't smiling, but it was lurking in the corners of his mouth, hiding behind his brown eyes.

'Because I wanted to see you.'

'We see each other all the time,' she pointed out. 'At the

197

hospital, and at your father's café.'

'There's always other people at the café. Perhaps I wanted to see you on your own.'

That shut her up. So did the way he was looking down into her upturned face.

'I thought your eyes were green,' he murmured, 'but they look grey right now – a beautiful soft grey. Don't look away.'

Discomfited by the compliment, she had dropped the eyes in question. She looked up again and blurted out a question.

'Are you a practising Catholic?'

'Yes. I'm hoping I'll get good at it one day. Might even be able to do it for a living.'

'Somehow I don't see you as a candidate for the priesthood.'

'Just as well,' he murmured, his eyes narrowing in amusement. 'If I were we most certainly wouldn't be having this conversation.' Then he grew serious again. 'Is that what bothers you? That I'm a Catholic and you're not?'

'Yes,' she said. 'That's what bothers me.'

'Answer me one more question then. The same way you answered that one. With simple honesty.' She was wearing a blue polka-dot shirt-waister dress with a big white collar. He took the edge of that between his finger and thumb and began to gently rub it. He was all but touching her, but Liz didn't dart back. She looked up into his face and knew exactly what he was going to ask her.

'Do you like me?'

Her whole future hung on the answer to that question. She could lie to him, nip this in the bud right now. It would make life much easier. It would make life bleak and empty.

'Yes,' she whispered. 'I like you. I like you very much indeed.'

'When it comes down to it, does it really matter what religion people are?' They were on the underground. Mario had bought the tickets for them both, asking only if Liz wanted to go to Partick Cross and walk up, or Hillhead and walk down. The hospital was equidistant between the two stops, the café slightly closer to Hillhead station.

'It matters if you're a Jew in Germany,' she replied, her voice sombre. 'Or Austria, or Czechoslovakia . . .'

'And probably Poland too in a couple of days,' he finished for her. 'That's my point,' he said quietly. 'Doesn't the way the Nazis are treating the Jews show what happens when religious prejudice gets out of hand?'

'Yes,' she agreed slowly. 'It does.' Preparatory to stopping, the train braked sharply. Sitting next to him on the cushioned seat which ran the length of the carriage, Liz curled her fingers round the upright pole on her other side. She didn't want to cannon into him when the train came to a halt.

Mario pressed the point, studying her face as she thought about what he had said. 'Your brother and your friend are made for each other. Religion doesn't seem to matter to them.'

And do you think you and I are made for each other? Is that what you're saying?

She didn't dare ask the question, nor did she point out that he wasn't quite right about religion not mattering to Helen and Eddie. It mattered to both of them a great deal – in diametrically opposing ways. Liz had been wondering for some time now how a good Catholic girl and an atheist who didn't believe in marriage were going to settle their future together.

'You're looking very serious.'

'These are serious times.'

'That's very true. We might all be dead by this time next week.'

Liz grimaced. 'Your point being?'

'My point being that if we're all going to hell in a handcart anyway – do not pass GO, do not collect two hundred pounds – why deny ourselves good company on the journey? Even if it isn't of an officially approved religion.'

'You're very plausible,' she told him. The train pulled away from Cowcaddens. Three more stops to go.

'It's my Italian charm.'

This situation called for the folded arms and the tapping foot. Hard to do when you were sitting down next to the culprit, the shoogly motion of the train occasionally tossing you towards him. Funny how it seemed to send him in the opposite direction – towards her.

Being shaken up like a sack of potatoes wasn't exactly conducive to maintaining your feminine dignity either. Nor did the mischievous twinkle in Mario's eyes help much.

'Have I worn down your resistance, then?'

'Maybe.'

He laughed out loud. 'You Presbyterians. You never give an inch, do you? Particularly if there's any danger of ending up doing something you might actually enjoy.'

That made Liz laugh too. Yes, she liked him. Not only the good looks and the charm, but the Mario who lay behind them, the man who saw the serious side of life all too clearly, but who preferred to laugh and make fun of it all.

'The pictures,' he said. 'On Thursday night. How about it? To take our minds off Poland and Czechoslovakia and little men with moustaches.'

It was what Adam had suggested too, but coming from Mario Rossi it caught her on the hop. Sitting next to him on a busy and well-lit subway train swapping wisecracks and smart comments was one thing. Sitting next to him in the darkness of the cinema was quite another.

'Hillhead next stop,' she said brightly as the train pulled away from Kelvinbridge.

He tapped his lips with one long finger. 'I know. I've been doing this journey for some time now. I think I know the way.'

It was what she had said to him earlier. Fatally, it also reminded her of the unfortunate comment Conor Gallagher had accidentally made last year, the one about Mario not going all the way with her. The memory made Liz blush and drop her eyes.

'Och, go on,' he said softly to her bowed head. 'Be a devil. Come to the pictures with me. It might be our last chance for a while. They're talking about closing the cinemas once war's declared. I'll even let you choose the flick. Pick a soppy one if you like. I don't mind.' His voice grew brisker. 'Our stop now.'

A soppy one, she thought as they went up to the street. He meant a romantic one. A love story. The sort of film which had people kissing in it. Definitely not. It might give him ideas.

Walking out into the sunshine of Byres Road with him, Liz lifted her chin. 'Not a soppy one. *Mars Attacks the Earth* – that's what I'd like to see.'

He stopped and turned to face her, a little smile dancing around his mouth. 'Flash Gordon,' he said. 'You want me to take you to a Flash Gordon film. For our first date.'

Liz put her hands on her hips. 'I like Flash Gordon,' she said.

'I suppose I should be grateful,' he murmured. 'Success at last. Even if the cinema is going to be full of wee horrors.'

He walked her down to the door of Outpatients. Liz stuck out her hand. 'Tomorrow night, then? Goodbye.'

Ignoring that businesslike hand, Mario Rossi smiled a lazy smile.

'Shouldn't we agree a time and place, Elisabetta?'

Oh, wow. Hearing his father say the Italian version of her name was one thing. Hearing it in his son's dark brown voice was something else entirely.

'Shall I pick you up at your house? Oh no, because your father would come out breathing fire and waving garlic at me.' That was something else Conor had said last year. Had Mario been reminded of the other comment too?

Liz managed to stammer out a meeting place. He suggested a time. Then he bent forward, as though to kiss her cheek. Liz took a step back. He frowned, but then he lifted her hand, bent his head and kissed it. In the middle of Church Street. Nobody had ever done that before.

'Liz? Are you asleep yet?'

She switched on her bedside light and sat up. Eddie was

201

standing in her bedroom doorway in his dressing gown.

'No,' she said softly. 'Come in.'

She tossed him one of her pillows and he sat down on the floor opposite her bed and put it at his back. Talking quietly, they began mulling over the events of the week. They moved quickly from the political to the personal.

'What are you going to do when they call you up next year, Eddie? Will you go?' She looked anxiously at him.

Not so long ago she would have known the answer to that question. Her brother would undoubtedly have been a conscientious objector. Things were different now.

'I'll go,' he said quietly. 'This has become everybody's war – a fight for democracy. I'm not a communist any more, but I still believe that socialism is the key to the future. First we'll sort Hitler out. Then we'll sort ourselves out. Create a better country and a fairer society. For our children and our children's children.'

His long legs stretched out in front of him, he was staring straight ahead, his eyes fixed on a large rose in the pattern of the bedroom wallpaper.

'What about your own future, Eddie? Yours and Helen's?'

He turned his head and brought his gaze back to her. 'I love her, Liz,' he said. 'She's the best thing that's ever happened to me.'

The simplicity and sincerity of his answer tugged at her heartstrings, but it didn't really answer her question.

'Are the two of you going to get married?'

His grey eyes were troubled. 'Liz, you know that I don't believe in marriage.' He changed the subject. 'I do want to introduce her to Ma and Father, though.'

'How would you broach it?'

She was aware of a growing uneasiness that wasn't entirely on Eddie and Helen's account.

Her brother's smile was wry.

'Oh, that's easy. Father, I'll say, I've fallen in love with a beautiful, kind, lovely girl. Clever too, with a mischievous sense of humour. She makes me laugh all the time. She's from a good family – not well off, but very respectable – and she and Liz are good friends. They get on like a house on fire. I'm sure you and mother will really like her too – just as soon as you get to know her.'

Liz, watching while he delivered this paean of praise, saw him cock one dark eyebrow. 'Oh, and by the way, Father – and I know this won't matter to you at all – her parents are Irish and she's a Roman Catholic.'

Liz felt her stomach lurch. 'And he'll say?' she invited.

'Son, if she's the girl you've chosen, that's fine by me.'

'I wish I could believe that, Eddie.' Liz shook her head. 'I really wish I could.'

'You don't think it might be different once he'd met her?' he asked. 'Perhaps if I introduced her to Ma first?'

'Ma would love her.' That wasn't in any doubt. Liz knew that while their mother might well be concerned about the religious difference, seeing how happy Helen and Eddie were together would be enough to overcome her misgivings. Unfortunately, it wasn't Sadie's reaction that mattered.

'How could anybody not love her?' asked Eddie in accents of amazement. 'Surely, Liz, when he sees how beautiful she is? Inside and out?'

'Eddie,' said Liz urgently, sitting up straighter in bed. 'He won't see any of that. All he'll see is that she's a Roman Catholic. You know that as well as I do.'

He'd caught something in her voice. His look became quizzical.

'Mario Rossi asked me out today,' she told him. 'And I said yes. We're going to the pictures on Thursday night.' Despite her concerns about their father, Liz smiled.

'So Father's got two shocks coming up? If you and Mario get serious about each other too?'

'It's only a first date, Eddie,' Liz mumbled – but she was still smiling.

Chapter 23

She walked beside Mario in miserable silence. Their first date. Their last one too, by the looks of it – and it was all her own stupid fault. It wasn't as if he'd tried to do anything so awful. He hadn't jumped on her – nothing remotely like that. There had been no undignified tussle in the back row.

He'd been the perfect gentleman, paying her in, buying her chocolates and letting her decide where they sat. She'd even sensed some amusement when she'd declined the double seats in the back row which were specifically designed for courting couples. The usherette had indicated them with her torch, but Liz had led the way to two separate seats a few rows further forward.

They'd laughed together at the trailers and at the plummy tones of the newsreel announcer, opened the sweets and settled down to watch Flash Gordon save the Earth from the Martian invaders.

Mario had tried to hold her hand a couple of times. That was all. Once he had slipped his arm about her shoulders. On each occasion Liz had shrunk away from him like a terrified rabbit.

She knew he was puzzled. He had a right to be. And it didn't help to be surrounded not by wee horrors, but by couples who seemed to have cast most of their inhibitions aside in the face of impending doom. Adolf Hitler had a lot to answer for.

When they came out of the picture house he said only one thing. 'Come on then, I'll walk you to your tram.'

They passed the café. Liz had thought they might have gone

there after the picture, but Mario kept on walking. She couldn't blame him.

Until this evening, she hadn't realised quite how much Eric Mitchell's unwelcome attentions had affected her. The memory of how she had felt when he had touched her breast and pulled her against him had stayed with her. It had fluttered up into full-blown panic tonight.

And yet she'd been wondering for weeks how it would feel to have her fingers intertwined with Mario's, what it would be like to be kissed by him . . . and to kiss him back.

She stole a sideways glance at him, walking gentleman-like on the outside of the pavement between her and the road. Should she tell him about Eric Mitchell? Try to explain her complicated feelings? Ask him to be patient?

Helen was the only other person who knew. Another girl could understand how it felt, that even though you hadn't invited it in any way, you were still expected to shoulder some of the blame for it. You must have led him on. No smoke without fire. All those horrible things people said. They reached the Botanic Gardens.

'This looks like a Clydebank tram coming now.'

Liz looked up at him. She should thank him for treating her, but she was tongue-tied with misery. She'd made a real mess of things tonight.

Mario gave an odd little laugh.

'You're very young, aren't you?'

She couldn't think of anything to say to that either.

'Here's your tram.' He lifted her hand and kissed it. Well, that was how it had started. It seemed miserably appropriate that it should finish that way too.

A short, wiry man was making a beeline for Liz. He had a girl of about twelve with him, her blonde hair tied up in two neat braids. The yellow ribbons which secured them matched the gingham frock she wore under a lacy white cardigan. When they reached Liz he propelled his reluctant daughter in from of him, work-gnarled hands resting lightly on her shoulders.

'This is Susan,' he announced. 'You'll look after her for her mother and me, won't you, Nurse?'

No point in telling him she wasn't a real nurse. Unkind, too. Despite Liz's youth, her uniform seemed to confer an authority on her which people found comforting. Susan's father's voice might sound firm. That didn't fool Liz for one minute.

'Of course we'll look after her,' she replied, instinctively adopting a brisk, no-nonsense tone of voice. The girl was upset, but she looked clever and bright. She did her best to respond to Liz's friendly smile, but her chin was wobbling furiously. She needed something to hang on to, some sort of a job to do. Liz had a sudden brainwave.

'In fact, Susan . . . I wonder if you might be able to help us out with something.' Half turning, Liz indicated the crowded platform. All the children wore luggage labels around their necks, identifying who they were. Quite a few folk had been having nightmares about children getting lost in transit like so many unclaimed parcels.

Adam Buchanan and Jim Barclay passed, ushering a group of children along and calling out, 'This way for the pleasure trip special!' Liz couldn't see Mario, but she'd better put him out of her mind anyway. She had work to do.

Susan was still tearful, but her face had grown more alert.

'We've got so many people to look after, and there's a wee girl I can think of who could do with a bit of cheering up,' said Liz. 'She's a bit younger than you and she's all on her own. I wonder if you might be able to look after her for us, Susan?'

The girl's chin stopped wobbling.

'I'll take her, MacMillan,' came a voice. It was Cordelia MacIntyre, back from settling the little girl Liz had been talking about into her seat on the train.

'So,' said Cordelia cheerfully, 'we're going to recruit you as one of our helpers for the day?'

Susan's father followed his daughter with his eyes. When

she climbed aboard the train after Cordelia, he put out his hand and shook Liz's.

'Thanks, hen. You're brand new – and that posh lassie.' He had tears in his eyes. 'That was a great idea. Giving her some responsibility, like. Her maw just couldnae face saying cheerio to her. Didnae want to see the train pull out, she said. Now I can tell her Susie went off happy.'

'You'll stay?' Liz asked him. 'To wave her off?'

'Well . . .'

'It would help all the children.'

He squared his shoulders.

'All right, hen – I mean Nurse. If it's for the sake of the weans. I'll let you get on wi' your work.'

Watching him as he moved to the back of the platform, Liz thought that maybe it helped everybody cope if they felt they had a useful job to do. Herself included. *Stop it, MacMillan, you've already decided you're not going to think about him today.*

Another family was hurrying along the platform to her. Liz put on the professional smile. The only way for any of them to get through today was to remain stubbornly cheerful.

It was Friday 1 September 1939 and Britain was sending its children to the safety of the countryside. The evacuation wasn't compulsory, but the government had recommended it strenuously to parents in the affected areas.

Those were the cities and towns huddled along the banks of the great shipbuilding rivers, the seaports, the great industrial conurbations of the Midlands and the north of England, London of course, Glasgow and Clydebank, Edinburgh and Dundee – all the places thought to be at imminent risk of German air attack.

The newspapers and the wireless and the press continued to repeat the official line. *The evacuation of our children does not mean that war is inevitable.* And the band played believe it if you like. Or so Eddie had sung at breakfast this morning.

'Well, Elizabeth?' boomed out Adam's mother as she came

sweeping towards her, another woman walking by her side.
'How are we doing?'

'Fine, Mrs Buchanan. Although I don't think the train's going to be full. A lot of folk seem to have changed their minds at the last minute.'

'Honestly, these people! When others have gone to so much effort for them. What *can* they be thinking of?'

The cut-glass accent, and the sentiments expressed in it, raised Liz's hackles immediately. She gave Mrs Buchanan's companion a level look.

'I expect they can't bear to be separated from their children,' she said. Amelia Buchanan threw her a curious glance and made the introductions. The disdainful lady was Lady Lydia MacIntyre – Cordelia's mother. She might have guessed. Liz wondered if she was supposed to curtsey.

'Can't bear to be separated from their children? How extraordinary! I had Cordelia packed off to boarding school when she was seven.'

Liz wondered fleetingly if the seven-year-old Cordelia had felt as nervous as young Susan when she had left home for the first time. She must have been homesick: as many of these children were soon going to be.

At least they weren't going to be subjected to her ladyship. Cordelia's mother wasn't coming with them on the journey. She'd just come down to wave them off. That was big of her.

Five minutes before the train was due to depart, a woman came rushing along the platform, four children trailing in her wake. Skidding to a halt in front of Liz and the two older women, she wheeled round to her offspring and grabbed the tallest of them by the elbow, thrusting him in front of her.

'This is Charlie,' she announced. 'He's in charge o' the others. I've tellt him they've no' to be separated.'

'We'll do our best, Mrs . . . ?' murmured Amelia Buchanan.

'Your best is no' good enough,' said the woman, thrusting out her hand. Liz recognised the crumpled letter she held in it

208

for one of the circulars about the evacuation arrangements which had gone out via the schools before the summer holidays. 'It says here that the children of one family are to be sent to the same place.'

'That's the problem with teaching the working classes to read,' came a soft murmur. Liz spun round and saw Cordelia.

'Sorry, MacMillan,' she muttered. 'Just trying to lighten the atmosphere.'

'They've no' to be separated,' Charlie's mother repeated. 'And that's final!' Liz recognised the belligerence for what it really was. The fierce Mrs Thomson was terrified at the prospect of sending her bairns off into the unknown but equally as scared of the dangers they might have to face if they stayed in the city.

Liz went forward and crouched down to say hello to the children. Besides Charlie, who looked to be about ten, there were twin boys and a wee sister, clutching a ragdoll as though her life depended on it. She was a pretty child, but the laddies were an unprepossessing lot, their clothes ragged, their faces none too clean. Liz had a horrible feeling she could see something moving in their hair . . .

Something else was moving – under Charlie's nose. As Liz watched, he drew his sleeve across his upper lip – not entirely successfully. His mother turned to her firstborn, wagging her finger at him.

'You've a' to stay together now! It's up to you, Charlie Thomson!'

'Aye, Ma,' he said. He was struggling hard to maintain a manful attitude. Poor wee soul, thought Liz, he's only a baby himself. Before she could think of something to cheer him up, Amelia Buchanan extracted a delicate handkerchief from the large handbag which she carried with her everywhere she went.

'Dear me,' she said to Charlie. 'Your nose seems to be running. A summer cold is such a nuisance, isn't it? Have a good blow now, young man.'

It was more of an almighty sniff than a blow, but it saved Charlie's face. Once she was satisfied that he had finished,

Amelia dropped the handkerchief back into her bag, apparently without a qualm. Cordelia's mother looked at her in horror.

The children were cheerful as the train pulled out of the station, looking around them with interest as they crossed the Clyde and passed through the southern outskirts of Glasgow. There were houses and factories to be seen, an environment they all recognised.

'You'll maybe be missing your lessons because of all this carfuffle,' said a helper, one of the few adult males on board the train. Charlie Thomson's reply flashed back at him like lightning.

'I'll not miss them at all, mister.'

It was a vestibule-type train, and the helpers moved through the open carriages, distributing the picnics donated by Glasgow bakers and packed into white cardboard cake boxes tied up with string. Smiling and chatting, they encouraged the children to relax and enjoy the trip.

It wasn't long before the train left the familiar surroundings of the city behind. Chocolate biscuits kept spirits high for a little while longer, but soon the children began to flag. The novelty had worn off.

Some of them were snuffling quietly, others doing their best to look brave. Amelia Buchanan raised her elegant eyebrows in a gesture which reminded Liz of her son. He and Cordelia were attending to the young passengers at the other end of the train.

'A sing-song, do you think?'

'That's a brilliant idea.'

Liz had really warmed to Amelia today. Any woman who could let a snotty-nosed wee toerag like Charlie Thomson use her finest lace-edged handkerchief without turning a hair was all right in her book. At the start of the journey her fair hair had been as elegant as her eyebrows, pulled back into a chic French roll. Now it was escaping from its pins, strands of it sticking to the sides of her face. One child, having eaten too many chocolate biscuits, had been sick down her front. That hadn't seemed to bother her very much either.

Liz thought about what this lot might want to sing. Inspiration struck. They'd probably be fans of Gene Autry, the singing cowboy. Softly at first, she started singing one of his hits, *South of the Border, Down Mexico Way.*

Amelia Buchanan joined in. She couldn't carry a tune, but that didn't matter. By the second verse, most of the children were singing along. By the second run-through they all were. Everybody had suggestions for the next song – and the next, and the one after that.

Sitting up in his seat and taking a renewed interest in the outside world, Charlie Thomson pointed at what he had just spotted through the carriage window.

'What's all that water out there, missus?'

Amelia Buchanan beamed at him.

'That, my dear Charlie, is the sea. You're going to really enjoy living by it.'

Several exhausting hours later, the public hall which had been the clearing house for evacuees and families prepared to offer them billets was half-empty, dusty and echoing. Most of the helpers had gone off for a well-deserved cup of tea or a breath of sea air before the train journey back to Glasgow.

A woman with two daughters of her own had taken young Susan and her friend in. That was going to be a noisy household as soon as the new arrivals found their feet!

Putting her fists into the small of her back, Liz arched her spine and let out a long sigh. She would go round and see Susan's parents tonight – the other girl's too – and tell them that they were both fine. She yawned. Or maybe she would leave it till tomorrow. It had been a long day, and it wasn't over yet. The Thomson children had still to be found a billet.

Clutching her rag doll in the crook of her elbow, the wee girl had her thumb stuck so tightly in her mouth you'd probably have needed a crowbar to prise it out. With her other hand she was gripping her big brother's hand.

'I'll take the little girl. I could probably scrub her up to something halfway presentable.' The woman who'd made the offer laughed, clearly expecting her remark to be taken as a good joke. Charlie's sister whimpered and redoubled her hold on his hand.

'We've got to stay together, missus,' he said firmly before any of the adults could speak. 'Ma ma'll leather me if we dinna.'

'Really!' exclaimed the woman, looking down her nose at him. 'Children should be seen and not heard, young man. One of my friends was saying that half of them haven't brought the right stuff with them, either. Are we supposed to provide all that, because their parents can't be bothered to? Don't these people care about their children?'

Liz, straightening up from her surreptitious health and beauty exercises, thought she might explode. She'd heard too many moans and complaints today, and not from the children either. She could understand it in one way. The folk who were taking the evacuees in were being asked to do a lot: opening their homes to youngsters who were complete strangers to them.

Some of them would have been badgered into it, persuaded to pull together in this time of national crisis. It must be difficult, being asked to turn your own house topsy-turvy to accommodate other folk's children.

But the complaints about them being badly kitted-out were unfair. As far as Liz was concerned, the people who made them were showing their own ignorance when they did so – like the people who'd drawn up the list of items evacuees should take with them to their new homes. They might have meant well, but the length and scope of that list had shown that too many people had absolutely no idea of the harsh living conditions endured by hundreds of thousands of their fellow citizens.

The evacuees were supposed to take 'a warm coat or mackintosh, a change of underclothes and stockings, handkerchiefs, night clothes, house shoes or rubber shoes, toothbrush, comb, towel, soap, face cloth and a tin cup'. As an afterthought they had also been asked to bring a warm blanket. Liz laughed when she read that list and then had to explain to Cordelia what was so funny.

What was so funny wasn't really funny at all: the reality that lots of children didn't possess a coat, let alone a warm one, that many of them had never owned night clothes, far less slippers, that while middle-class households might have several spare blankets, working-class families didn't have enough bedcovers to keep themselves warm at night as it was.

Liz glared at the woman who was regarding the Thomson children so disdainfully. How dare she look down her nose at these poor wee refugees? What they needed right now was a cuddle and some loving care – then they could have a bath and be scrubbed up.

Like the children, Liz was tired and upset and worn out by being at the centre of so much emotion throughout the day. Her own personal emotions stemming from last night's disastrous date with Mario weren't helping either.

'How dare you talk about these children like that?'

She crossed the floor to stand by the Thomsons, laying a comforting hand on young Charlie's shoulder. There was definitely something moving in his hair.

'People couldn't afford to supply half the things on that stupid list. That doesn't mean they don't care about their children. They care about them a lot. They're not used to sending them away, that's all. And how do you think you'd cope if you had to bring up a family in one room – your only washing facility a sink out on the landing, shared with several other families?' Liz gave the woman a head-to-toe appraisal. 'Not very well, I shouldn't think.'

There was a stunned silence. Nurse's uniform or not, nineteen-year-old girls weren't supposed to talk to their elders like that.

'Elizabeth,' said Amelia Buchanan quietly. She was digging in her handbag. Liz wondered if she was looking for her copy of the Riot Act, or perhaps a set of handcuffs – or a cat o' nine tails.

213

But she was wrong. With what could only be described as an air of triumph, Amelia found a brown leather horseshoe purse, extracted two half-crowns and extended them to Liz.

'Would you take Charlie and his brothers and sister out for an ice-cream, my dear? Come back in about half an hour.'

'Could I interest you in a cup of tea?'

Standing on the breezy station platform waiting for the train which would take them back to Glasgow, Liz turned at the sound of Adam's voice, forgetting for a moment that he would be able to see she'd been crying.

'Don't you want to sit in the refreshment room with the rest of them?'

'No. I want to stand out here in the fresh air with you.' He held out a chunky green Delft cup. 'Not the delicate porcelain you deserve, but it's wet and hot. One with sugar, one without. Which would you prefer? No saucers either, I'm afraid.'

'Which do you want?'

'I asked first.'

'I like sugar in my tea.'

'So do I,' he said. Overriding her protests, he handed her the cup holding the sweetened tea. 'You need the energy. It's been a hard day. Fancy a seat?' He indicated a bench behind them.

Holding his cup carefully, he lowered himself down, tilting his fair head back against the stone wall of the station buildings and closing his eyes.

'You're not upset about the Thomsons, are you?'

'No.'

She'd come back from the ice-cream parlour to find that his mother had done the impossible and found someone prepared to take all four children. No, she wasn't upset about the Thomsons. She was upset because she was tired and emotional and because of the argument she'd had with the stupid woman who wouldn't take the children. And because things hadn't worked out with Mario last night.

214

'Who was that woman who took them? She seemed a bit—'

'Eccentric?' Adam suggested, opening his eyes and giving her a tired smile. 'She's a friend of my mama's. Mad as a hatter, but in the nicest possible way. Got this huge house further down the coast where she lives with a husband who plays golf all day, an aged father and an equally aged and usually bad-tempered housekeeper who cooks like Escoffier. Not to mention two huge and hairy golden Labradors and an army of cats. When you ask her whether she likes children, she gives you the W.C. Fields answer. You know,' he said. 'Boiled or fried?'

'But will the children be all right there?' she cried, alarmed by this description of the household to which the Thomsons were now heading.

'They'll have a whale of a time,' said Adam confidently. 'She actually loves children, but she didn't volunteer to have any because she thinks she's no good with them.'

'Your mother used her legendary powers of persuasion on her?'

'You might say that. In actual fact, she's great with children. Treats 'em like little adults and they adore it – and her. Right now she's probably asking Charlie if he'd care for a brandy and soda after the exertions of his journey.'

Adam had closed his eyes again whilst he'd been speaking. Now he opened them wide, turned his head and looked Liz straight in the eye.

'After she's deloused him and the rest of his siblings, of course.'

She sighed and took a gulp of tea, feeling the relief of the warm, sweet liquid sliding down her throat.

'I know, I know. A few of them were verminous, a lot of them were pretty grubby, some of them had snotty noses – but that's not their fault, Adam! You might even argue that it's not really their parents' fault. When you see the terrible conditions that some folk live in, it's amazing how well so many of those children today were turned out. They weren't all toerags.'

215

'No,' he agreed. 'A lot of them were very neat and clean.'

'Some people have a real struggle. Lots of people need to be educated about things like hygiene.'

'I know,' he agreed again. She looked into his hazel eyes and thought that maybe he did. 'Drink your tea,' he said gently.

They sat in companionable silence for a few moments.

'We're two nations, aren't we? It's hard to see that anything positive could come out of a war, but if the country's going to ask everyone to get involved – men, women and children – then surely it owes something to those people when it's all over. Perhaps we might even manage to get rid of the blasted class system.'

He smiled at her look of surprise.

'Much though it might astonish you, Miss MacMillan, I think it holds us back too. You don't have to be a communist and want a revolution. There are peaceful ways of achieving change.'

The train was almost empty. They found a vacant compartment quite easily.

'I do like sugar in my tea,' Liz confided, making conversation about nothing because she was so tired, 'although I suppose I'll have to give it up if rationing comes in. D'you think it will?'

'Maybe,' he said vaguely. 'I don't know.' His voice was thick with tiredness, and she could feel his body settling into lines of fatigue as they sat back together on the cushioned bench seat.

Jim Barclay passed their compartment. He poked his head through the lowered window in the closed door.

'I knew there was a reason why I'd bought this *Glasgow Herald*,' he told Liz. 'There's a letter to the editor here suggesting that Britain and Germany should simply agree not to bomb one another's cities. How very civilised.' The sarcasm was heavy.

'So have we all been engaged on a fruitless journey and an unnecessary effort today? We could have left the wee horrors where they were?'

'I wish,' said the young man wearily. 'Going to find somewhere to stretch out, MacMillan. See you later.'

He gave her a wave and passed on up the carriage. He wasn't the only one who was dog-tired. As Jim had been talking to her, Adam's head had been gradually nodding towards her shoulder. It came to rest, warm and heavy and solid. Was he asleep? She tried to squint at his face to find out, but it was too close to her own.

'Adam?'

'Mmm?'

'Adam?' she asked again.

There was no reply. It would be cruel to disturb him. And on a day like today, when all of them thought they knew only too well what tomorrow might bring, there was something very reassuring about his closeness.

He was still asleep when the train got to Glasgow. Liz had been unwilling to waken him until the very last minute. If she were writing a prescription for him and Jim she wouldn't bother with sulphonamides or any new wonder drug. She'd go for regular meals and a few good nights' sleep.

As the train came to a halt she edged away from Adam a fraction – as much as she could with the weight of his head on her shoulder. Gosh, it was heavy. All that brain power, no doubt.

Tired as he was, he did have to get off the train. Liz lifted her free hand to give him a shake. The door of the compartment shrieked its protest as someone pushed it open abruptly.

Liz turned to give the noisy person a telling-off. The words died on her lips. It was Mario.

Chapter 24

He looked very serious, but his sombre expression lightened when he saw the sleeping Adam, dead to the world and still slumped against Liz. She felt the beginnings of a blush as Mario stood looking down at the two of them.

'Should I be jealous?'

'Don't be daft! It's only Adam.'

Ridiculous to think of anyone being jealous of her and Adam. Ridiculous that she was blushing. Why should Mario Rossi be jealous anyway? To cover her growing embarrassment she turned to Adam and gave him a shake.

'Adam. We're back in Glasgow. Wake up, Adam.'

His eyelids fluttered open. He gave her the sweetest of smiles, murmured her first name and closed them again. Mario laughed, bent forward and physically hauled Adam upright.

'Buchanan. You're leaning on my girl's shoulder. Shift yourself.'

My girl? Liz rose to her feet, moving her freed shoulder up and down to relieve the stiffness in it. She turned awkwardly in the confined space and stood as far away as she could from Mario. Which wasn't very far. It was a good job they had Adam to focus on.

'What?' He straightened up so quickly it was comical to watch. Then he sank back against the cushions, blinking. His thick fair hair mussed up from the prolonged contact with Liz's shoulder, he looked like a startled lion cub.

'You've been asleep leaning on Liz, you idiot,' said Mario, throwing a grin at her. She tried to smile back, but she imagined that she looked like a rabbit caught in the headlights of a car. Mr Rossi's smile ought to be registered as a lethal weapon. Thank God, once more, for Adam.

'What?' he asked again, yawning hugely. He looked up at the two of them. 'Sorry, MacMillan. I do beg your pardon.'

'Nae bother,' Liz said, smiling down at him. 'Nae bother at all.'

There was a commotion in the corridor outside. Mario stood hurriedly aside as Cordelia MacIntyre came hurtling into the compartment. She threw herself down next to Adam. One glance at her face was enough to know that she'd had some bad news: so bad she was incapable of expressing it in words.

With a cry of 'Oh, Adam!' she turned her face into his shoulder, breaking into loud sobs. His arm came round her in an instant.

'That's what I came to tell you,' said Mario. 'Looks like Cordelia's already found out. It's been all over the wireless today.'

'What has?' demanded Liz, looking with concern at Cordelia weeping on Adam's shoulder. She didn't much like the girl, but she couldn't witness such obvious distress and remain unmoved.

Mario took a grim pleasure in being the bearer of bad tidings. 'While you were having your trip to the seaside, my children,' he told them, 'enjoying the pleasures of the Ayrshire coast, the Germans were enjoying the pleasures of Poland. They marched over the border this morning.'

Adam tightened his grip on the weeping Cordelia and looked up at Liz and Mario, his mouth set in a grim line.

'So now it can only be a matter of hours.'

Persuaded by silent messages from both men that the most tactful course of action was to beat a strategic retreat and leave Cordelia to Adam, Liz got off the train and walked up the platform with Mario. She'd expected hustle and bustle, but the big station was eerily deserted, the few passengers coming off the train dispersing quickly and passing out under the portico into the September evening.

'Lots of trains have been cancelled, apparently,' said Mario when she commented on the unusual emptiness of the station. 'Most of the Clyde steamers are off too. They're running a skeleton service for the folk who live on the islands, but there'll be no pleasure trips this weekend.'

Amelia Buchanan passed them on the concourse, giving them both a cheerful wave.

'Is that why you came to meet the train?' asked Liz, watching Adam's mother going out of the station and disappearing round a corner out of sight. She must be heading for the taxi rank. Adam was probably going to drive Cordelia home to her flat in the West End once she had recovered. The Buchanans were a considerate family. She repeated her question.

'Did you come to meet us to tell us the news?'

'No.'

Funny how one little word could carry so much meaning. Mario smiled when he saw how she was mulling it over.

'Stop here for a minute,' he said, indicating a large pillar. 'Please?' Liz put her back to it and waited for him to speak.

'I came to apologise for last night.'

She couldn't think of what to say. He said it for her. At least, he articulated what he thought was the problem.

'You're very shy, aren't you?' His voice was soft. 'With boys, I mean.'

'I suppose I am,' she managed, and dropped her eyes.

'Look at me, Elisabetta. Please?'

His voice was like dark brown velvet, smooth, warm and comforting. She couldn't resist it: especially when he called her by the Italian version of her name.

'Would you like to try again?'

'N-not the pictures.'

He smiled ruefully. 'No, not the pictures. I thought we might try it the Italian way. How about having a meal with my father and me? This Sunday maybe, after your stint at the hospital?'

220

Liz liked the sound of the Italian way. A meal with his father as chaperone. She lifted her chin.

'I'd love to. Thank you.'

Before she had time to realise what was happening, a smiling Mario bobbed forward and pressed a swift kiss on her forehead.

'What big eyes you've got!'

He was laughing at her. Then he saw something in those big eyes which took the smile off his handsome face.

'Och, Liz. Don't panic. I'm not planning on going any further.' What he said next sent goosebumps racing up and down her spine. 'Not unless and until you ask me to.'

Liz swallowed. 'That might not be for a long time.'

'That's all right. I can be patient.'

Could he? Perhaps that was all she needed. And if she could work at getting rid of these silly inhibitions, perhaps she need never tell him about Eric Mitchell. But was it fair to keep him hanging on?

'Why are you bothering with me?' she asked. 'You could get any girl you wanted.'

'I don't want any girl. I want you. And don't you ever look in the mirror, Liz?'

That made her smile.

'You're as charming as your father – and as big a liar.'

Adam and Cordelia were walking slowly towards them. He had his arm draped about her shoulders.

'I'm taking Cordelia for a quick drink.'

Mario looked concerned. 'Should you not have something to eat as well, Cordelia? You look awfully pale.'

'She doesn't want to be home too late,' said Adam. 'She's very tired.' Cordelia seemed content to let him speak for her. 'You must be tired too, Liz,' he added, turning to her. 'If you want to come with us, I'll drop you off after I've taken Cordelia home.'

Liz shook her head. She couldn't imagine that Cordelia would welcome her company tonight.

'Thanks for the offer, but I'll be fine on the train.'

'I'll look after her,' promised Mario. 'See her safely on to it. How about we all come into town tomorrow night to see the blackout? We could meet up here.'

Amusement lit up Adam's weary face.

'To see the blackout? Isn't that a contradiction in terms?'

Stumbling bleary-eyed out of bed on Saturday morning, Liz pulled on her dressing gown, thrust her feet into her slippers and padded through to the kitchen. She would make herself some tea and take it back to bed with her. With a bit of luck nobody else was up yet.

Her hand on the round knob, she pushed the door open and stood there for a minute. Everybody was up: her mother, her father and Eddie. He gestured towards the *Glasgow Herald*, lying on the table in front of them, sliding the paper round so that she could read it. The headline stood out in heavy black letters: *GERMANY INVADES POLAND*.

Pulling out a chair, Liz sank down into it.

'I haven't been having a nightmare, then.'

Eddie shot her the oddest of looks across the table. There was something almost mischievous about it.

'No, you haven't been dreaming, Liz.' He gestured again to the paper. 'It says here that they flew down the Vistula yesterday, bombing all the bridges.'

'It's wicked,' said Sadie, shaking her head. 'Wicked. May God forgive that man Hitler.'

William MacMillan snarled at his wife. 'What would you know about it, woman?'

Sadie drew herself up and spoke with simple dignity.

'I know how I would feel if it was the Clyde.'

Liz gave her a silent cheer, and for a moment it was as if the Vistula was the river flowing past yards from the house.

Finding his wife – for once – refusing to be his victim, William MacMillan glared at his son. 'Why in the name of God should we go to war for a bunch of bloody foreigners? Even the Prime Minister said that, didn't he? *A faraway country*

222

of which we know little. Why? Answer me that!'

There was a pause. Liz knew what the answer was. Because Britain and France had let Hitler get away with it for too long. Because the two great democracies had a moral duty to their weaker neighbours. Because they couldn't simply stand by and watch as country after country fell under the jackboot of ruthless dictatorship. Because it was time to make a stand.

She knew that William MacMillan wouldn't understand any of that. She left it to Eddie to give his father the only answer which he could accept.

'Because if we don't, it'll be our turn next, that's why.'

Later that morning Liz went up to Glasgow with her mother and Mrs Crawford to a special service at Glasgow Cathedral. On the journey up, Annie Crawford spoke briefly about her brother Alan, who had fallen at the Somme during the Great War.

'He was only your age,' she told Liz sadly. 'Nineteen.' And Liz thought about Eddie, Mario and Adam – and all the other boys she knew.

They passed from the midday sunshine of Castle Street into the cool dimness of the ancient building in the shadow of the Royal Infirmary.

Out of the darkness into the light. But their entry into the cathedral had taken them in the opposite direction. It was the way the whole of Europe was going, teetering on the threshold of unimaginable disaster. Liz listened attentively to the two clergymen who were conducting the service. They prayed for calm, that 'we should hold fast to our principles and even in the cruelties and tragedies of war banish malice, bitterness and hatred'.

And Liz, knowing now that it was completely hopeless, bowed her head and prayed for peace.

'I am speaking to you from the Cabinet Room at Ten Downing Street. This morning the British ambassador in Berlin handed the German government an official note stating that unless we

223

heard from them by eleven o'clock that they were prepared at once to withdraw their troops from Poland a state of war would exist between us. I have to tell you that no such undertaking has been received, and that consequently this country is at war with Germany.'

The Prime Minister went on speaking, but Liz was having difficulty listening to his thin, reedy voice. The blood was thumping through her ears – *and that consequently this country is at war with Germany.*

War. They couldn't really be going to war. Could they? She looked up, experiencing a moment of intense panic. From across the day room of one of the empty wards where those on duty this morning had gathered, Mario winked at her.

As if it understood that events had taken a dramatic turn, the weather had decided to play along. A thunderstorm was raging over the Clyde valley.

Neville Chamberlain was coming to the end of his speech, his voice growing more and more portentous.

'Now, may God bless you all. May we defend the right. It is evil things that we shall be fighting against: brute force, bad faith, injustice, oppression and persecution, and against them I am certain that the right will prevail.'

Someone turned off the wireless. There was absolute silence in the day room. Then Adam cleared his throat.

'I love that bit about the evil thing *we* shall be fighting against,' he murmured. 'Nice of the Prime Minister to include us all. We wouldn't want anyone to feel left out, would we now?'

There were a few nervous laughs and shifting of positions. A split second later there was a vivid flash of lightning and peal of thunder. Liz felt as if she'd jumped about two feet into the air. She wasn't the only one.

'What? Are the Germans here already?' asked Mario. Everyone burst out laughing.

With Liz's approval, Mario made the invitation to a meal a

general one. Adam and Cordelia came. Jim and Naomi, too. Spotting the bust of Mussolini on the shelf next to the photograph of Mario's mother as they went through the door which led to the upstairs flat, Adam turned to Aldo.

'You'd better get rid of that, Mr Rossi.'

'You think so?' He looked surprised.

'You can't have anything connected with the enemy,' said Cordelia. 'It's not done.' She was very subdued.

'But Italy's not in the war,' said Liz.

'You forgot one word,' said Mario. 'Yet. Italy's not in the war yet.'

'Which side would you choose, Mario?' asked Jim Barclay.

He lifted his shoulders in a gesture which suddenly struck Liz as being very Italian. She'd never thought of him as a foreigner before. Not really.

'I hate fascism,' he said passionately, 'but how could I fight against my father's country? Against my own relatives, perhaps? How could I?'

None of his friends were able to give him an answer.

Chapter 25

The passenger ship *Athenia* left the Clyde on Friday 1 September bound for Canada. After leaving Glasgow she doubled back to pick up more passengers at Belfast and Liverpool. There were almost fifteen hundred people on board as she steamed out into the Atlantic on the early evening of the following Sunday. They were two hundred miles west of the Hebrides when the German submarine spotted them.

The U-boat captain had received his orders to commence hostilities against Britain at lunchtime that day, one hour after the declaration of war. Eight hours after that had been made, he gave the order to fire four torpedoes at the blacked-out *Athenia*. Only one of them hit her. One was enough.

On Tuesday morning five hundred survivors were landed at Greenock. Many of them were sent straight up to Glasgow: the uninjured to a hotel in Sauchiehall Street and the casualties to the Western.

Liz arrived at the hospital in the late afternoon, meeting Cordelia at the door to Outpatients and Casualty.

'This isn't one of your usual days,' observed Cordelia.

'No, but Mr Murray let me off work when we heard the news about the *Athenia* survivors being brought here. He thought I might be needed.'

'That's Uncle Alasdair for you. He's not a bad old stick.'

'Are you and Adam cousins then?' asked Liz as the two girls went into the building.

'Very distant ones. I call Alasdair my uncle but we're really second cousins – several times removed, I believe. The same as Adam and me. Oh!'

At first sight, the hospital looked to be in chaos, the corridors and waiting areas full of men, women and children. It was hard to tell what sort of condition they were in. Some were huddled silently in blankets, staring straight ahead of them with unfocused eyes. Others were chattering convulsively.

Cordelia spotted Mario and Adam. They were accompanying a patient on a trolley towards one of the big lifts further along the corridor which gave access to the wards above.

The patient was a middle-aged woman. Liz saw with relief that she didn't look too badly injured. Not wanting to delay her treatment in any way, she and Cordelia walked along beside her while they spoke to Mario and Adam. Adam was doing most of the pushing while Mario, carrying a bag of clothes and a brand-new set of hospital case-notes, was steering them round the corners and towards the lift.

Liz gave the woman a pat on the arm. Offering reassurance to anyone who seemed to need it was fast becoming second nature. The patient looked up at her.

'I feel kinda dizzy.'

'Och, that's just the trolley,' said Liz. 'It takes a lot of people that way. And you're in good hands. This pair'll look after you.'

'From what I can see of them, they sure are a couple of handsome fellas.'

'Don't,' pleaded Mario. 'You'll turn my head.' He grinned at Liz and Cordelia. 'What can we do for you ladies?'

'Tell us who to report to,' said Cordelia. 'We're not going to be in the way, are we?'

'Not a chance,' said Adam. 'It's all hands to the pumps today. I was here already, and Mario came across the road to see what he could do, and we were immediately dragooned into helping with the portering. Matron's about, and most of the senior sisters.'

His hands occupied with pushing the trolley, he gestured with his head towards the outpatient area.

227

'See if you can find one of them. They're along there somewhere. I'm sure they'll have something for you to do.' His tone of voice altered slightly, became brighter and more consciously cheerful. 'Right then, here we are. A ride up in the lift, and then you'll be there.'

We're all doing it, thought Liz, the reassuring voice and the professional smile. As long as it helped the patients – and it did seem to. The woman on the trolley was looking a lot happier.

She and Cordelia wished her good luck, promising to pop up to the ward later and see how she was getting on. Then they went looking for some marching orders. It was Sister MacLean they found first. She actually looked pleased to see them. That made a nice change.

'You can help us sort out the relatives,' she said. 'Follow me.' Liz and Cordelia scurried obediently behind her. Except in cases of direst emergency – and apparently even this didn't qualify – running in the hospital corridors was a crime. Sister MacLean had drummed that into them.

'It alarms the patients. A nurse must always convey an air of calmness and efficiency.'

However, Sister MacLean could walk pretty damn fast when the occasion demanded it. Almost out of puff, the girls only just managed not to cannon into her when she stopped abruptly in front of one of the outpatient clinics, a large room off the main waiting area. Two or three nurses were there already. They had their work cut out. The area was packed with people, most of them wearing a motley selection of garments.

'They're the survivors,' said Sister MacLean. 'Uninjured, but suffering from varying degrees of shock. Bring us through any you feel you can't deal with,' she said briskly, 'but try a cup of sweet tea and a biscuit first. That can often do a surprising amount of good. And listen to them. Let them tell you their stories.'

'Have we got relatives here too?' Liz asked. 'People who weren't on board the ship?'

Sister nodded. 'Yes – and they're all up to high doh. It's

understandable enough – but they're getting in our way while we're trying to deal with the casualties. One of the medical students is making a list of names and injuries, but he's not a quarter of the way through it yet. Everyone keeps interrupting him to ask about their own people. If you can get everybody settled – explain that they'll get the information as soon as we have it – that would be a big help.'

'Of course, Sister,' said Cordelia.

Sister MacLean nodded and walked smartly away. Cordelia smiled nervously at Liz. Liz didn't smile back. She was concentrating too hard on the way her heart was thumping. This was her first real test as a nurse. Would she be able to cope?

Cordelia seemed to be feeling the same. 'This is it then, Liz,' she murmured.

'Tea, Miss MacIntyre,' said Liz, sharper than she might have been because she was so nervous herself. 'Let's go and make the tea. Several gallons of it, I should think.'

'Miss MacMillan?' Cordelia's voice was very tentative.

'Yes?' said Liz shortly, pouring a jug of water into the big gas tea urn which sat in one corner of the small outpatients department kitchen. That would do for the first batch, but they would be as well filling the two big kettles which went on to the gas stove too. Was there some reason why that hadn't occurred to the Honourable Miss MacIntyre?

'You'll have to show me how to do it.'

'Show you how to do what?' asked Liz, still engaged in filling the urn.

'Make the tea.'

'What?' Wondering if she'd heard her right, Liz spun round. Cordelia was standing looking at her. Her normally elegant demeanour seemed to have deserted her. She looked like a diffident child who'd been caught doing something naughty.

'Oh, Liz, I don't know how to! I've never done it in my entire life. I can't even boil water, let alone an egg. Pathetic, isn't it?'

Liz stared at her, incredulous. How in the name of the wee man could anyone not know how to make tea?

'Absolutely pathetic,' she agreed, but her voice had softened. The other girl was close to tears. Her reaction seemed a bit extreme, but Liz could see that it was real enough. She was genuinely distressed.

Liz pointed to the big kettle. 'Take that to the sink and fill it.'

Cordelia perked up. Any minute now she'd start taking notes.

'Hot or cold tap?' she asked.

Ye gods. She really didn't know the first thing about it.

'The cold one,' said Liz with exaggerated patience. 'Then bring it over here and I'll show you how to light the gas and we'll take it from there. A master class in the art of tea-making. First lesson. Always take the pot to the kettle, never the other way round . . .'

Not all of the *Athenia* survivors wanted to talk. Some of them clearly felt they had to. There was a compulsion to go over the nightmare. As afternoon gave way to evening, Liz began to realise that many of them thought they owed it to those who hadn't made it. Their stories had to be told too.

The *Athenia* should have been taking them away from the danger zone, and there was bitter anger at how an unarmed passenger ship had been attacked a matter of hours after the declaration of war. In some people the rage was white-hot in its intensity.

'Surely they could see that we were harmless, Nurse! How could they do that to their fellow human beings – men, women and children? I don't understand. Have these Germans no humanity?'

Many of the survivors had spent hours in the water before they'd been rescued. They'd been landed at Greenock early in the morning – cold, hungry and exhausted. The women of the town had rallied round magnificently, supplying them with clothes out of their own wardrobes.

The survivors deeply mourned the loss of their fellow passengers. Some of them, alive when they went into the sea, had simply lost the unequal struggle with the cold waters of the North Atlantic.

An older man, shaking with emotion, told Liz of seeing children drowning all around him before he himself had been rescued by the *Southern Cross*, one of the ships which had gone full steam ahead to the rescue of the *Athenia*.

'It was bloody awful, Nurse,' he told Liz, his voice low and impassioned. 'Bloody awful. Why should a useless old man like me have survived when those kids didn't?'

She had no answer to give him, only a comforting hand on his shoulder. All she could do for him was listen to his story. That was hard. Not as hard as the telling.

'They were at the start of their lives,' he told Liz in an anguished whisper. 'And there was nothing we could do to save them. Nothing. We tried to get them to hang on to anything that was floating, but some of them just didn't make it.' He stared ahead, his eyes seeing it all again, reliving the horror. He reminded Liz of her grandfather. He had the same piercing blue eyes.

'God bless the crew of the *Southern Cross*,' he said fiercely. 'God bless them. But there was this woman,' he went on, his voice sinking to a tortured whisper. 'A young woman. She'd been rescued, taken out of the sea. It was so cold in the water, Nurse. So bitterly cold. She'd been saved, like me—'

He broke off, and let out a sob.

'It's all right. Take your time. You're fine.' Liz repeated the soothing words until he was able to go on.

'She stood up,' he said. 'She stood up and screamed and then she threw herself over the side. Deliberately threw herself back into the sea. Do you know what she was screaming, Nurse?'

Liz shook her head. He was rigid with horror and pain, his voice cracking.

'She was screaming, *My baby!*'

231

God forgive the Germans, thought Liz. Because I can't.

'Liz?' Adam's voice was very gentle. 'Are you all right?'

'I'm fine,' she said, but she didn't turn around to face him.

'We were worried about you,' came another voice. Cordelia MacIntyre. That was all she needed.

It was several hours later and the immediate panic was over. The casualties had been dealt with, the uninjured had been persuaded to board the bus which had been hired to take them to the hotel in Sauchiehall Street where the other survivors were staying, and Liz had found a quiet corner in which to gather her thoughts before she got the energy up to go home.

'Go away,' she told them both. 'I'm fine.'

'Och, aye,' Adam said. He came further into the room and stood in front of her. Cordelia followed him and stood looking at Liz with worried eyes.

'I can see you're fine,' said Adam with heavy irony. 'That's why you've got your arms wrapped about yourself and that's why you're shaking like a leaf, I suppose. You need some hot sweet tea – pronto! Doctor's orders, my girl.'

'I d-don't w-want any b-bloody t-tea.' She lifted a hand to point at Cordelia. That was a mistake. Her whole arm was trembling. 'She and I have served up enough of it tonight to launch a battleship.' That was a mistake too. She could have chosen a better metaphor. She didn't want to think about ships. Not tonight. Not for a long time to come.

'Coffee, then,' said Adam, his voice brisk. 'Up the road. In fact, we were already planning that. Mario's gone on ahead to warn his father that we're all about to descend on him.'

Liz saw Cordelia touch his arm.

'I'll go on ahead, Adam. The others are probably there by now. I'll let them know that the two of you are on your way.'

To Liz's considerable surprise, on her way out of the room Cordelia reached out and patted her arm too.

'You'll be all right, Liz. Adam'll take care of you. He's good at that.'

The comforting words. The reassuring touch. The professional smile.

'Isn't this where we came in, Liz? Last time it was me who couldn't face any more tea. We've had this conversation before. Remember?'

She looked up at him out of tear-filled eyes, hugging herself even more tightly.

'Please leave me alone, Adam. I have to sort this out by myself.'

He snorted and uttered one short but eloquent word.

'That's better,' he said, smiling at the surprise evident on her face. 'Now come and sit down, you wee daftie.'

She allowed him to lead her to the deep tiled windowsill. It was curtainless, blackout screens fixed directly against the window itself.

'You don't have to sort things out by yourself when you've got friends to help you,' he said as they sat down next to each other. 'Don't you know that, MacMillan?' His voice was very gentle.

'I know that I should be getting home.'

He shook his head. 'You don't have to. Matron says that any of the volunteers who live some distance away can sleep here tonight. They can fit you in at the nurses' home. Or Cordelia says you can go home with her.' He gave her one more alternative. 'Or I could drive you home. Whenever you're ready.'

'My parents will be worrying about me.'

Adam shook his head again. 'No they won't. Your brother Eddie came past – oh, hours ago—' He yawned, and put a hasty hand over his mouth. 'Excuse *me*. He thought you'd be here and that you might not get away at the usual time, so your folks know exactly where you are. Matron was there when he called, apparently, and she told him you might be staying over.'

Liz was looking very doubtful. Adam lifted her hand from her lap and on to the cool tiles of the windowsill, his own on top of it.

'Want to talk about it? I'm a doctor, you know. Well – almost. If I ever manage to pass my finals.'

'You'll pass. You'll make a great doctor.'

'You'll make a great nurse.'

'I don't think I'll make any kind of a nurse.' It came out in a rush of breath.

'How do you work that one out?'

'Just look at me,' she wailed. 'Look at the state I'm in!'

She began to cry, the painful lump in her throat dissolving into hot tears. Adam didn't move any closer to her, but he kept a tight hold of her hand and he said all the right things: the things Liz had been saying to people all evening.

'You're all right now. Just take your time. You're fine.'

She poured it all out to him. She'd wanted to be a nurse all her life. It had been the dream which had kept her going, the dream she'd refused to give up on, but when it came to the crunch she just wasn't up to it. Look at the way she was reacting now. Her first genuine emergency, and she'd gone completely to pieces.

He paid her the compliment of listening carefully and just as carefully considering what she had said.

'Think about it, Liz!' He gave her hand a shake. 'You're upset now, and it's only natural, but you didn't behave like this with the survivors, did you? You coped. And I'm sure – no, I know – that you did them a lot of good. You're being too hard on yourself. You've heard some heartbreaking stories tonight.' His mouth tightened. 'We all have. But the important thing is that you listened to the people who needed to talk without letting them see how it was upsetting you. You kept it inside until it was safe to let it out.'

'But look at me now!'

He gave her hand another encouraging squeeze. 'But that's what I mean. You've held it all in till now – so that you can let it out when you're among friends. There's nothing wrong with that, nothing at all.'

She turned to him then, her eyes huge.

'Isn't there?' She was like a little child seeking comfort and reassurance.

'No, in fact, if you weren't upset by everything you've heard today, you wouldn't make a very good nurse. Don't you know that all nurses and doctors feel like you do to begin with?'

'They do?'

'Definitely. I bet even Ming the Merciless has had her moments.'

'Now you are telling fibs.' Liz tried a smile.

Adam smiled back. 'She does resort to a wee brandy now and again, you know.'

'No!' Liz was incredulous.

'Well-known fact,' he said briefly. 'She keeps a bottle in her room. Fondly imagines the rest of us know nothing about it.' He released her hand and stood up. 'Come on, MacMillan, let's get up the road. I don't know about you, but I'm bloody starving.'

She shivered as they stepped out on to the pavement.

'Cold?'

'No. It's the blackout. I hate it already.' How well did she know this street? Like the back of her hand. But in this total darkness it was like stepping out into the abyss. 'I can't see anything. It all feels different.'

Adam's deep voice was reassuring. 'But it's not different. Everything's the same as it's always been. We can't see it at the moment, but it's all still there. Right, I think we're coming to the road. Step down now.'

'I can't. I'm scared I'll fall.'

'Off the pavement?' He sounded amused.

'Yes,' she said, 'and I know that's ridiculous, but I can't help it!' She froze, unable to go any further. He didn't tell her not to be so stupid. He simply waited, standing with her on the edge of the pavement.

'They were singing,' she said suddenly. 'Some of the children on board the *Athenia*. One of the survivors told me. Just before the torpedo hit them. They were on deck singing

"South of the Border".' She lifted her face to the night air. 'Like we did on Friday.'

'I know,' he said. 'I know.' His voice was husky. They stood for a minute or two in silence.

'I think my eyes are getting a bit more used to the dark,' she said at last.

'Take my arm,' he suggested. 'That'll help.'

Arm in arm, they stepped off the pavement and crossed the road.

'How long will it go on?' she asked. 'The war, I mean?'

'I don't know.' He squeezed her hand. 'But the lights will come on again. Don't you remember how they did at the Empire Exhibition?'

They paused briefly before they went through the door of the café, itself completely blacked out.

'Thank you,' said Liz.

She could just make out his smile.

'What for?' he asked.

'Taking time to comfort a gibbering wreck.'

'Any time, Liz,' he said. 'Any time.'

Inside the café, all was warm and bright. She headed for Mario's arms. That is to say, she would have, if he hadn't been engaged in setting tables. His hands full of plates and cutlery, he was unable to fasten them around her, but he looked pleased.

'Darling! This is so sudden.'

Trust him to make a joke of it, although it was as well that he did. Liz was embarrassed after she'd done it – in front of the others, too.

'The police came round to the café today.' It was an hour and a half later and Mario was walking Liz down the road to the nurses' home. As long as she got in by eleven o'clock, she'd been told. Naomi Richardson had passed on the message.

'Think yourself lucky, MacMillan. A late pass for us poor life prisoners is normally half past ten!'

The moon was up, the night much brighter now. She could

distinguish the buildings and make out the line of the road quite clearly – and the odd expression on Mario's face.

'The police? What on earth for?'

'My father's an enemy alien, Liz.' The tone of voice was equal parts rueful amusement and sarcasm. 'Sounds like something out of a Flash Gordon film, doesn't it?'

'An enemy alien?' she repeated. 'But your father's lived here most of his life.'

Mario shook his head.

'He was born in Italy, lived there till he was eighteen. That's enough. They're checking up on us all. In case we're a danger to the state.' He enunciated the final four words carefully, the sarcasm growing heavier by the second.

'That's ridiculous,' spluttered Liz. 'I never heard such nonsense in my life. How could your father be a danger to anybody?'

Then she registered exactly what Mario had said. *Us all?* She stopped dead. So did he, smiling wryly in the moonlight when he saw her reaction.

'Don't worry Liz, apparently we're both only Class C enemies of the state.' He was taking a savage delight in using the words.

'I don't understand,' she said. 'What does that mean?'

'That we're not considered *particularly* dangerous.' He struck a contemplative pose. 'Perhaps I should find that insulting. However, if Italy comes into the war . . .' He shrugged.

'Were you born in Italy?' she demanded.

'No, I was born here.'

'So you're Scottish: a British citizen. How can they possibly classify you as an enemy alien? And Mr Rossi's been here for ages. I don't see that, either.'

He smiled at her logic – and her loyalty to him and his father – but he told her the truth.

'Liz, I've got dual nationality: British and Italian. My father registered me with the Italian consul when I was born. Added to which, what I really am is half-Irish and half-Italian. Eire is probably going to remain neutral, but the Irish aren't very popular as it is. You know that as well as anybody. It'll be a case of he who is not for us is against us. And the chances of Mussolini coming into the war on the German side are pretty high. Italy could probably conscript me to fight for them.'

'But you wouldn't. Would you?'

He gave a quick frown. 'No, of course not. How could I fight against the country of my birth, against my friends? But like I told you before, I don't think I could fight against my own relatives in Italy either. So what happens when the authorities here ask me to prove my loyalty to Britain? By being disloyal to my father's country?' He stopped abruptly, and bit his lip.

She reached out a hand to him, clutched his sleeve. 'Oh, Mario. I'm so sorry.'

He looked down at her. For once he was completely serious.

'You've got a choice to make.'

'Me?'

He nodded grimly. 'Going out with me could cause you problems. It hadn't occurred to me last Friday when I met you at the station, but it sure has occurred to me now. That visit today from the boys in blue concentrated my mind wonderfully.'

He let her think about it for a minute or two. She did. Then she put a question to him as they stood together in the silent and deserted street.

'What do *you* want? No jokes, now. I want a straight answer.'

That made him smile, his teeth a flash of white in the gloom, but he did as she asked.

'I want *you*,' he said simply, 'but it's not too late for you to decide not to get involved with me.'

'I already am involved with you.'

He lifted her hands to his mouth and kissed her fingertips, first one hand, then the other.

'Thank you. You'll never know how much I appreciate that.' They smiled at each other. Then he became brisk. 'Come on. Time you were in your bed.'

238

They walked up to the door of the nurses' home. 'It's like a convent, this place,' Mario said conversationally. 'No man has ever been allowed to cross its hallowed portals. I've always wondered if there's human sacrifice of innocent young maidens behind these walls.'

'I'll survive,' said Liz, glad that he was joking again. 'I suppose I'd better be getting in. It must be nearly eleven.'

'Come to the café for your breakfast tomorrow?' he suggested.

'That would be lovely. Goodnight,' she said shyly, wondering if he was going to kiss her. He did, but on her forehead, the merest brushing of his lips against her skin.

'Goodnight, Liz.'

'Say it in Italian,' she urged. 'I love it when you speak Italian.'

His smile was very tender, and she saw how much he appreciated her request. Tonight of all nights. '*Buonanotte, Elisabetta.*' He put his lips to her brow a second time. '*Buonanotte, bellisima.* Sleep well.'

Chapter 26

'So,' Mario asked, his elbows on the table and his chin resting on his fists, 'when are you going to take me home to meet your parents?'

Liz mimicked his posture and pretended to consider. 'Well . . .' she began, 'how about some time after hell freezes over?'

'You really think your father would take it that badly?'

She gave him a rueful look. 'Why do you think I keep persuading Eddie to put off introducing Helen to my parents?'

That had to happen eventually. There were going to be fireworks that day, all right.

'Don't frown,' said Mario, shifting position and stretching across the table to rub his thumb gently along her lips. 'Why not take me to meet your grandfather instead?'

Liz straightened up and laid her hands flat in front of her. 'My grandfather? But you've already met him.'

'Not as your boyfriend, I haven't.' He smiled his lazy smile. 'Not as the young man you're walking out with.'

'I thought you preferred staying in,' she murmured, tucking a rogue strand of hair behind one ear. 'Judging from last night, that is. When you plied me with alcohol.'

'A glass of vermouth is hardly plying you with alcohol.' There was a gleam of mischief in his brown eyes. 'And if you're implying that I was trying to break down your resistance, I would have to point out that my strategy was spectacularly unsuccessful.'

Liz blushed and dipped her head. Mario reached for the hand

still lying on the table and gave it a little tug. She looked up and met his eyes again.

'I'm sorry. You've been very patient.'

She was surprised how patient he'd been. Not a little touched, too. She'd done her best to meet him halfway but progress, she would have to admit, had been slow.

'We'll get there eventually,' he said softly. 'Give us a kiss, beautiful.' Liz leaned towards him, eager to comply. Holding hands and gentle kisses were fine. More than fine.

Someone coughed. With a start, Liz broke the contact with Mario and looked up. Adam, Jim and Naomi had come into the previously empty café.

'Oh,' said Liz, 'I didn't see you there.'

Jim and Naomi were grinning, but Adam's voice was very dry.

'Evidently,' he said.

Liz was regaling Naomi Richardson with the story of Cordelia being unable to make tea the night the *Athenia* survivors had been brought to the Infirmary. A couple of months on from the event, the stories she'd listened to hadn't got any less vivid. She suspected they never would.

There had been a second tragedy in Scottish waters, up in the Orkneys, at the Royal Navy's anchorage in Scapa Flow. Supposedly impregnable, its defences had been breached by another German U-boat. It had sunk a battleship called the *Royal Oak*. Over eight hundred British sailors had been drowned.

When war had been declared it had been awful. It was going to be a struggle, a hell of a fight, but deep down everyone had assumed that Britain was going to win in the end. But if the Germans could get right into Scapa Flow . . . Liz couldn't stop thinking about the families of all those eight hundred men either.

She'd decided there was only one way to cope with it all. Pick out the funny stories and concentrate on them.

'Imagine!' she scoffed to Naomi. 'How could anyone not know how to make tea? I believe the Honourable Miss

MacIntyre had a very expensive education – boarding school in England, finishing school in Switzerland, a year in Heidelberg studying German. Yet she can't even make a cup of tea. Mind you, I suppose her mama would be horrified if she could!'

Adam was sitting in a corner of the outpatients' kitchen having a quick break. Many qualified doctors had already joined the Royal Army Medical Corps or gone off to military hospitals. That left the Infirmary's medical and surgical residents at full stretch, trying to reallocate the duties of the missing doctors as well as dealing with their own overcrowded schedules.

Some of the more capable senior medical students had been asked to help out by covering some sessions, both on the wards and in the outpatient clinics. Adam was one of them. He looked up from his reading – a medical paper this time – with a frown.

'You're a bit of a snob, MacMillan, aren't you?'

Stung by the note of reproach in his voice, Liz stared at him. 'A snob? Me?'

'Yes, you!' he said, standing up and running an angry hand through his hair. His fair locks were a bit untidy. He needed a haircut.

'Cordelia can't help her background any more than you can help yours. And it's as unfair for you to mock her for the way she was brought up as it would be for someone to look down on you for the way you speak. Cordelia's got the money to go and sit out the war in some funk-hole – yet she chooses to stay here and do her bit. Doesn't she deserve some credit for that? Or are you really so naïve that you believe that because she's well off she doesn't have any problems?'

He flung out of the room, his white coat billowing out behind him. Liz felt like bursting into tears. He'd never spoken to her like that before.

'You put your foot in it there, MacMillan,' said Naomi softly. 'I rather think you touched a raw nerve.'

Liz looked at her in dismay. 'Is he right?' she asked. 'Am I being unfair?'

The other girl shrugged. 'Well, you can say what you like

242

about the honourable Miss MacIntyre, but she is one of the world's workers, you'd have to give her that.' She stood up. 'Time I went back to the salt mines myself. See you later, MacMillan.'

She went out, leaving Liz alone with her thoughts. They weren't comfortable ones. She thought of Lady MacIntyre, whom she'd met the day of the evacuation. With a mother like that, maybe it was no wonder Cordelia hadn't a clue how to make tea – but she'd been more than willing to learn. She always was.

When she'd asked for help in tying her cap that first day, Liz had suspected she might be one of those girls who were attracted to the VADs because they wanted to swan about in a nurse's uniform. Liz had met a few of them. They didn't last long – till they were asked to give a patient a bedpan perhaps, or clean up after a child who'd been sick. Cordelia wasn't like that at all. She was always willing and always cheerful.

Adam had been perfectly right. She had been unfair. Unkind, too, making fun of Cordelia for something that wasn't her fault. And she'd offended Adam – worse, she'd upset him. She wouldn't have done that for the world.

Sphygmomanometer. She was to go the female medical ward up on the second floor and ask to borrow their sphygmo— How did the blasted word go again? *Sphygmomanometer.* There. She had it again. She'd better keep repeating it to herself.

Why did hospital corridors have to be so blinking long? Oh Lord, she'd forgotten it again. She could get as far as *sphyg—*, but the rest of the word had gone. Something like *meter* on the end of it. *Sphygmeter?* No, that wasn't right. She stopped short, biting her lip. She was going to look like a right eejit.

Especially as she was always sounding off to Sister MacLean about wanting to do more medical things. Especially as it was Sister MacLean who had sent her on this errand. Especially as it looked as if she was going to have to go back and ask her to write the word down.

'Stop biting your lip,' came an amused voice. It was Adam. He seemed to have regained his usual amiable disposition.

'Am I glad to see you!' said Liz. She was too, despite their recent encounter. A medical student would know the word for sure.

'What's the problem?'

'I've been sent on this message and I can't remember what for.'

'Short-term memory loss? At your age? Probably the first signs of madness, MacMillan. Do you think you should see a doctor?'

She scowled at him. 'I can't remember the word. It's the thing that measures blood pressure.'

'Oh, the sphygmomanometer?'

Liz put her hands on her hips. 'That's easy for you to say.'

He laughed again.

'For you too, MacMillan. If you split the word up. Like this: sphyg-mo-man-ometer. Easy.'

He made her repeat it two or three times. Then, before she could screw up the courage to offer him an apology, he spoke again.

'And MacMillan, by the way . . . I'm sorry I had a bit of a go at you earlier on. About Cordelia. I went over the score and I shouldn't have. I apologise.'

'No,' said Liz, the butterfly wings of her cap dancing as she shook her head. 'You were absolutely right. I'll mend my ways. I promise. I intend to become a reformed character.'

Adam's lips twitched.

'Don't change too much, MacMillan. I rather like you the way you are.'

Liz took Mario to visit her grandfather and was secretly amused to see how Peter MacMillan, prepared to do the stern patriarch act in the absence of her father, was so quickly won over by the Italian charm. Also, to be fair, by Mario's warm personality and genuine sincerity. She'd already observed that he was one of those men who got on as well with his own sex as with the opposite gender.

He was at home in any company too. From her grandfather's house, Liz took him down the road to visit the Gallaghers. He walked into the room, saw the picture of the Pope and immediately crossed himself. Helen introduced him to a beaming Marie Gallagher.

'Ma, this is Mario Rossi. He's a friend of Liz's.'

'You're Italian? A Catholic boy?'

Out of sight of her mother, Helen rolled her eyes at Liz. The Gallagher parents hadn't been exactly delirious when they'd found out that Eddie had metamorphosed from being the brother of their only daughter's friend into her steady boyfriend. Helen's father was only just managing to tolerate the mixed-religion romance.

'Yes, Mrs Gallagher,' said Mario, 'but I'm proud to say that my mother was Irish. Her family came from Cork.'

After that he could do no wrong. He charmed Marie, was respectful to Brendan, patted Finn on the head and told him what a handsome fellow he was, joshed about with the boys and taught Helen to sing an Italian song, insisting that Liz join her and make it a duet. A good time was had by all and, like Liz, he was given an open invitation to the flat in the Holy City.

'Well,' she said, as she walked him to the station, 'you were a big success. They really took you to their bosom, didn't they?'

As usual, she realised a split second too late that she had said the wrong thing. The look he gave her took her breath away.

'Perhaps you could consider taking a leaf out of their book, Liz. Patience has its limits, you know.'

She looked away guiltily.

Mario's limits were reached one snowy Sunday in January. They were spending the afternoon in the flat above the café playing records of Italian songs on the wind-up gramophone. Watching the snowflakes floating down past the big bay window, Liz was feeling warm and relaxed, enjoying the music and thinking happily that she wasn't expected home for a good few hours yet.

She turned from gazing out at the snow and looked indulgently at Mario. He was amusing himself by giving her extravagant translations of the words of the songs they were listening to, complete with theatrical – and very Italian – gestures.

'Mario, if I cut your hands off you wouldn't be able to speak.'

He pretended to take offence, slipping into an exaggerated Italian accent.

'Huh! Ze lady, she think-a I use-a my hands-a too much. Tell me, *bella scozzese*, how you describe a spiral staircase without-a you use-a your hands? Eh?' He reverted to his real accent, cocked his head to one side and folded his arms over his chest. 'Tell me that, my inhibited little Scotswoman.'

Chuckling at their antics, Aldo Rossi went back downstairs to attend to his customers. Liz was replacing one disc in its sleeve a minute or two later when she felt warm arms slide round her from behind, under her jumper. And the memories she tried so hard to suppress came shooting to the surface.

Spinning round in panic-stricken reaction, she saw Mario's face inches from her own.

'I can think of much better ways of using my hands than describing a spiral staircase,' he murmured. 'You have such a neat little waist – not to mention other parts of your anatomy which leave me cold when I see them illustrated in the textbooks, but which look very different when they come packaged as you. Kiss me, Liz.'

His voice husky with desire, he dipped his dark head towards her, one hand sliding up her body. Liz couldn't fight the urge to thrust him away. She did it with some force.

'Liz! For God's sake!' He stood where she had pushed him, in the middle of the room, and glowered at her, his dark eyebrows drawn angrily together.

'What *is* the matter with you? How many times do I have to tell you that I won't try to make you go too far? Can't you trust me by now? God, I've been so patient! Och, bloody hell, Liz!'

English obviously wasn't sufficient to express his irritation. He muttered an angry imprecation in Italian. It disconcerted her, reminding her of his foreignness, of the passionate nature usually hidden beneath the wisecracking Glaswegian side of his personality.

'You tell me you like me,' he said, beginning to pace about the room. 'You know that I like you. I like you a lot. We get on great together. And you're so lovely,' he said, wheeling round and coming to a halt in front of her.

The anger in his voice melted away as he stood gazing at her. 'And I don't want to do anything too naughty.' He smiled the smile which did indeed turn Liz's insides to melted butter. 'Well . . . maybe just a wee bit naughty . . .'

Deep inside her, something stirred into life. She ached to be able to relax into his arms, to let him touch her. She wanted to kiss him deeply and to be kissed passionately in return. She knew why there was a problem about that. He didn't.

She looked at him and saw the irritation fade once more. He never stayed angry with her for long. He took a step or two towards her.

'You look as though you're about to face a firing squad, Elisabetta.'

She could understand why he got annoyed with her, the way she seemed to welcome his touch, then suddenly started fending him off. Her behaviour would confuse anybody. Could she possibly tell him the truth?

'Trust me,' he said softly. 'I'm a doctor. Well, almost.'

Funny. Adam had said that once.

Mario moved closer. 'Oh, Liz,' he breathed. 'I could make it so nice for you . . . We could make it so nice for each other.'

She knew that. She knew there were delights. If she couldn't get over her problem they must remain forbidden fruit. She

liked him so much. She thought, maybe, that she loved him . . .
She cleared her throat and began.

'There's this chap where I work . . .'

'But why on earth would I think badly of *you*?' Mario asked
fifteen minutes later as they sat together on the settee, separate
but holding hands. She had told him the whole story: the way
Eric Mitchell had pounced on her almost as soon as she had
started at Murray's; the impossibility for a shy sixteen-year-
old of knowing how to cope with such unwanted attentions;
her fear of telling other people about his behaviour; how she
had finally stopped it from happening.

'I tried telling Miss Gilchrist once,' she explained, 'but she
more or less suggested that I was to blame in some way, had
led him on . . .'

'That's ridiculous,' snapped Mario. His brows were drawn
together again, but Liz understood that he was angry not at her,
but on her behalf. 'Anyone who knows you at all would see at
once that you're the last woman in the world to lead a man on
like that. I know that better than anybody,' he said ruefully,
lifting the hand he held and giving it a little shake.

'So, Doctor,' she asked, 'is there a remedy for my condition,
or am I a hopeless case?'

'Well, if the patient wants to be cured, that's half the battle.'
He tugged on her hand, but gently. She got the message. He
wanted her to come closer, but it would be her decision if she
did so. Not his.

She looked at him hungrily. He was so handsome, so funny,
so nice . . . and he was all hers. He'd made that plain. She
shuffled along the settee towards him. That got her the long,
slow smile, the one that lit a tiny candle gleam in his brown
eyes.

'A bit more,' he murmured.

She moved closer. He lifted one long finger and gently
touched her mouth, his voice a throaty whisper. 'Does the
patient want to be cured?'

'Yes,' said Liz, looking into his face, 'oh, yes!'

'Well,' said Mario, 'we have to take things very, very slowly, so that you get used to them very, very slowly. Shall we start with me putting my hand here?' He laid the lightest of hands on her neck, his fingers warm against her skin.

'How about that?' he asked. 'Is that all right?'

'It's fine.' She sounded like Minnie Mouse.

'Liar. Beautiful wee liar.'

'I'm not beautiful. You must need your eyes tested, Mr Rossi.'

'My eyes are perfect, Nurse MacMillan – and so are you.' He leaned towards her, murmuring softly in his dark brown voice. 'Don't close your mouth.'

That devastating instruction set Liz's insides all of a flutter, but his kiss was not invasive, merely a gentle nuzzling of his slightly parted lips against her own.

'I love you,' he whispered.

She gave the words back to him. *I love you.* She felt his mouth curve into a smile.

'Say that again.'

'I love you. What is it in Italian?'

'*Ti amo.* Repeat after me, class.'

'*Ti amo,*' she said. 'Kiss me again.'

This time it was deeper and more passionate. Liz could feel herself beginning to respond, kissing him back.

'Am I cured, Doctor?' she murmured.

'Almost, but I feel we need to keep practising, continue the treatment, I mean.' His lips were very close to her mouth. 'Now, don't you worry about a thing,' he murmured. 'Leave it all to your Uncle Mario.'

'Mr Eric Mitchell?'

'Who wants him?'

He turned, and felt a fist go into his face. Stunned by the speed of the attack, he was also unprepared for the fact that there was more than one assailant. In a few seconds they had him pinned up against the wall of the lane. Christ, there were four of them! And a huge bloody big dog.

No sooner had he registered that fact than one of the men who wasn't holding him against the wall drew his hand back and punched him in the stomach. Once. Twice. Winded, he slumped forward, stopped from falling to the ground only because he was being held up. His arms felt as though they were being ripped out of their sockets.

'That's enough,' came a voice he vaguely recognised. Then a mouth was against his ear.

'I hope it hurts,' the voice said pleasantly. 'And you might like to know there's plenty more where that came from.' The speaker paused for effect. 'Especially for people who use positions of authority to molest young ladies who're not interested in them. Tell anyone about this and I'll make sure Alasdair Murray knows how you pestered her. Do we understand each other? Now, we'll bid you goodnight.'

He was dropped like a sack of rubbish, left to sprawl on the rough and icy ground. As they sauntered off, he heard a couple of them start to sing.

'*Oh, we're all off to Dublin in the green, in the green . . .*'

Paddies. Micks. Fenians. And he had just remembered where he knew the other voice from. It was that Eyetie who had collected her from the office one night last autumn, just before the war had broken out. With a shaking hand, Eric Mitchell wiped the blood from his mouth and scrambled to his feet.

'Dear me, Mr Mitchell, what have you done to your face? And you seem to be walking rather gingerly too. Have you hurt yourself?'

'I slipped and fell on the ice,' he said, 'on my way home last night.'

Only half listening to the conversation, Liz lifted her head from her typewriter. Miss Gilchrist was clucking over Eric Mitchell, asking him if he'd been to the doctor, if she could get anything to make him more comfortable. He had an ugly purple bruise on his jaw, but the rest of his face was unmarked. It looked more like the after-effects of a punch, rather than a fall.

Liz froze. *Once I'd worked out what my fists were for.* Surely not. She gave herself a little shake. No. Mario would never do a thing like that. That had been when he was a wee daft laddie. He was a grown man now. She smiled.

Watching her, Eric Mitchell saw that smile, put two and two together and made five. So she hadn't been bluffing when she'd threatened him with a beating. No doubt she was spreading her legs for the wop. That would be how she'd have got him and his Paddy friends to do this to him.

He would get even with the fucking little bitch for this. This was going to be repaid with interest. However long it took.

Chapter 27

'No! I don't believe it.'

'It's true,' said Helen, her eyes sparkling. 'As I live and breathe.'

She was telling Liz about an incident at the first-aid post in Clydebank, set up in one of the local Church of Scotland halls – 'and me a good Catholic girl, too' – where she was a volunteer. Most of the incidents they were dealing with were casualties of the blackout: skinned noses and sore knees from walking into walls and other obstacles no longer visible during the dark winter nights. Tam Simpson had fallen foul of the lethal combination.

Determined, according to Helen, that the minor matter of being at war with Germany wasn't going to change his way of life, he had been wending his way homeward one Saturday night when the baffle wall in front of his own close – designed to stop flying debris from an explosion penetrating into the building – had decided to teach him a lesson.

'He'd had his usual wee refreshment, I take it?'

'He was refreshed out of his mind,' said Helen cheerfully, 'but you haven't heard the best bit yet.'

To Nan Simpson's eternal joy, she had been on duty when her husband – or, as she preferred to describe him, the wounded soldier – had been brought in. Blood gushing from his battered nose, he had decided there and then to take the pledge.

'He never did!' breathed Liz.

'He did,' Helen assured her. 'There he stands – well, he was actually sitting – and he looks up at Mrs S and he says, "Nan, this has been a lesson to me. I'm never touching the demon drink again.'"

'And what did she say?'

'She didn't crack a smile,' said Helen. 'She just looked at him and she said, "I'll believe you. Thousands wouldn't." They went off home arm in arm. It was hilarious, it really was.'

'She was probably holding him up. Trying to avoid any more baffle walls unexpectedly jumping up and hitting him in the face.'

'Probably,' agreed Helen with a smile.

The two girls were as close as they'd ever been. There had been a moment when Liz had feared that Helen would want to spend all of her time with Eddie, but that hadn't happened. Their friendship was important to both of them.

'Imagine me doing my bit in a Proddy church,' said Helen, turning her mouth down in mock dismay.

'Aye, right enough,' said Liz drily. 'I'm sure that priest of yours must be fearing for your immortal soul.'

She'd been visiting the Gallaghers one evening when their parish priest had called round. To say she hadn't taken to the man would have been putting it mildly. Once he found out that Liz was not of his own flock, it became clear that the feeling was entirely mutual. There was more to it than that. He made it obvious that he disapproved of Helen having such a close friend who was a Protestant.

'They're not all like that, Liz,' said Helen uncomfortably. 'We just happen to have got one who's a bit strict.'

'A bit strict? I got the distinct impression he was sizing me up for a nice burning at the stake.'

'Well, you did argue with him a bit,' Helen pointed out.

'I stood up to him,' said Liz with dignity. 'The man's a bully, clergyman or not.'

Helen grinned. 'You and Eddie have a lot in common, you know. Anyway, haven't you got some hellfire-and-brimstone ministers yourselves?'

Liz held up her hands in a gesture of surrender. 'I'll give

you that one. At least your lot don't think there's anything wrong with enjoying yourself on a Sunday. Although it's a good job your Father Whatsisname didn't call round on Sunday when Eddie was there. Can you imagine?'

'Only too well,' said Helen drily. 'He'd want to burn him at the stake as well. Me too, for consorting with him.'

'No doubt he'd think an atheist like Eddie is doomed to burn in hell forever anyway.'

'Eddie'll go to heaven,' said Helen definitely.

Liz looked at her in amazement. 'How do you make that out? How can an atheist go to heaven? Won't he have to go through Purgatory or something?'

'He's misguided,' said Helen confidently. 'Our Father in Heaven understands that, and I don't believe He's vengeful. Eddie's a good person. He's mistaken about religion, but it's out of good motives – because he's always questioning things.'

Liz went for the look of astonishment and an accent like Cordelia MacIntyre's.

'You have got it bad for my brother. You poor dear girl.'

Helen stuck her tongue out at her. Liz grinned.

'Tell me something. Have you put this point of view to Eddie?' She stirred the air with her index finger. 'About him being misguided in matters of religion, I mean?'

'Of course.'

'And he said?'

Helen tilted her head to one side and made a self-deprecating face. 'We argued all evening about it. I had to kiss him eventually, just to get him to shut up. It's the only thing that does. Shut him up, I mean.' She narrowed her eyes at Liz's reaction to those statements. 'Don't snort like that, MacMillan. It's unladylike.'

'Correct me if I'm wrong, Miss Gallagher, but I don't think I've heard you tell Eddie very often what a good person he is, have I?'

'Well,' said Helen with a sly smile, 'I have to keep him on his toes, don't I?'

254

The course of true love hit a serious reef one week later. Unable to stand it any longer, Brendan Gallagher exploded, demanding to know what Eddie's intentions were towards Helen. Fatally, he put the question of any Clydebank father who saw one of his offspring falling in love with someone of a different religion. Was Eddie going to turn? That is, was he going to become a Roman Catholic?

Eddie, passionate about his beliefs, and too honest for his own good, hadn't the sense to be diplomatic – or to know when to stop. Brendan Gallagher, normally the most peaceable of men, soon had steam coming out of his ears. Marie Gallagher and her sons – chiefly Conor, her most trusted lieutenant – had her work cut out calming her husband down.

Brendan's anger was not surprising, especially when you took into account that Eddie had told him exactly what he thought of all organised religions – particularly the Roman Catholic Church. Not content with that, he proceeded to tell the man who thought he was looking at a prospective son-in-law that he didn't actually believe in marriage and had in fact always been in favour of Free Love . . .

The lovers were banned from seeing each other. It took two weeks of the most strenuous intervention by Liz on the one side and Conor Gallagher on the other to persuade Helen's father to relax his edict. She and Eddie were allowed to meet again, but only under the strictest of conditions, as Eddie grumblingly explained to Liz.

'We can go dancing, but only if one of the Irish giants comes with us. We can have five minutes alone in the close together to say goodnight. Five measly minutes! We can go to the pictures, but only if you or one of the Irish giants comes with us. Preferably sitting between us,' he added gloomily. 'We can go for a walk in the hills, but only if Conor comes with us – and the hound of the bloody Baskervilles.' He drew a great sigh and ran a hand through his mop of hair.

'Do you know,' he went on, his voice full of righteous indignation, 'we were up there the other night and nobody was looking so I tried to hold Helen's hand.' He was the picture of injured innocence. 'That was all I wanted to do, Liz,' he said, 'hold her hand. The damn dog spotted me and do you know what he did?'

Liz shook her head, trying not to laugh.

'The beast fixed his beady eyes on me, and he growled. Every time I moved my hand closer to Helen's. Can you believe that?'

'Well, Eddie,' said Liz, amused by this description of Finn's behaviour, but exasperated with her brother at the same time, 'what do you expect? You can't go shooting your mouth off about Free Love and not believing in marriage and expect any father to welcome you in as his daughter's boyfriend. Can you, now?'

'I suppose not,' he said, heaving a great sigh, 'but I do have my principles, Liz.'

'And what's more important? Your principles or Helen?'

'We haven't done anything,' he mumbled in embarrassment. 'Not to speak of that is.' His pale skin went a beautiful shade of dark red. 'I love Helen and I've got too much respect for her.'

'Phooey,' said Liz. The breath expelled by the force of the exclamation lifted a lock of brown hair which had fallen over her brow. 'Respect doesn't come into it. I've seen the way you two look at each other. If I were Mr Gallagher I wouldn't let you out without a chaperone either.'

In the spring and early summer of 1940, despite a gallant struggle, Norway fell to the Germans. That made a lot of people stop and think. The Scandinavian country was Scotland's nearest neighbour across the North Sea, no distance away – particularly if you were a Luftwaffe pilot.

Denmark was already under Nazi control – large parts of Northern Europe too. Hitler's forces were beginning to look pretty unstoppable, resistance crumbling before them. That included the British Expeditionary Force, pushed further and further back until they were eventually evacuated from Dunkirk.

256

Heroic it certainly was, but it was also a defeat – a crushing one.

The crisis precipitated another fall – the end of Neville Chamberlain's career as prime minister. He was succeeded by Winston Churchill, who immediately proposed to the Labour Opposition that they should come in with the Conservatives and form a coalition government for the duration.

That made sense to most people, but it did little to calm growing fears of an invasion of Britain. News of devastating bombing attacks on the city of Rotterdam by the Luftwaffe and of German troops landing in Holland and Belgium by parachute fanned the flames of that anxiety. When France fell, that was it. Britain stood alone.

As spring gave way to summer, all sorts of wild rumours began to circulate. There had already been an aborted invasion. The bodies of German parachutists had been found on beaches on the south coast of England. The government was keeping it secret for fear of causing a panic. Parachute landings might take place anywhere, a silent descent by the enemy into the heart of Britain.

These Germans were clever. Even a handful of them could do untold damage, infiltrating towns, cities and villages and reporting back to their masters in preparation for the invasion of the British Isles. They might be men or women, or even men disguised as women. Any stranger might be a spy, particularly any foreigner. For a few panic-stricken months in 1940 the fear turned into xenophobia. It was an ugly many-headed hydra and it was to have terrible repercussions for many people.

'It's true, Doctor! Honest!'

Adam glanced at Liz over the woman's head. As the expected civilian air-raid casualties had not materialised, the Infirmary was busy dealing with what it had always dealt with: the ailments and emergencies of the community which it served. It was back to business as usual.

The woman had cut her hand on a broken milk bottle. Using

tweezers to lift out the shards of glass, Adam was cleaning the wound preparatory to its being dressed by Liz.

'German parachutists disguised as nuns? Do you not think that's a touch far-fetched?' he asked.

'We've all got to be alert,' the woman maintained. She looked furtively around her. 'Walls have ears, you know, and loose talk costs lives. But it's all right, Nurse,' she went on, turning her attention to Liz and nodding sagely. 'You can recognise the Germans because – although they speak very good English – they say *y* when they mean *j*. They cannae pronounce *j* properly.'

She herself pronounced the letter the Glasgow way: *jie,* to rhyme with tie.

Adam and Liz exchanged another look. They were getting good at it, the ability to silently share a joke.

Eddie sat his final exams in history and politics in May. There was a big push on to mark the papers quickly so that those students who were joining up would be able to graduate before they did so. Eddie had already received his call-up papers and his departure date was set. He was to leave Glasgow at the end of the first week in June, the day after the graduation ceremony.

In public Helen and he carried on as before, alternately laughing and arguing with each other. It made their friends laugh too, the way she seemed to prefer to tell him off rather than exchange sweet nothings with him.

In private Liz was pretty certain it was a different story. During the days and weeks before Eddie was due to leave, Liz often intercepted a wistful look passing between the two of them. It was as if they were trying to commit each other to memory. Not only looks, but every characteristic – voice, gestures, mannerisms.

She saw Helen watch the way Eddie tossed his unruly head before he launched into some political argument. She observed Eddie drinking in the mischievous smile Helen wore when she was telling a funny story.

Her heart aching with sympathy for them, Liz relaxed her chaperonage. She'd hated playing gooseberry anyway, but she was more willing now to yield to Eddie's pleading that he and Helen needed some time alone together.

The young lovers lost two other chaperones as well – Conor and Finn. Meeting Helen at Radnor Street one evening, Liz initially thought her friend's red-rimmed eyes had to do with Eddie's imminent departure, but that wasn't the source of Helen's distress this time. Conor had received his call-up papers too.

Dominic was too young, and Joe and Danny were in reserved occupations, having been taken on by the shipyard some time before. Working full tilt to replace British losses at sea, managers and foremen were less choosy now about the workforce's religious and ethnic backgrounds.

Conor, reluctant to surrender his independence in return for a regular wage packet, was the only member of the family to be conscripted. The consequences were entirely predictable. Unable to face the prospect of separation from his beloved dog, he'd done what he'd always said he would. He and Finn had taken to the hills.

'He was supposed to report to some office in Glasgow this morning, and he didn't, of course, so the police have been round to the house, and two military policemen as well, and Ma's so upset and they won't believe that she or I don't know where he is, and och, Liz, today's been bloody awful!'

Coming, finally, to the end of this rambling sentence, Helen burst into tears. Liz put a comforting arm around her shoulders and proffered a handkerchief.

'There, there, pet,' said Peter MacMillan, patting Helen's hand. 'I take it your brother deliberately didn't tell you or your mother where he was going?'

Helen blew her nose on Liz's hankie.

'Aye, to protect us, he said. He's going to try and slip back now and again, once the fuss has died down. Oh, but everybody's that upset about it, especially Ma and Daddy. What if something happens to him while he's out there living rough?'

Liz hastened to reassure her. 'Helen, Conor knows the hills like the back of his hand. He'll be fine.'

'Aye, but he's made himself a criminal, Liz. He could get into real trouble over this.'

Liz did her best to console her. So did Eddie. In the weeks between finishing his exams and getting his results, he took Helen for a run on the train to Balloch. They spent the day there, taking a picnic so they could wander through the dappled sunlight by the bonnie banks of Loch Lomond. They were by themselves, of course, without Conor or Liz – or the hound of the bloody Baskervilles . . .

Chapter 28

'Question,' said Mario, reading out from the newspaper. 'What should you do if you look up and spot a German parachutist floating down towards you?'

'Move out of the way before he squashes you to a pulp?' suggested Liz.

Mario gave her a dirty look. 'Thank *you*. No, according to this you should great him with a friendly *Heil Hitler!* He'll automatically raise his arm in the salute. Then you shoot the swine.'

There was general laughter, but one of the girls protested. 'Oh, what a pity! Shouldn't you check to see if he's good-looking first?'

'Are there any good-looking Germans?'

It was Liz who had spoken. Cordelia, who hadn't laughed with the others, gave her a cool look. 'I don't suppose it occurs to you that most Germans are people like us? They didn't all choose Hitler, you know.'

'They're a cruel race,' Liz insisted. 'Look at the *Athenia*. What sort of people attack an unarmed passenger ship full of women and children?'

'One man made that decision,' said Cordelia quickly. She was very pale. 'Perhaps he panicked and made the wrong one. It happens.'

Jim Barclay tactfully changed the subject.

'What was that story you were telling us about how you can recognise German spies by the way they pronounce their *jies*, Adam?'

That produced more chuckles, but Adam indicated that Liz should relate the story.

'Mmm,' said Mario thoughtfully after Liz had told the tale, 'hairy-handed nuns who're actually German parachutists. That's a neat combination of two prejudices: the sneaky Roman Catholic and the evil Hun.'

Cordelia excused herself. Adam rose too, but she waved him to sit down. He did, but continued gazing after her with a worried frown as she left the café.

Liz turned with relief to Mario. As usual he was choosing to see the funny side, putting on his cod Italian accent.

'As I was-a saying to my Uncle Benito ze ozzer day, I will do anything for my beloved Italia, but don't ask me to dress up as a nun. Think of the psychological damage.' He leered at Liz, lifted her hand and kissed it. 'Especially to my love life.'

'I don't think you should joke about it,' said Adam sharply. 'Do none of you realise how serious this could get? You most of all, Mario. It's people like you and your father it's going to affect. I'm going after Cordelia,' he announced. 'She's upset.'

He rose to his feet and strode briskly out of the café.

'Well,' commented Naomi Richardson, 'the Honourable Miss MacIntyre really does have our young Mr Buchanan on a string, doesn't she?'

Liz's heart was filled with pride. Eddie had passed his finals with flying colours. He'd got first-class honours.

'I'm pretty chuffed myself, Liz,' he told his sister with a diffident smile. 'Helen says I'm like a dog with two tails.'

'You deserve it, Eddie,' said Liz stoutly. 'You've worked hard for your degree.'

'So,' he asked, putting an affectionate arm around her shoulders, 'are you coming to Gilmorehill next Friday to see your big brother dressed up in silly clothes?'

She was, of course. She wouldn't have missed it for the world. The surroundings were magnificent – the Bute Hall of Glasgow University. It was all carved wood and heraldic shields and centuries of history and heritage. Liz wished she could have enjoyed the experience unreservedly, but she was filled with trepidation. Today was the day Eddie was going to introduce Helen to their parents.

No more procrastinating, he'd said. It was now or never. He'd proved himself more than equal to the academic challenge, surpassing every ambition his father had ever had for him. He was about to go off to fight for his country. There wasn't ever going to be a better time for his parents and the girl he loved to meet each other.

It was a reasoned and logical argument, but it had failed to calm Liz's anxieties. Helen was in another part of the hall throughout the ceremony, insisting that Liz had to sit with her parents. They'd all meet up again afterwards. And Liz was to stop worrying. Everything would be fine.

Afterwards, resplendent in his hood and gown, Eddie led Helen by the hand over the carefully manicured lawns of the University grounds towards his parents and sister. Helen was wearing the brown georgette dress and a new hat she'd spent months saving up for.

Liz's heart was thumping as she watched them approach. They were a handsome couple, Helen so fair and pretty and Eddie so dark and solemn in his academic robes. Liz darted a glance at her father. He was smiling. His wife, unable to contain herself, walked forward to greet Helen.

'I knew there was a special lassie!' she said triumphantly. 'I knew it. Och, and you're so bonnie too!' She seized Helen's hand. 'What's your name, my dear?'

'Helen, Mrs MacMillan. My name is Helen Gallagher.'

It was like watching time stand still – or perhaps go backwards. Liz knew, without having to look, that the smile had slid off her father's face. Sadie was frozen to the spot. Eddie too. Like his sister, he was transfixed, watching it all go horribly wrong. It was only Helen who kept moving. Taking her hand out of Sadie's grasp, she extended it to William MacMillan.

'Hello, Mr MacMillan, you must be very proud of Edward. I know I am.'

He ignored that outstretched hand, and the lovely and open face behind it. He ignored Helen Gallagher completely. Turning to his son, he asked one question.

'Is she a Fenian?'

Eddie spent his last night as a civilian at Queen Victoria Row only because Liz and Helen begged him to.

'For your mother's sake,' said Helen with tears in her eyes. 'For your mother's sake. And for mine too,' she added when she saw his face harden. 'Please, Eddie!'

'He insulted you,' he said, his lips compressed. 'He looked through you as though you weren't there! He wouldn't shake your hand. And you expect me to spend another night under his roof?'

But he gave in at last, unable to resist Helen's tears and Liz's pleading. He left after breakfast the next morning, although his train wasn't till the afternoon. He hugged his mother and refused his hand to his father, looking him straight in the eye before he left the house with Liz.

'You wouldn't take Helen's hand yesterday,' he said, his intelligent grey eyes cool and unforgiving. 'Why should I give you mine today?'

Liz and he spent the morning with the Gallaghers, enjoying a midday meal with Helen and her family as rumbustious as any that household had ever seen. William and Sadie MacMillan sat at their kitchen table alone and found nothing to say to each other for the rest of the day.

Liz couldn't speak. There was a lump in her throat the size of a tennis ball. It was the way they were looking at each other. When Eddie bent his head to kiss Helen for the last time, Liz turned her back and walked away from them. Then she heard her brother calling her name.

She turned, and saw that he had one arm about Helen's

shoulders and was extending the other to her. She ran back to him. There were only minutes until the train left. She stretched up to kiss his cheek.

'Look after each other,' he said huskily into her hair, squeezing her shoulder in farewell.

'We will,' Liz promised. 'Don't you worry about us.' She turned to Helen. 'We'll be out dancing with Polish soldiers every night, won't we?'

'Oh, aye,' Helen agreed. 'I'm told they've got *lovely* manners. Wouldn't dream of arguing with a lady. Unlike some people I could mention.'

'Ha ha,' said her sweetheart. 'Very funny.'

The whistle blew. A kiss on both girls' foreheads and then Eddie jumped aboard the train, slamming the door and swiftly pulling down the window so that he could lean out to give Helen one very last kiss. The train began to move and they separated. Arms linked, the two girls waved until they were sure he couldn't see them any longer.

'Come on, Helen,' Liz urged. 'Let's go.' Her friend seemed to have become rooted to the platform. Should she suggest the pictures for this evening?

'Oh, Liz!' said Helen, and burst into tears.

'I thought she was never going to stop crying,' Liz told Mario as she walked hand in hand with him in the sunshine of Kelvingrove Park the following day. 'I took her for afternoon tea after we'd seen Eddie off, and she was so upset she didn't argue with me when I paid for both of us. I don't think she even noticed, and that's not like Helen at all.'

Mario squeezed her hand. 'I know. It's tough. At least we don't have to be separated. That's one thing.'

When they got back to the café, they found it deserted, two irate customers waiting to be served. After he'd dealt with them, Mario ran swiftly up the stairs, pursued by a worried Liz.

'Papa?'

His father was sitting in the armchair by the fire, staring

into space. Mario crouched down beside him, Liz hovering nearby. Aldo Rossi looked up at them at last.

'I listened to the news,' he said. 'I always listen to the news.' They waited, both of them suddenly realising what was coming next. 'Il Duce has joined the Germans. Italy has declared war on Britain.'

Mario glanced up at Liz, his expression sombre. They'd been expecting it, but it was a blow nonetheless. She could see that he'd already started thinking ahead to the ramifications of the news. She didn't think his father had considered those yet. He was too shocked. The country of his birth and the country of his son's birth were now at war. That was enough to cope with.

The old man's eyes were wet. Mario put out a hand to him, but he pushed it aside. 'I go back downstairs,' he said. 'I cannot leave my customers unattended.'

Mario rose to his feet, shaking his head at Liz.

'I think he wants to keep going, pretend that nothing's changed,' he murmured. 'Maybe we can manage that for a wee while.' He grimaced. 'At least for the rest of today.'

They followed Aldo downstairs.

'Will you stay for a bit?' Mario asked quietly. 'Help me keep his spirits up?'

'Of course,' Liz said, giving his hand a quick squeeze. 'Nae bother.'

Chapter 29

One hour later a brick came flying through the window of the café. Aldo was serving coffee to two of his regular customers, an elderly couple sitting at the table nearest the door. The missile flew over them and struck the old man on the head.

The impact was sufficient to fell him, blood seeping from a wound on his forehead. Mario, hastily wiping his hands on the white apron tied round his waist, came rushing out from behind the counter and knelt down beside his father. Liz had been cleaning some tables at the back of the café, exchanging a few sentences with a single man who was the only other customer in at the time. She went forward too, the man rising to his feet and following her.

'Should ye no' get him down the road to the Infirmary, Mario?' asked the woman, now also on her knees beside Mr Rossi.

'Aye,' he said briskly, shaking off the initial shock. 'Liz, can you mind the store?'

She was about to say yes, of course, nae bother. The younger male customer spoke.

'I'm thinking you might not have a store to mind! Sorry, pal, but I'm getting out of here!'

He thrust open the door and was gone. That was when they became aware of the noise from outside. There were people out there. Lots of them.

'Don't waste any more time, laddie!' urged the elderly man. 'Get your father out now! And take the lassie wi' you! Come on!'

267

Between the four of them, they got Aldo to his feet and manhandled him out on to the pavement. It wasn't a crowd which had gathered there. It was a mob, ugly and menacing. Their very posture shrieked aggression.

'Aw, look,' shouted one voice. 'The old guy's hurt.'

Liz stared at them. She couldn't believe her eyes. If she blinked, would they go away? There were about thirty of them, mostly men but a few women also. They had a handcart in front of them. It was filled with bricks, and stones big enough to fit into a man's hand . . .

Had a ripple of sympathy run through them when they had seen Aldo, an old man with blood dripping from his head? If so, it didn't last long.

'Dirty Tallies!' shouted another voice.

'Tally bastards!' said someone else.

Mario, his shoulder under his father's arm, had gone white. Liz thought of Kristallnacht. Was this how it had started for the Jews in Germany? People calling them names? Men and women lifting stones, taking aim and getting ready to throw?

'We're no' wanting to hurt anybody,' came a man's voice. 'Let them through.' The mood shifted again. It came to Liz what made a mob like this so dangerous. You had no idea which way it was going to go next. First a brick through the window. Then sympathy. Then racist insults. And then more bricks and stones?

'Come on,' she urged Mario. 'Your father needs attention now.'

'You a Tally-lover, hen?'

She didn't know which one of them had said it, so she lifted her chin and looked at them all. The elderly man gripped her sleeve and whispered, 'Don't give them the opportunity, pet.'

He was right. Her head held high, but her heart racing with fear, Liz followed Mario as he moved across the pavement. A group of younger men blocked his path.

'Tally fucking bastard.'

The menace was unmistakable, all the more chilling because

the man who had spoken had said the words quietly, with slow and deliberate malice. He let a young woman push through in front of him. First she smiled at Mario. Then she spat in his face.

Supporting his father with both hands, he wasn't able to react. Trembling with fury, Liz took her handkerchief out of her pocket and wiped the spittle from his face. Locking eyes with the girl who'd done it, she crumpled the cloth up and dropped it in the gutter. The crowd parted and let them through.

When they came from Partick Police Station to arrest Aldo Rossi later that evening, he was still at the Western Infirmary. Some kind soul directed the police officers there. Aldo's injury had proved to be not too serious, but he was badly shaken. Cordelia MacIntyre, incensed by what had happened, folded her arms and looked down her aristocratic nose at the police sergeant and his constable.

'You can find Mr Rossi now, but where were you a couple of hours ago? There's been criminal damage done to his property, you know.'

'There's been criminal damage done to Italian businesses all over Glasgow, miss,' replied the sergeant. 'We cannae be everywhere at once.'

Over his son's voluble and frantic protests, they took the old man away. Mario was distracted. His friends had to restrain him or he'd have got himself into serious trouble. Adam and Cordelia managed to calm him down only by telling him several times that they would get their combined families on to the case, see what strings Mrs Buchanan, Mr Murray and Lady MacIntyre could pull. There must be something that could be done.

'We're not living in a police state, after all,' sniffed Cordelia, her cool eyes sweeping over the representatives of authority. 'I thought this was the sort of thing we're supposed to be fighting against.'

She could do the lady-of-the-manor act to perfection, thought

Liz admiringly. It helped wring one concession out of the police sergeant. Mario could visit his father the following morning at the police station, but not before then.

'Of course we'll not ill-treat him,' snapped the exasperated sergeant in response to another haughty question from the Honourable Miss MacIntyre. 'I've got a father of my own, you know.'

It was heartbreaking. The business which Aldo Rossi had struggled for years to build up lay in ruins, trampled and looted by a mindless mob. Silently, Liz followed Mario as he picked his way through the debris of his father's life.

The others had come too, offering to help clear up. Mario hadn't the heart for it. Not yet. Some of the boys had lent a hand with the boarding-up of the door and window and left it at that for the night.

'Watch your feet.'

Liz looked down. There was glass all over the floor. She saw the chrome lid of one of the straw dispensers lying in the middle of the mess. They had smashed the counter too, but the glass shelves behind it were intact, although all of the sweetie jars were gone.

'They probably took those home with them,' Mario said. 'Their children will be eating them right now.'

Liz's feet crunched on something else – not glass this time, but cones and wafers, their packets ripped open and tipped on to the floor. She wondered if they'd stood here and weighed up what to steal and what to spoil.

She blew out a long breath and ran her fingers through her hair. 'What sort of people could do something like this?' she asked him despairingly. 'It's such wanton destruction.'

Mario didn't answer her. He was crouching down, picking something up from the mess on the floor. It was a smashed photo frame.

'My mother's picture,' he said, his voice expressionless. 'Even my mother's picture.'

He had stood up again by the time Liz reached him, picking her way carefully over the mess on the floor. There was glass all over the photograph, too. His head bowed, he was carefully picking it off.

'My mother's picture,' he said again. Then he began to cry.

Somehow she got him upstairs to the flat. That, at least, was untouched. Once there, he laid the photo down carefully on a small table beside the settee and walked over to the window. He stood with his back to her, gazing down at the street.

Liz didn't follow him immediately, not sure how best to help him. Should she offer him comfort, or leave him alone with his thoughts for a while? While she was debating the point, he began to speak.

'My father served these people for years. Stayed open all hours to sell them ice-cream and sweets, cook them breakfasts and teas, help them celebrate their children's birthdays. And they reward him like this.'

Liz crossed the room and stood beside him. She couldn't bear the hurt in his voice.

'They didn't all do it, Mario.' She put a hand on his arm. 'It was only a few people who did this.' She paused, searching for the right words. There weren't any to describe the people who had wrecked the café below them. 'Stupid, mindless people,' she said wearily, and knew how inadequate the description was.

He was staring fixedly out of the window. 'And what about the people who saw it and heard it happening, and did nothing? What about them, Liz?' He turned to face her.

'Oh, Mario,' she breathed softly. 'Oh, Mario.'

She lifted her hand again to touch him, this time laying it flat on his chest. He jerked back as though to resist the consolation she was offering, and came up hard against the window.

'Ow!' he yelped. His eyes were watering. It must have hurt. Liz laughed softly.

'Let me kiss it better. I'm a nurse, you know.'

She pulled his head down and kissed the back of it, on his thick hair. Then she put her arms around him and held him.

'Mario?' she whispered.

It took him a long time to answer. When he did speak, his voice was muffled.

'Oh, Liz . . . Oh, Liz . . .'

He was crying again. She could feel the wetness of his tears on her neck. Her own eyes filled up and she took her hands from his shoulders and wrapped them around his waist. She held him as tightly as she could. Then she took him by the hand and led him over to the settee.

She found the vermouth bottle and poured him a generous measure. He finished it quickly, downing it in angry gulps. She took the glass from him and laid it on the small table, careful not to put it too near the photograph. It might get knocked over and the drops left in it spill on to the picture.

'Fancy a cuddle?'

He went into her arms again as though he were a small child, turning his face into her breast.

'Oh, Mario,' she breathed softly. 'I'm so sorry this has happened. I'm really sorry.'

He lifted his head.

'And I'm sorry for being such a milksop.' He had every right to be bitter, but he made an attempt at a smile. 'I can usually come up with a joke, can't I, Liz?' He bit his lip. 'Or some sort of smart comment.'

'You can,' she agreed.

He took a quick, hurried breath. 'Right at this moment I can't seem to think of a single one. Would you kiss me, Elisabetta?'

Wordlessly, she bent her head and did as he asked – trying to put everything into that kiss: love, compassion, understanding, support.

He lifted his head and looked into her face. She answered the question she saw in his by leaning back on the settee, pulling him with her.

'Liz?' His voice was husky as he looked down at her. 'Are you sure?'

'Yes,' she whispered. 'Yes. It's all right, Mario. It's all right.'

He was filled with contrition. It was around midnight and they were lying together on the floor of the living room. Mario had fetched the covers from his bed to put under and over them both. He had also set a well-shaded lamp on the floor beside them.

'Oh, God, Liz, can you ever forgive me?'

Secure in his arms, she smiled up at him. 'Forgive you for what?'

'Taking advantage of you, of course.' He looked really troubled.

'Nobody took advantage of anybody,' she said firmly. 'We made love. And it was beautiful.'

He lifted her hand from under the covers and kissed her fingertips, each one in turn. She laughed.

'But I hurt you,' he insisted. 'I made you bleed.'

She tapped his lips with her index finger. 'It only hurt at the beginning. Not after that. And of course I bled. You should have expected that, Signor Medical Student.'

'Real life's different from the textbooks,' he said a little grimly, and kissed her again. 'We'll get married,' he said after he raised his head. 'As soon as possible. Once we've got my father out.'

He was beginning to lose the worried look, but his words had reminded Liz of a problem of her own.

'Oh, God!' she said. 'What time is it? My father's going to kill me. And Ma'll be worried sick by now.'

'They'll think you've had an emergency at the hospital,' he said. 'Which, in a manner of speaking, you have.'

She frowned, and his voice grew gentler as he registered her concern.

'Remember you stayed over the night of the *Athenia*? That's what they'll think has happened, Liz. And you can dash home

273

first thing tomorrow morning before you go to work and set your mother's mind at rest.'

'Do you think?' She wasn't entirely convinced, but she didn't really see how she could travel home at this time of night either.

Mario's next words mirrored her thoughts. 'You're not going anywhere at this hour.' His voice was a little testy. Consciously or not, he moved one of his legs and laid it over both of hers, pinning her down.

'I just asked you to marry me, Liz MacMillan.'

'Oh, did you?' she responded with exaggerated surprise. 'I thought it was more like an official announcement. I didn't realise I was actually being consulted on the matter.'

He muttered something in Italian.

'Pardon? I'm afraid I don't speak that language.'

'Well, you'd better learn. After the war I'm taking you to Italy to show you off to my relatives.'

Their momentary spurt of amusement evaporated.

'After the war,' she said, and met the sudden pain in his dark eyes.

'We have to keep hoping,' he said lightly. 'Don't we?'

'Let's go to sleep,' she suggested. 'We've got a lot to do tomorrow.' Then, trying to think of a way to lift both their spirits, 'Unless you want to do it again, of course.'

Mario groaned.

'Not until after we're married. It would be dishonourable.' The mobile mouth quirked. 'But there's nothing to say we couldn't touch a little. How about if I put my hand . . . just . . . there? Is that all right?'

Liz gave a little moan of pleasure.

'Ah,' Mario said with some satisfaction. 'If you've lost the power of coherent speech, then it must be all right. More than all right, I would suspect.'

'Shut up,' she managed. 'Can't you think of anything better to do with your mouth?'

'What a thing to say to an Italian . . .'

Then he was too busy kissing her to say anything else.

They were woken at six o'clock by thunderous knocking on the boarded-up door of the café. Mario hastily pulled on his trousers and ran downstairs. Enveloped in his dressing gown, Liz followed him down.

'Mario Rossi? We have a warrant for your arrest.'

'You can't arrest him! He's got a British passport.'

'Aye – and he's got an Italian one, too.' It was a different sergeant from the day before.

'He's a British citizen,' Liz insisted. 'You can't take him away! You can't! Mario,' she said frantically, clutching his bare arm. 'Tell them they can't do this to you!'

The policeman's eyes were cold as his gaze flickered over Liz. They took in the dressing gown and the tousled hair, the knowledge that the two of them had spent the night here alone together.

'In case you hadn't noticed, miss, there's a war on. We can do what we damn well please.'

Ten minutes later, Liz flung into the hospital looking for help – five minutes after her father had got there, in search of his missing daughter after she'd failed to come home the night before. His eyes reminded her of the policeman who'd just taken Mario away.

They saw the same things he had: the hastily thrown-on clothes, the uncombed hair, the fact that she clearly hadn't spent the night in the hospital. They made the same judgement.

Chapter 30

'So what happened after that?' asked Helen in a tone of fascinated horror.

'All hell broke loose,' said Liz drily.

'A wee bit of a scene?'

'You might say that,' said Liz, trying to sound bright and cheerful and totally in command of the situation. 'I told him the truth.'

'Oh, Liz! Was that wise?'

'I was fed up with all the lies, Helen. And I was so upset I wasn't thinking straight.' She shrugged. 'So now I'm an ungrateful daughter, a loose woman, and I've broken my mother's heart into the bargain. Not to mention being a cheap little tart.'

Despite her bravado, her bottom lip wobbled. The expression her father had used had been a lot worse than that. In silent sympathy, Helen laid a comforting hand on her arm.

'I'm never to darken his door again,' said Liz flippantly. 'Or words to that effect.' Her voice shook. 'And I've not to try to get in touch with my mother. He's going to get her to pack my things in a couple of cases, and he'll drop them off at the Infirmary.'

A note of bleak bitterness crept into her voice. 'Not at my grandfather's house where I'm actually staying. He couldn't bring himself to do that.'

'Does your grandfather know what happened?'

'Not the gory details. Only what happened to Mario and Mr Rossi, and that I've fallen out with my father.'

Helen shook her head sadly.

'Your poor mother,' she said. 'That's her lost both her children. I'm so sorry, Liz.'

The two girls sat in silence for a moment or two. Liz, lost and alone, had come home to Clydebank for solace. Not to Queen Victoria Row, of course. That wasn't home any more. She'd gone to her grandfather, and to Helen. Peter had tactfully made himself scarce for an hour or two so that the girls could talk.

'Are they going to let you see Mario?'

Liz hunched her shoulders and wrapped her arms about herself. 'I hope so. Adam and Cordelia are getting their families to pull all the strings they can think of.' She looked at her friend. 'Say a wee prayer to St Jude for me, Helen. And one for Mario and his father too.'

He'd obviously slept in his clothes for the past two nights, and he was very pale and badly in need of a shave, but he was fit and unharmed and he was walking towards her with a typical Mario smile on his handsome face, his arms outstretched.

'Liz . . .'

'No touching,' said the policeman. It wasn't the sergeant who'd arrested Mr Rossi senior, but the one who'd come for Mario. The one who thought that Liz was a loose woman. 'One of you on either side of the table.'

Their eyes fixed on each other, they slid into the hard chairs. As soon as she was within reach, Mario grasped her hands.

'I said no touching,' came the voice of authority.

Mario tore his gaze away from Liz's face and turned to look at the man. He sat on a chair at a small table at right angles to them and the table at which they sat. There was no other furniture in the dingy room.

'Please, Officer. She's my girl. I only want to hold her hand. Please?' he asked again.

The man shot Liz a look of disdain. She knew what it meant. He thought she was a trollop. So did her father. She tried not to let it make her angry. They didn't know anything.

'Very well,' said the sergeant. 'But that's all. Do we understand each other?'

'Perfectly,' said Mario, lifting one dark eyebrow at Liz. I want to smother your face in kisses, that look said, but this numpty isn't going to let me do it. 'Eddie would love this, eh?' he murmured. 'The iron hand of the state.'

'Speak clearly, please.'

Liz closed her eyes briefly as she slid her hands into his. Funny to remember how she had once shrunk away from him. Now she would have let him touch her anywhere. That would shock the sergeant.

'Is your father all right?'

Mario shrugged. 'As well as can be expected.'

'Give him my love.'

'I will.'

'What are they going to do with you? Do you know?'

'They haven't told us anything. But I'm going to do my damnedest to stay with my father so that I can look after him. Whatever happens.'

Liz nodded. 'How are *you*?' she asked, putting as much feeling as she could into the simple question.

'All the better for seeing you,' he assured her, squeezing the hands he held. He ran his thumbs along her knuckles. 'And wishing I hadn't been so bloody noble the other night.'

Liz blushed and he laughed. The police officer coughed. Mario ignored him, his whole attention fixed on Liz.

'What about you?' he asked, his question also invested with deeper meaning. 'Are you all right?'

'I'm fine,' she said, answering his first question: *How have you been since we made love?* Then she dealt with the second one: *How are you coping with this?* She wouldn't tell him about her father.

'Everyone's looking after me,' she said, a catch in her voice. 'Helen, my grandfather, Cordelia and Adam.'

'Adam who?' came a voice from the corner.

278

Liz turned to look at the man. When she saw that he was making notes, she was outraged. Reading her reaction in her face, Mario gave her hands a warning squeeze.

'If you make a fuss he'll only throw you out,' he muttered. 'Adam Smith,' he said in a louder voice. 'He writes books. You'll find his *Wealth of Nations* in the library at the Uni.' He hadn't taken his eyes off Liz. 'We have good friends,' he told her. He grinned, his teeth flashing white. 'Even if some of them do belong to the aristocracy and the upper echelons of the bourgeoisie.'

'Keep the conversation in English, please,' came the voice of authority.

'He was clearly puzzled by the fit of the giggles his request provoked in the dangerous enemy alien and his girlfriend,' said Liz twenty minutes later as she sat in Adam's car on the way to his mother's house for a council of war on the Rossis' case. He had picked her up from the police station and they were calling in for Cordelia on the way out to Milngavie.

'Did they say if they would let you see him again?' asked Adam.

'They refused to say anything much,' she said wearily, gazing out at the shops and the passers-by. 'I'm so worried about Mr Rossi.' She turned and gave Adam a tired smile. 'And Mario too, of course.'

He steered the car into a space in front of Cordelia's house on Great Western Road and sounded the horn. The door opened almost immediately. She must have been watching for their arrival. Liz followed her slim figure as she ran down the front steps and came towards them.

'It's very good of you and Cordelia and your families to help. I'm so grateful to you all.'

'What are friends for?' asked Adam. He got out of the car to open the door for Cordelia.

In the end, however, it didn't matter how many strings were pulled by however many influential people. The invasion scare was at its height. The Italians were to be regarded as the enemy within, potential fifth columnists working behind the lines to pave the way for the German invasion.

The state apparently could not afford to recognise that many of them were profoundly anti-fascist and were absolutely no threat at all to the war effort. On the contrary, hundreds of Italian families actually had sons serving in the British armed forces.

Young and old, married and single, the men of Britain's Italian families were to be interned. The order came right from the top – from Winston Churchill himself. Some members of his war cabinet had asked if it wouldn't be possible to distinguish between the innocent and the guilty. Churchill's response was succinct. *Collar the lot!*

The string-pulling achieved one thing for Liz and Mario – permission to say goodbye to each other. Adam drove her to the police station. When they got there he turned off the engine and asked if she would like him to come in with her.

'Would you?'

'Of course,' he said gravely. 'If you want me to.'

The room was tiny, little more than a cell. Adam did his best to stand at a discreet distance from the lovers, but it was physically impossible for anyone in the room to be more than a few feet away from anyone else. Mario's velvet eyes were soft and warm and full of the pain of farewell.

'You've not to worry about me.'

'Worry about you? Perish the thought.' She was doing her best not to break down. She thought back to the night Eddie had taken his farewell of her and Helen.

'I'll be out dancing with Polish soldiers every night. I won't have time to worry about you, Mr Rossi.'

It was a gallant effort, but her voice was close to breaking.

Mario's smile was very tender. 'Are you about to cry, Miss MacMillan?'

Liz lifted her chin. 'I wouldn't give them the satisfaction.'

'That's my girl.'

'Time up,' said the policeman. It was the sergeant who had come to arrest Aldo Rossi.

Mario took Liz into his arms and embraced her passionately. Adam, the unwilling observer, coughed and studied the wall.

'Let's be having you then, son,' said the policeman. He didn't sound unkind.

'Just let me give her one last kiss, Sergeant,' Mario pleaded. The policeman hesitated, then gave him a little nod.

Now that the moment had come, Liz clung desperately to him, all her brave resolutions about letting him go without a tear crumbling into nothing.

'*Ti amo,* Elisabetta,' he whispered. '*Amore mio.*'

The sergeant didn't tell him to stick to English.

'Liz, Liz . . . you've got to let me go . . .'

But she wasn't responding to his words, only to his lips and his arms and the anguish of having to separate from him.

Mario lifted his head. 'Adam, will you take her, please?'

She was being transferred from one set of supporting arms to another.

'Look after her for me, old friend.'

'Aye,' said Adam. 'Don't worry about her, Mario. I'll take care of her.' His voice had gone husky, but he recovered himself. 'I'll not let her mope.'

Over the top of her head, she felt Mario's hand go out to squeeze Adam's shoulder. It came back to rest briefly on her hair, like a benediction. Then he was gone.

PART III

1940-1941

Chapter 31

'Sorry! I was away in a dwam. Did you say something?'

'The flicks,' said Adam. He was half in and half out of the door, one hand lightly gripping the frame. 'This afternoon. You're off, aren't you?'

Liz nodded. She was a full-time auxiliary nurse at the Infirmary now, being paid a pittance and living at the nurses' home. She had resigned from Murray's when her father had kicked her out.

Neither the low wages nor the restrictions on her freedom bothered her. Nothing much bothered her at the moment. Except Mario. And sometimes her mother – when she allowed herself to think about her.

'But what about you?' she asked Adam. He didn't have much free time. Effectively doing a resident's job, he was also studying hard for his finals next year. He came into the room and perched on the edge of the table at which she was checking the belongings of a patient about to be discharged, making sure everything tallied with the list made when the woman had been admitted.

'Believe it or not, my dear girl, I've actually managed to get someone to cover for me this afternoon.'

'What's on at the pictures anyway?' she asked, satisfied that everything was in order and glancing up at him.

'Who cares?'

Liz looked at him anxiously, hearing the note of something more than tiredness in his voice. He'd been so good to her since Mario had been taken away, keeping his promise not to let her

285

mope. Cordelia MacIntyre had been kind, too.

When news had come through at the beginning of July of the sinking of the *Arandora Star*, a ship carrying hundreds of Italian internees to prison camps in Canada, the two of them had held her hand, literally and metaphorically, for days. Over seven hundred men had drowned when the vessel was torpedoed by the same U-boat commander who had sunk the *Royal Oak* at Scapa Flow not long after the start of the war.

Six anxious weeks later, a mysterious unsigned note with a Liverpool postmark had arrived for Liz care of the hospital. *Your friend reached the other side of the water safely.* That was all it said. It was enough. For a while at least.

'Shall I make you a cup of tea?' she asked Adam now. 'You look all in.'

'Work to be done before that.' He pushed himself up off the table. 'But thanks for the offer. Maybe later. I can't remember when my last cup of tea was. Some hours ago, I believe.' He ran a hand through his hair. 'Maybe even yesterday.'

It was a joke, but it wasn't a joke.

'When did you last have a proper meal?' Liz demanded. 'Or a decent night's sleep?'

He gave her a weary smile. 'Sleep? What's that? I don't think I'm familiar with the concept.'

Her expression was a mixture of concern and rebuke.

'Wouldn't you prefer to snatch a couple of hours this afternoon instead of going to the pictures?'

'Nope.' He shook his head as though to clear it and headed for the door. 'You might have to elbow me in the ribs if I start snoring, though.'

'Meet you at one o'clock, then?'

'Yes,' he said. 'Oh, and Liz,' he added, already halfway out of the door. 'Thanks.'

'What for?'

'Tea and sympathy,' he said. For the briefest of moments, a smile lit up his face. 'Well, sympathy anyway.' With a wave of his hand, he plunged back into the fray.

'And to think,' Liz said softly to herself and a sparrow which was sitting on the outside windowsill, 'that I once dismissed Adam Buchanan as one of the Idle Rich. I've never seen anyone work so hard.'

He was more relaxed by the time they came out of the cinema that afternoon, laughing about the film they'd seen.

'Didn't you love the way the German spies were so stupid, and the British were so clever? And they were all so terribly stiff-upper-lip— Uh-oh!' The air-raid siren had started up.

'Probably a false alarm,' he said, but there was a question in his voice.

'Maybe we'd better be safe than sorry,' said Liz.

'You're right. There's a shelter in the crypt of the church at the top of the road.' He held out a hand to her and they ran.

Glaswegians had at first been blasé when air-raid warnings had started to sound. There were a lot of false alarms, but the attacks which took place in the middle of September had quickly made most folk see sense. The German planes dropped a mixture of bombs and incendiaries, starting fires and causing a great deal of damage all over the city.

One raider scored a direct hit on HMS *Sussex*, berthed at Yorkhill Quay, not far from the Western. Slicing through her, the bomb had exploded directly over her oil tanks, causing a fierce fire to take hold immediately. Sixteen sailors had died and twenty-nine had been injured. After that, people began to take the sirens more seriously.

Sitting in the pitch black of the shelter, Liz was terrified. Her stomach was churning and her skin was clammy. This definitely wasn't another false alarm. She could hear the German planes overhead.

They sounded different to the British ones. Distinguishing the various aeroplanes was a skill many people had picked up. Dominic Gallagher had become quite an expert. He could tell a Heinkel 111 from a Junker 88 and was quite happy to explain the differences to anyone who cared to listen. Usually at some length.

It didn't sound as though there were a lot of planes up there. Liz thought back to HMS *Sussex*. It only needed one. She felt warm male fingers wrap themselves around her own.

'All right, MacMillan?' murmured Adam.

'Not really,' she whispered back, her lips close to his ear so that the people around them wouldn't hear. There were at least two children in here. She didn't want to alarm them.

That was a joke. The air-raid siren was bad enough in itself – that whooping, banshee wail. The noise and vibration of the first sticks of bombs dropping, uncomfortably close to where they sat, was – well, you could think of a lot of words. None of them came close to describing the mind-numbing terror Liz was currently experiencing.

Adam gave her hand a squeeze.

'Time to show an example, I think.' He waited till there was a brief pause in the bombardment.

'I think it's so vulgar to make loud noises, don't you?' he asked the assembled company, his voice firm and carrying, but deliberately languid. 'These Nazis are terribly uncouth.'

Despite her fear, Liz felt a bubble of amusement surface. Vulgar. That was Adam Buchanan's favourite criticism. He was such a snob. How had she, a true Red Clydesider, ever got mixed up with a man like this?

'Let's sing some rude songs,' he suggested.

'Oh, aye, mister,' came an enthusiastic young voice.

'Nothing too rude,' came an anxious female one.

'Of course not.' That was Adam again. 'One has one's standards, after all. Even if there is a war on. Let's see now. Here's one.' To the tune of 'My Bonnie Lies Over the Ocean', he began singing.

> *My mother's an ARP warden,*
> *My father makes counterfeit gin,*
> *My sister goes out every evening*
> *Oh, how the money rolls in.*

It was the first time Liz had laughed since they had taken Mario away.

'Och, Helen, why didn't you tell me before?'

'Because you had your own problems, Liz. You didn't need mine as well. You were so worried that Mario might have been on board that ship. I couldn't burden you with this – not until you'd got that message and I knew you were feeling a wee bit happier.'

'Och, Helen,' Liz said again. Not knowing quite what to say next, she took refuge in a practical question.

'Next March,' replied Helen. 'My date's the nineteenth. I've been to the doctor and all that.' She grimaced. 'One who doesn't know me. But I'm taking care of myself – and the baby.' Her hand went protectively to her still flat stomach. 'I just haven't told my parents, that's all.'

'That's all?' Liz's voice was a squeak. 'Does Eddie know?'

Helen nodded, a lopsided smile on her face.

'And he's left you to cope with it on your own?' The pitch of Liz's voice rose even higher.

'Don't blame him, Liz,' pleaded Helen. 'He didn't have much choice. And,' she said with a blush, but looking Liz straight in the eye, 'he didn't make me do anything I didn't want to do. It takes two to tango. You know that as well as I do.'

Liz couldn't think of an answer to that one. 'It was the day you went to Loch Lomond, I suppose.'

Helen's face grew soft with remembrance. 'Aye. Oh, it was lovely, Liz. He asked me to sing the song for him, and he read me some poetry . . .'

'But at some point you stopped serenading him and he put his poetry book down,' said Liz drily.

'Elizabeth MacMillan!' cried Helen. The pink glow on her cheeks deepened to scarlet.

'So,' demanded Liz, 'are you going to do something about it when he's home on leave next week?'

'He says we're going to discuss it all properly,' said Helen breathlessly. 'I got another letter from him today.'

Liz frowned. 'Helen, I think the two of you need to do something more than talk about it.'

'That's why I'm asking for your advice, Liz. I need to work out what I'm going to do when the baby comes – where the two of us are going to live and what we're going to live on. All that sort of thing.'

'Helen, that's Eddie's responsibility too. Not just yours.'

'Och, Liz,' the girl burst out, no longer pretending to treat the subject so nonchalantly. 'Don't you think I know that? But he doesn't believe in marriage, does he?' She stopped, biting her lip, then continued in a calmer voice. 'He's never made any secret of his views. I knew how he felt from the beginning. And I don't want to worry him too much. Not when he's got to go back to the army.'

'Don't want to worry him?'

'Liz,' said Helen, darting a nervous glance at Liz's thunderstruck expression. 'Promise me you won't go on at him when he gets home. He'll only have a few days. I want him to enjoy them.'

'Want him to enjoy them?'

'Would you stop repeating everything I say? And,' Helen pleaded, 'will you come to the station with me when I meet him?'

'Oh, I'll come,' said Liz, folding her arms and scowling ferociously. 'I'll certainly come. Wild horses wouldn't stop me from meeting my dear brother. An entire regiment of German parachutists wouldn't stop me from meeting Edward MacMillan.'

Helen looked alarmed.

'Liz, you'll not lay into him as soon as he steps off the train, will you?'

'I'm promising nothing,' said Liz.

Eddie's train was due into Glasgow at nine o'clock the following

Friday evening. Helen would call past the hospital to meet up with Liz when she finished her shift at eight. Then they would catch the tram into town together.

Helen arrived shortly after eight as arranged. Liz, who'd been standing talking to Adam while she waited for her, turned to say hello. Helen burst into tears. Alarmed, Liz pulled her into an empty outpatient clinic and sat her down on a chair, Adam following the two girls in.

'Helen . . .' asked Liz, taking a seat beside her. 'What's wrong?'

Helen's eyes welled with fresh tears.

'Oh, Liz, my parents have found out about the baby!'

'Eddie?' asked Adam. He didn't appear too shocked by the revelation of Helen's pregnancy.

Liz rounded on him. 'Well of course Eddie,' she snapped. 'Who else would it be?'

'Don't shout at Adam! It's not his fault! It's all my fault!'

Adam sat down beside Helen and took one of her hands in his. His lips twitched. 'Well, I think Eddie might have to accept some of the blame.'

'Would you stop being so bloody calm and reasonable?' said Liz. Adam glanced across at her. His expression was mild enough, but there was reproof in his hazel eyes. 'Her hand's a bit cold,' he murmured.

The reminder was enough. Helen was in a state of some distress. She was an expectant mother. At this precise moment, that made her their patient. Liz took hold of her other hand.

'How did they find out, Helen? Did you tell them?'

Helen gulped and shook her head. Her mother had noticed that – she darted an embarrassed glance at Adam – a certain thing which should happen every month hadn't happened. She had confronted her daughter about it and had then told her husband. Shocked and dismayed, Brendan Gallagher had turned to his Church for help. The parish priest had called in after tea this evening.

'Or, as some of us know him, Torquemada the Grand

Inquisitor,' murmured Liz. 'Don't tell me – he *is* planning to burn you at the stake.'

Adam looked faintly surprised at Liz's robust approach, but it seemed to be working. Helen had a bit more colour in her cheeks and she was talking more coherently.

'He thinks I should go into this home for unmarried mothers at some convent on the south side of Glasgow.' Her sense of humour bobbed briefly to the surface. 'Probably run by the Sisters of Absolutely No Mercy.'

Adam gave a short bark of laughter.

'He kept praying at me,' said Helen. 'Telling me I had to confess my sin. I told him I hadn't committed any sin.'

'You did?'

She started crying again. 'He told me my baby was a bastard, conceived in sin and degradation, and that I . . . that I was a . . . was a . . .' It took her a few attempts to get it out. 'That I was a whore and a harlot.'

On Helen's other side, Liz was aware of Adam wincing at the words. Damn the bloody Church, she thought. Damn all bloody churches, with their certainties about right and wrong, their refusal to allow people to make mistakes. She gazed at Helen, whose fair head was now bowed in absolute dejection.

'Listen to me, Helen,' she said urgently. 'You made a mistake, that's all. A mistake made for the best reasons. Because you love Eddie. What the two of you did wasn't a sin. You're dead right about that.'

Helen lifted her head.

'It wasn't?'

Liz squeezed the hand she held.

'The two of you have created another life, Helen. Out of your love for each other. How can it be a sin to do that?'

'I didn't think it was, Liz,' said Helen pathetically. 'I thought it was something beautiful.' She let out a sob. 'But the priest thinks I'm a whore and a harlot.' Her voice dropped to a tortured whisper. 'And now my daddy thinks that, too. And the boys. I cannae bear that.'

Damn them again, thought Liz fiercely, all these men who pontificate about how warm and passionate men and women should act, and who judge them when they fall short of their ludicrous standards.

'Helen, your brothers adore you. They could never think badly of you. Your father loves you too. At the moment he thinks what the priest tells him to think. Because he doesn't know what else to do.'

Helen looked at her, her expression mournful, clearly racked by doubts. Liz took a deep breath.

'Helen, you know that Mario and I went to bed together. I don't think that makes me a whore. I was lucky. We made love, but we didn't make a baby.' Her urgent grip on Helen's hand loosened, and her voice cracked. 'Sometimes I wish we had. At least then I would have something – someone – to remember him by.'

'Oh, Liz!' cried Helen, animated at last, starting up in her seat in a movement so quick it had all three of them up on their feet. She flung her arms around Liz's neck. Despite her pregnancy, she was very thin. They'd have to make sure she ate well from now on, thought Liz, got the proper nutrition she needed, for her own sake and the baby's. Eddie's baby. Liz's flesh and blood too.

She lifted her head, wanting to share the moment of relief with Adam. He looked pale, and very serious.

'Come on,' he said. 'We'd better get to the station.'

'Helen and I are going for the tram,' she said, glancing up at the clock on the wall. They'd need to get a move on if they were going to make it on time.

Adam's voice was sharp. 'Don't be so bloody stupid,' he said. 'I'll drive you, of course.'

'You can stay at my grandfather's,' said Liz as they drove between the Kelvin Hall and the Art Galleries on their way into town. She twisted round to look at Helen, sitting in the back seat of Morag. She'd got a bit more of the story on the way to the car.

Helen's parents had tried to stop her from going to meet Eddie off the train, but she had defied them. Brendan Gallagher had thundered at her that if she went out of that door tonight, she shouldn't bother coming back. Ever.

'He'll think better of it tomorrow,' insisted Liz. 'I'm sure he will. Give him some time to cool off. For tonight, Grandad and Eddie can have the back room and you'll fit into the kitchen.' Since he was still estranged from his father, Eddie planned to spend his leave at Peter MacMillan's house. 'As long as you don't mind being roasted, of course.'

Helen did her best to return Liz's grin.

'Helen can stay at Milngavie if she wants to. My mother would gladly take her in.'

Liz looked across at Adam. It was a very generous offer. She put a hand on his wrist. He shook it off.

'I'm trying to drive.'

'Oh,' she said. 'I'm sorry.'

The railway station was like all railway stations these days, full of men and women in uniform saying hello and goodbye to each other. There were soldiers and sailors and airmen – British, Polish and French – wives and mothers and girlfriends and children too.

The three of them pushed their way through the crowd to the ticket barriers. They were late. Eddie's train was already in.

'I hope we havenae missed him.' Helen's eyes were flickering nervously over the dismounting passengers. An army officer was walking towards them. Liz glanced at him without much interest. He was very smart, tall and straight with a neat haircut. She looked again. It was Eddie.

He saw Helen about the same time as she saw him. He stopped dead, dropped his kit on the platform and opened his arms wide, his face suffused with joy. With a little cry, Helen ran towards him and was enveloped in his embrace.

Liz frowned. This was all very well, but her brother had some explaining to do. So close together that they looked as if they were taking part in a three-legged race, he and Helen came towards her. Eddie had a rather shamefaced grin on his face.

'They made me an officer,' he mumbled. 'Because of my degree. How am I ever going to live it down?' He dropped his bag again and held out both hands to his sister. Helen, smiling all over her face, took a step or two away to allow brother and sister to great each other properly.

Liz ignored Eddie's outstretched hands. Her voice was full of reproach. There was little doubt what she was talking about.

'Oh, Eddie! How could you?'

His smile grew even more rueful.

'How could I? Well, you're the nurse, Liz. You know how human reproduction works.'

Liz slapped his face. Then she burst into tears, fending Eddie off when he took a step towards her.

'What are you going to do about it, Eddie? Eh? You'll marry her, that's what!'

'Liz,' said Adam, 'stop it.'

Eddie was more than capable of answering his sister himself. He took a step forward and planted a swift kiss on her forehead.

'I thought I'd get that in before you hit me again,' he murmured. 'Now, shut up for a minute, would you?'

He turned to Helen, who'd been watching this interchange with a look of growing distress on her face. Ignoring Liz and Adam, Eddie went down on one knee on the dusty platform. He reached for Helen's hand.

A few feet away a pigeon fluttered up in a great flapping of wings. Nobody noticed it. Eddie spoke very clearly.

'Miss Gallagher, would you do me the honour – the very great honour – of becoming my wife?'

Helen stood like a statue. The hand Eddie wasn't holding rested protectively on her stomach. A solitary tear rolled down one smooth cheek.

'But Eddie,' she whispered, her voice breaking, 'you don't believe in marriage.'

'No,' he agreed. His emotions written on his face for all to read, he looked up at the girl he loved. 'But I believe in you.'

Liz suddenly couldn't see very well. She felt hands on her shoulders, swivelling her round and marching her down the platform.

'This is private,' said Adam. 'We'll wait for them by the car.'

Chapter 32

'I'm sorry,' mumbled Liz into the thick cloth of her brother's uniform jacket. 'I just breenged in, didn't I? Opened my big mouth and put my equally large foot right in it.'

Eddie gave her a final hug and let her go.

'With the best possible motives, wee sister. I understand that.'

The wedding was already booked – in the registry office at two o'clock the following afternoon. With the help of his commanding officer, Eddie had arranged it all from a distance. With a faintly embarrassed air, he told Liz how swiftly red tape could be sliced through when it came to helping a serving army officer get wed.

'Huh!' said Helen. 'Assumed a lot, didn't you, Mr Lieutenant MacMillan? What if I'd turned you down?' But her blue eyes were sparkling with life again.

Eddie grinned and pulled her arm through his.

'And you understand that I can't get married in a church, don't you?'

His wife-to-be nodded, but Liz saw the regret in her face. Helen's devoutly Catholic parents weren't going to attend a registry office wedding.

'We'd like you to be our witnesses,' said Eddie, smiling at Liz and Adam. 'Will you do that for us?'

'We'd be honoured,' said Adam, giving Eddie a little bow. 'Oh, hell,' he said and they all laughed at his formality. Eddie stuck out a hand and Adam shook it with a smile. He turned to Helen.

'Do I get to kiss the bride?'

She blushed and proffered her cheek.

'It's most irregular,' the registrar was saying.

'But look, he's dressed for a wedding, so he is.'

Looking half strangled in collars and ties, the Gallagher boys had turned up at the registry office. All of the Gallagher boys. Conor and Finn were there too. Peter MacMillan had taken it upon himself to call on Helen's family first thing in the morning to inform them that the ceremony was taking place that afternoon. Liz had suspected for some time that Conor's brothers knew exactly how to get hold of him in the event of a family emergency.

The bride was radiant as a bride should be, in a knee-length cream dress which Eddie had bought her that morning. He'd wanted her to wear white, but she'd refused point blank to do so. A brief but spirited argument had ensued in the middle of Sauchiehall Street.

Naturally, Helen had won. Liz had been snorting quietly for most of the morning, amused at how the pair of them had slipped back into their usual affectionate arguing. It was as if Eddie had never been away.

Seeing her brothers smiling diffidently at her when she arrived at the registry office had, however, silenced Helen completely. Her eyes had filled with tears.

'Here we go again,' said Eddie irreverently. 'You'd think it was her execution she was going to, not her wedding.'

The registrar was a little concerned about the canine guest, but as Conor had said, the dog *was* dressed for a wedding. At his master's side as always, the wolfhound had a pink carnation tucked into his collar. All four boys sported similar blooms in their buttonholes and the same flowers made up the posy they'd brought along for their sister to carry. Liz wondered if the owner of the garden they had come out of had missed them yet.

The registrar was prevailed upon to allow Finn to remain and the brief ceremony commenced. When it was finished,

Conor kissed his sister, shook Eddie warmly by the hand, winked at Liz and disappeared with his dog.

'You're all coming home with us,' announced Dominic Gallagher. His older brothers seemed happy to let him do the talking.

'Oh, no, Dom, I don't think so,' said Helen, her face soft with regret. 'Ma and Da wouldn't have me.'

'Wouldn't they now?' asked her younger brother. He seemed much older than his fifteen years. Although too young to join the forces, he was doing his bit for the war effort by acting as a bicycle messenger boy for the ARP.

'And will you have me going back and telling our mother that you're not coming when she's been baking solid since first light? Ever since Mr MacMillan came round to give us the news about the wedding?'

'But they didn't get wed in church,' said Brendan Gallagher dolefully.

'Sure, we'll just gloss over that part of the story,' said his wife with female practicality, bustling around attending to her visitors. 'She's a respectable married woman. That's what matters. Will you have some shortbread, Mr Buchanan?'

Eddie and Helen spent their brief honeymoon in Milngavie. Adam's mother offered them the use of her spare room, insisting she had planned to be away for the next four days anyway. Liz suspected she had cleared out on purpose, leaving the new Mr and Mrs MacMillan to start married life on their own. Apart, that was, from Mrs Hunter, the resident cook-housekeeper. She was a somewhat formidable lady, but unlikely to interfere much with the house guests.

'I don't know what it is about cooks,' mused Adam. 'I've known a few who were quite ferocious.'

Liz was reminded of his words when she turned up at Milngavie on the day before the end of Eddie's leave. Amelia Buchanan was coming home that night and she wanted to give the young couple and their friends a special meal as a send-off to Eddie. He had asked Liz to come along a bit early. It was Mrs Hunter who opened the door to her. She had a large knife in her hand and she was scowling.

'A celebration meal. That's what Mrs B wants. Without any proper ingredients?'

Liz blinked, taken aback to be the recipient of the complaint before the woman had even said hello to her.

'The gentleman who sometimes helps me out with a few bits and pieces hasn't turned up yet,' moaned the cook. 'I thought you might be him, but you're not. Pity.'

Gentleman. No doubt she meant her black-market supplier. She could have done with the poaching services of Conor and Finn.

'If I don't get them on time it'll all go to pigs and whistles. Come in, then,' she said irritably, beckoning Liz off the doorstep. 'You're letting cold air into the house.'

It was the end of October and the weather was beginning to turn chilly. The cook went on complaining, gesturing alarmingly with her knife towards the upper regions of the house.

'Not that Love's Young Dream notices what's put in front of it. Honeymooner's salad, that's all that pair want. Lettuce alone.'

Hearing a footfall on the stairs, Liz looked up and saw Eddie. He must have caught the last comment. He was smiling broadly. The cook went off, still grumbling.

'Into the dragon's lair,' murmured Eddie, running nimbly down the last few stairs to greet his sister. 'How are you, Liz?'

'All the better for seeing you. How's Helen?'

'I've persuaded her to take a nap,' he said.

Liz opened her eyes wide. 'What did you use? Thumbscrews?'

Eddie grinned. 'Why don't you and I go out for a good walk?'

They went up on to the moors, turning when they reached a decent height to look back towards Milngavie, and further afield to Clydebank and Glasgow in the distance.

They walked and talked for well over an hour, discussing it all. How could they win their parents round to the marriage? They didn't come up with many answers to that one. Their grandfather had also taken it upon himself to inform Sadie of the wedding. Liz knew that Eddie was bitterly disappointed that his mother hadn't turned up to see him marry Helen.

'It was a Saturday,' she pointed out. 'Father would have had to know about it.'

He sighed heavily. 'I know, but don't you sometimes wish that she would just stand up to him?'

'I used to think that, Eddie.' Liz's eyes were fixed on a beautiful rowan tree in front of them. It was heavy with red berries. That was supposed to mean a hard winter ahead. 'But it must be difficult. He's bullied and badgered her for so many years. I think she's lost any courage she ever had. And now we're away from home it must be even worse.'

He gave her a plaintive look. 'You feel guilty about that too?'

She asked how he was coping with life as an officer, albeit a junior one.

'It's not as bad as I thought it would be, Liz,' he said. 'A lot of the chaps have quite left-wing views.'

She suppressed a smile at that *chaps*. His accent was still very Scottish, but it had undergone a subtle shift. Liz was sure he was quite unaware of it.

'I'm running a series of lectures,' he went on, 'on politics and the causes of the Great War – stuff like that.'

Liz retied her woollen scarf. It was beautiful up here, crisp and clear, but it was cold.

'Do you think you'll go in for teaching after the war?'

'I'd like to,' he said enthusiastically. 'What greater goal can there be than the education of young minds?'

'Health,' she suggested. 'Making everybody healthier. Educating them about how to do that.'

'That's your department,' he said with a smile.

'How do the senior officers react to your politics?'

He shot her a sideways glance. 'Och, they think I'm a bit of a rebel.'

'Who'd have thought it?'

Eddie pulled her to him in a great bear hug. 'Och, Liz, I've missed you! I'm so sorry about Mario,' he added. 'You won't have heard anything of him, I suppose?'

'Only that message I told you about. Nothing since then.'

Damn, there was a lump in her throat.

'I'll see if I can find anything out,' he promised, 'but there's an awful lot of secrecy about some things. You're cold,' he said, looking down at her. 'Let's go back to the house and see if we can persuade the dragon to make us a hot drink. Do you think there's any chance the army might send me somewhere nice and warm for the winter?'

They descended the path arm in arm.

'Adam's very fond of you, you know,' remarked Eddie as they approached the front gate of the house.

'I'm very fond of him,' said Liz.

In the days and weeks following Eddie's departure, Liz thought back often to that walk on the moors. He had talked about his plans for the future, once the war was over. What were her own? She missed Mario dreadfully and longed for his return. She worried constantly about his and his father's well-being, and her dreams were full of him. And he had spoken of marriage.

Liz wasn't sure about that. Did she want to get married? Would he still want to when he came back? *If* he came back . . . but she mustn't let herself think like that.

One thing she knew. She couldn't make her main aim in life waiting for him to come home, however much she ached for that to happen. Liz thought long and hard about it, and eventually came up with a decision.

She would apply to do her nursing training, starting the following autumn. She'd be twenty-one by then, legally an adult. Her father wouldn't be able to stop her. Perhaps he wouldn't have stopped her this year either, but there was no way Liz was going back to Queen Victoria Row to ask for his permission. No way on earth.

Adam was delighted when she told him of her decision. So was Cordelia. She'd decided to apply to start her training the following year too.

'That's great, MacMillan. Sister MacLean will have to address us as *Nurse* then, won't she?'

'I wouldn't put money on it,' said Liz with a smile.

The weather outside was atrocious, but no one was bothered by that. They were giving their full attention to the concert party which the doctors and nurses were putting on for them in honour of it being New Year's Day of 1941.

That friendly young Dr Buchanan had got himself up like a charlady. He was wearing a dress with a pinny on top, something stuffed down the front to give him a huge bosom, and a red and white spotted scarf tied round his head, knotted at the front. You wouldn't have taken him for anything other than a man, a tall and broad-shouldered one at that – but it was a good laugh all the same.

They finished one song and then, having agreed the programme in advance beforehand, launched into the next. It was 'My Wee Gas Mask', one of music hall star Dave Willis' great hits.

> *Wi' ma wee gas mask,*
> *I'm working oot a plan,*
> *Though all the kids imagine,*
> *That I'm just a bogeyman . . .*

Adam was giving it laldy. Waving his arms about, he encouraged all the patients to join in with the chorus.

> *Whenever there's an air raid,*
> *Listen for my cry,*

An airyplane, an airyplane,
A way way up a 'ky!

Going round the beds afterwards to wish all the patients individually a happy new year, Liz found one man wiping tears of laughter from his eyes.

'You're a wee gem, hen,' he told her. 'You all are. It's very good of you to do this for us. We know how hard you all work.'

Adam, back in his white coat, peered over her shoulder. 'This one especially,' he told the man, resting a hand briefly on Liz's shoulder. 'She works like a wee Trojan.'

The patient smiled at him and nodded towards the exit from the ward. 'There's some mistletoe over there, Doctor. Hanging above the doors.' Then he winked at Liz.

'How about it, Nurse MacMillan?' Adam asked lightly.

Liz blushed and moved away.

Liz's face was wreathed in smiles. She looked as if she was about to burst with happiness.

'I got another message,' she told Cordelia, breathless with the joy and excitement of it. She was telling her because she was the only person she could find, and she had to tell someone. Coming off duty in the early afternoon, she had popped her head into the nurses' common room to see who was there.

'A message?'

The words came spilling out.

'This man bumped into me not long after I came on duty this morning. He was on his way out of Casualty. I didn't think anything of it at the time.' That wasn't quite true. She had felt the stranger's hand graze her body, an unpleasant reminder of Eric Mitchell. Now she understood why he had touched her.

Her hand trembling with excitement, Liz held out a piece of paper. 'He must have put this in my pocket, under my apron.'

Cordelia bent her head and read the few words written on the scrap of paper.

A certain person is alive and well and being treated well.

304

He sends Elisabetta his love. The old man is also well and not too far away.

'Oh,' said Cordelia.

Liz was disappointed by her reaction. 'Don't you understand? *Not too far away.* That probably means that Mr Rossi's on the Isle of Man. My brother managed to find out that's where some of the Italians are interned. And at least I know now that Mario is being well-treated. Isn't it exciting?'

Cordelia handed back the precious scrap of paper.

'Yes, Liz, I can see that it's exciting for you.' She turned her head away and stared across the room. 'I'm glad to hear that Mr Rossi's all right. Mario too, of course.' There was a brief silence.

'Cordelia,' said Liz. 'Is there something the matter?'

With ineffable slowness, Cordelia turned her head back to look at Liz. An expression of deep sadness passed over her face.

'I suppose I'm a bit jealous, Liz. That's all. You've had a second message about Mario. I've got no idea what's happening to the man I love.'

Liz digested this piece of information. Cordelia was using the present tense. Whoever he was, he obviously hadn't been killed in action. She tried to think who he might be. Not Adam. Cordelia knew exactly where he was and what he was doing. And Liz had stopped believing there was a romance between the two of them a long time ago.

'Did he . . . I mean, is he with someone else now? Did you have an argument, break up with each other?' She wondered if the other girl wanted to talk about it. Would she be better to go away and leave her alone?

There was a long pause. Then Cordelia spoke.

'He's German,' she said.

Chapter 33

They were in Cordelia's room. She was sitting on the narrow bed while Liz was in a small armchair by the window.

'I met him at Heidelberg before the war. I was studying German and he was training to be a doctor.'

She gave Liz a sad smile. 'That's one reason why I volunteered to be a nurse. Felt it would connect us in some way, I suppose.'

'And you've no idea where he is now?'

Cordelia lifted her shoulders. 'How could I have?' She bit her lip. 'There was one phone call – the weekend war was declared. The night we came back from taking the evacuees down to Ayrshire. You remember how upset I was? That was why I wanted to get home quickly that evening. I knew he'd get in touch with me if he possibly could. That's what he's like, kind and thoughtful.'

Tears were sliding down her cheeks. Liz leaned forward, her voice earnest.

'Cordelia, don't talk about it if it makes you so unhappy . . .'

Cordelia gave a huge sniff and wiped her nose with the back of her hand. Like a child. Liz had a sudden memory of young Charlie Thomson.

Yes, she remembered how upset Cordelia had been that day, and how Adam had comforted her. He must have known all along about her German boyfriend. And there had been other occasions when Cordelia had been distressed . . . it was all very clear now.

'But I want to talk about it, Liz,' she was saying. 'It's such a relief to be able to tell another girl about him.' She was right then. Adam did know.

'What's his name?' she asked gently.

'Hans-Peter,' said Cordelia, pathetic in her eagerness to talk of her forbidden lover. 'I-I've got a photo of him here.' The snapshot was in her bedside drawer, well hidden under scarves and stockings. Herself, a year or two younger, a tall and fair young man standing beside her. They were beaming at the photographer, both wearing breeches and jerseys, knapsacks on their backs.

'You were hiking?' asked Liz, studying the picture. She couldn't get very enthusiastic about a German, but he was handsome enough, she supposed.

'Yes, near the River Neckar,' agreed Cordelia. 'That was a lovely day.' Her voice broke. 'And now I've no idea where he is – or how he is – or what he's doing.' Her eyes were naked with longing and the need for comfort. 'Oh, Liz, how do I know that he's not been hurt' – she took a quick little breath – 'or that he's not helping to kill Jews?'

'Oh, Cordelia!' Awkwardness forgotten, Liz crossed to the bed and crouched down in front of her. 'If you love him, I'm sure that he's a good person. I'm sure he is.'

She was surprised when she realised that she had meant exactly what she had just said. She patted Cordelia's knee until the other girl had stopped sobbing.

'I get so lonely without him,' said Cordelia, as she wiped the tears from her cheeks. 'Although Adam's been a brick all through this. An absolute rock.'

Liz smiled. 'I used to think you and Adam were an item.'

'Adam and I!' Cordelia sounded completely incredulous. 'You really thought that? Well, that explains . . .' She broke off. 'Adam and I are like brother and sister – always have been.'

'He's great, isn't he? He's been such a good friend to me too.'

Cordelia gave her an odd look. 'And you really thought he and I were . . .' She left the sentence unfinished. 'I've always liked you, Liz,' she went on, giving a rueful little grimace. 'I'm sure I've offended you sometimes in the past. Please believe me when I say that I've never meant to. I hear myself coming up with these dreadful Lady Bracknell-type expostulations, and it's really my mother talking. But I get nervous, and I think I should say something. Unfortunately it's usually the wrong thing.'

Liz stared at her. How often in her life had she felt that she'd opened her mouth and put her foot right in it? Lots of times. She came up from the floor and sat down suddenly on the bottom of Cordelia's bed, one arm curled round the bedpost as though for support. She looked at the other girl.

'I've been hard on you sometimes, haven't I?' And, she thought, I've said some incredibly tactless things. Things which must have hurt Cordelia a lot. 'I'm sorry,' she said. 'I apologise.' She stuck out her hand, but Cordelia leaned forward and gave her a swift hug. Separating, the two girls looked at each other. Then they both laughed.

'Sorry for the emotional display,' said Cordelia.

'What happened to the stiff upper lip?' queried Liz with a smile.

'Bugger the stiff upper lip,' said Cordelia robustly. 'We're all people, aren't we? With feelings and emotions?'

'Yes,' said Liz slowly, considering it. 'Whatever kind of accent we speak with. Whatever kind of background we come from.'

The army did send Edward MacMillan somewhere nice and warm. With several thousand others he had embarked for Egypt in the late autumn to join the forces of General Wavell, commander-in-chief for North Africa. The goal was the preservation of Britain's access to the Suez Canal. The Italian army was in possession of most of Libya, plus the fortress of Sidi Barrani, well inside the Egyptian border. General Wavell decided that Mussolini's 'new Roman legions' had to be driven back.

Eddie was one of the men deployed on what was known as Operation Compass. Under Major General O'Connor he took part in the recapture of Sidi Barrani and its surrounding forts, and the push into Libya. It all seemed to happen with embarrassing ease. In three days the British took forty thousand Italians prisoner.

Eddie felt sorry for most of them. They looked so utterly dejected. He wondered if any of them were Mario Rossi's relations.

There were more successes in the new year. The fortress of Bardia fell to the British – and another forty-five thousand prisoners. Then there was a bit of a lull. Eddie took the time to catch up on his correspondence.

He composed a long letter to Helen. There was the little in it about the campaign which he thought would get past the censors, something about the conditions in which the local people lived and a great deal about his feelings for his wife.

My wife. He was surprised how much pleasure those two little words gave him. He was a lucky man. He found a funny postcard to send to Liz and wrote a cheerful message on it. He knew the two girls would compare notes and that Helen would tell Liz what was in the letter.

Some of it at any rate, he thought with a smile. Not the romantic passages. The soppy bits, as Liz would call them. His writing finished, he went to the doorway of the tent and stood looking out over the desert.

He wondered idly if the baby would be a boy or a girl. He didn't mind either way – a healthy baby and a happy Helen, that was all he wanted. And surely his parents would come round when they saw their grandchild for the first time. His mother would love to have a baby to fuss over.

He didn't suppose he could hope to get home in time for the birth. It was good to know that Liz would be there to help Helen when the time came.

Although there were to be many reverses later, particularly after Rommel and his Afrika Korps arrived on the scene, the

British initially continued to have success in North Africa. On 23 January 1941, British and Australian forces stormed and took the strategically important fortress of Tobruk. The generals considered it a remarkably easy victory. They lost only five hundred men.

As Eddie had surmised, Liz and Helen got together to share the correspondence from him. Spending the afternoon with the Gallaghers, Liz had been teasing Helen over the way she would be reading out from Eddie's letter then suddenly stop, blushing.

'Another romantic passage?' Liz sighed. 'Dear me.'

They were laughing over Eddie's postcard when the knock came at the door. Brendan Gallagher got up to answer it.

Some sixth sense made Liz turn her head as he came back into the room. He had something in his hand. He was holding it gingerly, as if it were poisonous.

'It's a telegram,' he said. 'For Helen.'

He handed it to his daughter. Terror raging in her blue eyes, she gave it to Liz.

She managed two words: 'Deeply regret . . .' Then she broke down. Helen was calmer than she was.

'We have to tell your mother. We don't know if she'll have been informed. Eddie said he was going to put me down as his next-of-kin. Come on, Liz. We'll go to her now.'

They called at Annie Crawford's house first, taking her with them to help break the news to Sadie. When Liz's mother opened the door and saw the three of them standing there, nothing needed to be said. Her daughter and daughter-in-law went into her arms.

Mrs Crawford disappeared briefly to dispatch another neighbour to the yard with a message for William MacMillan, then returned to hover anxiously around the three women. They were still standing locked together when he came into the house ten minutes later.

'Get those two out of here.'

'William,' pleaded his wife. 'This lassie's carrying Eddie's baby – our grandchild.'

There was no emotion in his eyes. Liz thought they looked dead. Like broken glass on a beach, washed opaque by the waves.

'Father,' she said. 'Please.' As she had done as a child being taken to hospital, she turned and stretched her arms out to him. He looked through her. As though she weren't there.

'William,' said Sadie again.

'I'll have no Catholic bastard under my roof.'

Helen drew herself out of her mother-in-law's embrace and faced him unflinchingly.

'My child is no bastard, Mr MacMillan. Eddie and I are married.' She corrected herself. 'I mean, Eddie and I were married.' Her face crumpled, the full horror of it hitting her with the use of that one little word. She turned to her friend. 'Oh, Liz!'

William MacMillan ignored her. It was as if she hadn't spoken. Liz took Helen's arm.

'Come on, Helen,' she said. 'Let's go. You don't belong here.' She looked at her father. 'And neither do I. I'll not set foot in this house again. Sorry, Ma.'

Chapter 34

Helen insisted on seeing Liz down to the street when she left. Conor came with them so that his heavily pregnant sister could lean on his arm when they went back up the stairs to the flat. It was March now and she was near her time, but so far nothing seemed to be happening. Liz was reluctant to leave her, but she was covering at the hospital this evening for Cordelia, who was in Edinburgh, attending some family party.

Liz had made Conor promise he would go to a phone box and call the Infirmary as soon as Helen showed any signs of going into labour. He'd come home late last night, escaping the cold March nights up in the hills. Concerned about his sister, he was also wrestling with another problem.

'Better men than me are fighting for their country,' he'd told Liz this afternoon, his good-natured face sombre. 'Better men than me are dying for their country.' He was in tears at the thought of separating from his beloved dog, but he was seriously considering turning himself in – since he'd heard the news from North Africa.

Liz and Helen had become closer than ever in the weeks since Eddie's death, clinging to each other in their shared grief. It wasn't getting any easier.

First there had been a paralysing numbness, a refusal to accept the fact that he was never coming home again.

Then, for Liz at least, there had been anger. She directed it mostly against governments and politicians and warmongering dictators – the whole German nation, too. She knew very well that it had been an Italian bullet which had killed Eddie, but somehow she didn't blame them so much. They'd just got themselves into a mess, whereas it was the Germans who had started this awful war.

She railed against God too. Why had he allowed a boy from Clydebank who hated war to die in the sands of North Africa? It was stupid, a senseless sacrifice of her brother, with his brains and his passion and his hopes for the future with Helen and their baby. Some days Liz feared that the rage would consume her completely.

It was one emotion Helen seemed not to feel. Devastated as she was by her loss, in the midst of her terrible grief there was a strange calmness about her. She said it was because of the baby. Liz thought she was probably right. The imminent arrival of Eddie's child was a little pinprick of light in the desolation and darkness which had surrounded them both since the end of January.

As she stepped out of the close on to the pavement, Liz felt Helen shiver.

'Away back upstairs. Don't get cold.' The girls hugged. 'Look after my nephew or niece,' Liz said. She stretched up to give Conor a peck on the cheek and patted Finn on the head.

She was at the end of the street when she heard her name being called. Helen was standing in the close mouth, one hand resting on Finn's head, the other raised in farewell. Conor stood behind her. They were both smiling at her. She could have sworn that Finn was smiling too.

'Goodbye, Liz,' called Helen. 'I'll see you tomorrow.'

'Aye.' Liz returned the smile and the wave, turned the corner and walked the few yards along Kilbowie Road to the railway station. She clattered down the steps on to the platform, hoping the train wouldn't be late. Stations could be such lonely places.

As Liz waited on the platform at Singer's station, two hundred and fifty Luftwaffe pilots in France, northern Europe and Scandinavia were making their final preparations for take-off.

The German airmen had excellent maps. They showed tonight's target in minute detail.

The aerial photographs made by earlier spy flights pinpointed the shipyards and the docks, the industrial and commercial targets, the power station, the oil depots and the munitions factories. They showed the streets and houses of the town too, the tenement buildings and little terraced houses which were home to almost fifty thousand people.

British civil defence knew the attack was coming. Several weeks earlier they had intercepted and decoded German radio signals which indicated that an air assault on Clydebank was being planned. On the morning of Thursday 13 March 1941 they detected Luftwaffe radio navigation beams over central Scotland. Then individual German planes made reconnaissance flights, checking the weather conditions. That confirmed it. They would be coming that night.

A decision was taken not to inform the populace. They would only panic, probably start trekking up into the hills. That could cause all kinds of confusion, give the authorities some real headaches.

And these were Red Clydesiders after all. The news might lead to disturbances, riots and civil unrest. Much better to leave them in a state of blissful ignorance about what was heading their way.

At around six p.m., about the same time as Liz was boarding her train, the German pilots began taking off from their different airfields. While they droned their way over the sea, gradually forming up into a huge squadron, the people of Clydebank got on with whatever they normally did on a Thursday evening.

A young man who lived close to Liz's grandfather in Radnor Street, an apprentice at the Singer factory, caught the same train as her, heading for his weekly evening class at the Tech in Glasgow.

In the Holy City, while Marie Gallagher joyfully prepared a meal for her prodigal son, Helen and her other brothers sat by the fire talking with him. Everyone was making a big fuss of

314

Finn. Conor complained that the dog was getting a better welcome than he was.

In Queen Victoria Row, Sadie MacMillan was also sitting by the fire, but the scene was far from joyful. Her husband sat opposite her, ostensibly reading the evening paper. He'd been staring at the same page for the past twenty minutes.

He had refused to talk about their son's death, denying his grieving wife even the silent refuge of his arms. They slept in the same bed, but there was no physical intimacy between them. There hadn't been for a long time.

Sadie yearned for comfort and consolation. William MacMillan gave her none. Not a touch. Not a kind word.

They had loved each other once. It had been after little George's death that he had changed. Now they had lost a second son – and Lizzie too, by the looks of it. He had forced their daughter to walk out on them – and the bonnie girl Eddie had loved. Not to mention the bairn. Their grandchild. Sadie wondered how much more of this she could take.

'Hi, there,' said Adam, standing up as Liz walked into the empty casualty department. He'd been sitting at a table poring over a textbook. 'How's Helen?'

'Oh, she's all right.'

'When's her date – next week sometime?'

Liz nodded. 'Wednesday. Nothing happening yet, though.'

'Well,' he said comfortingly, 'first babies can often be late.'

Liz nodded again. *First babies*. There weren't going to be any subsequent ones, not for Helen and Eddie. Adam put a solicitous hand on her shoulder.

'And how's Liz?' His voice was very gentle.

She managed a tight little smile. 'Bearing up. Were you swotting when I arrived? Don't let me stop you.'

He made a face. 'My finals do seem to be approaching at a rate of knots. Less than two weeks to go till the first exam.'

'Do you want me to ask you some questions?'

'Yes, if you can be bothered.'

315

She sat down in front of the book. 'It'll pass the time,' she said. 'It looks like it's going to be a quiet night.'

At ten past nine the air-raid siren went off.

'Ignore it,' Adam advised. 'Ask me another.'

'Aye, we've had a lot of false alarms, haven't we?' responded Liz, scanning the page to see what topic she could test him on next. 'There's a lad lives near my grandfather – he's an apprentice at Singer's. I came in on the train with him tonight. He was telling me that they have a sweepstake every day in the factory on when the siren's going to go off that night.'

Adam smiled.

'Right,' said Liz, 'tell me—'

'—what that noise was,' he said, straightening up abruptly in his chair.

'It sounds like doors banging,' said Liz in puzzlement, putting her finger in the textbook to keep her place and lifting her head towards the sounds which had so rudely interrupted them.

Adam rose to his feet. 'That's not doors banging, MacMillan. Those are bombs. Bloody hell!'

Peter MacMillan, as a volunteer ARP warden, had been attending his weekly training night. He had just got home and undressed when the siren went off. Bugger. He'd been looking forward to an early night. He enjoyed his war work, but he wasn't getting any younger. Ach well, it was back down the road for him, to the control centre in the basement of the public library.

With a muttered curse, he reached for the trousers he'd laid over the back of a chair. In the blackout that was easier said than done. The material evaded his groping fingers and the trousers slid off the chair on to the floor. It took a few more seconds to locate them and get them the right way up.

First one leg, then the other. What the hell was the matter with the bloody things? They felt far too tight. They'd been fine five minutes ago. Then he fell over. Fortunately he made it into the chair rather than going all the way to the floor. Feeling more than faintly ridiculous, he realised that he had put both legs down the same trouser leg. He swore colourfully. It was a good job Lizzie wasn't here.

As the whooping wail of the siren faded, all hell began to break loose. Flares were the first thing to come down, bathing the whole town in an eerie greenish glow. Then, to make the target yet more visible for their comrades, the German pathfinder units dropped hundreds of incendiaries. They let go of a few high-explosive bombs too, aiming to force the population down below into the shelters as soon as possible. That wasn't done for any humanitarian reason. The more people there were in the shelters, the fewer there would be to put the fires out.

Some people came back out to look at the incendiaries dropping, floating gracefully down in a shower of sparks like fairy lights on a Christmas tree. Afterwards they were to wonder if they'd been off their heads, especially when they heard stories of people being permanently blinded by the glare.

The pathfinder units were followed by the main bombing force. Some were flying up the Irish Sea, carrying their hideous load from Beauvais in northern France. The majority were approaching over the North Sea, from Holland, northern Germany, Norway and Denmark. The drone of their engines could be heard as far south as Hull and as far north as Aberdeen. On the east coast near Edinburgh, people heard wave after wave coming over. Every ten minutes there were more of them.

By about half past nine the main phalanx of Luftwaffe planes had arrived over Clydebank. Then they started to unloose their deadly cargo.

The accident and emergency department was busy enough now. A steady stream of injured and shocked people were being brought in. Bombs were dropping not only on Clydebank but on the West End of Glasgow too. A landmine had fallen on

Dudley Drive in Hyndland, no distance from the Infirmary. The hospital buildings had shaken in sympathy, and several windows had been shattered.

Casualty was busy not only with patients, but also with medical staff and students. They were duty-bound to turn out to help after a raid, once the all-clear had sounded, but many of them had headed for the Infirmary as soon as they realised that there was a heavy bombardment taking place.

A lot of doctors had turned up as well: too many. Adam had been due to go off duty at ten o'clock anyway, but he was considerably frustrated by being summarily ousted from his duties by a qualified doctor. He and his fellow students were left to cool their heels in the corridor. Liz, also now officially off duty, stood with them.

'There's too many of us here,' said Jim Barclay.

'We're just getting in the way,' agreed another student.

'It's all right,' said one of the staff nurses as she passed them, misinterpreting the concern on their faces. 'Apparently it's Clydebank that's really getting it.'

Liz clutched Adam's arm.

'Helen . . . my parents . . . my grandfather . . .'

He was interrupted before he could attempt to reassure her.

'There's a girl here,' shouted Jim. 'A nurse who's brought in a badly injured baby. She says there's no doctors down in Clydebank. I vote we go with her. Is anyone else game?'

Dominic Gallagher was unable to give much thought to whether the planes overhead were Heinkel 111s or Junker 88s. By quarter to ten, fifteen minutes after the main Luftwaffe squadron had arrived, all of the telephones were out – not to mention the electricity and water supply. Communication was crucial and the team of teenage messenger boys were standing by, ready to criss-cross the town on their bikes.

'But Liz! You can't come with us! It's not safe.'

Adam shook his head. 'Don't waste your breath, Jim. You'll

318

get nowhere with this one. She's stubborn as a mule.' He gave Liz a swift smile, doing his damnedest to put some reassurance into it. 'I'll take my car. Jim, you'll come with me. You too, Liz. That'll leave more room in the ambulance for the others.'

'We'll need supplies,' she said. Her voice sounded odd. Rusty, as though she hadn't used it for a while.

One of the sisters was there before her, making up bundles of bandages and dressings, wrapping them up in hospital sheets like so many washerwomen's bundles. She put one into Liz's hands.

Adam turned to the woman and kissed her on the cheek. 'Sister MacDonald, you're a brick. Have we got morphia in here? I imagine pain relief's going to be quite crucial.' His voice was grim.

It was Sister MacLean who answered him. 'We are not permitted to give you morphia.' Her voice was carefully expressionless. 'You're all students. The Medical Superintendent insists, therefore, that you are not qualified to administer it. Furthermore, he declares that he will accept no responsibility for anything which any of you do tonight.'

The students looked at her for a moment in shocked disbelief. 'Then may God forgive him,' said Adam fiercely. 'Come on, Liz!'

Nowhere was safe. Not even the shelters. Several of them took direct hits, killing everyone inside. Terrified of suffering that fate, many people had elected to stay in their buildings. Neighbours gathered together, some in their reinforced closes, others in ground-floor flats. They sat in lobbies and hallways if they had them. If they didn't, they picked a spot as far away as possible from the windows and the awful dangers of flying glass.

Other people rushed out into the open, terrified by the thought of sitting on the ground floor of three- and four-storey tenements with all that masonry above them. Some of them spent the night in the park – and lived.

One of the planes which had taken off from Stavanger in Norway dropped a parachute mine on one of the Holy City terraces. The front wall was completely blown off and thrown across the street. Helen Gallagher, tucked between Conor and her father as the family sat in the reinforced tenement close, was sucked clean out of the building by the blast. Her last recollection was of her father trying to grab her. Then nothing. Only blackness.

First-aid posts had to be hurriedly moved to other sites when their original locations were hit. A school which housed one of them was one of the first places to go up. Along with the timber store at Singer's, it made a wonderful beacon for the incoming German pilots, guiding them to their prey.

'At least,' said Peter MacMillan laconically to a fellow warden, 'we've got enough light to see by. It makes a nice change.'

'Why are we going this way?' asked Liz, as they headed along Highburgh Road towards Great Western Road, following the ambulance. She was breathless after the run to Morag. Fortunately, the little car had been parked not too far away. 'Wouldn't Dumbarton Road be quicker?'

'Think about it, Liz,' urged Adam. 'We'll have to go into Clydebank from the top – along the Boulevard and drop down that way. Dumbarton Road could well be impassable. They'll be trying to hit John Brown's and Rothesay Dock, although they'll be going for Singer's too, I expect— Oh, hell, I'm sorry.'

He took his hand briefly off the wheel and laid it on her own. She was convulsively clutching the bundle of dressings and bandages.

John Brown's and Rothesay Dock. Her parents' house was sandwiched between the two. And Helen's home was only yards away from Singer's.

Oh, please God, let Helen and the baby be safe. And Mother and Father. And Grandad too. With a guilty start, Liz realised that everyone would be sending up the same sort of prayer. *Not at the expense of anyone else, God. Oh God, not that.*

'Are you sure you're all right about this? About coming?' Adam swung the wheel to turn them from Hyndland Road into Great Western Road.

'I'll have to be, won't I? I'm not going to be much bloody use to anybody otherwise.'

'Good girl.'

They drove in silence past the handsome villas on Great Western Road and the grounds of Gartnavel, the rambling Victorian psychiatric hospital set in its own grounds behind Bingham's Pond. They passed through the man-made cavern of the red sandstone tenements at Anniesland Cross. When they emerged from them they got a full view of the night sky over Clydebank.

'God Almighty!'

'What pretty colours,' drawled Jim Barclay from the back seat. Liz rounded on him, eyes blazing as brightly as the flames in front of them.

'That's my home town that's burning.'

The lad's face crumpled and he stretched a hand forward to her. 'Och, MacMillan, I'm sorry. I'm really sorry. I'm just trying to pretend that I'm not scared to death.'

She found his hand and squeezed it.

'I know,' she said, her voice breaking. 'I know.'

'Maybe we should all say a wee prayer,' muttered Adam. Youthful cynicism forgotten, they did so.

'Shall I try St Jude as well?'

'Every saint you can think of,' said Adam. 'We're not proud. I can think of a poem which might be appropriate, too. *Into the valley of death rode the six hundred*, perhaps. What the fu—'

Liz blinked. She'd rarely heard him swear. Given that he'd stamped down hard on the brakes in order to prevent Morag disappearing down a large crater which had appeared before them, she was disposed to let it go. Just this once.

He reversed and swerved over on to the other carriageway

of the Boulevard to get around the obstruction. Liz glanced over at the fields to her left. The open area between the road and East Kilbowie was full of bright lights.

'Incendiaries, I think,' muttered Jim Barclay. 'At least they won't do much harm there.'

'Here goes,' said Adam a few minutes later, as he pulled off the Boulevard into Kilbowie Road. 'Where to, Liz? I'm not sure how far we'll be able to take the car.'

'Radnor Park Church Hall,' she said breathlessly. 'There's a first-aid post there. It's not far. Keep going along Kilbowie Road as far as you can.'

There were people everywhere: lying on stretchers, slumped in chairs, being brought in by rescue parties. First-aiders were doing what they could, but the relief was palpable when the white-coated medical students entered the room. A shout of welcome went up.

'Nice to be appreciated at last,' muttered Jim Barclay. As they passed through the rows of stretchers and camp beds, heading for the people who seemed to be in charge, a middle-aged man, his face smeared with grime and streaks of blood, lifted a hand and gripped Adam's sleeve.

'God bless you for coming, son. God bless you.'

Adam patted him gently on the shoulder. It was the one part of him which seemed to be uninjured. Standing behind Adam, waiting for him to move on, Liz glanced down at the grey blanket which covered the lower half of the man's body. It was curiously flat. Then she realised. He had lost his legs.

She wanted to be sick. Behind her, Jim gripped her elbow. She heard Adam's voice through a buzzing in her ears.

'We'll be right with you, sir. Just give us a minute or two to get organised.'

He moved on, his white sleeve now stained red. *The patients come first. The patients come first.* Liz forced down the bile rising in her throat and plastered a smile on to her face.

'God bless you too, pet. We need a few bonnie nurses to go

with the handsome doctors, is that no' right?'

Like Adam, she put a comforting hand to the man's shoulder. 'Nae bother,' she said. 'We didnae want to miss out on the excitement.'

Incredibly, the blood-stained face broke into a smile. 'Aye, better than Guy Fawkes Night this, eh, hen? Imagine yon young doctor calling me sir! And him so well-spoken too.'

Half an hour later he died in Liz's arms. She laid him gently down and went on to the next person who needed her. She was desperately worried about her own people: her parents, Helen, her grandfather. Every moment she dreaded turning round and seeing one of her own loved ones lying there with terrible injuries.

She dealt with it in the only way she knew how – in the only way possible. As the bombs fell all around them, Liz cleaned wounds, bandaged limbs, applied dressings and gave what reassurance she could to dazed and distressed people.

In a strange way she was helped by the sheer awfulness of it all. Was she really in Clydebank, her own familiar little home town? Could this horror actually be happening?

It was a night when she saw the best and the worst of humanity. A line of Robert Burns came back to her: *man's inhumanity to man*. She wondered about the people who had chosen to unleash this awful suffering on a civilian population, snug in their houses on a cold March night, listening to the nine o'clock news on the wireless.

She tended a mother who was desperately clutching a baby. Liz suspected the poor little mite was dead. It was . . . and Liz persuaded the girl to let go of her precious burden.

'We have to identify the dead, Nurse,' someone murmured in her ear, *sotto voce* so that the young mother didn't hear. 'As far as we can. Some luggage labels for you.' And so, dry-eyed, Liz coaxed the Christian name and surname of the child – a little girl – out of the shocked mother, and tied a luggage label around the tiny blood-stained wrist.

There was inhumanity on the ground too: people who

thought only of themselves, who wanted their injuries treated *now* – before others who were much more seriously hurt. Liz also knew there would be people out there taking advantage of the situation. There would be looting going on. But her abiding memory was of people's courage and care for each other.

The messenger boys were risking their young lives to keep the control centre and the first-aid and ARP posts in touch with each other. Ambulance drivers were taking their lives in their hands to transport the badly injured to hospitals outside the danger zone.

Rescue workers, dashing from close to close as the bombs dropped, were saving other people's families whilst desperately worried about their own. They spoke also of men and women crawling back into the wreckage of their ruined buildings to comfort neighbours who were trapped.

There were the badly wounded people who, seeing the fear in others' faces, made jokes in the midst of their pain. As she moved among the injured, Liz heard little snatches of conversation.

One man reported being blown out of his house and waking up to find himself surrounded by packets of tea.

'What did you do?'

'Stuffed a few of them in my pockets, of course. Would you like one, Doctor?'

Another, garrulous with relief because both he and his wife had survived a bomb which had buried several of their neighbours, was now making fun of his better half.

'We were in the close and she wanted to go back up to the hoose. To check that the fire was still in, if you please! Well, says I to her – it's Jerry who's keeping the home fires burning for us the night! And he's making a bloody good job of it, tae!'

Shortly before midnight they heard that the whisky bond at Yoker Distillery had got a direct hit. That provoked an unreasonable amount of hilarity.

'I expect we're all delirious,' said Adam, glancing up from the little girl he was attending to. 'Going a bit hysterical.'

An hour or so later, they realised that the noise overhead had diminished a little.

'Just when we were beginning to get used to them too,' said Jim Barclay.

'There's no reason to suppose they won't be back,' came the grim response.

The lull allowed the removal of more of the injured to hospital. Liz was asked to accompany two of them to Canniesburn Hospital in Bearsden. The phones being out, she was also to ask how many more they might be able to take. Local hospitals like Blawarthill had filled up quickly. The injured were going to have to be taken a bit further afield.

'Cup of tea before you go back into the lion's den, Nurse?' asked the sister at Canniesburn, who then persuaded Liz and the ambulance driver to take five minutes to drink one. The sister laid a hand on both their shoulders.

'God speed.'

When she got back to the first-aid post, Liz stood back to allow a stretcher to be carried out to another ambulance.

'Hello, Liz,' said the boy lying on it.

'Dominic! Are you all right?'

'I've buggered my leg,' he said cheerfully. 'There was I, cycling along minding my own business, when this dirty great piece of timber falls on top of me. Knackered the bike as well.'

'Are they taking you to Canniesburn?'

One of the stretcher-bearers answered for him. 'No, he's heading for Killearn. Some fresh country air for this lad.'

'It's a bit far out,' said Dominic, with a quick frown. 'It'll be difficult for anyone to visit me.'

'We'll manage somehow,' said Liz. 'There's buses go out that way.' He was being put into the ambulance now, struggling to sit up so he could still see her.

'Liz, will you let them know at home what's happened? Ma'll be real worried about me.'

'I will,' she promised.

'Oh, and Liz,' he said. 'Don't tell Ma that I said my leg was

325

buggered. I don't want a cuff round the ear when she comes out to visit me.' He grinned. 'Put it a wee bit more politely.'

'Nae bother,' she said. She gave him a wave and a smile before the ambulance doors were slammed shut.

The first person Liz spotted when she went back into the church hall was her grandfather in his ARP uniform. She flew to his side.

'It's all right, hen,' he told her after he had given her a hug which took her breath away. 'I think your mother and father are probably all right. They seem to have missed Brown's. There's been some damage, but no' as much as you might expect.'

Relief flooded through her. In the morning I'm going down there, she thought. I'll make it up with them. It's not worth it. This is no time to bear a grudge.

'What about the Holy City, Grandad? Do you know what's happening there?'

His face betrayed his knowledge.

'They've taken a hell of a beating, hen.'

Helen and the baby! Oh, please God, let them be all right! Terror made her angry, snapping her out of her previous unnatural calmness.

'Well, is anybody doing anything to help them? Let me past, Grandad, I've got to go and see for myself!'

The old man gripped her shoulders with a strength which belied his years.

'Lizzie! You cannae. It's bloody dangerous out there. There's enough folk risking their necks as it is. And you're needed here!'

The bombardment started again. The merciless pounding of the town went on for another four hours.

Chapter 35

It was half past six in the morning and it was over at last. The all-clear had sounded some time ago and dawn had broken. A large convoy of ambulances had arrived to ferry the remaining casualties out. Hospitals all around Glasgow were taking them in.

More help had arrived in the devastated town, not least a squadron of mobile canteens, many of them run by the Women's Voluntary Service.

'Thank God for the WVS,' said one of the medics wearily. 'What would we do without you, ladies?' He lifted his cup in a toasting gesture.

'What would we have done without you, young man?' replied the woman, offering Liz a cup of tea as she sat slumped at a table with her head in her hands.

She shook her head and stood up.

'No thanks. I have to go and see if my friend is all right. And my folks.'

'I'll come with you,' said Adam, 'but we're going to drink a cup of tea and have something to eat first. A quick bite – a roll or something.'

'I don't want anything.'

'Liz, you've been up all night. And you'll be no use to anybody if you collapse of exhaustion.'

She gave in. She could see she wasn't going to get anywhere unless she did. She bolted down a couple of mouthfuls of bread roll and drank the tea so fast it scalded her mouth.

Her ears were still ringing with the remembered noises of

last night: the crashing and whooshing and booming of the bombs dropping, the screams and cries of the injured. The sounds were all the louder in her head because of the eerie quiet which now lay like a pall over the town. It was uncanny. Clydebank was a place of bustle and industry. She had never experienced such stillness.

In increasing distress, she took in the devastation wrought by the raid. All around, burned and blasted houses were smouldering. There was a bigger fire somewhere close at hand, too. At Singer's, she thought. They passed Radnor Street. The buildings were extensively damaged.

'Looks like your grandfather's going to have to find somewhere else to sleep tonight.'

They had seen him again this morning, after the all-clear had sounded. It was a relief to know that he, at least, was all right.

'Look at the tram lines,' said Adam. 'It's like a piece of avant-garde sculpture.' Liz looked. Exploded from their moorings, the lines were standing up like jagged vertical spears. Water mains had burst too. Kilbowie Road was running like a river. And there was a peculiar smell in the air – not only from all the fires which were still raging, but something faintly sweet.

'It'll be from the distillery at Yoker,' said Adam, indicating the direction with a lift of his chin. 'Remember someone told us last night that it had taken a hit? Looks like they got Rothesay Dock, too.' He turned his head and looked in the other direction, to where a huge pall of smoke was hanging over the Clyde. 'That looks like oil burning. Where would that be?'

'Old Kilpatrick,' said Liz, her words slurred with tiredness. 'There's an oil depot there.' But she wasn't really listening to him. Her eyes were fixed on the rubble, slates, broken furniture and glass which lay strewn about the street. With a horrible sense of foreboding of worse to come, she picked her way through it, Adam occasionally gripping her elbow to guide her.

Worse was to come.

'Don't look,' he said. He reached out an arm, trying

physically to turn her head away, but he was too late. It was the body of a small boy, clearly dead. Her head tucked into Adam's chest, Liz spoke in an anguished whisper.

'Shouldn't we do something? Lift him and take him somewhere?'

She felt him shake his head.

'No, Liz, that's not our job. Someone'll come and get him soon.' He stopped, and she knew from the way he held her that he had something else to say, something which he was trying to phrase in the kindest way possible. In the end he chose simple words.

'He won't be the only one. I think I can see a squad down the road. They'll come up for him soon. They've . . . I think they're getting someone else at the moment.'

Held close against him, Liz nodded her head. He was right, of course he was. She pulled out of his embrace and looked up at him, dry-eyed. He cupped her face with his hands, his hazel eyes soft with compassion.

'All right?'

'All right,' she replied.

They turned a corner – and it was like all the newsreel reports she'd ever seen of London and Coventry and Liverpool. She remembered Guernica and the Spanish cities too.

There were the same surreal pictures: houses which stood like hollow teeth, as though scooped out with a spoon: buildings where the fronts had fallen off, leaving the rooms behind exposed to view. It was pitiful. Liz saw a precariously poised black-leaded range, a big kettle still sitting on it. There were dogs and cats running about everywhere, panicked by the events of the night. She saw with relief that there were people rounding them up.

She thought about Conor and Finn. She'd have given anything to see the two of them coming towards her. Liz had never been able to decide if Conor had copied his long loping stride from Finn, or if the dog had taken it from his master. Their mutual devotion seemed to make either possible.

Liz rubbed her eyes. They were playing tricks on her. Small wonder. After all she had seen last night and this morning it would be odd if they weren't. But she was confused all the same. She would ask Adam. He always had a sensible answer to everything.

'Where's Helen's close gone, Adam? I can't see it at all.'

'Oh, Liz,' he said. 'I'm so sorry.'

He tried to take her in his arms again, but she side-stepped him. What was he on about? What was he so sorry about? All they had to do was find Helen's close and then find out how she was – and Mr and Mrs Gallagher and the boys too, of course. Finn as well. They had to be all right. They just had to be.

'Adam,' she said. He was very pale. Poor soul, he must be exhausted. 'You've got to help me find Helen's close. The entrance has to be here somewhere.'

'Oh, Liz,' he said again.

Now she was getting angry. She began shouting. She ran towards what was left of the houses.

'Liz! Come back!'

She ignored him, but she was forced to stop when he caught up with her and grabbed her roughly by the arm. He swung her round to face him.

'Helen!' she shouted. 'She's in there somewhere! Let me go, Adam. Please! We've got to get her out. She's pregnant! With Eddie's baby. Don't you know that?'

Adam seized her other arm and held her fast. 'Yes, I know that – and there are people trying to get her out,' he insisted. 'People who know what they're doing, who know the best way to go about it. We don't.' He saw from her face that she needed convincing.

'You and I are both exhausted, too tired to make proper judgements. About anything much. We might do something stupid – simply because we're so desperate to get to Helen and her family. The buildings will be extremely unstable. Digging the wrong way could do more harm than good. It could bring more masonry down on everyone in there.'

Privately, he had a horrible fear that there was no one left alive. He'd never seen such devastation. The human body could be very resilient, but not against the damage which had been done here.

It was Liz he was concerned about now. She needed rest to enable her to cope with whatever was coming next.

'Do you hear me, Liz?' he asked, gripping her arms and forcing her to meet his gaze. 'Do you understand what I'm saying to you?'

He repeated his arguments, shaking her in an attempt to get the message across. They weren't experts. Think of all the different things in a building: plaster, wood, heavy furniture. Moving something the wrong way could do more damage to the folk trapped in the buildings. She took it in eventually, slumping briefly against him before straightening up and looking around her.

'Let's see if we can help the people they bring out, anyway.' He nodded. It was the best he was going to get. She really needed her bed. So did he, but he would go along with this for a while. A very little while. Then he would insist.

They were still there at ten o'clock, when the rescue parties brought out a big man and a large grey dog. Finn was greyer than usual, himself and his master covered in plaster. Both he and Conor were quite dead.

'Oh, no,' whispered Adam. 'Oh, God Almighty, no.'

'This lad was lying over the dog,' said one of the rescuers, scratching his head in puzzlement. 'He had his arms around him, like he was shielding him. Can you believe that?'

Numb with exhaustion and grief, Liz took the luggage labels out of her pocket and began writing the names: *Conor Gallagher* and *Finn Gallagher*. It was the last thing she could do for them.

Her fingers didn't seem to be functioning properly. She managed Conor's label, her writing big and round as it had been when she had first learned her letters in primary school. On the second one, she got as far as *Finn*. Her fingers locked. She couldn't seem to write any more.

Adam leaned over Liz's shoulder, plucked the labels and pencil out of her grasp and finished the job. He crouched down to attach the labels. Someone laughed.

'We'll not be needing to identify the dog, lad.'

'Yes we do!' Liz shouted. 'Yes, we bloody well do! They were friends, these two. The best of friends! They've got to stay together! They've got to! Adam! Tell him they've got to stay together!'

The man who'd brought Conor and Finn out shot a warning glance at his mates and put a hand on Liz's shoulder.

'Aye, lass. We need to know who they both were. You're right enough.'

She crouched down beside the bodies, laying a hand first on Conor's hair, brushing the grey dust off to reveal the burnished copper underneath. His face was unmarked. Then she laid a hand on Finn's head.

'Well, my boy, you'll not be stealing any more gingerbread.'

The man who had told her to go ahead with the labels was looking down at her, compassion written all over his face. His cheeks and forehead were streaked with dust and blood.

'I'll make sure they stay together, lass. You can trust me.'

Liz looked up at him. She was like a little child.

'Where you found them . . . is there anybody else in there? Alive?' she whispered.

'I don't know, lass, but we're going to keep digging until we find out.'

As the morning wore on, the rescue parties were joined by a group of miners from East Lothian. They had made their way over to the west as soon as they'd heard the news early that morning.

'Of course it only said a Clydeside town on the wireless,' Liz overheard one of them saying in his sing-song east-coast accent, 'but we knew where it would be.'

They quickly changed the thrust of the rescue process. Instead of clearing away masonry and wooden beams from the top of the rubble, they tunnelled in from the sides – and began hearing cries for help. The knowledge that there were people still alive under the debris gave everybody fresh hope and fresh heart.

'It's no' going to be a quick job to get any o' them oot, mind,' warned one of the miners. 'We'll be taking this real slow.' He spoke to Adam. 'I'd take the lassie home, son. Yourself too. Away and get some rest.' His eyes swept over Liz's blood-stained uniform, Adam's filthy white coat. 'I hear the two o' you had a bit of a busy night.'

'You could say that,' said Adam drily. He wrote something on one of the luggage labels which he'd slipped into his own pocket and handed it to the man.

'Can you try to get a message to us at this address? If you find anyone by the name of Gallagher or MacMillan? Particularly a heavily pregnant young woman.'

He turned to Liz. 'Come on, you,' he said gently. 'I'm taking you to your mother's.'

Liz thought her mother was never going to stop hugging her.

'Oh, hen, I was that worried about you.' She let her daughter go at last, standing back to look at her with tears in her eyes. 'What about Eddie's lassie?' she asked anxiously.

Adam explained the situation. 'So if Liz could have a wash and a rest here? Maybe something to eat?'

Sadie squared her shoulders. 'And where else would she go to do that, I might ask? You'll stay too, Dr Buchanan.' It wasn't a question.

Adam smiled. 'Thanks very much, Mrs MacMillan – but I'm not a doctor yet, you know.'

Sadie MacMillan fixed him with a look, taking in the blood which streaked his face and his white coat. The coat which had been white last night. 'You're a doctor, son. Don't let anyone tell you otherwise. Now,' she said briskly, 'let's have that coat and I'll get it washed. Your uniform too, Lizzie.'

* * *

It was six o'clock that evening before a boy on a bicycle pushed open the gate at Queen Victoria Row. They'd got Helen out, but she was in a bad way. She'd been taken straight to Rottenrow, the maternity hospital up in Glasgow. With all forms of public transport disrupted, and Morag abandoned up near the Boulevard, it took Liz and Adam over two hours to get there.

By the time they did, Helen was in theatre having an emergency Caesarean. They were left to wait in the corridor outside. About half an hour after they arrived at the hospital, the air-raid sirens went off.

The first bombs fell on Drumchapel shortly before nine. Ten minutes later a punishing bombardment of Radnor Park, Kilbowie and Dalmuir started. The second raid wasn't unexpected. It had been the pattern in other places.

With thousands of others, Liz's parents and her grandfather had left the town for the night, taking advantage of the buses laid on to take people to temporary rest centres outside the danger zone. There had been no news about the rest of the Gallagher family.

Liz and Adam stood by a window looking in the direction of Clydebank. Last night they'd been in the thick of it. It was strange to be watching it from a distance like this. A sister passed them and told them off for being so stupid as to stand by a window while there was bombing going on.

Adam apologised sheepishly for both of them and they moved away to sit on a bench in the corridor outside the operating theatre. Liz was glad he was with her. He was a tower of strength and she told him so.

He lifted her hand to his lips and kissed it.

'Nae bother,' he said. 'Nae bother, hen.'

The baby – a fit and healthy girl – had been safely delivered. The midwife brought her out to them and Liz forced back the tears. She wanted to look at her niece. She was perfect. She had blue eyes like Helen's and a shock of thick hair as dark as her father's had been.

'Poor wee mite,' said the woman. 'An orphan of the Blitz.'

'She's not an orphan,' shouted Liz, clutching the precious bundle to her. 'She's got a mother! Her mother's in there!' Holding the baby tight, she slid round on the wooden bench, turning her body in the direction of the operating theatre.

'Nurse,' said the midwife sternly, 'there's no need for that. Really.'

It was Adam's words which calmed her down. Sliding his arm around her shoulders, he pulled her and the baby into him. 'Wheesht,' he said. 'You don't want Helen to hear you, do you? What is it Sister MacLean always says?'

Liz turned to him, her eyes glittering like emeralds in a face as white as paper.

'The patients come first.'

'Exactly. Hang on to that, and hang on to the baby. They'll let us see Helen as soon as they can.'

They sat with the baby and waited. They were like proud parents themselves, admiring the perfect little creature. Then the surgeon who'd operated on her mother asked to speak to them both. A midwife took the baby from Liz and she and Adam followed the man into his office.

'Sit down, please. A drink?' He didn't wait for an answer. Chunky whisky tumblers were pressed into their hands.

'Drink it,' he said. 'You're going to need it. What is your relationship to the patient?'

'She's my sister-in-law,' said Liz. 'The baby's my niece.'

'Your brother's wife? Where is he right now? Drink some whisky,' he added.

Liz did, spluttering as the fiery liquid went down her throat.

'He was killed in action. North Africa.'

'Her parents?'

'Missing since last night, sir,' said Adam. 'In the bombing. The whole family, it appears. Apart from her younger brother.'

The surgeon shook his distinguished head.

'I'm sorry, lass,' he said to Liz, suddenly sounding much

335

less exalted and much more down-to-earth. 'She hasn't got long. Maybe an hour. Maybe less.'

Adam held her while she wept, the surgeon looking sadly on. Then she pulled herself out of Adam's embrace. Straightening up, she wiped her eyes.

'I'm a nurse. Helen's a patient, and the patients come first. Come hell or high water.' She looked across at the surgeon. 'Is there somewhere I can wash my face before we see her?'

Just before they were shown into the room, Liz's courage almost failed her. 'Adam, I don't know if I can do this!'

He put his hand on her shoulder and gave it a shake, but his voice was as gentle as she'd ever heard it.

'Come on, Liz. You can do it. If I can.' He raised his fair brows in the gesture she knew so well. 'I'm only an effete member of the middle classes after all. You're a Red Clydesider. Tough as old boots. Tempered in steel. Forged in the fire.'

'Oh, Adam! The Clyde's red in another way now, isn't it?'

'Aye,' he said carefully. 'But it'll run clear again. Come on, now. Helen needs you. You can't fail her at the last.'

She looked very small. Tucked into the hospital bed, sheet and blanket folded back neatly over her chest, her soot-blackened hair was just visible beneath a white cap into which it had presumably been tucked while she had undergone the Caesarean. She smiled when she saw them and tried to reach out a hand. Choking back the tears, Liz approached the bed. She had to bend down to hear the words properly.

'Ma and Daddy? The boys? Finn?'

'They're fine,' said Liz, rushing in before Adam could speak. He brought forward an upright chair from a corner of the room and Liz sank down on to it, grinning in sheer relief that Helen could still speak. People who were about to die couldn't speak coherently and ask sensible questions, could they?

She swallowed. Sensible they might be. Easy to answer they weren't. She told Helen about Dominic. Then the lies started spilling out of her mouth.

'Well, Finn's pretty scared of course and the rest of them are not exactly fine. Cuts and bruises. That sort of thing. You'll see them soon.' Was she gabbling?

A faint smile touched Helen's mouth. There was a bruise at one side of it.

'Aye . . . that I will.' She turned her head on the white pillow and fixed Liz with one of those clear blue looks of hers, her voice all at once clear and strong. 'You're a terrible liar, Elizabeth MacMillan. You're no good at it at all.'

Liz could think of nothing to say to that.

'I've thought of trying a prayer to St Jude,' Helen went on conversationally, 'but I don't think he can help me. There's a limit even to his powers.' With agonising slowness, she raised her eyes to Adam, standing behind Liz's chair.

'Hello, Adam. I'm glad you're here.'

'Hello, Helen.' His voice sounded very deep in the quiet of the room. 'How are we feeling?'

That raised another smile. 'The doctor's question. I think we both know the answer to that one, don't we?' A look passed between the two of them. 'I'd like to see someone. Do you think there's any chance?'

'You want a priest of your own faith?'

Helen nodded.

'I'll get you one,' he said decisively. His hand squeezed Liz's shoulder briefly before he swept out of the room. Turning her head to follow his departure, Liz looked back to the bed to find Helen's candid gaze once more fixed on her. She took her friend's hand gently in her own and Helen's lids flickered closed.

'I'm not hurting your hand, am I?'

Helen replied without opening her eyes.

'No, it feels nice.'

'Don't worry,' said Liz, doing her best to adopt the brisk and no-nonsense voice. 'I don't know how the hell he'll do it in all this, but he'll get you a priest. Adam never lets anybody down.'

She had thought – hoped perhaps – that Helen was drifting off to sleep, but her eyes flickered open again.

'You know his worth, then?'

'I know his worth.'

Helen seemed to be about to say something else, but then her eyes clouded and lost their focus. She managed a few more words.

'You'll not leave me, Liz?'

'You don't get rid of me that easily, Helen MacMillan,' Liz assured her.

A smile touched the bruised mouth.

'Even if it was only the registry office,' Helen murmured, 'I'm still a respectable married woman.'

'Of course you are,' said Liz. 'My sister-in-law. My very dear sister-in-law.'

She could barely make out the reply, but she smiled when she did.

'Don't go all soppy on me, MacMillan.'

'Perish the thought,' said Liz.

Adam was back within ten minutes. The hospital's Roman Catholic chaplain had been on the premises. He showed the clergyman in, then gently ushered Liz up from her chair.

'We'll sit over here in the corner,' he said. 'Then Father Fitzgerald can do what he has to.'

'Shouldn't we leave the room?'

The priest looked kind. 'Not necessary, my child. Mr Buchanan advises me that there probably isn't time for me to hear her confession.'

Liz glanced at the still figure lying in the bed. Helen's eyes were closed, but she could have sworn she'd muttered three little words. *Just as well.*

What the priest did next had no meaning for Liz, but she could see that Helen welcomed it. When it was over, she once more took up her position by the bedside. It wouldn't be long now. She'd seen that look too many times, so she was surprised when Helen's voice rang out.

'I want to see the baby.'

The look of tenderness on Helen's face when the small white bundle was placed in her arms was almost too much to bear. She held her daughter for a few short minutes. Then the nurse came forward, murmuring something about all the babies being down in the basement tonight for safety during the raid. Would she maybe take the wee one now?

Helen pressed her lips to the baby's forehead and allowed the midwife to lift her gently out of her arms. Her eyes followed them as they left the room. She murmured something, but her strength was fading fast. Adam leaned over, straining to catch the words. He looked up in surprise.

'You want the baby baptised a Protestant?'

Helen nodded, and her eyes swung round to Liz.

'Going to be brought up by damned Proddies, isn't she? It'll be for the best. No offence, Father.' Her words trailed off into a mumble.

Liz scowled. 'You'll be looking after her yourself, Helen. What rubbish you do talk.'

Helen's eyes shifted to Adam.

'For an intelligent woman, she can be awful stupid sometimes, can't she?'

'A complete numpty,' he agreed.

'Look after her for me, Liz. You and your mother.' Helen smiled faintly. 'Don't let your father make her hate Catholics.'

'What rubbish you talk,' Liz said again. 'You'll be looking after her yourself.'

'Don't tell lies, Elizabeth MacMillan. You're no good at it.'

Those were almost the last words she spoke. Only at the end, when Liz could no longer deny what was happening, did she ask, 'The baby, Helen. What shall we call her?'

'Hope,' said the dying girl. 'Hope Elizabeth MacMillan.' Her voice was as clear as a bell. 'Give me your hand, my dearest friend . . . Don't cry, Liz . . . Don't cry. I'm going to see Eddie.' For the last time in this world, the old mischievous smile lit up

339

her features. 'He'll not be an atheist now . . .'

Then, her hand in Liz's, the smile still on her face, she slipped away.

Chapter 36

It was strange to be away from the bustling routine of the hospital: odd to find herself governed once more by the quieter rhythms of a home, even if a rather more luxurious one than the house in which she had grown up. Liz and baby Hope were staying with Amelia Buchanan in Milngavie.

She took Hope to Clydebank every weekend, but despite her mother's pleading she refused point blank to take her home to live at Queen Victoria Row. Sadie insisted that things had changed. Liz remained to be convinced.

Certainly some astounding things had happened. For a start, Peter MacMillan was staying with his son and daughter-in-law until he was rehoused or his own building in Radnor Street was rebuilt. As far as Liz could see, the two men existed in a state of armed neutrality, William barely acknowledging his father's presence in the house. The fact that he was tolerating it at all was quite amazing.

He did so because his wife had insisted on it: another breathtaking development. Something had happened to her parents' relationship since the Blitz. To Liz's surprise, her father had been much more shaken up by the bombing than her mother had. Literally. His nerves were shattered by the experience, and it had been weeks before he'd been able to hold a cup and saucer without them rattling from the tremor in his hands.

In contrast, her mother seemed to have found a new strength. She delighted in the brief visits of her granddaughter, cheerfully fighting with her father-in-law over who should have the privilege of holding the baby. William MacMillan, on the other hand, barely glanced in Hope's direction.

Liz found that hard to forgive and, in private, she reminded her mother what her father had said about not having a Catholic bastard in his house.

'He could be persuaded,' said Sadie, further astonishing her daughter – although it wasn't enough to persuade Liz to come home.

Her situation in Milngavie was far from ideal, but it had been the only thing she could think of at the time. Having practically no money, especially after she stopped work at the Infirmary, Liz had asked Adam's mother if she could perhaps do some chores around the house in return for her and the baby's keep.

Amelia Buchanan, whose war work had introduced her to some colourful turns of phrase, told her to go and boil her head. She would be delighted to have the two of them and she didn't expect anything in return. Mrs Hunter wouldn't tolerate any interference in the running of the house anyway. Liz and the baby were welcome to stay for as long as they wanted.

She fitted up a bedroom at the back of the house as what she called Liz's boudoir. It had French windows looking out on to the garden, now given over mainly to the growing of vegetables, although the elderly gardener who came in twice a week had left a small square of grass for use as a drying green. Liz and Hope sat out there on a blanket when the weather got warmer. The room itself had a cot for Hope, a comfortable bed for Liz and an upholstered rocking chair.

Liz spent much of her time there, especially in the evenings. After she had given the baby her bath, she would rock gently backwards and forwards, enjoying the warm and solid feel of the healthy little body lying on her chest.

Her life had shrunk – sometimes she thought it had come right down to the feel of Hope's downy head under her lips as she kissed her goodnight before laying her gently in her cot. At times she wept into her soft dark hair, but she tried not to. As Helen's daughter, Hope deserved better than that. Liz

342

thought often of her friend's sense of humour and indomitable spirit.

Liz told the baby all about Helen and Eddie and chatted to her constantly as they went through their day. The housekeeper shook her head and muttered that no good ever came of talking to babies. It only made them go funny. Liz smiled at Amelia Buchanan over Mrs Hunter's head, and went her way rejoicing.

Or not quite. She knew their sojourn in Milngavie could only be a stopgap arrangement. She couldn't expect Mrs Buchanan to keep them forever. And then there was her nursing training, due to start in the autumn. Liz was in a real quandary about that.

Her mother desperately wanted to look after Hope. If she did, that would allow Liz to start back at the Infirmary as a student nurse, fulfilling her lifelong ambition. Then she would remember how she'd been brought up experiencing nothing but coldness from her father. She wasn't prepared to subject Hope to that.

But if things really had changed at Queen Victoria Row . . . that might be different. Liz knew very well there was a decision to be made. She kept putting it off.

She had discovered that looking after a baby could be a tiring business. Not that she grudged one moment of it, especially when Hope looked at her one day and smiled. Adam said it was wind. Both Liz and his mother told him to go and boil his head. They knew a smile when they saw one.

Liz visited Dominic Gallagher at Killearn Hospital twice a week, taking the bus out from Milngavie. He had cried in front of her once. Now, with the resilience of youth, he played happily with his niece and talked of when he would be old enough to join up. Killearn was a military hospital. He was surrounded by wounded heroes, all of whom relished the opportunity of telling their tallest stories to the admiring lad.

Liz privately prayed that the war would finish before Dom was old enough to march off. That seemed unlikely. And she had to admit that if he joined the forces it would solve the

343

problem of where he was going to stay when he eventually came out of hospital.

Under pressure as ever at the Infirmary, Adam did his best to get home to Milngavie two or three times a week, but they were usually flying visits. Perhaps because of that, he didn't pick his words as carefully as he might have done one Sunday in July.

Coming through the French windows from the garden, he found Liz sitting in the old rocking chair which had been his father's, gently crooning Hope into her afternoon nap. Hearing his step, she looked up and put a warning finger to her lips.

'As pretty as a picture,' he said softly. 'Both of you, I mean. Shall I put her in her cot?'

'Gently,' said Liz as he lifted Hope out of her arms without waiting for an answer. He laid the baby down, tucked the covers around her and turned, a slightly pained expression on his face.

'I have handled a baby before, Liz.' His next words were rather unwise. 'You're a bit proprietorial about her, don't you think?'

Liz drew her breath in. It was rare for Adam to criticise. Feeling fragile, she answered him back more sharply than she might have. 'I'm all she's got. She's all I've got.'

'That's not true, Liz. You've got friends.'

He walked over to the French windows and stood looking out over the garden, his back to her. 'Friends who care about you very much.' He swung round and looked at her. 'And you've got parents. Hope's got grandparents. And a great-grandfather. Isn't it a bit unfair on her and them that they don't get to see very much of each other?'

She didn't answer him. He walked forward, crouching down beside the rocking chair. His last comment had hit a nerve. She did feel guilty about that.

'Liz . . . I don't want to see you throwing your life away like this.'

She bristled immediately. 'I'm not throwing my life away. I'm looking after my niece. Helen and Eddie's daughter.'

'And Helen wanted your mother to bring the baby up. With you helping her, of course.'

She turned her face away from him. 'How do you work that out?'

'Liz,' he said, his voice very gentle, 'I was there. I heard what Helen said. She of all people wouldn't have wanted you to sacrifice your own future, give up something you've always longed to do. And she knew how much your mother would long to care for Eddie's child.'

Liz still facing away from him, squeezed her eyes tight shut for a moment. He'd got that bit right.

'Why do you think Helen asked for Hope to be baptised a Protestant? Did that not strike you as extremely odd?'

She looked at him then. 'Yes, it did. She cared so much for her own Church.'

Adam nodded, his face full of sympathy for Liz and the dilemma with which she was wrestling. 'And did you come to any conclusion about that?'

He reached for her hand, but she moved it out of his grasp, stood up and walked a few steps into the garden. He followed her out, standing a pace or two behind her. She had worked out exactly why Helen had made that dying request: because she had known very well that William MacMillan wouldn't tolerate any child in his house being brought up a Catholic.

Helen had made an enormous sacrifice so that her daughter could be raised and loved by Eddie's mother. Perhaps also, thought Liz sadly, for my own very unworthy sake. To allow me to follow my dream.

She'd given Adam no response. He came round to stand in front of her.

'What about the future, Liz? How are you going to support her?'

Angry with him for making her confront something she'd been trying to avoid for weeks, her voice was sharp as broken glass.

'I don't know. I'll cross that bridge when I come to it.'

345

'So you're quite happy to let my mother keep you and Hope for the moment?'

No, she wasn't happy about that, and he knew that perfectly well. Too many of his darts were striking home today.

'That's not fair.'

He was watching her intently. 'Isn't it?'

She tossed her head. 'Your mother says we can stay as long as we want. She likes having us here.'

Adam looked at her for a long moment. When he spoke his voice was stiff and formal.

'I'm off to wash and change. I'll see you at lunch.'

'Would you pass the milk, please?'

'Certainly.' Liz's voice was frosty.

Amelia Buchanan finished her cabinet pudding and placed her spoon in the dessert bowl with some force. There was a ringing sound as silver struck porcelain.

'Honestly! What's wrong with you two today? You've barely said a civil word to each other.'

Liz pushed her own bowl away, her pudding half eaten. She'd get a ticking-off from Mrs Hunter for wasting food. 'Your son thinks I'm taking advantage of you.'

Adam let out an exasperated sigh.

'I did *not* say that.'

'Yes you did,' wailed Liz, and burst into tears.

'My dear,' said Amelia, rising immediately from her chair to comfort her. 'What's wrong? Why are you so unhappy?' Frowning, she glanced at her son. 'Adam, what is this all about?'

He told her. Then Liz poured out her side of the story. She spoke in short, jerky sentences, the words interspersed with sobs.

'I love looking after Hope,' she said, 'but I do want to do my training. I'm not sure what to do for the best. I know my mother would love to have her, but I don't know if that's the right thing to do. For Hope, I mean. That's what matters. And I'm tired,' she said, 'I'm so tired. I'm not in any fit state to

346

make a decision. And that's not fair on Hope either!'

'Of course you're tired,' said Amelia. 'She's not sleeping through the night yet. That's exhausting.' She gestured towards Adam. 'This lump was ten months old before he slept right through.'

She smiled at her son. He didn't smile back, his hazel gaze fixed on Liz. She had bowed her head and put her hands over her face. She sat like that for a few minutes. When she raised her head at last, she looked directly at him.

'He's right, of course. The only thing that makes any sense is for Hope to go to my mother. He's right,' she said again. 'Damn him.'

'So infuriating,' agreed Adam's mother. 'When men are right about something. We never hear the end of it, do we?'

Liz and Adam were still looking at each other. Liz sniffed and swallowed and lifted her chin.

'I can't manage to take Hope and all her bits and pieces on my own,' she said quietly. 'Will you give me a lift?'

'Of course,' he replied, his expression as grave as hers. 'Do you want to go today?'

Liz shook her head. 'No. Let me have another week with her on my own. I'll write to my mother too, let her know we're coming. She'll want to get beds and blankets aired. All that sort of thing.'

'Fine,' he said politely. 'Next weekend, then.'

In the old days, Liz had often observed how her mother seemed to grow smaller when she had done something to provoke her husband's disapproval or anger. Now she was witnessing the opposite. Sadie seemed to be growing taller.

Liz sat up in her chair, suddenly alert, all her senses perked up and waiting to see what was going to happen. She could still change her mind about this. If her father said one word which made her think that Hope wasn't welcome in his house, she was fully prepared to.

Walking over to her daughter, Sadie held out her hands for

347

Hope. Once the two women had carefully transferred the baby, Sadie walked across to her husband, two fingers gently pulling down the blanket from Hope's chin so that her small face could clearly be seen.

'Look at her, William.'

Her voice was quiet but determined. Her husband started to bluster, but Sadie stood her ground.

'Look at her, William,' she repeated. 'And keep your voice down so that you don't frighten her. She's our granddaughter, Eddie's daughter. All we have left of him. And I want you to hold her.'

Liz held her breath. This was going too far. He'd never do it. Her mother had locked eyes with her husband. That was another first. As it was when it was William MacMillan who dropped his gaze.

'I can't,' he said at last. Incredibly, he dashed a hand across his eyes.

'Yes you can,' said Sadie softly. 'Look. She's reaching out for you.'

She was right. A little hand was extended towards him. Liz had to surreptitiously wipe her eyes. Nothing moved in the kitchen. For how long? Thirty seconds? A minute? A lifetime of bitterness and misunderstanding? Then her father spoke.

'I've forgotten how to hold a baby, Sadie. I'm scared I'll hurt her.'

Liz let out the breath she didn't know she'd been holding and listened to her mother speaking in a firm, confident voice.

'You'll not hurt her, William. Put your arms out. The way I've got mine.'

Gently, she placed Hope into his arms.

'She's coming to live with us, William. I'm going to look after her. That way Lizzie can start her nursing training. What she's always wanted to do.'

Her husband didn't reply. He was too busy looking at his granddaughter. Hope Elizabeth MacMillan completed his downfall. She smiled at him.

PART IV

1944-1945

Chapter 37

It was Hope's third birthday, and there was to be a family tea party. As Liz climbed the steps from the platform of the railway station she saw her grandfather waiting for her at the top of them. Although back now in a house of his own, he remained a regular visitor to his son's home.

'Sadie sent me out for some lemonade,' he explained, 'so I thought I'd hang on and see if you were off that train.'

'Changed days,' Liz observed as they fell into step together. 'You and me walking along to Queen Victoria Row together. In broad daylight, too.'

The glance Peter shot his granddaughter had something in it which might have been reproach.

'D'you not think you should give your father a bit more of a chance, Lizzie?'

Hurt, she returned his look.

'Did he ever give me one?'

'He's changed a lot since Hope came to stay.'

'I can't say that I've noticed,' she said tightly and looked away, out over the street. That was a lie. There had been a huge change in William MacMillan over the last two and a half years. Outwardly he was as stiff and formal as ever, but anyone who knew him well could see the difference.

Little Hope was a constant joy – a cheerful and happy child with her mother's blue eyes and her father's dark hair. It was a devastating combination, especially when that hair grew into a mass of brown curls. And as she grew older, the sense of fun Liz knew she'd inherited from her mother was beginning to show itself. That enchanted everybody, including her grandfather. However much he tried to hide it.

As she had grown and blossomed, there had been a kind of blossoming in him too. He could be brusque with her sometimes, but that seemed to be water off a duck's back to Hope. She just laughed. And there had been many other occasions when Liz had noticed him watching his granddaughter with a little smile on his face.

He was even known to smile at his wife these days, usually over something funny Hope had said or done. The little girl had connected them again, given them a focus, allowed them to carry on some sort of family life together. For their granddaughter's sake.

Liz's own relationship with her father remained a distant one. Correction, she thought. We don't have a relationship. Not one worthy of the name.

'And have the two of you resolved your differences?' she demanded now of her grandfather. He shrugged.

'We're never going to be best pals, but we did have a long conversation last New Year's morning. It might have been the whisky talking, of course, but we got some things sorted out.'

'So what did the two of you fall out about?'

There was a pause, and a curious look passed over Peter's face. 'It's best left alone, lass.'

'No,' Liz insisted. She stopped dead in the middle of the pavement, forcing him to stop too. 'I think I've a right to know. It affected me, after all. Wouldn't you say?'

He turned to face her slowly and with obvious reluctance.

'You'll mind that he and I had an argument around the time your granny died?'

'Yes.' She remembered it well: the raised voices and the slammed doors, her mother in tears and completely distraught. 'But Eddie and I never knew what it was about.'

'Jenny was in the back bedroom,' he said, his voice very soft. 'It was the morning of the funeral. Your mother had come downstairs before we set off for the cemetery to . . . to pay her

352

last respects.' His voice had gone husky, and he had to swallow before he could go on. 'She was that fond of your granny, you know?'

'I know,' said Liz gently, putting a comforting hand on his arm. 'And Granny loved her too.'

'Aye,' he said, 'and you too, pet. She had lost three of her own children. Bruce was sailing the seven seas and Bob was on the other side of the world. Your father . . .'

His mouth tightened and the sentence went unfinished. 'You and your mother and Eddie . . . well, you were all very precious to my Jenny. And to me,' he said. 'And to me.'

Unable to speak, Liz squeezed his arm. Her grandfather gave her a faint smile. Then he shifted his gaze to something he saw over her shoulder.

'Your mother began to sob. Your father told her to pull herself together, that he hoped she wasn't going to behave like that at the service and at the graveside. He didn't want her disgracing the family in public.' Peter's voice had grown very dry.

Liz looked up at him, but he seemed unwilling to meet her gaze, his eyes focused on something only he could see.

'I asked him what kind of a man he was, that he could stand dry-eyed by his mother's coffin, that he could watch his wife breaking her heart over it and offer her no comfort. I asked him why he had no heart. I told him he was the one who was a disgrace to the family.'

Peter paused, and swallowed again. There was pain in every word that he spoke. 'I told him I was ashamed to call him my son.' He stopped, his face working. Liz saw anguish there. She saw something else too. Regret.

'Oh, Grandad,' she breathed, gripping his arm once more. 'Oh, Grandad.'

He looked at her at last. There was more to come. His voice was so quiet she had to strain to hear the words. 'And I told him his mother had been ashamed of him too, because of how hard he was on his family. Especially you, Lizzie. Especially you.'

Liz remembered another conversation she'd had with her grandfather. *Your father has strong feelings,* he'd said. *About a lot of things.* Don't we all? she thought bitterly. Don't we all?

Her words were clipped.

'And now you think it's up to me to forgive him? Don't you think that's asking a bit much?'

'I'm asking you to have a bit of understanding, lass. Because you're capable of it. He's not.'

Liz's voice was bitter. 'He shuts himself off from me, but he's opened up to Hope.'

Peter's piercing gaze saw far too much. 'And are you a wee bit jealous of that?'

She watched her father that afternoon, saw the smile on his face as her mother played peek-a-boo games with Hope, looked on when the little girl clambered up on to his lap, the smile growing as she laughed up at him. Liz wondered if he'd ever been like that with her. She searched her memory and came up with one long-lost image of being hoisted up on to his shoulders.

She seemed to remember they'd both been laughing then. Had they been watching a launch? The *Queen Mary* perhaps? No, it must have been earlier. The recollection was of herself as a much smaller child – before she had contracted the scarlet fever.

Watching his face now as he looked at Hope, Liz wondered if her grandfather might be right. Was she jealous?

Troubled by the thought, she was restless and unhappy when she took her leave of her family after the party. About to head back for Riverside station, she turned the other way instead, obeying some inner compulsion to walk up to the ruins of the Holy City houses. She would get the train back to Partick from Singer's and then take the tram along. It was growing foggy. She didn't want to have to grope her way all along Dumbarton Road.

She loved Hope to bits. The thought that she might be jealous of the attention her father was giving her was an extremely uncomfortable one.

Sometimes Liz felt as though she were two separate people. There was the cheerful and competent student nurse MacMillan, calm and efficient, always ready with a joke or a comforting word. And then there was wee Lizzie, so terribly lonely when so many of the people she had cared for were gone.

As she reached what remained of the Holy City, she forced down the lump in her throat. She stood staring at the rubble, at the sheer bloody mess of what had once been homes full of families. It had taken weeks to bring all the bodies out. Some had never been found – or at least never identified. Liz tried not to think too much about that.

No one was entirely sure how many people had died in the Blitz. Officialdom, with the justification of not wanting to spread gloom, despondency and panic, had deliberately underestimated the numbers, quoting a figure of five hundred deaths. One of the rescuers who'd lived through those terrible nights responded to that with a bitter question. 'Five hundred? Which street do they mean?'

Despite the devastation wrought – only seven houses in Clydebank had escaped damage of some description – the town was rising from the ashes. Buildings which could be saved were being repaired and rebuilt. Industry was recovering, getting back into production. In some cases that had happened astonishingly quickly. John Brown's and a few other places had been working again only days after the Blitz. The German bombs had done great damage, but people told each other gleefully that Jerry had missed a hell of a lot as well: the Singer's clock, for one thing. It had come through the onslaught intact, a symbol of survival.

And because it was Clydebank, people found things to laugh at. There had been government compensation for losses sustained in the bombing. Some folk had worked out very quickly how to milk the system. As Annie Crawford had drily remarked, 'You'd never have guessed there were so many pianos in Clydebank.'

On her last visit home, Liz had bumped into Nan Simpson. She'd been up in arms about the compensation too.

'Her downstairs from me claimed for window blinds. That woman never had blinds on her windows in her life!'

All of that passed through Liz's mind as she stood in the rubble. It was all mixed up together – life and death, laughter and tears. She was visualising it too, the horror of the Blitz, the Gallaghers singing and teasing each other, Marie and Brendan arguing incessantly about which part of Ireland they were going home to, Finn stealing the gingerbread and getting away with it, Conor's pride in his faithful companion.

Then she saw Helen and Eddie on the day of his graduation. Her big brother had been so handsome in his hood and gown, love and tenderness in his eyes as he had looked at Helen in the brown georgette dress. What an effort it had been getting the independent Miss Gallagher to accept that!

She thought of Mario. Would they ever see each other again? Maybe not in this world . . .

He'll not be an atheist now. Helen's voice was ringing round her head, happy because she was going to be reunited with Eddie. Oh, God, she missed them all so much!

Turning to leave, her eye was caught by a flash of yellow. Curious, she picked her way through the rubble. Clinging on to a rough piece of masonry, in much less earth than you would think it needed to survive, was a daffodil, flowering bravely in the misty March air. A fragment of blue earthenware pot still stuck to it. It had to be one of Helen's.

Liz stood for a moment, remembering the pots of flowers which had dotted the Gallaghers' living room. That had been so Helen, brightening up her surroundings, making the best of things, never complaining about the hand which fate had dealt her.

She reached for the daffodil, then stopped herself. She should leave it here, a tiny memorial to the brave girl who had been her friend. Eyes blinded by tears, Liz stumbled back to the main road. She was cold. Terribly, terribly cold.

She shouldn't have taken the short cut. It was a stupid thing to have done, but she was anxious to be on time for Adam, now a senior house officer at the Infirmary. They had agreed to meet outside the nurses' home and go for an early evening drink and a bite to eat somewhere up Byres Road.

As if the blackout wasn't enough, the fog was now a pea-souper, blanketing everything in thick yellow folds. Her wee torch, carefully pointed downwards so she didn't get yelled at to 'Put out that light!', wasn't making much of an impact. Liz coughed, and drew her woollen scarf further up around her mouth.

The trouble with fog was that it disorientated you – made familiar surroundings unfamiliar. She'd hopped off the tram at the front entrance to the University on Dumbarton Road. Instead of going the long way round to meet Adam, along to Church Street and then up and around, Liz had decided to cut through the hospital complex, past the Andersonian Institute and round behind the ophthalmology department.

That ought to have brought her round the back of Outpatients and then out on to University Avenue, but she'd taken a wrong turning somewhere. She suspected she was near the mortuary. That was a happy thought.

From somewhere in the gloom came a rustling noise. Liz gave a little shriek, and jumped.

'Is there anybody there?'

Her words bounced back off the walls. The narrow beam of her torch didn't illuminate much either. The rustling noise continued, transformed now into a kind of scuffling sound. A rat, of course. What else? Liz shuddered, remembering how they had appeared from everywhere in Clydebank after the Blitz, flushed from their tunnels and nests by the bombs and the noise.

She quickened her step. The sooner she found Adam, the

357

better. It felt so lonely out here.

There must be lots of people mere feet away from her, but they were inside the buildings which rose around her like the walls of some giant cavern. Those walls were thick, built to last. There were wards above her head but their windows would be tightly shut against the night and the fog, the blackout blinds securely in place. Liz knew they were there, but the patients and staff inside would have no idea that she was out here.

Unbidden, she heard a voice in her head. It was one of the student nurses, a girl from the Outer Isles. When Liz had once confessed that walking past the mortuary gave her the creeps, the girl had chided her gently, her accent as soft and lilting as Sister MacLean's.

'Och, no, Liz, you shouldna worry about that. Dead people will never hurt you.'

She'd meant it to be comforting. The memory of her words was having entirely the opposite effect.

Liz shivered again, quickened her step, and walked into something solid and warm. Not something. Someone. Could it be Adam, come looking for her? Instinctively, she reached out for him – and felt herself roughly grabbed and spun round, her torch pulled from her grasp and flung to the ground. Its narrow beam was extinguished immediately. A male arm clamped itself hard across her throat and shoulders, hurting her. Not Adam, then.

Chapter 38

'Want to hear a joke?'

It was four years since she'd heard that voice, but she'd have recognised it anywhere. Horrible, unwanted memories swamped her, rendering her incapable of speech, struggle or resistance.

'I spotted you coming down the stairs at Partick,' said Eric Mitchell. 'You didn't notice me on the tram, did you now? Or following you up through here?' His voice sank to a hiss. 'And little Lizzie always thought she was so clever.'

The words dripped malevolence.

His hand was on her neck, his fingers caressing her flesh. She tried not to shrink from his touch. If she kept calm, maybe he would too. Not do what she feared was on his mind. Panic threatened to overwhelm her.

Then a picture of Hope popped into her head. Somehow the thought of her little niece gave her strength.

'Sure. I'd like to hear a joke,' she said. Her voice sounded perfectly level. That was funny. Funny peculiar, that was, not funny ha-ha.

'Sensible girl,' he said. His voice was a growl of soft menace. 'Heard the one about the new utility knickers?'

'No,' she whispered, 'I haven't.'

His lips were touching her ear. 'One Yank and they're off,' he murmured. 'Only in your case it would be an Eyetie, wouldn't it?'

She had heard the joke. She'd thought it mildly funny at the time. It didn't seem at all amusing now.

'Wouldn't it?' Eric Mitchell asked in a louder voice, his hand tightening painfully on the bones in Liz's neck. 'What's wrong with a good Scotsman, eh?'

Anger boiled up in Liz. Four years she'd put up with him. And for at least two of those years she'd had to be constantly on her guard. Two years of being nervous and jumpy every minute of the day. She'd had enough of being Eric Mitchell's victim.

'Nothing,' she snapped. 'Only I can't seem to see one right now.' She knew where one was, though. Probably only a few hundred yards away. Would he have started to worry about her yet? Come looking for her?

'You can't see anything,' said Eric Mitchell silkily, 'and neither can anyone else. No one's going to hear you if you scream either. Not on a night like this, with all the windows closed.'

Liz squeezed her eyes tight shut in the blackness. *St Jude, can you get me out of this one?*

His hand was moving. He pulled her scarf out of the way, began unfastening the top buttons of her coat. His fingers, cold and rough, were in the V-neck of her blouse . . .

A tiny torch beam played over Liz's face.

'You know, I really don't think the young lady wants you to do that.'

Buckling at the knees with sheer relief, she felt Eric Mitchell's hold on her slacken as he turned round to face Adam, but if he had recognised the voice as belonging to his boss's nephew there were no signs of it.

'Fuck off, pal. Mind your own business.'

'Afraid I can't do that, *pal*,' said Adam. 'You see Miss MacMillan is a friend and colleague of mine and I really think you should take your filthy hands off her. Right now. And you're on hospital property too – without, so far as I can see, any valid reason to be here.'

He sounded his usual languid self. Perhaps that was why Mitchell was caught so much by surprise when Adam lunged forward and grabbed Liz by the arm. He swung her round behind him with such force that she crashed into the wall, banging her elbow painfully against the stonework.

It made her head swim for a moment, and in the confusion which followed she was aware of two punches being thrown, then the sound of running footsteps. She could hear heavy, laboured breathing. It was her. Beside her, someone else's breath was also coming too fast.

'Adam?' she said into the fog. 'Please tell me it's you who's still here.'

'It's me,' he said grimly. 'I don't know where my bloody torch is though.'

Liz reached for him, patting the darkness with her hands and finding his face.

'You're bleeding!' she gasped.

'Ten out of ten for diagnosis. Come on, let's get inside and shed some light on the subject.'

'He could have had a knife,' Liz said sternly ten minutes later.

'Well, he didn't,' replied Adam, looking remarkably cheerful for a man who'd just taken a punch. 'Ouch!'

'Keep still, then. How can I clean you up if you won't stay still?'

'Oh, you're so sympathetic, Nurse,' he grumbled. 'No wonder Sister MacLean used to make you clean floors and lavatories all the time and never let you near the patients.

'My turn,' he said with some satisfaction when she'd finished with him. 'Where's the damage?'

'Just my elbow, I think.' Liz rolled up her sleeve and let him have a look at it. 'You did that,' she said lightly, 'but I'm rather glad that you did.'

'Mmm.' He cleaned it and applied some ointment, then put his hands on her shoulders and peered anxiously down into her face. 'Are you really all right, Liz?'

'Yes, of course I am,' she said brightly. In fact, she felt full of beans. She'd been miserable a couple of hours ago; now she felt absolutely great. Strange. A surge of adrenaline because she'd narrowly escaped a fate worse than death?

'You look very thoughtful,' said Adam.

'Mmm. I expect I do.' She smiled up at him.

'Right,' he said briskly. 'Do you want to go to the police station now or tomorrow morning?'

'Not at all.'

'Liz, you've got to report it!'

She'd given him the whole story whilst she'd attended to his injuries. He had listened without comment, but she'd seen the tightening around his mouth, known without him having to spell it out that he was outraged by what she'd had to put up with while she was working at Murray's.

She bit her lip. 'Do I have to report it? Don't you remember that woman we had in A and E who'd been raped and beaten up by her boyfriend? I worked with Eric Mitchell for four years. I didn't make a single complaint about his behaviour. Not an official one, at any rate. Can you imagine what they would make of that?'

They'd both been appalled by the way the police had treated the girl, as though she were the guilty party rather than the victim. And it had occurred to Liz that she might find herself reporting the assault to the sergeant who'd arrested Mario . . . the one who thought she was a loose woman.

'Please, Adam,' she pleaded. 'I'd rather do nothing about it.'

He spluttered. 'Liz, he can't be allowed to get away with it! Let me at least go and see my Uncle Alasdair. Does Mitchell still work at Murray's?'

'I've no idea,' she said. 'I'm not in touch with anybody there.'

'I'll find out tomorrow,' he said determinedly. 'In the meantime, d'you still fancy that drink and a spot of supper?'

He reported back to her the next afternoon. Eric Mitchell had left Murray's exactly one week before, having joined up.

According to Lucy Gilchrist, he'd shown his mettle by signing up voluntarily. Alasdair Murray had a different interpretation of events.

Mitchell had been trying unsuccessfully to get his job as a shipping clerk categorised as a reserved occupation. He'd been in dispute with the authorities for some time over it. His time had run out a couple of weeks before.

Lucy Gilchrist knew he'd been due to leave Glasgow on the overnight train to London the day before. His contretemps with Liz and Adam had taken place in the early evening. He'd probably caught that train.

'We could try to find out from his wife where he is,' said Adam, frowning at Liz. 'Otherwise, it's a case of tracing him through the Army, and that could take time. And if you're reluctant to press charges . . .'

'I'm a lot happier knowing he's away from Glasgow,' said Liz, thinking about it. 'Let it go. For the duration, at least. Maybe we can do something about it after that.'

Adam gave her a look. 'Why do I get the feeling that you're trying to pacify me, MacMillan?'

Reaction set in the next day. The catalyst was tripping over the threshold of one of the ward kitchens and dropping a tray full of dirty cups and saucers.

Cordelia, standing at the draining board drying dishes which another student nurse was washing, turned with a smile.

'Would you like a hammer, Liz?' She crouched down to assess the damage, plucking the cups and saucers which had survived out of the mess of broken crockery.

'Hey,' she said, glancing up and seeing Liz's stricken face. 'Come on, now. It was an accident. Even the old battleaxe will understand that.'

'To whom might you be referring, MacIntyre?'

Cordelia glanced up guiltily as Sister MacLean swept into the kitchen.

'I-I don't think MacMillan's very well, Sister.'

363

Sister MacLean took one look, pulled Liz over to a chair and fired out an instruction to the anxiously hovering probationer.

'Is Dr Buchanan in the hospital?'

'I-I think so, Sister.'

'Well, go and fetch him. Now!'

He came striding into the room, the pupil nurse having to run to keep up with him.

'Liz?' he asked gently, crouching down in front of her. 'Liz, sweetie, what's the matter?'

His voice penetrated her distress. She lifted her head, clutching the sleeves of his white coat.

'Oh, Adam! It's all just hit me.'

'What's just hit her?' demanded Sister MacLean. Cordelia explained.

'Delayed shock then,' said Sister briskly. 'Some form of sedation, Doctor?'

'No,' said Adam decisively. 'She needs her bed.'

He rose to his feet, scooped Liz up in his arms and headed for the door, turning pointedly when he got there and waiting for one of them to open it for him.

'You're not taking her there yourself!'

His lips twitched. 'I know there hasn't been a man in the nurses' home since Florence Nightingale was a girl, but this is an emergency, Sister.'

'And anyway,' put in the student nurse, doing her best to be helpful, 'it's not really a man – it's only Dr Buchanan.'

Adam lifted his fair brows. 'I'm not quite sure how to take that. But will somebody please open this bloody door!'

Sister MacLean could do the eyebrow-raising trick too. 'There's no need to swear, Dr Buchanan,' she said primly. She opened the door and walked beside him as he carried Liz along the corridor. He gave her a formal little nod.

'I apologise for my language, Sister. Now, can we have some of that brandy you keep for emergencies?'

'By all means,' said Sister MacLean with dignity, apparently not at all fazed by the fact that he knew about her secret drinks supply. 'How much?'

'Well,' he said, waiting again whilst she opened the door which led into the nurses' dining room, on the other side of which lay the home. 'Why don't we all have a glass?'

'Certainly, Doctor.'

He was there when she went to sleep and he was there when she opened her eyes again the next morning.

His long length was propped uncomfortably in a chintz-covered armchair which had always seemed a reasonable size but which looked far too small with him sitting in it. He was ruffled and unshaven, but when she opened her eyes and wished him good morning he shot up out of the chair to feel her pulse and lay his hand against her forehead.

'Hmm,' he said, after a minute. 'That all seems normal enough. How are we feeling, sleeping beauty?'

'Well, I don't know how you're feeling,' she said, half closing one eye and regarding him through the other, 'but I'm starving. I'm that hungry I could eat a scabby dog.'

He laughed. 'Och, MacMillan, see you and your way with words? Scrambled eggs on toast?'

Liz shuddered.

'Yellow liver? No thanks.' She was one of the many who found the slab-like concoction made from dried egg powder completely unpalatable. 'You know what I'd really like? A bacon roll.'

'Then a bacon roll you shall have. Even if I have to go out and wrestle wild pigs the length of Byres Road to get it. Back in two shakes. I'll get Cordelia to come and sit with you.'

In the event, he didn't have to go that far. He managed to sweet-talk one of the hospital cooks into parting with two thin slices of precious bacon and putting them into two rolls for him. He carried them back triumphantly to Liz's room, Cordelia tactfully disappearing when he got there.

Liz told him to eat one of the rolls himself, and they sat

365

chatting quietly over their impromptu breakfast.

'What about Sister MacLean? Does she want me to report what happened?'

'Apparently not,' he said, between mouthfuls of roll. 'Cordelia told her what you'd said and she can understand your point of view.' He looked contemplative. 'She's not a bad old stick sometimes.'

Liz smiled. 'I suppose not, though I'll deny ever having said that.'

'Eat up,' he said. 'You're still looking a bit pale.'

She obeyed the instruction but then, distracted by the cooing of a pigeon which was sitting on the window ledge outside, turned and looked in the direction of the sound. She studied the bird for a long time. When she eventually spoke, her eyes were still fixed on it.

'I wonder where Mario is right now,' she said. Her voice was full of wistfulness.

Adam laid his half-eaten bacon roll back down on the plate, a dull ache in his jaw. The punch which Eric Mitchell had thrown at him two days before had just begun to throb.

Chapter 39

'Join the Army!'

'Well, the medical corps,' he said. 'The RAMC.'

'But why, Adam? Why now?'

He shrugged. 'Because I reckon it's time I did my bit, I suppose.' He turned to look out of the window of the ward kitchen.

Liz came round in front of him, peering up into his face.

'But you're doing your bit here. None better. You've worked like a dog since the war started. Right from the *Athenia*, through the Blitz, all of that.'

He shrugged again. 'Maybe I fancy myself in a uniform.'

She recognised the flippant answer for what it was. She was looking at a man who'd set his mind to a course of action and who wasn't going to be dissuaded from it. For some reason which he wasn't prepared to share with her.

'I'll miss you,' she said at last.

'Will you?' He hadn't moved from the window, standing there staring out, his arms folded across his broad chest.

'Of course I will. How am I going to cope without you?'

'You'll survive.' He turned at last from his contemplation of the rooftops of Partick.

'Look, Liz, I've got to get on. I'll see you later.'

The door swung closed behind him. Liz stared at it in dismay. She'd become so used to his company, so accustomed to taking her troubles to him and having him make them better. Had she put too much pressure on him when he already had so many stresses in his work? Was it her fault he was going away?

She tried discussing it with Cordelia, but she seemed unable to shed much light on Adam's decision.

'Perhaps it's the soldiering bit,' she suggested eventually. 'Sooner or later it gets to most of them. They feel they should be out there – doing their bit for king and country, defending their womenfolk against the vile Hun, that kind of thing.' She grimaced.

Liz looked at her doubtfully. 'But he's doing his bit here. You know how hard he works.'

Cordelia, uncharacteristically unhelpful, shrugged.

'I wondered if it had anything to do with me, Cordelia.'

'Eh . . . how exactly do you mean, Liz?'

'He's helped me so much,' she replied, 'always been there for me. Maybe I've asked too much of him.'

'In which case,' Cordelia pointed out, 'I'm as much to blame.'

'So you don't think that's what's making him want to go away?'

'No, Liz, I don't think that's what it is.' She squinted down at the watch pinned on the bib of her apron. 'Good grief! Is that the time? I really must be getting on.'

Central Station was thronged as usual when Liz saw Adam off. At her insistence, he found himself a seat, deposited his things on top of it to book it and then jumped back out on to the platform. He'd said his farewells to his mother earlier that morning in Milngavie. Liz was surprised that Amelia wasn't here now – nor Cordelia either – but Adam told her how upset his mother had been, although doing her best not to show it.

'Maybe I should have taken French leave,' he said, 'like they did the night before the Battle of Waterloo.'

Liz struck a dramatic pose. 'Well, we could go for the scene in the romantic film where you say—'

'It's not goodbye, darling, it's only *au revoir*,' he supplied. 'Or maybe we'll all be saying *auf Wiedersehen* if things don't look up.'

She punched him lightly in the chest.

'Nonsense. Now the Army's got you on its side, we'll have the war finished in a fortnight. Winston doesn't know it yet, but he's got a new secret weapon.'

'I'm touched that you have such faith in me,' he murmured. There was a pause. 'Liz . . .' he began, but she had started speaking at the same time as him.

'You look very dashing,' she said, taking in the picture he presented in cap and uniform, his tall frame surmounted by a casually unbuttoned greatcoat.

'I don't feel very dashing,' he confessed. 'Why don't you and I go down the coast together instead? A walk on the beach and lunch in a pub with a roaring fire?'

'Sounds lovely, but it'll have to wait till you come back.' There was a pause.

'What were you going to say just now? I think I interrupted you.'

'Oh . . . nothing really. Mind your back.' He pulled her out of the way of a raucous group of sailors who were heading up the platform complete with attendant girlfriends.

'You will write, won't you?' Liz asked, once the noisy crowd had passed. 'Keep me posted. It's bad enough having to worry about Dominic Gallagher.' For Dominic, appropriately enough for a Flash Gordon fan, was now a trainee pilot in the RAF.

'You don't have to worry about me,' said Adam lightly. 'I'm a medic, remember? I'm the one who'll be patching up the other chaps.'

'So you won't go and fling yourself in front of any bullets?'

'Would you care?'

'I would care,' she assured him, uncomfortably aware of the tiny pause before she had answered him. She glanced away. To their left one of the sailors and his girlfriend were locked in a passionate embrace. Adam followed Liz's gaze.

'Looks like he's trying to perform a tonsillectomy,' he muttered. 'By suction.'

'Maybe I should give *you* a kiss. For luck.'

Adam turned his attention away from the couple and looked down very intently at Liz. And there was another of the pauses which seemed to be characterising this conversation.

'Kissing in public is vulgar, MacMillan,' Adam drawled, the blandest of expressions on his face. 'Don't you know that?'

'Kiss my hand, then,' she suggested, extending it to him with a gaiety she was very far from feeling. 'Like the gentleman you are.'

Mario had kissed her hand in all manner of extravagant ways. From Adam Liz expected the swift equivalent of a peck on the cheek, perhaps a joking comment to go with it. Instead, he took her hand, lifted it to his mouth and pressed a long kiss against the softness of her palm. He had his eyes closed, his eyelashes, much darker than his hair, thick and feathery against the smooth skin underneath them. She was reminded suddenly of a wet night in Buchanan Street.

She stood and watched his train pull out, waiting till it went out of sight. Then she wished she hadn't. It gave her a real empty feeling. She would miss him, of course she would. He was a good friend. She just hadn't been prepared to miss him quite so much.

Adam wrapped his greatcoat more tightly about himself and settled into a corner of the compartment. The train was bloody freezing. The junior Army officer sitting opposite him was telling another – in great detail – what he'd got up to with a girl he'd picked up during his leave.

The young lady had clearly been very accommodating, but Adam didn't think any woman deserved to be talked about like that. He loathed men who boasted of their conquests. The naval officer sitting beside him was, however, listening in with interest. It looked as if he'd be pitching in with his own story soon.

Great, he thought glumly, exactly what I need – God knows how many hours locked up in a train full of sexually frustrated and overtalkative servicemen.

Honesty compelled him to admit that he himself might not be much better. When it came to sexual frustration he was something of an expert. He could write the bloody book.

He had promised Mario he would look after her. He had kept his promise well. Whenever he had seen that she was tired or fed up or depressed, he had offered a drink, or a trip to the cinema. Nobody, not even Cordelia, had ever known what it had cost him to spend so much time in her company and be forced to treat her like a sister.

And now he had left her: because he just wasn't able to stand it any longer. He knew she would be all right now. There was a core of steel in Elizabeth MacMillan.

He suspected he had started falling in love with her the very first time he had met her – that soaking wet night in Buchanan Street. She'd been all shining hair and passion.

But he had seen how shy she was, suspecting there was something more to it than mere reserve. He'd been willing to wait. And while he'd been standing back, behaving like a bloody gentleman as usual, Mario had got there before him.

It made no difference to him that she had allowed Mario to make love to her. He shifted uncomfortably on the cushioned seat. Who was he trying to kid? Certainly not himself. When he had found out about that he had been overwhelmed by his feelings. A tidal wave of pure sexual jealousy, he supposed, which had left him empty and despairing.

It hadn't stopped him loving her. He wished it had been him, that was all. How many times had he sat next to her in the cinema, hoping that her hand would accidentally brush against his? Hoping that her hand would deliberately brush against his . . .

How often had he longed to slip his arm around her shoulders, put his fingers under her chin and lift her face towards him for a kiss?

'You all right, old man?'

'What?'

'You groaned,' said the naval officer. 'Thought you were in pain or something.'

'N-no,' stuttered Adam. 'I'm fine.'

I must have invented some new meaning of fine, he thought bitterly. And yes, he was in pain, but not the sort he could cure with his own medical skills.

She didn't love him, of course. Oh, she liked him as a friend, an amiable twit, someone who made her laugh. That was all. It was Mario she loved. Even in his misery, Adam found something to admire in that. Her constancy to her lost lover shone like a diamond.

He stared out of the window and saw nothing of the countryside flashing by. All he could see was her lovely face, smiling as she wished him farewell, sending him off to war with a cheerful word and the offer of a kiss.

He nearly groaned again. What sort of an idiot was he anyway? She had made the offer and he had turned her down.

As the train picked up speed after Motherwell, all he could think of was that squandered opportunity. She might have put her arms around him. He could have felt her body against his, experienced the softness of her breasts against his chest—

He pulled himself up. What was the use?

Adam propped his chin against his fist and stared at the fields rushing past outside the window. He had held her in his arms, of course, when she had been distressed and in need of comfort. She had permitted him to do that. But it was Mario she loved. Not him. It would never be him.

Chapter 40

'I'm not nursing a German.'

Liz hadn't raised her voice. She'd said the words perfectly calmly. Judging by the determined set of her mouth, however, she meant business. Unfortunately, so did Sister MacLean.

'I'm not asking you to nurse a German, MacMillan.'

Her accent had become more lilting. That was a well-known danger signal. It made no difference to Liz.

She waved an unsteady hand in the general direction of the bed further down the ward where the young German sailor lay. It had shaken her badly to find him there when she'd come on duty tonight. He'd been picked up in the sea after his vessel had been torpedoed by a British ship.

'He was out there trying to kill our boys.'

'Our boys were out there trying to kill him,' came the implacable answer. 'That's war. On this occasion they killed a lot of his comrades. Sometimes it's the other way round. A stupid way of sorting things out if you ask me,' Sister said briskly, 'but that's the male of the species for you. What I meant is, I'm not asking you to nurse a German. I'm asking you to nurse a patient.'

Stung, Liz met the older woman's eyes.

'The man in that bed is our patient, as much as anyone else in here. If Adolf Hitler were admitted to this ward, I'd expect you to nurse him too. With medical competence and human compassion. Do I make myself understood?'

The night was crawling past. Liz took a walk round the ward.

She hadn't quite perfected the silent glide of the most experienced staff nurses and sisters, but she was getting better at it. All of the patients were sleeping soundly, including the German. She walked back to her table.

Her books were lying open on it. Night duty was a good opportunity to catch up on some studying. Half an hour later she realised she'd been staring at the same page for a full ten minutes without taking in one word of it.

Night nurse's hysteria. That was what one of the old hands had told her it was called. When your thoughts went rattling off in a hundred different directions. To Mario, naturally. Italy had surrendered in June, had now joined the Allies. Surely that meant he would be released? But it was September now and she'd heard nothing. There had been no more messages.

She'd had the occasional cheerful, if brief, missive from Adam, but they'd dried up completely over the past few months. The last one had arrived the morning after they'd had the thrilling announcement that D-Day had come at last. Which meant that young Dr Buchanan was probably on the continent – patching up the other chaps, as he'd put it. In the danger zone.

One of those who had died in the battle to free Europe was Eric Mitchell. Liz found that out by accident when Miss Gilchrist turned up in Accident and Emergency one night, having twisted her ankle during the blackout. She greeted Liz like a long-lost daughter, all but falling on her neck. Liz treated her with professional courtesy.

According to Lucy Gilchrist, Eric Mitchell had died a hero. Somehow Liz doubted that, but she was sorry for his wife and child.

The Allies were making progress – Paris had been liberated the week before – but they were meeting fierce resistance from the Germans every step of the way. Getting to Berlin wasn't exactly going to be a stroll through the country. Liz worried a lot about Adam. If only he would write!

And then there was her father. Her grandfather had

challenged her to apply her knowledge of psychology to the problem.

'Some men hit the bottle when the going gets rough. Your father didnae, but he got all closed in on himself, tried to shut the rest of us out. Particularly after wee Georgie died and when he was laid off from the *Queen Mary*. That sort of thing hits a man hard, you know.'

'And he took it out on his family?' Liz asked, unable to keep the bitterness out of her voice.

'His family was the one area of his life that he could control. Or thought he could. Until you rebelled.'

It did make some sort of sense. Liz could see already that Hope – like her mother a born diplomat – wasn't going to have the same problems she'd had growing up in her father's household.

Understanding that she herself had been a constant challenge to her father was one thing. Forgiving him for how he'd dealt with that was a different matter.

Liz's head snapped up at the faint moan coming from one of the beds. She made the patient comfortable, soothed him back to sleep, then returned to her textbook, closing it in quiet exasperation ten minutes later. She couldn't seem to concentrate tonight.

For some reason it was Marie Gallagher who was filling her thoughts now. Clear as day in her mind's eye, Liz could visualise the cramped flat in the Holy City before the parachute bomb had devastated it.

She could see its neatness and cleanliness, Helen's pots of flowers, the holy pictures on the walls. Her brain focused in on that one she'd always loved so much of Christ knocking at a door: His face full of understanding, His eyes full of compassion for all the world.

She remembered how Helen's mother had noticed her studying it. '*The door to our hearts*,' Marie had said. '*All we have to do is let Him in.*'

Liz glanced at her watch. An hour and a half to go till her break.

'*Schwester?*'

The sibilant whisper was startlingly loud in the night-time silence of the ward. She knew exactly which bed it had come from: the one occupied by the German sailor. She walked swiftly but quietly up the ward, careful not to rouse any of the other patients. They'd be woken soon enough, poor souls.

As she reached the foot of his bed, he said the word again, more quietly now that he could see her. He didn't seem to want to waken the other patients either.

'*Schwester?*'

Could it mean sister? That was what it sounded like. Had he perhaps been dreaming of his own sister back in Germany and woken up confused, still half-asleep? She supposed Germans did have sisters.

She had a sudden brainwave. Perhaps *Schwester* was the German word for sister in the nursing sense. Well, she thought wryly, at least someone here knows my true worth, even if it is only a filthy Hun.

He didn't look much like a filthy Hun, lying back quietly on a white pillow, gazing up at her in mute appeal. He looked like a boy. Some mother's son. Some sister's brother. His eyes were very blue. Like Helen's.

He indicated the jug of water which stood on his locker. Both of his hands were heavily bandaged.

'Water? You want a drink of water?'

'*Ja,*' he managed. '*Wasser.*' He tried to say it in English. '*Votter.*'

She poured out a glass, and since there was no way he could hold it himself, she put an arm round his shoulders, lifted him up and helped him drink. As she lowered his head carefully back on to the pillow, she could see that the effort of sitting up had been considerable.

'*Danke, Schwester. Danke schön.*'

He was thanking her. That much she could understand. And he was trying to smile.

'Can I do something else for you?'

She wasn't sure if he understood her or not, but he said something which sounded like *photograph*. He kept repeating the word and pointing towards the top of the ward. Of course. His personal possessions, such as they were, must be in the locked cupboard up there where such things were kept.

She told him in sign language what she intended to do and was back in five minutes with what looked like a home-made waterproofed wallet. His eyes lit up when he saw it and he indicated that Liz should open it. The photo inside, only slightly spotted by sea water, was of a young woman holding a baby.

'Your wife and child?'

He wasn't sure about that, so she rephrased it, pointing to the photograph and then at him. 'Your wife and baby?'

He nodded. Liz pretended not to notice the wetness in his eyes. She found a spare chunky glass tumbler inside his locker and propped the photo up against it, securing it with a New Testament laid on its side, pushing the locker so that it was inches from his head.

'Then you can look at them while you fall asleep again,' she said softly. She was sure he hadn't understood any of that, but she could see that he appreciated what she had done.

'Thank you,' he said, although it came out like *zank you*. Liz laid a cool hand on his brow. He shut his eyes, like an obedient child who'd been told to go to sleep.

'Nae bother,' she said.

'*Nae bozzer,*' he repeated, opening his eyes briefly again and looking up at her.

Liz smiled.

Handing over to the day shift, Liz briefed Naomi Richardson, now a staff nurse, on the condition of the various patients. She told her about the German sailor and the events of the night.

'Cordelia speaks German. I'll ask her to pop in sometime this morning to talk to him. In fact, I'll go and see if I can catch her now, before she goes on duty.'

Cordelia came back from the young sailor's bed with a big smile on her face.

'He comes from Hamburg, although his wife is staying with relatives out in the country somewhere. They were bombed out by our lot. I told him we'd try to get a letter to her via the International Red Cross. He's really pleased about that and he wants to know who the angel was who gave him a drink of water in the middle of the night. He says you tried to talk to him, even though he doesn't speak any English and you don't speak any German. And he says thank you, from the bottom of his heart. He was feeling really lost and lonely, and you helped.'

Liz went pink with pleasure. It was nice to be appreciated, even if it was by a filthy Hun – but she wasn't thinking of him that way any more. She'd go and have a quick word with him before she dragged her weary body off to bed – well, a quick point and smile anyway.

She did that, then made her way out of the ward, waving to Naomi as she headed for the door.

'That's me away off to have my beauty sleep!'

'Some of us need it more than others, MacMillan,' responded Naomi.

'Huh,' said Liz, turning and taking a few steps backwards as she went out through the double doors. 'I'll have you know I've already been called an angel this morning. Oh, sorry.'

Turning around to see who she had bumped into, the apology on her lips faded when she saw Sister MacLean. She'd been talking to Cordelia, who now beat a hasty retreat, heading smartly towards her own ward.

Liz was for it. Walking backwards? That was nearly as bad as running. No rebuke was forthcoming, however.

'No problems during the night?'

'None, Sister.'

'Sleep well then, Nurse MacMillan.'

Liz was halfway along the corridor before it registered. She turned and saw Sister MacLean smiling at her. That was a big enough miracle, but the first one was even more significant.

She had called her *Nurse*. For the first time ever. Liz went off to bed with a spring in her step.

She'd been dreaming again. That wasn't unusual. She still occasionally had nightmares about the Blitz, but there were pleasanter dreams too. She often saw Helen and Eddie with Hope. She liked those dreams. It made her think that the two of them were still around somewhere – somehow – and watching over their daughter.

Lately, however, she'd been having dreams about Helen and Adam together, the two of them walking towards her. Helen would lift his hand and extend it towards Liz, as though she were introducing the two of them to each other.

You know his worth, then? That was the question Helen had put on the night she died. Of course she did. If this was some sort of message, she didn't need it. She knew very well how much he had done for her. They had been through a lot together, Adam and her, and she missed him dreadfully.

The first time she had the dream, she woke in a panic, fearful that something had happened to him, but the uneasiness had soon worn off. However, the frequency of the dream began to concern her.

Coinciding at teatime the following day in the nurses' dining room, Liz asked Cordelia if she ever dreamed about Adam.

'Occasionally. Not very often. Why?'

'I seem to be dreaming about him a lot lately.'

Cordelia had a very peculiar smile on her face.

'I dream a lot about Hans-Peter, Liz.'

'MacMillan!'

Liz looked up. Someone was calling her name from the other side of the room. It was Naomi Richardson, beaming all over her face. When Liz reached her, she grabbed her by the hand.

'Come with me,' she said. 'And don't ask any questions.' Curious, Liz allowed Naomi to pull her out to the hallway. 'Turn around, Liz,' the girl said when they got there. 'Turn your back and close your eyes.'

Intrigued by her obvious excitement, Liz did as Naomi asked. She heard someone else come into the hall. The footsteps approached her. A man, she thought. Two long-fingered hands came over her eyes.

'Guess who?' said a dark brown voice.

She whirled round. 'Mario? Oh, Mario, you're home at last!'

Chapter 41

He hadn't told her much yet: only the bits which made good stories. After their arrest they'd found themselves in a transit camp in the north of England. There had been all sorts there, from captured German sailors to Jews who'd come to Britain fleeing from the Nazis. And there had been a few Italians who were convinced fascists.

Mario had laughed at them, making light of the threats they'd issued to their fellow internees who they thought were opponents of Il Duce. Anyone who criticised Mussolini, expressed left-wing views or thought the Allies might win the war had been warned that their names were being noted for reprisals after the supposed German and Italian victory.

'So for a brief period,' he told her with a smile, 'I was an enemy of both the Italian and the British states. Some doing, eh? Aren't you proud of me, Liz?'

He was choosing to see the funny side, as he always had done, but there were fine lines on his brow which hadn't been there when he had left, and after he told her the story his lips settled into a tight line. Liz was sure the threat had seemed all too real at the time, but she took her cue from him, and didn't press him to tell her anything he didn't want to.

They were sitting in the flat above the café. Although very dusty and more than a little grubby, it was intact and secure. Someone had cleared up the café too, sweeping up the worst of the broken glass and mess. Friends of his father, Mario thought, from one of the Italian cafés or restaurants which had managed to ride out the storm.

Apparently willing to forgive and forget, the Italian community was once more in the business of serving its adopted city. Mario would set about finding out exactly who had organised the clearing-up the following day, so that he could thank them for what they had done.

'From the bottom of my heart,' he said quietly, lifting Liz's hand and kissing her fingertips.

Some of their guards, he told her, had been none too gentle at first, believing the internees were all fascists or fifth columnists or worse. Then one soldier at the camp, exasperated by his inability to give instructions to a group of Polish Jews, had yelled out in the broadest of Glasgow accents: 'Is there naebody here who speaks the King's English?'

'Aye, pal,' Mario had called out in reply. 'Come over here. We're all frae Glesca.'

After that they'd got much better treatment, although he had been forced to split up from his father.

'Oh, Mario,' said Liz with quick sympathy. 'That must have been awful for you both. Is he all right?'

He was keeping a tight hold of her hand. 'He's fine.' He shot her a glance and she saw the yearning for sympathy in it. 'It was bloody awful, Liz, but it's all right now. They took him to the Isle of Man, and the people there treated him very well.'

'He's still there?'

Mario nodded. 'Yes, I've got him digs with a local family. I want him to rest up for a bit before I bring him home.'

'I knew you were in Canada,' she told him. 'I got a message.'

Mario nodded thoughtfully. 'That would have been one of the sailors on the ship that took us over there. A Liverpudlian. An older man – in his fifties. He thought we were being very shabbily treated and he was sympathetic. He asked if there was anyone who would be worrying about me . . .'

Mario swallowed and gave Liz's hand a squeeze.

'Someone else must have been sympathetic,' she said gently. 'I got a second message, telling me that you and your father were all right. Do you know who might have sent that?'

He thought about it.

'They sent out people to investigate, not long after we got to Canada.' He smiled. 'Not a bad advert for British democracy, that. In the middle of a war, the powers-that-be still found time to investigate individual injustices.' He grimaced. 'Not that it did me much good at the time. But there was a clerk, a young chap, about the same age as myself. He and I had a chat. I told him how worried I was about my father.' He paused. 'I told him about you.'

'And he took it upon himself to find out about your father and also get a message to me? That was kind,' Liz said. 'That was very kind.'

'Yes. People like that . . . they kind of restore your faith in human nature, don't they?'

'Thank God for them,' said Liz passionately. 'I worried myself sick when news came through about the *Arandora Star*.'

'You and thousands of Italian families,' said Mario, and for the first time there was bitterness in his voice. 'There were no passenger lists for those ships. We were herded on to them like cattle. I missed going on the *Arandora Star* by about twenty men, Liz. That's all.'

They looked at each other solemnly.

'Oh, Mario,' she said again, leaning over impulsively to kiss him. 'So when did you come back from Canada?'

'Last year. When Italy surrendered. I was in line for release anyway. Conditional release. I had to agree to come home and do work relating to the war effort. I did it in the Isle of Man, to be with my father. But now,' he said brightly, sitting up and squaring his shoulders, 'I'm a free man. I'm going to get the café sorted out for my father coming home. My brother and his family too, once the war's over. And then I'm going back to finish my degree. Take up where I left off.'

'Once the war's over,' she repeated, remembering another time they had been together and alone in the living room of the flat. They smiled shyly at each other.

'And your story, Liz,' he said softly. 'Tell me your story.'

383

He listened patiently, encouraging her gently when she faltered, holding her close when she spoke of Helen and Eddie and the Blitz. When she had finished, he wrapped his arms even more tightly about her and let her sob, his own eyes wet, his face pale and shocked. He didn't speak until her tears had subsided to quick and shallow little breaths. Then he planted a long, cool kiss on her brow.

'I thought *I* was suffering,' he told her, his voice sombre. 'Now I see how lucky I've been. Eddie and Helen . . . Helen's family . . . the poor dog, too. I can't take it in . . .' He bit his lip, and it was a minute or two before he could go on.

'Oh, Elisabetta, I'm so sorry you had to go through all of it alone.' His voice was anguished.

Held fast and secure in his arms, she sought to comfort him.

'I wasn't alone,' she said simply. 'Adam was here.'

Mario's dark eyes were soft with emotion: shock, pain, sympathy for her. He pressed his lips once more to her forehead. 'I'm very glad that he was.'

'And Hope has been a great consolation.'

His face lit up. He'd been overjoyed to learn of the existence of Hope Elizabeth MacMillan. 'So when,' he asked, 'do I get to meet this wonderful child?'

Liz patted his chest and pulled herself out of his arms, curling her legs underneath her on the sofa.

'I'm supposed to be taking her out tomorrow. We usually go to the Botanic Gardens and then for our afternoon tea somewhere in Byres Road. She loves that.' Responding to something she saw in his face, she asked anxiously, 'Would you mind doing that tomorrow? I don't want to disappoint her. But if you want it to be just the two of us . . .'

He laid a warm hand on her knee. She glanced briefly down at it. Mario smiled. 'No, Liz, I wouldn't mind at all. Now then, why don't we go out for a meal?'

They got back about half past eight and spent twenty minutes downstairs assessing the damage, calculating how much time and money it was going to take to put things right again.

Professional help would be needed. That was obvious.

'But we can sort the flat out,' said Liz, as they went upstairs. 'It needs a damn good clean, that's all.' They walked into the living room and stood looking about them. 'If we wash the curtains and leave the windows wide open during the day for a while, that'll get rid of the foosty smell. I'll get some supplies tomorrow.'

She moved through to the small kitchen and opened a food cupboard.

'Yee-uch! You'll need to throw most of this away. Shall I bring some stuff in with me tomorrow morning? What will you need? Coffee, definitely. Will you trust me to buy the right sort? All depends what I can get, of course. Mario?'

Liz went to the kitchen door. He was standing where she had left him, in the middle of the living room.

'Come here,' he said. 'And stop talking about coffee.'

She hesitated, but when he held out his arms, she went to him. His arms locked around her and she looked shyly up at him. He was older. There was a greater maturity in his features. They were as attractive as they'd always been.

'Do you remember,' she whispered, 'when we said goodbye at the police station?'

His eyes were very tender. 'I remember, Elisabetta, I remember.'

And because she remembered too, and because she could hear the pain in his voice, she returned his kiss with all the passion she could muster. As the arms which held her tightened, she felt his body begin to respond to hers. Was this something else he wanted to take up where he'd left off?

His grip loosened, enough to allow them to look at each other. He didn't say anything, but she could read the question in his face. They had both, after all, been here before: the time that wordless request had first been made – and answered.

'Mario . . .'

He said nothing. He was waiting for her. She laid a hand flat on his chest.

'Mario . . .' she said. 'I'm sorry . . . Could we take this slowly?'

It was a terrible thing to ask a man who'd been deprived for so long . . . but Mario's arms further slackened their hold.

'It's been a long time,' he said at last.

'Yes,' she agreed. 'It's been a long time.'

There was a pause.

'You must be tired, Liz,' he said gently. 'Too much emotion for one day.' He dropped his arms completely and took a step back. 'Come on, then,' he said. 'I'll walk you back down the road to the nurses' home.'

The next afternoon, Mario tactfully waited outside on the pavement while Liz went in to fetch Hope. Her mother, however, came out to say hello. Like her grandmother, Hope was shy at first, but within half an hour she was calling him Uncle Mario.

'You haven't lost your touch with the ladies, then,' said Liz teasingly as they walked hand in hand round the gardens. It was a beautiful day, the autumn sun dappling through the trees as they strolled along the paths.

'I certainly hope not,' he said lightly. 'Looks like Hope's made a friend.'

Scampering on in front of them, the little girl was patting a golden Labrador puppy being taken for a walk by a middle-aged couple. Liz and Mario stood back and watched.

'We'll have to be getting on,' said the woman eventually, smiling down at Hope. 'We'll maybe see you another day. Away back to your mummy and daddy, now.'

Mario held out a hand to Hope. 'I suppose we do look like a family,' he said. 'We're all the same colouring. Any children we might have will probably look a bit like Hope. Apart from the blue eyes, of course,' he mused.

Startled, Liz stared at him. Watching Hope with the playful little dog, she'd been thinking about Conor and Finn.

Children we might have?

* * *

'Right,' she said briskly the next morning. 'Coffee and tea, milk, sugar and one of my mother's fruit loaves. I told her what we were planning to do today, and she thought we would probably need more sustenance than a packet of biscuits.'

She glanced at Mario, who was leaning against the cooker watching her empty her bag out on to the small kitchen table. 'You made a hit there too,' Liz said with a smile. 'As well as with Hope.'

'So the grandmother and the grandchild like me. I hope the aunt does too.'

Liz's smile grew brighter. 'Don't lean back too far on that cooker,' she instructed. 'It's filthy. I'll tackle that this morning as well. Once I've soaked the curtains in the bath.'

'Liz,' he said. 'Shut up. And come here.'

He held out his arms for her, but she shook her head. 'We've got work to do. Where do you want to start?'

He dropped his arms, his expression grave. 'By talking to you,' he said quietly.

'I thought you just told me to shut up.'

'About cookers and curtains and cleaning, yes. You and I have more important things to discuss.'

She pushed the milk bottle she'd brought in with her away from the edge of the table. It might fall if she left it there. She felt, rather than saw, that Mario had pushed himself up off the cooker.

'Liz,' he said quietly. 'Look at me.'

She heard the implacable tone in his voice and knew that this couldn't be delayed any longer. Lifting her head, she did as he had asked. He smiled faintly and crooked a finger at her.

'Elisabetta,' he said. 'Come here. Right now.'

Chapter 42

The war was over at last, at least in Europe. Liz was conscious of a deep thankfulness, but as the city around them exploded into one giant street party, neither she nor Mario felt very much like celebrating. He was anxiously waiting for news from Italy of his brother and his family. Liz's mood was sombre and reflective, her thoughts full of Eddie and Helen.

For a few days the pain of their loss was as acute as it had ever been. It was so unfair that they hadn't lived to see this day or enjoy their daughter growing up. Then Liz seemed to hear Helen's voice in her head. *Get on with it, MacMillan! You've got exams to pass!*

So she buckled down and got on with it, and she passed with flying colours. She was Elizabeth MacMillan, RGN. Mario gave her a beautiful silver fob watch to replace the more workaday one she wore on her apron, and they went out for a celebratory meal together. She and Cordelia and the other new registered general nurses had a night out too. Liz completed the marking of her achievement by spending a riotous afternoon with Hope at Queen Victoria Row.

Sadie baked a cake and they sat and ate it in the front room. Hope kept asking why they were in there when it wasn't someone's birthday. Liz laughed, and tried to explain it to her. It was a party of a different sort.

In that case, Hope said, they ought to play some party games. An hour and a half later, Liz was convinced they'd done the hokey-cokey and ring-a-ring-of-roses a hundred times. At the very least. Peter MacMillan and Annie Crawford both pleaded their age and left them to it.

Sadie pleaded her age too, although she looked far too young to be a grandmother. She sank down laughing into an armchair opposite her husband and watched Liz and Hope sitting on the hearth rug playing row-your-boat. Hope loved it when her aunt allowed her body to go slack so that the little girl could pull her easily towards her. Then, despite the protests, it was bedtime.

'I'll come and read you a story,' Liz promised. 'Once Grandma's tucked you in.'

Hope skipped over to her grandfather.

'Kiss,' she demanded.

'Away with your nonsense,' he said, but he leaned forward and submitted to the little arms coiling around his neck, Hope's rosebud mouth pressing a kiss against his cheek.

'Night, night, Grandad,' she said cheerfully, apparently not at all put out by his gruffness. She never was. She and Sadie left the room. And an uneasy silence settled.

'The place seems empty now, doesn't it?'

Still sitting on the rug, Liz darted a quick glance up at him, then looked away. Did he have any idea how she felt?

'You were like that, you know. Bright as a button.'

She scrambled to her feet and stood in front of the fire, pretending to check her hair in the mirror. 'Was I?'

'Aye, you were a right bonnie wee thing, too. D'you remember when you had the scarlet fever?'

Liz stopped pretending she was looking in the mirror and turned to face him.

'That was one of the worst days of my life,' he said quietly. She stared at him. One of the worst days of *his* life?

There were things she wanted to say to him then. Like: *how do you think I felt, Daddy? When I reached out for you and you turned away from me?* She said nothing.

'Seeing you going into that ambulance . . .' her father said. The words weren't coming easily. He stopped and swallowed, and went on, not looking at Liz, 'We'd just lost your brother . . .'

There was another pause. She had to strain to hear what he said next. 'I was terrified we were going to lose you as well.'

There wasn't a sound in the room except for the crackling of the fire. But you did lose me, she thought sadly, you did lose me. And it's too late now for apologies. If that's what this is.

He raised his eyes to his daughter, standing so rigidly in front of him. 'I had two sisters died of the scarlet fever. Did you know that?'

His next words seemed to be a complete *non sequitur*.

'You've done well,' he said, 'at the Infirmary. Your mother's very proud of you.'

Liz waited, but it appeared that her father had nothing to add.

'I-I'd better go up,' she said. She tried not to let the bitterness swamp her. It was stupid of her to be expecting anything else from him. 'Hope will be wondering what's happened to me.' She crossed to the door and curled her fingers around the knob.

'Your mother's very proud of you,' he said again. Liz opened the door. 'So am I,' he added quietly.

Too late for apologies. She should go out of the door, close it behind her, turn away from him as he had once turned away from her. Was it ever too late? He was looking intently at her.

'Thank you, Father,' she said gravely. 'Thank you.'

The patient in Male Surgical looked as if he was about to die of embarrassment. Liz didn't blame him. Not only was she going to give him a blanket bath, she was also demonstrating the art to a group of probationers under the supervision of Sister MacLean. Poor man. She'd try to make it as easy as possible for him.

Gathering together the relevant bits and pieces, she glanced out of the long windows of the ward. It was almost Christmas again – the first Christmas of peace – but there was no seasonal snow. A persistent drizzle had been falling all day. Och, well, there was Cordelia's party to look forward to this weekend.

Like herself and Mario, Cordelia hadn't felt much like

celebrating on VE day. She'd been too worried about Hans-Peter. Two weeks ago, however, she'd got a letter from him. It was going to be some time before the necessary formalities would permit their reunion but, absolutely ecstatic, she had decided to throw a party for her friends anyway.

Mario had also received some good news. His brother Carlo, now a father of three, would be coming over with his family in the new year. The expectation of seeing his grandchildren was giving Aldo Rossi a new lease of life. Mario was over the moon about it too. Both he and Liz were really looking forward to Cordelia's party.

Her old friend Janet Brown, now married, was going to be there, as was Dominic Gallagher, due home on leave tomorrow night and staying with the family of his WAAF girlfriend in Paisley. He was quite the young man now, planning a career in commercial aviation. That was the future of travel, he'd told Liz enthusiastically during his previous leave. Everyone, it seemed was coming home. Well . . . apart from one person.

Adam was working at a military hospital in southern England. Liz had received a brief letter from him in September. The war might be over, he'd written, but there were still wounded to be cared for. He had said nothing about when he might be coming back to Glasgow. Or even if he was coming back to Glasgow. She had no idea what his plans were.

Carrying a large tray with all the necessary paraphernalia on it, Liz approached the patient. The student nurses were already gathered round his bed. If any one of them giggled, she'd have their guts for garters. Always supposing Sister MacLean didn't get there before her.

'You're working well, MacMillan,' observed a light, mocking voice from behind her.

Liz spun round so quickly that she dropped the tray. It appeared to fall in slow motion, taking what seemed like minutes to hit the floor. It bounced when it got there, its contents leaping gracefully into the air before spilling in a series of crashes and clatters.

'Quite spectacular,' observed Adam once the noise had finally died away.

Sauntering forward, he stood on the other side of the debris. He was in civilian clothes, elegant in a belted trenchcoat, his fair head bare. She'd forgotten how tall he was.

No she hadn't. She hadn't forgotten a single thing about him. Not the height, not the thick fair hair, not the hazel eyes – currently surveying the damage with an elegantly quizzical air.

The probationers stood open-mouthed. Sister MacLean's mouth also opened, but Adam pre-empted her. Reaching out, he coiled his fingers around Liz's wrist and pulled her towards him, angling her so that she side-stepped the mess on the floor.

'I want fifteen minutes with Nurse – I beg her pardon – Staff Nurse MacMillan, Sister.'

'You can have five, Dr Buchanan.'

'Ten.'

'As long as it takes this lot to clear up the mess. Not a second more.'

He didn't waste any time, leading Liz out of the ward and into the corridor. When they got there, he backed her up against the wall, but then the forceful decisiveness seemed to desert him, and he took a step back.

'Look, Liz,' he said. 'I've got something to say. Will you hear me out? Not say anything till I've finished?'

He ran a hand through his hair and darted a quick glance at her from under his fair brows.

'I had a speech all rehearsed,' he said quietly. 'Worked it out on the train home.' He gave her that odd little look again. 'Right now I can't seem to string two coherent words together.'

Liz was having some difficulty in speaking herself.

'Tell me the most important bit,' she whispered.

'The m-most important b-bit?'

She had never known him to stutter. He was always so self-possessed, in command of whatever situation he found himself in. Then, all at once, she realised what that nervous stammer meant. Adam Buchanan was scared: of what he was going to say next.

Before she could think of a way to help him, he squared his shoulders, looked her straight in the eye, and came out with it.

'I love you.'

There had been no stutter that time.

Liz saw that she'd been wrong. It wasn't those three little words which frightened him. It was her reaction to them. When he dared to say them again, she felt a lump form in her throat.

'I love you. That's all.' He took another step back, so that he was standing in the middle of the corridor. 'That's what I wanted to say, Liz.'

The look on his face was breaking her heart.

'Liz,' he pleaded. 'Say something.'

She pushed herself off the wall and took a step towards him, lifting her hands, both for the sheer pleasure of touching him and to reassure herself that he really was here, that this wasn't happening in one of her dreams.

When she trailed her fingertips lightly over his jaw and his mouth, he froze. Then he closed his eyes, and muttered something under his breath.

Liz found her voice at last.

'I love you too, Adam.'

His eyes snapped open, but he wasn't prepared to believe her. Not yet. He grabbed her wrists, drawing her hands away from his face.

'And Mario?' he asked tightly.

'A very dear friend. No more, no less.'

He went on as though she hadn't spoken. 'Hope wrote to me.'

'I know,' she said, bemused by this apparent change of subject. 'I gave my mother your forwarding address so that she could write the envelope for her. I expect it followed you around for a while until you got it.'

He nodded impatiently. 'Yes, but she sent me this drawing. It was very colourful. It showed her Auntie Liz in the Botanic

Gardens. With her Uncle Mario. Hand in hand.'

'I expect we were holding hands when she drew it,' Liz said evenly. 'That was just after Mario came home.' She paused. 'When he and I were still trying to pretend that everything was exactly the same as it had been before.'

Adam was watching her closely. 'And it wasn't?'

Liz smiled, remembering that day in the kitchen of the flat, when Mario had told her to stop talking about washing curtains, when he had crooked his finger at her, more or less ordered her to come to him.

'It was the day after that walk in the Botanic Gardens,' she told Adam now. 'Mario and I were in the flat above the café, getting ready to start cleaning it up. He kissed me,' she said. 'Very passionately.'

The blood drained from Adam's face and his fingers tightened on her wrists. 'Liz . . . please . . .'

He had to hear this. She forced herself to go on.

'I did my best to respond, but it wasn't working. For either of us,' she said softly. 'And Mario made a very interesting observation.'

'Which was?' Adam's voice was raw.

'He told me that it was pretty hard to make love to someone who was quite obviously in love with someone else.'

She saw it then in his hazel eyes: equal parts hope and fear. He took refuge in flippancy.

'Anyone I know?'

'Someone into whose arms he'd once put me. Quite symbolic that, he thought,' she said lightly. 'At Partick police station – if that helps you work out who he was talking about.'

Her eyes dropped to his very beautiful mouth. When had she first started imagining what it would feel like on her own?

'The last time I offered you a kiss, you turned me down. Would you refuse me now?'

Adam shook his head. The corners of that beautiful mouth began, very cautiously, to lift.

'Oh, Adam!'

He pulled her roughly into his arms, the forcefulness back. His kiss was thorough, and everything she had dreamed it would be. When he released her they stayed in each other's arms.

'I love you,' she said again. 'Do you believe me now?'

Someone coughed. It was one of the pupil nurses, very embarrassed and apologetic.

'Sister MacLean's compliments, and she'd be extremely obliged if you could possibly find the time to step back into the ward. Sorry, Staff,' said the girl a lot less formally. 'She told me to say it exactly like that. And we tried to take as long as we could clearing it all up, but you know what she's like!'

'Don't we just,' murmured Adam, taking a firm grip of Liz's hand. He gave the probationer a dazzling smile. 'Lead on, Macduff.'

It was obvious that their reappearance had been eagerly awaited. Every head was turned towards them. Sister MacLean spoke, insincerity dripping from every lilting syllable.

'How kind of you to rejoin us, Staff Nurse MacMillan. I do hope you've finished sorting out your private life?'

Adam grinned. 'Not quite, Sister.'

She gave him a steely look. 'She'll be off duty in one hour, Dr Buchanan. If you're going to wait for her, kindly do so out in the corridor.'

'Och, Sister,' he said. 'Have a heart. She's just told me that she loves me.' With an impish grin, he walked up to the nursing tutor and, before she had time to object, kissed her on the cheek. 'And we all know you're not as hard-hearted as you'd have us believe.'

'Dr Buchanan!'

Liz, watching the reactions of the probationers, was pondering the fact that their mouths had once more quite literally fallen open when Adam walked over to her, pulled her to him and kissed her – briefly, but full on the mouth.

'Enough!' yelled Sister MacLean. 'I won't have my doctors and nurses kissing and canoodling and putting the patients off their recovery.'

'The patients are enjoying it, hen,' came a voice from one of the beds. 'This is better than the pictures.'

Laughter ran round the ward.

'Anyway,' Adam told Sister MacLean cheerfully, 'I'm not one of your doctors any more. I'm a free agent. Thinking of going into general practice. I thought Clydebank might be able to stand another doctor or two. I'd need a practice nurse, of course. What do you say, MacMillan?'

'She says,' broke in the man whose blanket bath had been postponed, and who was hoping that everyone had forgotten about it by now, 'do you only want her for your nurse or are you planning to make an honest woman of her?'

The laughter died away, the patients sat up straighter in their beds and the student nurses stood stock still. Even Sister MacLean was quiet.

'Liz,' he said, 'I love you. Will you marry me?'

You could have heard a pin drop in the ward. They were all waiting for her reply. She had eyes only for him. She thought of all they had been through, of all they had meant to each other – of all the future might hold for them. Together.

'Yes,' she whispered. 'I will.'

A cheer went up in Male Surgical. As it subsided, Sister MacLean drew a sigh of theatrical proportions.

'Could we possibly get on with our work?' Her gaze swept over Adam and Liz. 'I suppose,' she said in her lovely Highland accent, 'that we have to be grateful that Staff Nurse MacMillan has finally seen what has been staring her in the face for a long time. Several years, by my estimate.'

Liz and Adam looked at her. Then they looked at each other. Then they burst out laughing.

'You look perfectly lovely,' he said.

Liz dropped her head in pleased embarrassment at the admiration evident in Adam's eyes. 'Turn around,' he commanded, 'so that I can have a good look at you.'

Laughing, she did as she was bid. Her dress was of wine-coloured velvet, simply shaped, with a small matching cape over her shoulders.

'The material was a gift from a grateful patient,' she said. 'No questions asked. No clothing coupons, either.' She squinted down at herself. 'Maybe I shouldn't have made the cape, though. Then the dress could have been a wee bit longer.'

'I wouldn't want it any longer,' he growled, and Liz laughed again. His appreciative gaze travelled up to her head. 'What do you call that thing you're wearing on your hair?'

'A snood.' She put a hand to the back of her head and patted the heavy black crocheted lace which contained her hair below her ears. 'Do you like it?'

'Mmm . . . Maybe.' He walked round her to examine it from the back. 'It's very chic.'

'But?' She went to turn, but his hands came on to her shoulders, holding her where she was. 'What are you doing?' she laughed.

'Checking to see how it's secured.' He allowed her to turn to face him, but his hands remained where they were, resting lightly on her shoulders. 'So I know exactly how to loosen it later. Did you enjoy yourself yesterday evening, by the way?'

'Couldn't you tell?' she murmured. 'I must say it was very tactful of your mother to suddenly remember a previous engagement.'

'Wasn't it? You know,' he said, his mouth very close to hers, 'I'm having a terrible problem. I find I can't stop smiling. D'you think I should see a doctor?'

Liz shook her head. 'Only one thing cures a propensity to smile too much,' she advised. 'An intensive programme of kissing. Trust me. I'm a nurse.'

He trusted her for the next few minutes.

'Eh . . .' said Liz, a little uncertainly. She was finding it hard to concentrate with Adam's arms around her waist and his hands beginning a little cautious exploring. 'We've got a party to go to.'

'And?'

'Things are escalating, I feel.'

'And?'

'Well, we had a bit of a problem stopping last night, didn't we?'

The roaming hands stopped moving. He sighed and placed them in a more neutral position, but he was still having the smiling problem. Liz addressed her next comments to his black bow tie, her hands flat on the lapels of his coat.

'Thank you for stopping last night. Thank you for not assuming that . . . because . . . well, you know what I mean . . .'

'I love you,' he said simply. 'I've loved you for a very long time, and I'm prepared to wait. I'm good at that.' His voice grew dry. 'I've had a lot of practice.'

She lifted a hand to his face. He turned his head and kissed her palm. 'You keep touching my face,' he observed.

'I want to make sure you're really here.' She told him about her dream and he listened thoughtfully.

'Helen knew how I felt about you,' he said simply when she had finished. 'From the start. She was a very perceptive person.'

Seeing Liz's emotion, he pulled her into his arms.

'Do you mind me touching your face?' she asked him a few moments later.

'I love you touching me anywhere,' he assured her. A gleam of mischief crept into his eyes. 'Do it as much as you like. Wherever you like.'

'Adam . . . What that patient said . . . about you making an honest woman of me. Well . . . it wasn't you who made a dishonest . . . well, what I mean is . . .'

'Liz,' he advised, 'that hole you're digging for yourself? It's getting bigger by the second. If I were you, I'd stop shovelling.'

She looked anxiously up at him. 'You mean it really doesn't bother you about Mario and me?'

'I'm jealous as hell,' he said swiftly. 'But only because I wish it had been me who was your first love. That's all.'

'You'll be my last love.'

'I'm going to need a lot of reassurance about that,' he said.

She touched his face again. 'As much as you want, my love. As much as you want.'

'Well,' said Cordelia, as she opened the door to them. 'About time too. That's all I can say.' Then she threw her arms about Adam's neck and greeted him properly.

'Why does everyone keep saying that to us?' he asked with a faintly puzzled air. 'My mother said something very similar.'

'Why do you think she and I didn't come to see you off when you joined the medical corps?' asked Cordelia cheerfully. 'We were hoping that if we left the two of you alone you might actually get round to saying something to each other.'

She had been off visiting relatives in Edinburgh for the past couple of days, but Liz had given her the good news by phone, wanting her to be one of the first to know. Beaming at both of them, her face suddenly took on a guarded look. Liz turned, and saw Mario.

He came forward and greeted her before turning to Adam. They looked at each other a little warily, then Adam laughed and held out his hand. Mario shook it warmly and clapped him on the shoulder.

'Welcome home, old friend. I understand congratulations are also in order.'

'Be my best man?'

'If you'll do the same for me.'

'Is this the one?' Liz asked eagerly, peering over Mario's shoulder. 'Where is she?'

He had told her last week that he was bringing someone special with him tonight. He'd had two or three girlfriends since he and Liz had agreed to part. When he had forced her to admit how she felt about Adam, she had asked him anxiously about himself. Was there someone?

'Not yet,' he had said, 'but I'm going to have fun looking for her!'

'Come on,' he said now, with a pride which boded well for

this new relationship. 'I'll introduce you both to her.'

'Everything all right, Liz?'

'Fine,' she replied, turning her face away from the lights of Great Western Road. She patted the window seat beside her. 'Come and join me for a minute, Mario.'

He sank down beside her. 'Your mother and Mrs Crawford brought Hope to the café again today.'

'It's becoming quite a regular outing for them, isn't it?'

Mario nodded. 'Maybe we'll even get your father in sometime.'

'I doubt it,' said Liz with a rueful smile. 'But you never know, I suppose.'

'How is it with you and him these days?' Mario's eyes went to Adam. He was on the other side of the room, laughing at something Dominic Gallagher had said. Mario's new girlfriend was talking to Naomi Richardson and Jim Barclay. 'I presume he approves of your engagement?'

'Wholeheartedly.' She shrugged. 'And we communicate. After a fashion. It's not great, but it's better than it was.'

There was a certain wistfulness in Mario's voice.

'Do you regret it, Elisabetta? Us, I mean?'

'Not a single moment of it. It was something very special – and very romantic.'

His face lit up. 'It was, wasn't it?' His eyes went to his girlfriend. 'It's romantic this time too . . . but different somehow.'

'Deeper,' Liz suggested. 'Something that's going to last.'

Mario's glance lit on Adam, then came back to her. 'We've both been lucky, Liz.'

'Yes,' she agreed, smiling into his eyes. 'Now go back to her,' she said gently. 'I'll be fine. Adam and I are going soon.'

Mario leaned over and kissed her on the cheek – an affectionate salute between old friends.

'Will the two of you come for a meal with us and my father? To celebrate your engagement?'

'Thank you,' she said. 'We'd love to.'

She was still sitting on the window seat when Adam came looking for her later. He had to say her name twice before she heard him. He helped her into her coat and they took their leave of their hostess. As they walked down the steps on to the pavement he headed for Morag, but Liz pulled on his sleeve.

'Could we walk for a bit? Would you mind?'

They walked in silence till they reached the café, dark now and shut for the night. Liz stopped.

'This is where it all started. When you brought me for a coffee that day.'

'The very first time I was jealous as hell, you mean?'

'Were you really?'

'I could see how you were reacting to Mario,' he said lightly. 'I didn't care for that one little bit.' He lifted her gloved hand and put his lips to it, sliding his other arm around her waist. 'I was already falling in love with you, you see.'

'I'm sorry,' she said. 'I was blind, wasn't I?'

'On numerous occasions,' he said wryly.

'The last night of the Empire Exhibition?'

'Yes. The night of the *Athenia*, too. When I had to stand back and watch you go into Mario's arms. Not mine.'

'I'm in yours now,' she said earnestly. 'And I intend to stay there.'

'I'm very glad to hear it.'

'I think Eddie knew about us too, you know,' she said. 'He said something to me once about you being very fond of me.'

'Did he? That's nice to know. Almost as though I have his blessing. Was that who you were thinking about back at Cordelia's? Absent friends?'

Liz nodded, and would have said more, but her eyes had filled with tears. Adam pulled her head against his shoulder. She wasn't at all surprised that he had guessed. He had always been sensitive to her feelings. She sniffed and looked up.

'Sorry.'

'Don't be,' he said comfortably. 'That's one of the things I'm here for.'

'We won't forget them, will we?'

The hazel eyes were very tender. 'How could we, my love? They live on through Hope, for one thing. And through our memories of them. They'll always be part of our lives. Come on,' he said. 'It's getting cold.'

They turned, and began to walk up Byres Road.

'Cordelia's had a second letter from Hans-Peter. Did she tell you? They're going to try and get together as soon as they can.'

'That's good,' said Adam. He squeezed her hand. 'I'm glad you and she have become such good friends.'

'She's going to be my bridesmaid,' said Liz. 'Naomi too, of course – and Janet. Well, Janet will have to be a matron of honour, since she's already married. Hope will be the flower girl, of course—'

She was brought up short by the look of sheer male panic on Adam's face.

'This wedding,' he said, 'it's not going to get out of hand, is it?'

Liz chuckled. 'You'll have to speak to my mother about that – and your own. You wouldn't want to spoil their fun too much, though, would you?'

'Big weddings take longer to arrange,' he grumbled. 'I said I could wait – but not that long. When are we seeing your minister?'

'Tomorrow afternoon.'

'We're going to tell him that we want to get married very soon. Very, very soon,' he repeated. 'Oh, damn. Come in here for a minute.' He pulled her into a shop doorway.

'I thought kissing in public was vulgar,' she said, some considerable time later.

'What idiot ever said that?' he mumbled. 'I find I can't keep my hands off you, Elizabeth MacMillan.'

'Good,' she said blithely. 'Now that I've got you in a

weakened state, I've got some things to say. First of all, an early wedding is fine by me. Secondly, after we're married, I'm going to keep working.'

'I'm counting on it,' Adam said. 'You're going to be in charge of our health education programme at the practice.'

She beamed at him but he sent her a warning look.

'We could court controversy there, you know. Especially when we start giving advice about birth control.'

Liz lifted her chin. 'I've never been afraid of a fight. Especially in support of a just cause.'

'I know,' he said admiringly. 'That's one of the many reasons why I love you.'

He got another kiss for that. Then Liz continued to enumerate her list of requirements.

'If we have children I'm going back to work once they're old enough.'

'Fine by me,' he said equably.

'Are you going to agree with everything I say?' she demanded.

'Oh, no!' His eyes crinkled at the corners. 'I'm looking forward to some really good arguments.' He raised his eyebrows at her. 'Especially the making up afterwards.'

Liz dropped the belligerent attitude. 'Oh, Adam Buchanan, I love you!'

'You will keep telling me that, won't you?' He glanced across at the streetlight on the edge of the pavement. 'Do you remember the night of the *Athenia*?'

'I'll never forget it. We walked up the road arm in arm in the blackout and you told me that one day the lights would come on again. And they have,' she finished happily, smiling up at him.

'For both of us,' he agreed. He held out his hand. 'Come on, Liz. Let's go home.'

A Mersey Duet

Anne Baker

When Elsa Gripper dies in childbirth on Christmas Eve, 1912, her grief-stricken husband is unable to cope with his two newborn daughters, Lucy and Patsy, so the twins are separated.

Elsa's parents, who run a highly successful business, Mersey Antiques, take Lucy home and she grows up spoiled and pampered with no interest in the family firm. Patsy has a more down-to-earth upbringing, living with their father and other grandmother above the Railway Hotel. And through further tragedy she learns to be responsible from an early age. Then Patsy is invited to work at Mersey Antiques, which she hopes will bring her closer to Lucy. But it is to take a series of dramatic events before they are drawn together . . .

'A stirring tale of romance and passion, poverty and ambition . . . everything from seduction to murder, from forbidden love to revenge' *Liverpool Echo*

'Highly observant writing style . . . a compelling book that you just don't want to put down' *Southport Visitor*

0 7472 5320 X

HEADLINE

At The Toss of a Sixpence

Lynda Page

At eleven years of age, Albertina Listerman loses her parents in a terrible accident. Approaching her twenty-first birthday, she experiences further tragedy: her half-brother commits suicide, having squandered the family fortune, and Ally is no longer acceptable in the elegant Victorian society of her childhood.

Robbed of her very last penny, Ally is thrust into a world of hardship for which she is ill-prepared. Her only salvation comes from meeting Jack Fossett during one of the worst rainstorms in Leicestershire's history. Jack is a kind, caring young lad who takes pity on the beautiful, bedraggled girl, and he and his younger brother and sister welcome Ally into their hearts.

But Jack's mother, Flo, is deeply resentful of all gentlefolk. And time must pass and secrets must be revealed before Ally and Flo can see eye to eye – particularly when they discover that Ally is in fact not as destitute as she thought . . .

0 7472 5504 0

HEADLINE